The Best British Mysteries IV

The Best British Mysteries IV

Edited by

MAXIM JAKUBOWSKI

First published in Great Britain in 2006 by
Allison & Busby Limited
13 Charlotte Mews
London W1T 4EJ
www.allisonandbusby.com

This paperback edition published in 2007

A CIP catalogue record for this book is available from
the British Library.

10 9 8 7 6 5 4 3 2 1

ISBN 978-0-7490-8199-7

Typeset in 10.5/15 pt Sabon by
Terry Shannon

Printed by Creative Print and Design, Wales

Contents

Introduction

Already our fourth annual volume presenting the best crime and mystery short stories written by British authors in the past year and it's another veritable cornucopia of thrills, dirty deeds, clever plots, evil villains, determined sleuths, psychological torment, confounding puzzles, and almost every shenanigan under the sun (or, in many instances, the moon...).

The ingenuity of crime writers never ceases to amaze me as they plumb the hidden depths of the human psyche and explore that tenuous territory that sometimes separates good and evil in which characters much like you and me can sometimes get away with it, or not, as the case may be. Murder, deceit and wrongdoing are fertile grounds, though, for splendid entertainment, as a recent statistic confirmed, showing that British library readers now read more mysteries than romance; the first time this has historically happened. Whether you read crime books for the intellectual crime-solving element, or for their often fascinating insight into human nature or, more simply, for the sheer pleasure of a good read where the plot effortlessly goes from A to Z with many a roadside attraction during the journey, there is no more satisfying form of entertainment and the mystery short story embodies all these virtues in a concentrated format which proves a challenge to good writers and a particular delight to readers. And, forgive me for just a touch of gentle chauvinism, British crime and mystery writers certainly rule the roost in this regard.

This year's batch of stories sees some grand names joining our ranks, who had not appeared in previous volumes: the delightful Alexander McCall Smith with, naturally, an African tale; the slick creator of Jack Reacher, British expatriate Lee Child, whose thrillers live on the bestseller list; the urbane Robert Goddard who actually seldom pens short stories; Allan Guthrie, Kevin Wignall, Adrian McKinty and Ray Banks, all an integral part of the recent, impressive new wave of hardboiled British Crime writers; ex-Crime Writers' Association Chairperson Danuta Reah, whose story won the CWA Short Story Dagger this year, the collaborative duo of Simon Avery and Ian Faulkner...

Alongside these relative newcomers, I am also pleased to be able to feature for the first time tales by such stalwarts of British crime and mystery fiction as Catherine Aird, Paul Charles, Natasha Cooper, Simon Brett and Chris Simms. And, of course, last but not least, our always welcome repeat offenders, some of whom are making a dangerous habit of featuring in these pages: Morse creator Colin Dexter, Peter Robinson with a Xmas Inspector Banks story, John Harvey, Ken Bruen, Martin Edwards, Robert Barnard, Michael Z Lewin, Gillian Linscott, Barbara Cleverly, Edward Marston, Peter Tremayne, Judith Cutler, Amy Myers, Anne Perry, Peter Lovesey, Peter Turnbull.

A scintillating, if murderous menu...

Enjoy the fruits of their crimes.

Maxim Jakubowski

Resnick was unable to sleep. All those years of living alone, just the weight of the cats, one and occasionally more, pressing lightly down on the covers by his feet or in the V behind his legs, and now, with Lynn away for just forty-eight hours, he was lost without her by his side. The warmth of her body next to his, the small collisions as they turned from their respective dreams into a splay of legs, her arm sliding across his chest. 'Lay still, Charlie. Another five minutes, OK?' Musk of her early morning breath.

He pushed away the sheet and swivelled round, then rose to his feet. Through an inch of open window, he could hear the slight swish of cars along the Woodborough Road. Not so many minutes short of two a.m.

Downstairs, Dizzy, the oldest of the four cats, a warrior no longer, raised his head from the fruit bowl he had long since appropriated as a bed, cocked a chewed and half-torn ear and regarded Resnick with a yellow eye.

Padding past, Resnick set the kettle to boil and slid a tin of coffee beans from the fridge. A flier announcing Lynn's course was pinned to the cork board on the wall – *Unzipping the Agenda: A Guide to Creative Management and Open Thinking*. Lynn and forty or so other officers from the East Midlands and East Anglia at a conference centre and hotel beside the A1 outside Stevenage. Promotion material. High fliers. When she had joined the Serious Crime Unit a little more than two years ago, it had been as a sergeant; an inspector now and barely thirty, unless somehow she blotted her copy book, the only way was up. Whereas for Resnick, who had turned down promotion and the chance to move onto a bigger stage, little more than a pension awaited once his years were in.

While the coffee dripped slowly through its filter, Resnick opened the back door into the garden and, as he did so, another of the cats, Pepper, slithered past his ankles. Beyond the allotments, the lights of the city burned dully through a haze of rain and mist. Down there, on the streets of St Ann's and the Meadows, armed officers patrolled with Walther P990s holstered at their hips. Drugs, of course, the cause of most of it, the cause and the core: all the way from after-dinner cocaine served at trendy middle-class dinner parties alongside the squares of Green and Black's dark organic chocolate, to twenty-five pound wraps of brown changing hands in the stairwells of dilapidated blocks of flats.

Bolting the door, he carried his coffee through into the living room, switched on the light and slid a CD into the stereo. *Art Pepper Meets the Rhythm Section*, Los Angeles, January 19th, 1957. Pepper only months out of jail on drugs offences, his second term and still only thirty-two. And worse to come.

Resnick had seen him play in Leicester on the British leg of his European tour; Pepper older, wiser, allegedly straightened out, soon to be dead three years shy of sixty, a small miracle that he survived that long. That evening, in the function room of a nondescript pub, his playing had been melodic, and inventive, the tone piping and lean, its intensity controlled. Man earning a living, doing what he can.

Back in 'fifty-seven, in front of Miles Davis's rhythm section, he had glittered, half-afraid, inspired, alto saxophone dancing over the chords of half-remembered tunes. 'Star

Eyes', 'Imagination,' 'Jazz Me Blues'. The track that Resnick would play again and again: 'You'd Be So Nice To Come Home To'.

For a moment Pepper's namesake cat appeared in the doorway, sniffed the air and turned away, presenting his fine tail.

Just time for Resnick, eyes closed, to conjure up a picture of Lynn, restlessly sleeping in a strange bed, before the phone began to ring.

It was the sergeant on duty, his voice stretched by tiredness: '...ten, fifteen minutes ago, sir. I thought you'd want to know.'

That stretch of the Ilkeston Road was a mixture of small shops and residential housing, old factories put to new use, student accommodation. Police cars were parked, half on the kerb, either side of a black Ford Mondeo that, seemingly, had swerved wildly and collided, broadside-on, into a concrete post, amidst a welter of torn metal and splintered glass. Onlookers, some with overcoats pulled over their night clothes and carpet slippers on their feet, stood back behind hastily strung-out police tape, craning their necks. An ambulance and fire engine stood opposite, paramedics and fire officers mingling with uniformed police at the perimeter of the scene. Lights flashing, a second ambulance was pulling away as Resnick arrived.

Driving slowly past, he stopped outside a shop, long boarded-up, *High Class Butcher* in faded lettering on the brickwork above.

Anil Khan, once a DC in Resnick's squad and now a sergeant with Serious Crime, came briskly down to meet him and walked him back.

'One dead at the scene, sir, young female; one on his way to hospital, the driver. Female passenger, front near side, her leg's trapped against the door where it buckled in. Have to be cut out most likely. Oxyacetylene.'

Resnick could see the body now, stretched out against the lee of the wall beneath a dark grey blanket that was darker at the head.

'Impact?' Resnick said. 'Thrown forward against the windscreen?'

Khan shook his head. 'Shot.'

It stopped Resnick in his tracks.

'Another car, as best we can tell. Three shots, maybe four. One of them hit her in the neck. Must have nicked an artery. She was dead before we got her out.'

Illuminated by the street light above, Resnick could see the blood, sticky and bright, clinging to the upholstery like a second skin. Bending towards the body, he lifted back the blanket edge and looked down into the dead startled eyes of a girl of no more than sixteen.

Fifteen years and seven months. Alicia Ann Faye. She had lived with her mother, two younger sisters and an older brother in Radford. A bright and popular student, a lovely girl. She had been to an eighteenth-birthday party with her brother, Bradford, and his girlfriend, Marlee. Bradford driving.

They had been on their way home when the incident occurred, less than half a mile from where Alicia and Bradford lived. A blue BMW drew up alongside them at the lights before the turn into Ilkeston Road, revving its engine as if intent on racing. Anticipating the green, Bradford, responding to the challenge, accelerated downhill, the BMW in close pursuit; between the first set of lights and the old Radford Mill building, the BMW drew alongside, someone lowered the rear window, pushed a handgun through and fired four times. One shot ricocheted off the roof, another embedded itself in the rear of the front seat; one entered the fleshy part of Bradford's shoulder, causing him to swerve; the fourth and fatal shot struck Alicia low in the side of the neck and exited close to her windpipe.

An impulse shooting, is that what this was? Or a case of mistaken identity?

In the October of the previous year a gunman had opened fire from a passing car, seemingly at random, into a group of young people on their way home from Goose Fair, and a fourteen-year-old girl had died. There were stories of gun gangs and blood feuds in the media, of areas of the inner city running out of control, turf wars over drugs. Flowers and sermons, blame and recriminations and in the heart of the city a minute's silence, many people wearing the dead girl's favourite colours; thousands lined the streets for the funeral, heads bowed in respect.

Now this.

Understaffed as they were, low on morale and resources, policing the city, Resnick knew, was becoming harder and harder. In the past eighteen months, violent crime had risen to double the national average; shootings had increased fourfold. In Radford, Jamaican Yardies controlled the trade in heroin and crack cocaine, while on the Bestwood estate, to the north, the mainly white criminal fraternity was forging an uneasy alliance with the Yardies, all the while fighting amongst themselves; at either side of the city centre, multiracial gangs from St Ann's and The Meadows, Asian and Afro-Caribbean, fought out a constant battle for trade and respect.

So was Alicia simply another victim in the wrong place at the wrong time? Or something more? The search for the car was on: best chance it would be found on waste land, torched; ballistics were analysing the bullets from the scene; Bradford Faye and his family were being checked through records; friends would be questioned, neighbours. The public relations department had prepared a statement for the media, another for the Assistant Chief Constable. Resnick sat in the CID office in Canning Circus station with Anil Khan and Detective Inspector Maureen Price from Serious Crime. His patch, their concern. Their case more than his.

Outside the sky had lightened a little, but still their reflections as they sat were sharp against the window's plate glass.

Maureen Price was in her early forties, no nonsense, matter-of-fact, wearing loose-fitting grey trousers, a zip-up jacket, hair tied back. 'So what do we think? We think they were targeted or what?'

'The girl?'

'No, not the girl.'

'The brother, then?'

'That's what I'm thinking.' The computer print-out was in her hand. 'He was put under a supervision order a little over two years back, offering to supply a class A drug.'

'That's when he'd be what?' Khan asked. 'Fifteen?'

'Sixteen. Just.'

'Anything since?'

'Not according to this.'

'You think he could still be involved?' Resnick said.

'I think it's possible, don't you?'

'And this was what? Some kind of pay-back?'

'Pay-back, warning, who knows? Maybe he was trying to step up into a different league, change his supplier, hold back his share of the cut, anything.'

'We've checked with the Drug Squad that he's a player?' Resnick asked.

Maureen Price looked over at Khan, who shook his head. 'Haven't been able to raise anyone so far.'

The detective inspector looked at her watch. 'Try again. Keep trying.'

Freeing his mobile from his pocket, Khan walked towards the far side of the room.

'How soon can we talk to Bradford, I wonder?' Resnick said.

'He's most likely still in surgery now. Mid-morning, I'd say. The earliest.'

'You want me to do that?'

'No, it's OK. I've asked them to call me from Queen's the minute he's out of recovery. There's an officer standing by.' She moved from the desk where she'd been sitting, stretching out her arms and breathing in stale air. 'Maybe you could talk to the family?' She smiled. 'They're on your patch, Charlie, after all.'

There were bunches of flowers already tied to the post into which the car had crashed, some anonymous, some bearing hastily written words of sympathy. More flowers rested up against the low wall outside the house.

The victim support officer met Resnick at the door.

'How they holding up?' he asked.

'Good as can be expected, sir.'

Resnick nodded and followed the officer into a narrow hall.
'They're in back.'

Clarice Faye sat on a green high-backed settee, her youngest
daughter cuddled up against her, face pressed to her mother's
chest. The middle daughter, Jade, twelve or thirteen, sat close
but not touching, head turned away. Clarice was slender, light-
skinned, lighter than her daughters, shadows scored deep
beneath her eyes. Resnick was reminded of a woman at sea,
stubbornly holding on against the pitch and swell of the tide.

The room itself was neat and small, knick-knacks and
framed photographs of the children, uniform smiles; a
crucifix, metal on a wooden base, hung above the fireplace.
The curtains, a heavy stripe, were still pulled part-way across.

Resnick introduced himself and expressed his sympathy;
accepted the chair that was offered, narrow with wooden
arms, almost too narrow for his size.

'Bradford – have you heard from the hospital?'

'I saw my son this morning. He was sleeping. They told me
to come home and get some rest.' She shook her head and
squeezed her daughter's hand tight. 'As if I could.'

'He'll be all right?'

'He will live.'

The youngest child began to cry.

'He is a good boy, Bradford. Not wild. Not like some. Not
any more. Why would anyone…?' She stopped to sniff away
a tear. 'He is going to join the army, you know that? Has been
for an interview already, filled in the forms.' She pulled a
tissue, screwed and damp, from her sleeve. 'A man now, you
know? He makes me proud.'

Resnick's eyes ran round the photographs in the room. 'Alicia's father,' he ventured, 'is he…?'

'He doesn't live with us any more.'

'But he's been told?'

'You think he cares?'

The older girl sprang to her feet and half-ran across the room.

'Jade, come back here.'

The door slammed hard against the frame.

Resnick leaned forward, drew his breath. 'Bradford and Alicia, last night, you know where they'd been?'

'The Meadows. A friend of Bradford's, his eighteenth.'

'Did they often go around together like that, Bradford and Alicia?'

'Sometimes, yes.'

'They were close then?'

'Of course.' An insult if it were otherwise, a slight.

'And his girlfriend, she didn't mind?'

'Marlee, no. She and Alicia, they were like mates. Pals.'

'Mum,' the younger girl said, raising her head. 'Licia didn't like her. Marlee. She didn't.'

'That's not so.'

'It is. She told me. She said she smelled.'

'Nonsense, child.' Clarice smiled indulgently and shook her head.

'How about Alicia?' Resnick asked. 'Did she have any boyfriends? Anyone special?'

The hesitation was perhaps a second too long. 'No. She was a serious girl. Serious about her studies. She didn't have time for that sort of thing. Besides, she was too young.'

'She was sixteen.'

'Too young for anything serious, that's what I mean.'

'But parties, like yesterday, that was OK?'

'Young people together, having fun. Besides, she had her brother to look after her...' Tears rushed to her face and she brushed them aside.

The phone rang and the victim support officer answered it in the hall. 'It's Bradford,' he said from the doorway. 'They'll be taking him back up to the ward any time.'

'Quickly,' Clarice said to her daughter, bustling her off the settee. 'Coat and shoes.'

Resnick followed them out into the hall. Door open, Jade was sitting on one of the beds in the room she and Alicia had obviously shared. Aware that Resnick was looking at her, she swung her head sharply towards him, staring hard until he moved away.

Outside, clouds slid past in shades of grey; on the opposite side of the narrow street, a couple slowed as they walked by. Resnick waited while the family climbed into the support officer's car and drove away... *A good boy, Bradford. Not wild. Not any more.* The crucifix. The mother's words. Amazing, he thought, how we believe what we want to believe, all evidence aside.

On the Ilkeston Road, he stopped and crossed the street. There were more flowers now, and photographs of Alicia, covered in plastic against the coming rain. A large teddy bear with black ribbon in a bow around its neck. A dozen red roses wrapped in cellophane, the kind on sale in garage forecourts. Resnick stooped and looked at the card. *For Alicia. Our love will live forever. Michael.* Kisses, drawn in red biro in the shape of a heart, surrounded the words.

* * *

Resnick was putting the last touches of a salad together when he heard Lynn's key in the lock. A sauce of spicy sausage and tomato was simmering on the stove; a pan of gently bubbling water ready to receive the pasta.

'Hope you're good and hungry.'

'You know…' Her head appearing round the door. '…I'm not sure if I am.'

But she managed a good helping nonetheless, wiping the spare sauce from her plate with bread, washing it down with wine.

'So – how was it?' Resnick asked between mouthfuls.

'All right, I suppose.'

'Not brilliant then.'

'No, some of it was OK. Useful even.'

'Such as?'

'Oh, ways of avoiding tunnel vision. Stuff like that.'

Resnick poured more wine.

'I just wish,' Lynn said, 'they wouldn't get you to play these stupid games.'

'Games?'

'You know, if you were a vegetable, what vegetable would you be? If you were a car, what car?'

Resnick laughed. 'And what were you?'

'Vegetable or car?'

'Either.'

'A first crop potato, fresh out of the ground.'

'A bit mundane.'

'Come on, Charlie, born and brought up in Norfolk, what do you expect?'

'A turnip?'

She waited till he was looking at his plate, then clipped him round the head.

Later, in bed, when he pressed against her back and she turned inside his arms, her face close to his, she said: 'Better watch out, Charlie, I didn't tell you what kind of car.'

'Something moderately stylish, compact, not too fast?'

'A Maserati Coupé 4.2 in Azuro Blue with full cream leather upholstery.'

He was still laughing when she stopped his mouth with hers.

The bullet that had struck Bradford's shoulder was a 9mm, most likely from a plastic Glock. Patched up, replenished with blood, Bradford was sore, sullen, and little else. Aside from lucky. His girlfriend, Marlee, had twenty-seven stitches in a gash in her leg, several butterfly stitches to one side of her head and face and bruises galore. The BMW was found on open ground near railway tracks on the far side of Sneinton, burned out. No prints, no ejected shell cases, nothing of use. It took the best part of a week, but thirty-seven of the fifty or so people who had been at the party in The Meadows were traced, tracked down and questioned. For officers, rare and welcome overtime.

The Drug Squad had no recent information to suggest that Bradford was again dealing drugs, but there were several people at the party well known to them indeed. Troy James and Jason Fontaine in particular. Both had long been suspected of playing an active part in the trade in crack cocaine: suspected, arrested, interrogated, charged. James had served eighteen months of a three-year sentence before being released; Fontaine had been charged with possession of three kilos of amphetamine with intent to supply, but due to alleged contamination of evidence, the case against him had been dismissed. More recently, the pair of them had been suspected of breaking into a chemist's shop in Wilford and stealing several cases of cold remedies in order to manufacture crystal meth.

James and Fontaine were questioned in the street, questioned in their homes; brought into the police station and questioned again. Bradford spent as much as fourteen hours, broken over a number of sessions, talking to Maureen Price and Anil Khan.

Did he know Troy James and Jason Fontaine?

No.

He didn't know them?

No, not really.

Not really?

Not, you know, to talk to.

But they were at the party.

If you say so.

Well, they were there. James and Fontaine.

OK, so they were there. So what?

You and Fontaine, you had a conversation.

What conversation?

There are witnesses, claim to have seen you and Fontaine in conversation.

A few words, maybe. I don't remember.

A few words concerning...?

Nothing important. Nothing.

How about an argument... a bit of pushing and shoving?

At the party?

At the party.

No.

Think. Think again. Take your time. It's easy to get confused.

Oh, that. Yeah. It was nothing, right? Someone's drink got spilled, knocked over. Happens all the time.

That's what it was about? The argument?

Yeah.

A few punches thrown?

Maybe.

By you?

Not by me.

By Fontaine?

Fontaine?

Yes. You and Fontaine, squaring up to one another.

No. No way.

'There's something there, Charlie,' Maureen Price said. 'Something between Bradford and Jason Fontaine.'

They were sitting in the Polish Diner on Derby Road, blueberry pancakes and coffee, Resnick's treat.

'Something personal?'

'To do with drugs, has to be. Best guess, Fontaine and Ford were using Bradford further down the chain and some way he held out on them, cut the stuff again with glucose, whatever. Either that, or he was trying to branch out on his own, their patch. Radford kid poaching in The Meadows, we all know how that goes down.'

'You'll keep on at him?'

'The girlfriend, too. She's pretty shaken up still. What happened to Alicia. Keeps thinking it could have been her, I shouldn't wonder. Flakey as anything. One of them'll break sooner or later.'

'You seem certain.'

Maureen paused, fork halfway to her mouth. 'It's all we've got, Charlie.'

Resnick nodded and reached for the maple syrup: maybe just a little touch more.

The flowers were wilting, starting to fade. One or two of the brighter bunches had been stolen. Rain had seeped down into plastic and cellophane, rendering the writing for the most part illegible.

Clarice Faye came to the door in a dark housecoat, belted tight across; there were shadows still around her eyes.

'I'm sorry to disturb you,' Resnick said.

A slight shake of the head: no move to invite him in.

'When we were talking before, you said Alicia didn't have any boyfriends, nobody special?'

'That's right.'

'Not Troy James?'

'I don't know that name?'

'How about Jason? Jason Fontaine?'

The truth was there on her face, a small nerve twitching at the corner of her eye.

'She did go out with Jason Fontaine?'

'She saw him once or twice. The end of last year. He came round here in his car, calling for her. I told him, he wasn't suitable, not for her. Not for Alicia. He didn't bother her again.'

'And Alicia…?'

'Alicia understood.' Clarice stepped back and began to close the door. 'If you'll excuse me now?'

'How about Michael?' Resnick said.

'I don't know no Michael.'

And the door closed quietly in his face.

He waited until Jade was on her way home from school,

white shirt hanging out, coat open, skirt rolled high over dark tights, clumpy shoes. Her and three friends, loud across the pavement, one of them smoking a cigarette.

None of the others as much as noticed Resnick, gave him any heed.

'I won't keep you a minute,' Resnick said as Jade stopped, the others walking on, pace slowed, heads turned.

'Yeah, right.'

'You and Alicia, you shared a room.'

'So.'

'Secrets.'

'What secrets?'

'Jason Fontaine, was she seeing him any more?'

Jade tilted back her head, looked him in the eye. 'He was just a flash bastard, weren't he? Didn't care nothin' for her.'

'And Michael?'

'What about him?'

'You tell me.'

'He loved her, didn't he?'

Michael Draper was upstairs in his room: computer, stereo, books and folders from the course he was taking at City College, photographs of Alicia on the wall, Alicia and himself somewhere that might have been the Arboretum, on a bench in front of some trees, an old wall, Michael's skin alongside hers so white it seemed to bleed into the photo's edge.

'She was going to tell them, her mum and that, after her birthday. We were going to get engaged.'

'I'm sorry.'

The boy's eyes empty and raw from tears.

* * *

Maureen Price was out of the office, her mobile switched off. Khan wasn't sure where she was.

'Ask her to call me when she gets a chance,' Resnick said. 'She can get me at home.'

At home he made sure the chicken pieces had finished defrosting in the fridge, chopped parsley, squashed garlic cloves flat, opened a bottle of wine, saw to the cats, flicked through the pages of the *Post*, Alicia's murder now page four. Art Pepper again, turned up loud. Lynn was late, no later than usual, rushed, smiling, weary, a brush of lips against his cheek.

'I need a shower, Charlie, before anything else.'

'I'll get this started.' Knifing butter into the pan.

It had cost Bradford a hundred and fifteen, talked down from one twenty-five. A Brocock ME38 Magnum air pistol converted to fire live ammunition. .22 shells. Standing there at the edge of the car park, shadowed, he smiled: an eye for an eye. Fontaine's motor, his new one, another Beamer, was no more than thirty metres away, close to the light. He rubbed his hands and moved his feet against the cold, the rain that rattled against the hood of his parka, misted his eyes. Another fifteen minutes, no more, he'd be back out again, Fontaine, on with his rounds.

Less that fifteen, it was closer to ten.

Fontaine appeared at the side door of the pub, calling out to someone inside before raising a hand and turning away.

Bradford tensed, smelling his own stink, his own fear; waited until Fontaine had reached towards the handle of the car door, back turned.

'Wait,' Bradford said, stepping out of the dark.

Seeing him, seeing the pistol, Fontaine smiled. 'Bradford, my man.'

'Bastard,' Bradford said, moving closer. 'You killed my sister.'

'That slag!' Fontaine laughed. 'Down on her knees in front of any white meat she could find.'

Hands suddenly sticky, slick with sweat despite the cold, Bradford raised the gun and fired. The first shot missed, the second shattered the side window of the car, the third took Fontaine in the face splintering his jaw. Standing over him, Bradford fired twice more into his body as it slumped towards the ground, then ran.

After watching the news headlines, they decided on an early night. Lynn washed the dishes left over from dinner, while Resnick stacked away. He was locking the door when the phone went and Lynn picked it up. Ten twenty-three.

'Charlie,' she said, holding out the receiver. 'It's for you.'

I could have shot you in one ear and out the other from a thousand yards. I could have brushed past you in a crowd and you wouldn't have known your throat was cut until you went to nod your head and it rolled down the street without you. I was the guy you were worrying about when you locked your doors and posted your guards and walked upstairs to bed, only to find me already up there before you, leaning on the dresser, just waiting in the dark.

I was the guy who always found a way.

I was the guy that couldn't be stopped.

But that's over now, I guess.

None of my stuff was original. I studied the best of the best, long ago. I learned from all of them. A move here, a move there, all stitched together. All the tricks. Including the greatest trick of all, which I learned from a man called Ryland. Back in the day Ryland worked all over, but mainly where there was oil, or white powder, or money, or girls, or high-stakes card games. Then he got old, and he slowly withdrew. Eventually he found the matrimonial market. Maybe he invented it, although I doubt that. But certainly he refined it. He turned it into a business. He was in the right place at the right time. Getting old and slowing down, just when all those Californian lawyers made divorce into a lottery win. Just when guys all over the hemisphere started to get nervous about it.

The theory was simple: a live wife goes to a lawyer, but a dead wife goes nowhere. Except the cemetery. Problem solved. A dead wife attracts a certain level of attention from the police, of course, but Ryland moved in a world where a guy would be a thousand times happier to get a call from a cop than a divorce lawyer. Cops would have to pussyfoot around the grief issue, and there was a general assumption that when it came to IQ cops were not the sharpest chisels in the box. Whereas lawyers were like razors. And, of course, part of the appeal of a guy like Ryland was that evidence was going to be very thin on the ground. No question, a wife dead at Ryland's hands was generally considered to be a lottery win in reverse.

He worked hard. Hit the microfilm and check it out. Check newspapers all over the States and Central and South America. Look at Europe, Germany, Italy, anyplace where there were substantial fortunes at stake. Look at how many women went missing. Look at how old they were, and how long they had been married. Then check the follow-up stories, the inside pages, the later paragraphs, and see how many hints there were about incipient marital strife. Check it out, and you'll see a pattern.

The cops saw a pattern too, of course. But Ryland was a ghost. He had survived oil and dope and money lending and hookers and gambling. No way was he going to get brought down by greedy husbands and bored wives. He flourished, and I bet his name was never written down in any cop's file. Not anywhere, not once. He was that good.

He was working back in the days when billionaires were rare. Back then, a hundred million was considered a threshold level. Below a hundred mil, you were poor. Above, you were respectable. People called a hundred mil a unit, and most of Ryland's clients were worth three or four units. And Ryland noticed something: rich husband, rich wife. The wives weren't rich in the sense their husbands were, of course. They didn't have units of their own. But they had spending cash. It stands to reason, Ryland said to me. Guys set them up with bank accounts and credit cards. Guys worth three or four units don't like to trouble themselves with trivia down at the six-figure level.

But the six-figure level was where Ryland worked.

And he noticed that the blood he was spilling was dripping all over minks and diamond chokers and Paris gowns and perforated leather seats in Mercedes-Benzes. He started searching purses after a while. There were big checking balances in most of them, and platinum cards. He didn't steal anything, of course. That would have been fatal, and stupid, and Ryland wasn't stupid. Not stupid at all. But he was imaginative.

Or so he claimed.

Actually I like to believe one of the women handed the idea to him. Maybe one a little feistier than normal. Maybe when it became clear what was about to transpire she put in a counter-offer. That's how I like to think it all started. Maybe she said: 'That rat bastard. I should pay you to off him instead.' I know Ryland's ears would have pricked up at that. Anything involving payment would have gotten him interested. He would have run the calculation at the same hyper speed he used for any calculation, from a bullet's trajectory to a risk assessment. He would have figured: this chick can afford a six-figure coat, so she can afford a six-figure hit.

Thus, the greatest trick of all.

Getting paid twice.

He told me about it after he got sick with cancer, and I took it as a kind of anointment. The nomination of an heir. The passing of the baton. He wanted me to be the new Ryland. That was OK with me. I also took it as a mute appeal not to let him linger and suffer. That was OK with me too. He was frail by then. He resisted the pillow like crazy, but the lights went out soon enough. And there it was. The old Ryland gone, and the new Ryland starting out with new energy.

First up was a stout forty-something from Essen in Germany. Married to a steel baron who had recently found her to be boring. A hundred grand in my pocket would save him a hundred million in hers. Classically, of course, you would hunt and strike before she ever knew you were on the planet. Previously, that would have been the hallmark of a job well done.

But not anymore.

I went with her to Gstaad. I didn't travel with her. I just showed up there the next day. Got to know her a little. She was a cow. I would have gladly killed her for free. But I didn't. I talked to her instead. I worked her around to the point where she said, 'My husband thinks I'm too old.' Then she looked up at me from under her lashes. It was the usual reassurance-seeking crap. She wanted me to say. 'You? Too old? How could he think that about such a beautiful woman?'

But I didn't say that.

Instead, I said, 'He wants to get rid of you.'

She took it as a question. She answered, 'Yes, I think he does.'

I said, 'No, I know he does. He offered me money to kill you.'

Think about it. How was she going to react? No screaming. No running to the Swiss cops. Just utter stunned silence, under the weight of the biggest single surprise she could have heard. First, of course, the conceptual question: 'You're an assassin?' She knew people like me existed. She had moved in her husband's world for a long time. Too long, according to him. Then eventually, of course, after all the other questions, the inevitable inquiry: 'How much did he offer you?'

Ryland had told me to exaggerate a little. In his opinion it gave the victims a little perverse pleasure to hear a big number. It gave them a last shot at feeling needed, in a backhanded kind of a way. They weren't wanted anymore, but at least it was costing a lot to get rid of them. Status, of a sort.

'Two hundred thousand US dollars,' I said.

The fat Essen bitch took that in and then started down the wrong road.

She said, 'I could give you that not to.'

'Wouldn't work for me,' I said. 'I can't leave a job undone. He would tell people, and my reputation would be shot. A guy like me, his reputation is all he's got.'

Gstaad was a good place to be having the conversation. It was isolated and other-worldly. It was like there was just her and me on the planet. I sat beside her and tried to radiate sympathy. Like a dentist maybe. When he has to drill a tooth. I'm sorry…but it's got to be done. Her anger built, a little slow, but it came. Eventually she got on the right road.

'You work for money,' she said.

I nodded.

'You work for anyone who can pay the freight,' she said.

'Like a taxicab,' I said.

She said, 'I'll pay you to kill him.'

There was anger there, of course, but there were also

financial considerations. They were forming slowly in her mind, a little vaguely, but basically they were the exact obverse of the considerations I had seen in the husband's mind a week previously. People like that, it comes down to just four words: all the money, mine.

She asked, 'How much?'

'The same,' I said. 'Two hundred grand.'

We were in Switzerland, which made the banking part easy. I stuck with her, supportive, and watched her get her fat pink paws on two hundred thousand US dollars, crisp new bills from some European country's central reserve. She gave them to me and started to explain where her husband would be, and when.

'I know where he is,' I said. 'I have a rendezvous set up. For me to get paid.'

She giggled at the irony. Guaranteed access to the victim. She wasn't dumb. That was the single greatest strength of Ryland's idea.

We went for a walk, alone, on a snow-covered track rarely frequented by skiers. I killed her there by breaking her fat neck and leaving her in a position that suggested a slip and a fall. Then I took the train back to Essen and kept my rendezvous with the husband. Obviously he had gone to great lengths to keep our meetings secret. He was in a place he wouldn't normally go, alone and unobserved. I collected my fee and killed him too. A silenced .22, in the head. It was an article of faith for people like Ryland and me. If you get paid, you have to deliver.

So, two fees, and all those steel units cascading down to fractious heirs that would be calling me themselves, soon enough. All the money, mine.

It went on like that for two years. Check the microfilm. Check the papers. North America, Central, South, all over Europe. Cops in a lather about anarchists targeting rich couples. That was another strength of Ryland's idea. It rendered the motive inexplicable.

Then I got an offer from Brazil. I was kind of surprised. For some reason I imagined their divorce laws to be old-fashioned and traditional. I didn't think any Brazilian guy would need my kind of help. But someone reached out to me and I ended up face to face with a man who had big units from mineral deposits and an actress wife who was sleeping around. The guy was wounded about it. Maybe that's why he called me. He didn't strictly need to. But he wanted to.

He was rich and he was angry so I doubled my usual fee. That was no problem. I explained how it would work. Payment after the event at a discreet location, satisfaction guaranteed. Then he told me his wife was going to be on a train, some kind of a long private club-car journey through the mountains. That was a problem. There are no banks on trains. So I decided to pass on Ryland's trick, just this one time. I would go the traditional single-ended route. The old way. I checked a map and saw that I could get on the train late and get off early. The wife would be dead in her sleeper when it rolled into Rio. I would be long gone by then.

It was comforting to think about working the old way, just for once.

I spotted her on the train and kept well back. But even from a distance I saw the ring on her finger. It was a gigantic rock. A diamond so big they probably ran out of carat numbers to measure it with.

That was a bank right there, on her finger.

Traceable, theoretically, but not through certain parts of Amsterdam or Johannesburg or Freetown, Sierra Leone. Potentially a problem at customs posts, but I could swallow it.

I moved up the train.

She was a very beautiful woman. Skin like lavender honey, long black hair that shone, eyes like swimming pools. Long legs, a tiny waist, a rack that was popping out of her shirt. I took the armchair opposite her and said, 'Hello'. I figured a woman who sleeps around would at least give me a look. I have certain rough qualities. A few scars, the kind of unkempt appearance that suggests adventure. She didn't need money. She was married to it. Maybe all she needed was diversion.

It went well at first and I found a reason to move around the table and slide into the chair next to her. Then within an hour we were well into that train-journey thing where she was leaning left and I was leaning right and we were sharing intimacies over the rush of the wind and the clatter of the wheels. She talked about her marriage briefly and then changed the subject. I brought it back. I pointed to her ring and asked her about it. She spread her hand like a starfish and let me take a look.

'My husband gave it to me,' she said.

'So he should,' I said. 'He's a lucky man.'

'He's an angry man,' she said. 'I don't behave myself very well, I'm afraid.'

I said nothing.

She said, 'I think he wants to have me killed.'

So there it was, the opening that was often so hard to work around to. I should have said, 'He sure does,' and opened negotiations. But I didn't.

She said, 'I look at the men I meet and I wonder, is this the one?'

So then I got my mouth working and said, 'This is the one.'

'Really?' she said.

I nodded. 'I'm afraid so.'

'You're not the first,' she said.

That threw me a little. But I came back with, 'But I'm the best.'

'You are?'

'I'm the one who can't be stopped.'

'I carry insurance,' she said.

She raised her hand again and all I saw was the diamond. Hard to blame myself, because the diamond was so big and the stiletto's blade was so slender. I really didn't see it at all. Wasn't aware of its existence until its tip went through my shirt and pierced my skin. Then she leaned on it with surprising strength and weight. It was cold. And long. A custom piece. It went right through me and pinned me to the chair. She used the heel of her hand and butted it firmly into place. Then she used my tie to wipe the handle clean of prints.

'Goodbye,' she said.

She got up and left me there. I was unable to move. An inch left or right would tear my insides out. I just sat and felt the spreading stain of blood reach my lap. I'm still sitting there, ten minutes later. Once I could have shot you in one ear and out the other from a thousand yards. Or I could have brushed past you in a crowd and you wouldn't have known your throat was cut until you went to nod your head and it rolled down the street without you. I was the guy you were worrying about when you locked your doors and posted your guards and walked upstairs to bed, only to find me already up there before you, leaning on the dresser, just waiting in the dark.

I was the guy who always found a way.

I was the guy that couldn't be stopped.

Then I met Ryland.

And that's all over now.

Alexander McCall Smith
He Loved to Go for Drives with His Father

I

This took place some time ago, in a country called Swaziland, a small landlocked kingdom in southern Africa. It is a country of great beauty, rising from a swathe of low country in the south to highlands in the northwest. When viewed from a distance, these northern hills seem impossibly blue, fading into the sky as gently as mist shades into the contours of the land. Along the east side of the country there is a range of mountains, the Lebombo Mountains, from the ridge of which one may look down into Mozambique below, and beyond that, when conditions are right, to the line of blue which is the Indian Ocean.

At that time, which was in the nineteen fifties, the country was a British protectorate, presided over by a Paramount Chief, Sobhuza II, who was later to be referred to as the king. He was a man of considerable wisdom, much admired by his people, who were an offshoot of the Zulu nation and who were proud of their heritage.

The Paramount Chief lived in a sprawl of buildings between the two main towns of the country, Mbabane, which was the capital, and Manzini, which was close in to the airstrip and the few factories which the country had. The Paramount Chief's place was at the foot of a small group of hills which was sacred to the Swazi nation, being the place where leaders were traditionally buried in caves, wrapped in the hides of their finest oxen. Nobody was allowed to scale those hills except on the occasion of a royal burial or similar ceremony.

II

There was a Scottish doctor who took up a post as government medical officer in Manzini. He was based at the hospital there – a rambling collection of buildings next door to a hotel called the Uncle Charlie Hotel. This hotel, which had a bar and a long veranda, also boasted a dining room in which a striking mural had been painted. This mural showed a great African lake, with palm trees and mopani forests about its edges. Giraffe and zebra were depicted moving across the savanna. Nobody paid much attention to this mural, which had been painted as a shallow strip around the top of the walls, just below the ceiling, but every now and then a visitor who saw its merits would stand and stare at it. Such people said that for some reason the mural made them sad. 'It shows the beauty of Africa distilled,' said one such visitor. 'And it shows us what is being lost.'

The doctor had been allocated a house in the town, close to the tennis courts. It was a good house, commensurate with his position in the community, and it boasted a particularly attractive garden. The previous medical officer, who had been a bachelor, had spent all his spare time in the garden and had stocked it colourfully and imaginatively. He had been particularly fond of bougainvillea, which grew in profusion along the side of the house and around the kitchen garden. The local man who helped him in the garden did not like the bougainvillea, which he said attracted snakes. Nor did he like that doctor's collection of aloes, which he said were poisonous, and which he hoped would die of neglect. But aloes thrive on neglect, and they continued to grow.

The new doctor appreciated the garden but did not take a strong interest in it. He enjoyed playing chess, and he would sit for hours on the veranda, working out chess problems using a set made by Italian prisoners of war. His wife, who was not interested in chess, was a keen member of the tennis club. She was a strong player and would give lessons to any of the other tennis-playing wives who were eager to improve their game. She never played with her husband, who said that he found tennis a dull game after the first few services had been knocked over the net.

After chess, the doctor's other passion was cars. He was something of an amateur mechanic, and he would sometimes spend the whole weekend tinkering with the engine of the old green Pontiac which he had bought in Cape Town and driven all the way up to Swaziland. This car was his pride and joy until it was badly damaged in an accident on the road that ran from Manzini to Mbabane. This was a notoriously dangerous road, with its hairpin bends, and numerous vehicles had simply dropped over the edge, careering down through the undergrowth until they came to a ruinous halt against a tree or a granite boulder. In the accident which destroyed the doctor's car, neither he nor his wife was seriously hurt, although they were both shaken by the event.

'I don't want to drive anywhere at night in this country,' said the doctor's wife to one of her tennis partners. 'It's just too dangerous.'

III

After the loss of his green Pontiac, the doctor was obliged to buy a much less interesting car, a Volkswagen, which, although reliable and well suited to the country's unpaved roads, was dull to drive. The engine was not very powerful, and the doctor liked to be able to accelerate more quickly in order to pass trucks. Trucks, particularly the large cattle trucks, threw up a large cloud of dust behind them, and the doctor hated having to drive in that. But there was not a very wide choice of cars in Swaziland at that time, and the doctor could not lay his hands on anything more interesting.

Some months after the doctor's road accident, the manager of the Uncle Charlie Hotel went off to Johannesburg for a weekend. This man was a thin-faced Englishman whose wife had left him because she could not bear what she described as the boredom of living in a colonial backwater like Swaziland. She had gone to Nairobi, where she had a cousin, and where she soon met and married a wealthy farmer. The manager of the Uncle Charlie Hotel was philosophical about this. 'She never loved me, anyway,' he said. People who heard him talk this way were shocked into silence. It was difficult to know what to say in the face of such a personal revelation.

When he went off to Johannesburg for his weekend, the doctor's wife said: 'Poor man, he deserves a bit of fun after putting up with that flighty woman. Let's hope he meets somebody in Johannesburg.'

The hotel manager did not meet somebody in Johannesburg, but he did come back with a different car from the one in which he had set off. This was a Mercedes-Benz, which, although not new, was a car of considerable character and charm. It had beige leather seats and a marvellous wooden steering wheel. It was one of the most striking cars in the whole country, and it was even said that the Paramount Chief had seen it on the road and asked whose it was and had expressed a desire to have a car like that at some point.

Everybody talked about his new Mercedes-Benz. It stood parked in front of the Uncle Charlie Hotel, where one of the junior waiters was detailed to wash and polish it every day, paying particular attention to the shiny chrome bumpers and the silver three-point symbol at the top of the radiator.

The doctor was particularly taken with this car. A few days after its arrival he was seen by somebody in the dining room of the hotel to pull up beside it in his Volkswagen, get out, and peer through the window, like a schoolboy. And some time after that he was heard to say to the hospital pharmacist, 'I'd kill for a car like that. I really would.'

The doctor's wife was indifferent to vehicles of any sort. 'Men are ridiculous,' she observed at the tennis club one afternoon. 'They love those bits of machinery as if they were…as if they were women. It's ridiculous.'

'I'd prefer my husband to have a love affair with a car than another woman,' said one of the other tennis players.

'That's true,' said the doctor's wife. 'But I still wish that men would just grow up. They're so immature.'

IV

When the wife of the manager of the Uncle Charlie Hotel had gone off to Kenya, she had left behind a child. This was a boy of eleven, who suffered affected brain development. This boy could walk unaided, but could not utter more than a few words. But he was not troublesome. He did not scream or wail, as can happen with some of these distressing conditions. He merely gazed out of the window and pointed at birds and animals which attracted his attention. He took particular pleasure in looking at cattle and would make a mooing sound in imitation as he watched them. The manager of the Uncle Charlie Hotel would drive his son out in the Mercedes-Benz at the end of the working day and take him for a short spin along the Siteki Road, slowing down when they came to cattle grazing at the side of the road. Then they would drive back before it got dark, which happens so suddenly in those latitudes. One minute it will be light and the next the sun will have disappeared behind the hills and the night will be filled with the screech and chirrup of nocturnal insects.

The boy loved the Mercedes-Benz. He would stand beside it for hours, looking into its gleaming paintwork as if it were a mirror.

V

Six months after the manager had gone to Johannesburg to fetch the car, there was an awful row one morning at the Uncle Charlie Hotel. The Mercedes-Benz, which had been parked at the front of the hotel overnight, was missing from its place. The manager called the police immediately, and the police inspector himself came over within twenty minutes in his grey Land Rover.

'Car theft,' said the inspector. 'It happens, you know. It'll be over the border by now, I'm afraid, probably taken into South Africa, although it might have been spirited up to Lourenço Marques. I'm very sorry about this, but I fear that's that. Have you got the chassis number, by the way?'

The manager did not have the chassis number. He had bought the car in a private sale, and he had not been given proper registration documents. So there was no record of this vital piece of information.

'Then it will not be possible for us to get the cooperation of the people over the border,' said the police inspector. 'We wouldn't be able to prove that it was stolen, even if they found it.'

The manager of the Uncle Charlie Hotel swore violently when he received this news. This did not please the police inspector, who told him to watch his tongue. 'I understand how you feel,' he said. 'But you don't swear like that in front of me. Understand?'

Everybody sympathised with the manager over his loss.

'It's a terribly sad thing,' said one of the members of the tennis club. 'He used to take that boy of his for those runs on the Siteki Road. I saw them. It was rather touching, I thought, with that little boy sitting there looking out of the side and smiling in that way of his. Poignant really.'

'The insurance will pay up,' said another.

'Maybe. But you can't replace those cars just like that.'

'True. You can't.'

VI

The doctor's wife was aware of the fact that her husband was working on a project with his friend Ed, a mechanic who had a small garage on a dirt road that led to the Umbeluzi River. She had met this man once before and did not like him. There was something about his eyes which made her uncomfortable. The whites of his eyes looked yellow.

'Fatty deposits in the eyes,' said the doctor. 'His cholesterol is out of control.'

'I still don't like him,' she said.

The doctor shrugged. He did not like some of the women at the tennis club, but he did not think it helpful to say so. 'We're fiddling about with an engine,' he explained. 'It's an old Rover and we're stripping it right down and reboring it. Complicated stuff. But Ed's good at that sort of thing and he's teaching me a lot.'

She said nothing to this. She was not interested in that sort of thing and she did not mind if that was how he wanted to spend his spare time. It was better than drinking, which was what a lot of people did in the evenings, out of sheer boredom.

Then one evening the doctor announced to her that he had managed to acquire a new car through Ed. It was a Mercedes-Benz, he said, and he was sure that she would like it. It was the same model as the one which had belonged to the manager of the Uncle Charlie Hotel, but it was a different colour. The manager's car had been red; this one was black.

'How much did it cost?' she asked. 'Was it expensive?'

The doctor hesitated for a moment – just a moment. 'No,' he said. 'It was a very good bargain.'

He brought the car back to the house the following evening. He parked it in front of the veranda and invited her to inspect it.

'It runs beautifully,' he said. 'I'll take you up to Mbabane in it if you like. We could go right now.'

'No thanks,' she said. 'I don't want to travel at night. And you shouldn't either, or this one will end up down the hill like the Pontiac.

VII

The manager of the Uncle Charlie Hotel was astonished when he saw the doctor driving around in the Mercedes-Benz. 'It's the same model as mine was,' he said. 'Different colour. But otherwise the same. He's lucky to get a car like that.'

He asked the doctor one day whether he would mind if he

had a look at his new car. 'I'm pretty envious of you, doc,' he said. 'You know I had one just the same as that. I know how nice they are to drive. Lovely cars.'

'Yes,' said the doctor. He did not seem to be enthusiastic about showing his car to the manager, but he could hardly refuse. He drove it around one Saturday afternoon, and let the manager sit behind the wheel.

'Lovely workmanship,' said the manager, caressing the steering wheel. 'Beautiful.'

'Built to last,' said the doctor. 'I loved that old Pontiac of mine, but this is in a different league.'

'Take good care of it,' said the manager, ruefully. 'These things get stolen. And I suppose it's pretty easy to whip them away and then repaint them.'

The doctor nodded. 'I'll be careful,' he said. 'I put it away in my garage at nights, you know. That's the safest thing to do. And when I take it to the hospital, I park it right outside the main entrance where the porter can keep an eye on it.'

'Very wise,' said the manager. He fingered the steering wheel again, as if making contact with an old friend – an old friend who had been lost and was much regretted.

VIII

The doctor's wife left the household finances to her husband, who was good with accounts. She did not have a head for figures and simply drew on the housekeeping accounts that they kept in a small lock-up cupboard in the doctor's study. But one afternoon she was in the study, looking for an envelope, when she came across a file of bank statements. She decided, out of idle curiosity, to look at the regular withdrawals for obvious purposes: the payment of the account at the general store, the payment of the insurance premiums, and so on. That was all unexceptional. But then it occurred to her that it was strange that there was no payment for the new car. The money from the sale of the Volkswagen had been paid in, but nothing had gone out to pay for its replacement.

She reflected on her discovery that afternoon, and it suddenly occurred to her that the only explanation was that the car had cost him nothing. And then, while she was standing on the veranda, looking at a frangipani tree, the thought struck her: her husband must have stolen the car, taken it to Ed's, and repainted it. All he would have had to pay for was the paint, with perhaps a small amount for Ed's time and connivance. He could have managed to pay that out of his normal pin money.

She stood quite still for a while, trying to reach another, less disturbing conclusion; but she could not. She went out into the garden and walked about in the daisies that had been planted by the previous doctor. She sought another answer in the flowers, but there was none to be had. It appalled her to think that she lived with a man who was prepared to do that. But then she thought: do I really know him all that well? He never talks to me about the things that really move him. He never does that. He is a stranger in so many ways. Men are a different continent, she thought; distant, unpredictable. Perhaps I should not be surprised.

Then she debated with herself what she should do. She could not tell the manager of the Uncle Charlie Hotel that they had his car. She could not bear the shame that would follow. She imagined what they would say at the tennis club, what would be said behind her back. It would be intolerable to be the subject of such gossip. She would rather die than be disgraced in that way.

She would have to punish him herself, she thought. She would have to show him that he could not get away with a crime like that. She would be the agent of justice.

IX

The doctor's wife was not a keen driver, but she did occasionally drive the Mercedes-Benz to the tennis club or into town to buy meat and vegetables. Now she said to the doctor, 'I'd like to drive up to Mbabane some time next week to visit Jennifer. She's not been well and I want to catch up with her.' He said, 'That's fine. I'll get one of the hospital drivers to pick me up. You take the car.'

She went off that day. She drove up towards Mbabane and stopped near the top of the long incline, near a place where the road bent sharply. She got out to stretch her legs and looked down over the edge. The ground fell away sharply, down to a stand of eucalyptus trees far below. She heard the sound of their leaves in the wind, a sound that drifted up on the warm afternoon air. It was a beautiful country, she thought. There was so much beauty in Africa, but such wickedness too.

She returned to the car. The road was deserted, and so there was nobody to see her drive very slowly to the very edge of the road and then get out. She leaned against the car, the engine of which was still idling. She pushed, and very slowly it moved forward and then, in a sudden lurch, slipped over the edge. There was a crumbling of sand and dust from the edge of the road and a sound of crushing metal and the breaking of small trees. She watched as the car went down, turned over, and broke into flames. She leant down, picked up a handful of dust, and rubbed it into her face and hair. Then she tore her dress, and scratched at her arm with a stick until a small, bright line of blood appeared.

X

The doctor said to her, 'I'm so glad that you weren't hurt. It's you I care about. I don't care about the car.'

She said, 'You don't care about the car? Are you sure of that?'

He shook his head. 'No. Human life is more important than a machine. The important thing is that you weren't hurt. Well, hurt a tiny bit, but not much.'

She was silent for a moment. Then she said. 'You don't care about the car?' She paused, then, quite softly, as if remarking on something unimportant, she said, 'Well, I suppose it wasn't really your car in the first place, was it?'

The doctor said nothing. They had been sitting on the veranda and he now rose to his feet and walked over to peer at one of the bougainvillea bushes that twisted itself around one of the veranda pillars. Then he looked back at her. She saw that his face was drawn, aghast, uncomprehending.

'That poor little boy,' she said. 'He loved to go for drives with his father.'

Robert Goddard
Toupee for a Bald Tyre

A Misadventure from the Motor Trade Years of Harry Barnett

Swindon, 24 September 1970

If he had stayed in the pub, even for another five minutes, it probably would have been all right. Rillington had more or less said as much, which only made the thought more tantalising. Another five minutes; another pint; another gently blurred afternoon; for once, they would have added up to prudent business practice. Instead, Harry had returned dutifully, if far from soberly, to Barnchase Motors at half past two that afternoon – and found a visitor waiting for him.

'I was just about to give up on you, Mr Barnett,' Rillington explained, smiling thinly.

Harry sensed it was the only kind of smile that ever crossed his face. Rillington was a lean, sombre, narrow-eyed man of sixty or so, grey-suited, grey-haired, grey-*skinned*. On the early morning train journey to work that Harry imagined him taking, he would attract no one's attention, draw no one's glance, challenge no one's preconceptions. Yet here, seated stiffly on the other side of Harry's desk, briefcase clasped flatly in his lap, pursed lips emphasising his trimmed moustache, he did pose some kind of challenge. That much was already certain.

'Your secretary didn't seem to think it was worth my while waiting.'

'No?' Harry caught Jackie's eye through the glass partition

between his office and the outer room where she fitted occasional typing and telephone-answering into her nail-filing regime. Her devotedly plucked eyebrows arched meaningfully. 'She must have misunderstood. With my partner away for the day—'

'That would be Mr Chipchase.'

'Yes. He, er...'

'Is cheering on a horse at Newbury even as we speak, I dare say.'

'Ah, you—'

'Your secretary mentioned he was...entertaining some clients at the races.'

Clients? If only, Harry thought. But all he said was, 'Quite,' grinning manfully and shooting a glare at Jackie, who by chance or contrivance was no longer looking in his direction. His gaze reverted glumly to Rillington's card, which lay before him on the blotter, forming a small oblong of orderly typography in a jungle of scrawled telephone numbers, jotted mark-up calculations and obscene doodles.

C E Rillington
Motor Repairs Standards Assessor
H M Ministry of Transport
St Christopher House
LONDON SE1
Tel: 01-928-7999

'So what can I...do for you, Mr Rillington?'

'I'd like you to clarify a few points for me, Mr Barnett.'

'Oh yes?' Harry lit a cigarette, hoping he would appear what the advertisement for the brand promised – as cool as a mountain stream – but gravely doubting it. 'Smoke?' He proffered the pack to Rillington.

'I prefer a pipe.'

'Well...'

'Shall we get on, Mr Barnett? I'm sure we're both busy people.'

'Right.' Harry took a spluttering draw on the cigarette. 'Of course.'

'I popped into your workshop while I was waiting.'

'You did?'

'Young fellow called Vince showed me around.'

'Excellent.' I'll strangle Vince with a fan-belt, thought Harry. Slowly. 'Helpful lad.'

'Indeed. Not that he could help me with the...statistics of your operation.'

'No?'

'Your province, I rather think. Yours and...Mr Chipchase's.'

'Statistics, Mr Rillington? I'm not...'

'They can be the very devil, I find. But they tell a story. There's been a push to apply them to my field in particular since this government came into office. Computers are the future, Mr Barnett. We're only nibbling at the edges of what they can achieve.'

'Really? I don't know much about that kind of—'

'Take the Korek, for example. Feed its findings to a computer and—'

'The what?'

'The Korek, Mr Barnett. Not heard of it?'

'Dr Who's latest enemy?'

'Very amusing.' Rillington looked anything *but* amused.

'It's a machine that pulls out crushed car bodies, using air-operated rams to reverse the effects of a crash. We can then check the manufacturer's dimensions against the final size and shape.'

'Amazing.'

'And revealing. If the car fails to reach those dimensions, it's generally because it never did. Now, why might that be, do you suppose?'

'Can't imagine.'

'You're aware of the disreputable practice of welding together the intact halves of two damaged cars to produce what looks, to a hapless buyer's eye, like a pristine ready-to-drive-away bargain?'

'Well, I...'

'The Korek finds that trick out every time.'

'Does it?' Harry distractedly tapped ash off his cigarette and locked eyes hopelessly with Monsieur Michelin, who beamed up at him from his perch on the rim of the ashtray. 'How very clever of it.'

'Now, taken together with a separate investigation of tyre blow-outs where the driver, if he or she is lucky enough to emerge in one piece, reports recently fitting remoulds which, upon inspection—'

'What have remoulds got to do with body welding?'

'At first glance, nothing, Mr Barnett. But therein lies the beauty of the computer. It correlates the statistics, you see. It crunches the numbers and spits out...overlaps.'

'Overlaps?'

'Common sources...of cars that fail the Korek test...and tyres that have been remoulded a couple of times too many. At *least* a couple of times.'

'I see.' Dimly and queasily, Harry did indeed begin to see. The blind eye he had long turned to Chipchase's profitable innovations on the repair front had suddenly descried a disturbing vision.

'Bad luck? Bad workmanship? Or something more sinister? That's what we're bound to ask ourselves when the statistics point us so compellingly to a particular garage.'

'Well, I...' Harry puffed out his cheeks. 'I suppose you would be.'

'Vince and his less talkative colleague...Joe is it?'

'That's right.'

'They both seemed competent enough to me. Capable, even. Well capable.'

'Oh...good.'

'And I don't believe in luck.'

'You don't?'

'Which brings us—'

'Here's that tea I promised you, Mr Rillington,' trilled Jackie, as she toed the door abruptly open and entered with a tray bearing two cups and saucers and a plate of digestive biscuits. 'And coffee for you, Mr Barnett.' *Mr Barnett?* Jackie was evidently on her best behaviour, a small mercy for which Harry could not summon much gratitude. 'Black, I reckoned. Was that right?'

'Spot on,' mumbled Harry, noticing as Jackie plonked the tray down on the desk that Rillington's gaze left him and slid appreciatively up Jackie's long and shapely legs to the hem of her miniskirt, which at that height Harry judged could scarcely be concealing very much. The man was evidently not immune to temptation. A chink in the armour, perhaps? But a small chink, in evidently thick armour.

Jackie minced out. Rillington's eyes swung back to Harry. 'Sugar?' Harry ventured.

'No thank you.'

'Biscuit?'

'Just the tea, I think.' Rillington took a sip.

'Righto.' A gulp of strong black coffee cleared the last of the fog from Harry's brain. But clarity did not furnish inspiration. 'So, where, er…were we?'

'How long have you and Mr Chipchase been in business together, Mr Barnett?'

'It's, er…five years now.'

'Did you take this place over from someone else?'

'Knight's Motorcycles. They, er…went bust.'

'And how long had *they* been in business?'

'Oh, seven or eight years. Until the late Fifties there were fields here. The Belmont Brewery used to graze their dray-horses—' Harry broke off, smiling awkwardly. 'I'm sure you don't want a local history lesson.'

Rillington turned and squinted out through the window into the serried ranks of Barnchase Motors' used cars, gleaming in the sunshine on the forecourt laid where Harry had once as a child fed carrot-tops to Belmont's magnificent beast of burden. 'Sounds like a veritable lost Eden,' Rillington murmured.

'I wouldn't go that far.'

'And we can't turn back the clock anyway, can we, Mr Barnett?'

'Fraid not.'

'Good Lord.' Rillington's squint honed itself into a concentrated peer. 'Is that an E-Type you have out there?'

'Yes. I, er…believe it is.' A midnight-blue 1962 Jaguar E-

Type 3.8, to be precise. A snip at four hundred and ninety-nine guineas. A snip, indeed, at whatever price Rillington might be willing to pay. 'Fancy a test drive?' Harry asked impulsively.

'I wouldn't mind...taking a look.' A tinge of pleasurable anticipation had crossed Rillington's face. He sipped his tea, but his eyes remained fixed on the shimmering come-hither bonnet of the E-Type. Here was a second chink in his armour, one Harry was far better placed to exploit than the fleshy allurement of Jackie Fleetwood. 'I wouldn't mind at all.'

No more than a few minutes later, the two men were seated side by side in the car, Rillington's hands sliding slowly round the steering-wheel while Harry jingled the ignition key against the Jaguar's-head fob in what he judged to be a tempting tintinnabulation.

'Nought to sixty in seven seconds,' he purred. 'Top speed of a hundred and fifty. Really blows the cobwebs away.'

'I'm sure,' said Rillington.

'I could do a very special deal...for someone in your position.'

'No doubt.'

'What do you normally drive, Mr Rillington?'

'A Hillman Imp.'

'Well...need I say more?'

'Probably not.'

'Why don't you take her for a spin?'

'It's an idea.' Rillington smiled, less thinly than before, and moved his left hand from the steering-wheel towards the dangled ignition key. 'But not as good as *my* idea.' His hand froze.

'Sorry?'

'Once my report on this place hits the appropriate desk, you'll be for the high jump, Harry.' *Harry?* 'You and your race-going chum, Barry. It could be a police matter. It could be...the end of the line.'

Harry swallowed hard. 'Surely...not.'

'Oh yes.'

'But...'

'Cut as many corners as you have here and, sooner or later, you're bound to come to grief.'

'But...'

'Fortunately for you, there's a way out.'

'There is?'

'And it doesn't involve me taking this overpowered heap of junk off your hands.'

'No?'

'No. It involves something more...*recherché*. Which isn't French for remould.'

'I, er...don't...'

'Need to say a thing. Just listen. While I tell you a little story.' Rillington leant back in his seat. 'I used to do a bit of cycling, you know. Took it seriously. CTC membership. Fifty miles every weekend. Eighty every other. Proper racing bike. No half measures. Then, one Sunday morning, the bike let me down. The gears seized solid. There wasn't a thing I could do with it. I hadn't got far, so I wheeled it home, planning to strip it down in the garage. I got back several hours before I was due, of course. Bit of a surprise for the wife. More of one for me, though. I caught her with the husband of one of her Townswomen's Guild friends. In a compromising position, you might say. Very compromising. In fact, so compromising

I'd never even thought of it. An eye-opener. Yes. You could certainly call it that. Now, why am I telling you this pitiful tale of the cuckolded suburbanite?' Good question, Harry thought. 'Well, you may be surprised to learn that Mrs Rillington and I are still together. It was a simple choice really. I preferred trying to satisfy her exotic tastes to indulging my hurt pride and turning into a bitter and lonely old man. To tell the truth, I *enjoyed* trying to satisfy her tastes. And, if I say so myself, I succeeded beyond her expectations. She no longer needed to look elsewhere. Oh my word no. But continued success required continuous innovation. Mrs Rillington has recently expressed her interest in unusual locations for lovemaking. Bearing in mind her enthusiasm for all things rubber, I think I may have found an ideal venue. Your workshop, Harry. Plenty of tyres, most of them bald enough to avoid tread marks, adaptable to any required height or juxtaposition. And plenty of authentic, grease-smeared, petroleum-scented atmosphere. I can see it now. I almost feel it now. As for Mrs Rillington...' Rillington released a long, slow anticipatory breath. 'Enough said, I rather think.'

'You want to...use our workshop to...'

'It's her birthday today, Harry. We're making a long weekend of it. Starting tonight.'

'*Tonight?*'

'Why not?'

'Well, I...'

'Barnchase Motors can get a tick in every box from me. *If* you help me out. But if you're going to go all prissy on me...'

Harry smiled nervously. 'There's no question of that. I mean in this line of business, the customer is always right.'

'Glad to hear it. So...' Rillington flicked the still suspended ignition key with his forefinger. 'I don't think that's the right key. Do you?'

'Didn't think you'd get rid of him so easily,' said Jackie when Harry returned to the office after giving Rillington his key to the side-door of the workshop. 'I told Barry he had bad news written all over him.'

'Barry?'

'He phoned while you were out on the forecourt. Wanted to make sure everything was going smoothly, apparently.'

'I trust you told him it was.'

'Not exactly, no. Well, I didn't think it was, did I?'

'So, will Barry be rushing back to bale me out?'

'Didn't get that impression. Anyway, you don't need baling out now, do you?'

'No. As a matter of fact, I don't.'

'How *did* you get rid of him, then?'

'Who?' Harry countered coyly.

'Rillington. The guy with the wig.'

'Wig?'

'That hair's never natural. Didn't you notice?'

'Can't say I did.'

'Creepy, I'd call him. Could be a bit of a pervert on the quiet.'

'You reckon?'

'With that wig? And those X-ray eyes of his? Definitely kinky, I'd say.'

'Would you?' Harry yawned, exhaustion pouncing on him now the crisis was past. He could feel a doze coming on. 'Would you really?'

* * *

Harry was the last to leave Barnchase Motors that afternoon. Chipchase had not returned, which would have been unsurprising in the normal course of events but was utterly predictable given what Jackie had told him. MoT officials were not his company of choice. He was probably skulking in a pub in Newbury, fearing the worst. The thought gave Harry some small amount of pleasure. He would have to have a serious word with him about what Joe and Vince had been getting up to at his instigation. Harry would have to put his foot down. Firmly.

But that could wait. There was an evening of gentle recuperation to be passed first. A pint at the Beehive; collection of dirty washing from his house; delivery thereof to his dear and doting mother, followed by consumption of one of her steak and kidney puddings; several more pints at the Glue Pot, and an earlyish night. Just the therapy his frayed nerves needed. As for what might be happening in the workshop back at Barnchase Motors while he was thus engaged, he could only imagine. With relief as well as incredulity.

Chipchase finally put in an appearance as Harry was nearing the end of his first pint at the Glue Pot, entering the bar with his coat collar turned up and the brim of his racing felt angled over his eyes as if he was intent on being taken for a fugitive.

'Hellfire, Harry,' he said as he sat down. 'Am I pleased to see you.'

'Worried about me, were you Barry?'

'You bet.'

'But not enough to hurry back and face the music with me?'

'Well, pulling the wool over some nitpicking bureaucrat's

64   ROBERT GODDARD

eyes is more your speciality than mine. I didn't want to cramp your style.'

'That a fact?'

'And you look chipper enough, so I'm guessing you got said bureaucrat off our backs.'

'You guess right.'

'How'd you manage that?'

'All in good time, Barry. Let's begin with *why* he was on our backs in the first place.'

Chipchase's response to Harry's account of Rillington's visit to Barnchase motors was a characteristic blend of bombast and blandishment: Harry had never wanted to know exactly how the profits he shared in had been generated and it was too late to start now, even supposing there was any substance to Rillington's accusations, which naturally there was not; but Harry's negotiation of a solution to the problem qualified as a redeeming masterstroke.

'Wouldn't mind being a fly on the workshop wall tonight, hey? You played a blinder there, Harry old cock, you really did.'

'I'm glad you think so.' Harry was finding censoriousness difficult to maintain as pint and lurid images filled his mind.

'Got a mental picture of Mrs Rillington, have you?'

'Big woman, I should think.'

'Yeah. With a bit of a spare tyre.'

Harry finally cracked at that and descended into tearful mirth. 'Several spare tyres tonight,' he managed to say.

'In all kinds of juxtapositions,' Barry hooted.

'Oh dear, oh dear.' Harry dried his eyes as best he could. 'I wonder if his toupee'll stay on.'

'I doubt it.'

'*Did you say toupee?*'

They did not at first appreciate that the question had come from a third party. Eventually, however, as the gale of their laughter blew itself out, they noticed a man staring at them round the corner of the settle. He was a small, shrunken, whey-faced fellow of indeterminate age, dressed in a threadbare ratcatcher's coat and a greasy pork-pie hat.

Without waiting for an answer, he slid round, Mackeson in hand, and joined them at their table. 'Sounds like you could be talking about a mate of mine.'

'I doubt it,' said Harry.

'Fred Christie. Streaky, hawk-eyed bloke with a 'tache but not a strand of hair north of his eyebrows to call his own.'

'Never met him.'

'Are you sure about that? Only—'

'What does your mate do for a living?' put in Chipchase.

'How d'you mean?'

'Simple question, old cock. What's his line of work?'

'Well…'

'And what's yours, while we're about it?'

'Look…' The man leant forward and lowered his voice. 'I need to find Fred. Pronto. If you know where he is, I could, er, make it worth your while to point me in the right direction.'

'But Harry's already told you. We've never met him.'

'He, er, could be using a false name.'

'Oh yeah? Why might that be?'

'Let's just say…there are reasons.'

'Then we'd best be hearing what they are.'

'They're, er, private. Between him and me.'

'Not any more they aren't.' Chipchase gave the man a less than genial wink. 'Not if you want to get a chance to talk them over with Fred.'

'Are you saying you know where he is?'

'I'm saying we'll come clean if you'll come clean.'

The man squinted at each of them in turn. He did not look persuaded of the case for soul-baring.

'Have a think about it,' Chipchase continued. 'Harry and I are just off. We'll wait in my car. It's the Wolseley parked over the road. Two minutes.' He raised a pair of fingers. 'Then we skedaddle. So...don't think about it too long.'

'What are you playing at, Barry?' Harry demanded as soon as they were outside.

'Following my nose, Harry. Always a good policy.'

'You can't seriously think that creep really is a friend of Rillington's.'

'The description matched, didn't it?'

'That's rich. I was the one who met Rillington, not you.'

'Thin. Moustache. Toupee. You telling me that isn't Rillington?'

'I'm telling you—'

Chipchase whipped the driver's door open and flung himself in, slamming it behind him. Harry sighed heavily, opened the passenger door and clambered in.

'I'm telling you,' Harry resumed in a level tone, 'that there isn't a single good reason to believe a word this bloke says.'

'No?'

'Of course not.'

'How about your MoT man's choice of moniker?'

'What?'

'According to our friend, his real name's Christie.'

'So?'

'Like the murderer.'

'Like the actress too. And the whodunit writer. I don't see—'

'Never mind them. Where did Christie the *murderer* live, Harry? Tell me that. Surely you remember. It was all over the papers.'

Enlightenment dawned slowly on Harry in the Swindonian night. Christie the murderer. Of course. Harry had even flicked through a book about the case his mother had borrowed from the library. He really should have remembered the title. His pseudo-civil-servant visitor of earlier in the day clearly had. 'Ten Rillington Place,' he murmured.

'Exactly.'

'Bloody hell.'

'Looks like you've been had, Harry. And here comes the man who can tell us why.' A shadowy figure in a pork-pie hat had just emerged from the Glue Pot. He peered suspiciously about him, then headed towards them. 'Leave this to me.'

As the man slid into the seat behind them, Harry sensed all was not quite right.

Long before he could have said why, however, he felt something cold and hard pressing into the back of his neck.

'Yes, Harry, it's a gun,' said Fred Christie, aka C E Rillington of the Ministry of Transport. 'One false move by you or Barry and your brains will be all over the windscreen.'

'Bloody hell.'

'Exactly. Very bloody indeed.'

'Calm down, mate,' said Chipchase, characteristically recommending a course of action he was obviously not following himself. 'There's no—'

'I'm not your mate, Barry. And I'm perfectly calm, thank you. But I *am* a little short of time and patience, so we'll dispense with the niceties. I tried the roundabout route and it didn't work. How much did Arnie tell you?'

'You mean the owner of that hat?'

'The very same.'

'Well, nothing really, except he knew you…and…'

'You weren't from the MoT,' Harry finished off, swallowing hard. 'We, er, stepped out here for a word in private.'

'And that's what we're having, Harry. Arnie's collecting his thoughts in the Gents. He'll be collecting them for quite a while, actually, so there's no immediate rush, but we do need to press on. Once I'd checked the workshop, I realised we'd have to resume our conversation on a more realistic basis. I asked after you at the pub where you take your liquid lunch and the mention of several other watering holes where I might find you. This was second on the list. I imagine Arnie came here because it's close to the station. He'd have been hoping to get some directions. Geography's not his strong point. Never was.'

'You and he…go back a long way, do you?'

'Too long. But let's get to the point. Where's my money?'

'Money?'

'Don't act dumb with me. I kept a careful mental note of the burial spot. It was a tricky exercise, pacing out across your yard and workshop what I originally paced out across a field. But there's not a shadow of a doubt. I checked and double-checked. The inspection pit is exactly where I buried the money – and several feet deeper than I dug. Well, Arnie did most of the digging, to tell the truth, but that doesn't give him any prior claims in my judgement, considering I went down for a longer stretch and we'd have been caught in possession, but for me thinking on my feet. Now, you said Knight's Motorcycles owned the site before you, didn't you, Harry?'

'Yes,' came a hoarse response in what Harry barely recognised as his own voice.

'Did they have an inspection pit?'

'No.'

'So, you installed it?'

'Yes.'

'In that case, I return to my original question: where's my money?'

'We don't know,' said Chipchase.

'You dug the pit. Harry's just admitted it. You couldn't have avoided finding the money.'

'*We* didn't dig it. We got a builder in.'

'Sharland,' said Harry, his heart sinking as he realised the significance of the builder's identity.

Now it was Chipchase's turn to say, 'Bloody hell.'

'What about Sharland?' snapped Christie.

'Our workshop was the last job he ever did,' Chipchase replied. 'He had a big Pools win straight after and retired.'

'A Pools win?'

'So he said.'

'And where did he retire to?'

'Spain, wasn't it, Harry?'

'Florida, I heard.'

'*Shut up.*' The pressure against Harry's neck increased. 'Why should I believe any of this?'

'Well, there's the fact that Sharland's bronzing himself in

some palatial villa in the sun...' Chipchase began.

'While we're still stuck here in Swindon,' Harry rounded off.

'Bit of a choker for all of us,' Chipchase went on. 'No wonder the last time I saw the bloke he was grinning like the cat that's got the cream. Not that I know how much cream there was, of course.'

Christie said nothing. Harry's heart was thumping in his ears. A rivulet of sweat was inching down his temple. His breaths came fast and shallow.

'What now?' Chipchase asked eventually.

'Now?' Christie responded, as if from some more distant place than the rear seat of the car. 'You'd better start driving.'

'Where to?'

'Head west. Towards the motorway.'

'There's not a lot more we can—'

'*Just drive.*'

'OK, OK.'

The bleak thought formed in Harry's mind that this was likely to be a one-way journey. Either Christie believed them, in which case he was probably planning to kill them before going after Sharland. Or he did not believe them, in which case...

'That's funny.' Chipchase had got no response from the starter. He turned the ignition key off, then back on and tried the starter again. To no effect. 'The engine's dead.'

'Don't play games with me,' said Christie. 'Start the bloody car.'

'I can't.' There was another futile wrestle with ignition key and starter. 'It's dead as a doornail.'

'Do you take me for a fool? *Get this thing moving.*'

'I can't, I tell you.'

'Barry,' Harry put in, 'for God's sake—'

'I'm not kidding, Harry. It's kaput.'

'But you've just driven it from Newbury.'

'I know, I know. It doesn't make sense.' Chipchase glanced back at Christie. 'Why don't I take a look under the bonnet. There must be a loose connection.'

'There'd need to be a loose connection under *my* bonnet to fall for that one.'

'It's God's honest truth. I don't know what's the matter with the thing. Let me give it the once-over. You'll still have Harry as hostage. I'm not going to leg it with an old mate's life on the line, am I?'

Harry closed his eyes for a second, praying silently that Chipchase might once be relied upon.

'All right,' said Christie after a long and breathless moment's thought. 'Go ahead.' He pushed his door open. 'But remember: I'll have time to plug you as well as Harry if you try to scarper.'

'OK. Understood.' Chipchase climbed out, moved round to the front of the car and raised the bonnet, obscuring their view of him.

'*Stand where I can see you*,' shouted Christie.

Chipchase edged back into view round the nearside wing. He secured the bonnet-strut, then peered down into the engine.

'*Now you know how it feels*.'

The voice had carried distinctly through the still night air, though where it had carried *from* Harry could not have said. His eyes swivelled in search of the source.

'That Zephyr you sold me conked out the second trip I

took in it.' The source materialised in Harry's field of vision, striding towards Chipchase along the pavement. 'And what did that mealy mouthed partner of yours say? Not our problem. Well, it is *now*.' It was Mr Gifford, outraged and out-of-pocket buyer of one of Barnchase Motors' less durable used cars. Harry recalled a recent conversation with him. It had not ended harmoniously. 'Since I can't drive my car, I don't see why you should be able to drive yours, *Mr* Chipchase.'

Chipchase seemed lost for words. He glanced up at the approaching figure of Gifford – a bullet-headed, square-shouldered fellow carrying some weight he looked intent on throwing around – then gaped helplessly back at Harry through the windscreen.

'There's *Mr* Barnett as well,' roared Gifford, pointing an accusing finger at Harry. 'Get yourself out here and join the fun, why don't you?'

'Bloody hell,' murmured Harry.

'Come on.' Gifford yanked Harry's door open. 'Let's be having you.'

'Bugger it,' said Christie. Quietly and decisively.

Harry flinched at the words and closed his eyes, reckoning the odds were heavily weighted in favour of Christie pulling the trigger at that moment.

But he did not pull the trigger.

The pressure was suddenly removed from Harry's neck. There was a scuffling sound behind him. Then a pounding of running feet on paving stones. He opened his eyes. Both Chipchase and Gifford were looking past the car along the street. Harry turned to look in the same direction.

Just in time to see the pork-pie-hatted, toupee-sporting

figure of Fred Christie vanishing at a trot round the corner into Faringdon Road.

'Who's that?' demanded Gifford.

'You don't want to know,' Chipchase replied, leaning back against the wing of the Wolseley and tipping up the brim of his hat to wipe the sweat off his brow. 'Believe me.'

'I thought...he was going to shoot me,' Harry said unevenly. He made to climb out of the car, but his legs buckled beneath him. Gifford had to help him out in the end, frowning in puzzlement at his sudden conversion from saboteur to saviour.

'What's going on?' Gifford asked, almost solicitously.

'Long story,' said Harry.

'He dropped the gun,' said Chipchase, pointing to a dark shape lying a few feet away in the gutter. 'Can you believe it? He dropped it and ran.'

'Gun?' Gifford stared at them in astonishment. 'You mean there are customers of yours even more pissed off than me?'

'In a sense,' mumbled Harry.

'But a *gun*? That's a bit strong.' Gifford stepped towards the discarded weapon, then stopped – and laughed.

'What's so funny?' growled Chipchase.

'This gun.' Gifford stooped and picked it up.

'Be careful with it.'

'Don't worry. It's not connected.'

'Connected?'

'It's a petrol-pump nozzle.' Gifford held it up for them to see. And a petrol-pump nozzle was indeed what they beheld. 'Gallon of thin air for you two?'

'Bloody hell,' said Harry.

'He must have filched it from the workshop,' said Chipchase.

'Let's hope that's all he filched.'

'*Where's he gone?*'

The shout had come from the doorway of the Glue Pot. They turned to see Arnie, bare-headed and even wobblier on his feet than Harry, staring blearily across at them and rubbing what was presumably a tender spot behind his left ear.

'That way,' said Harry and Barry in unison, pointing in the direction Christie had taken off in.

'He won't give me the slip this time,' Arnie declared optimistically before setting off in tepid pursuit.

A brief silence, borne of general disbelief, fell upon them. Then Chipchase said, 'Maybe we should phone the police.'

'Never thought I'd hear those words coming out of your mouth, Barry,' Harry responded, truthfully enough.

'Neither did I.' Chipchase shrugged. 'Anyway, I only said *maybe*.'

'What about my car?' Gifford cut in, seeming suddenly to remember his grievance.

'What about *mine*?' Chipchase countered.

'Listen.' Harry's spirits had revived sufficiently for him to assume the role of conciliator. 'Come to the office tomorrow, Mr Gifford, and I'll give you a full refund for the Zephyr, plus ten per cent for the inconvenience you've been put to.'

'If you think you can fob me off with a rubber cheque, you've got—'

'Cash in hand. And call it quits. Provided you replace whatever vital part you took out of this Wolseley, of course.'

'Well...' Gifford softened. 'I suppose...that'd be all right.'

'Hold up, Harry,' said Chipchase under his breath. 'I know you've just had a nasty experience, but don't you think you're getting a bit carried away? A *full refund*?'

'In the circumstances, I reckon we can afford to be generous.'

'Yeah? Well, there's generous and there's over-generous and then there's plain bloody crazy. We don't have to—'

'Tell you what, Barry. You can stay out here and haggle with Mr Gifford if you like. Or you can join me in the pub. But I need a drink. And it won't wait.'

So saying, Harry turned and steered a straightish path across the street towards the Glue Pot, tossing back a concluding comment over his shoulder as he went.

'It's up to you.'

Frank Stout was a serial killer. He hadn't intended to be – he'd always planned to be an accountant. But instead, he became a serial killer who raised maggots.

This is how it happened.

Some of us – a few – are born to maggots. Some of us – most, in fact – achieve maggots eventually. And some of us have maggots thrust upon us. Frank's father, Harry Stout, achieved maggots earlier than most. He was thirty when he lost his job as a clerk in a local tax office. He read through his notice of redundancy with a growing sense of dread. He and his wife, Cynthia, had just bought, at more expense than Harry had ever imagined, a small semi on a modern housing estate at the edge of town. They would have to sell up. They would have to move, though Harry couldn't think where. Cynthia would not be happy.

She wasn't. Jobs were scarce, and Harry had not been able to find other employment. Cynthia was still expanding on her displeasure six weeks later over breakfast. 'It's no wonder no one wants to take you on,' she was saying as she cracked the shell of her egg with a sharp rap. 'Look at you. You're…'

The letter box rattled, and Harry escaped to collect the post. There were three letters, all addressed to him. Cynthia opened them. One was from a credit company offering to lend them improbable amounts of money at interest rates that were very small, at least as far as the font size went; a letter in a somewhat larger font told them that if they didn't pay off their mortgage arrears they would be evicted; and there was a third letter. Cynthia studied the envelope. 'Cowlishaw and

Thring,' she said. 'Solicitors.' She fixed her husband with a suspicious gaze. 'What have you been up to now, Harry?'

Harry concentrated on his cornflakes. She opened the envelope and slowly unfolded the sheets of paper inside.

Harry hadn't been up to anything. It was his uncle, Ted Stout, who had, or rather, who wouldn't be up to anything much any more. He had died, leaving his nephew as his sole surviving relative and the heir to his estate, the smallholding and farmhouse that Harry had visited when he was a child.

'Meadowsweet Farm,' Cynthia said, after she had read the letter. 'Meadowsweet Farm, Honeysuckle Lane, Lark Meadows...' She looked at her husband with more favour than she was generally given to. 'Well. I've never lived in the country. I suppose it will have to do.' And she consented to leave the tiny semi and move north to take over the tenancy of Meadowsweet Farm.

Harry had vague memories of the farm. As he, Cynthia and their six-year-old son, Frank, drove north, he let himself dream a little, about meadows full of wild flowers and hills in a misty blue distance. He was a man who had yet to learn the danger in dreams.

Times had changed since his childhood visits. The road that led to the farm was still called Honeysuckle Lane, the area where the farm stood was still called Lark Meadows, but the signpost pointing in the direction of the farm said, perhaps unintentionally, all that was needed: Municipal Dump.

The fields had vanished under industrial shacks, the hedgerows had been grubbed out, the lanes had become roads, and the pastures where the cows used to graze had become a landfill site, run by Meadowlands Waste Management, plc.

'You've made me move to a rubbish tip,' Cynthia sobbed to her husband as he unpacked their bags from the car. 'My mother told me you'd never amount to anything, but I didn't listen to her, fool that I was!'

Uncle Stout's old dog, Mortimer, uncurled from the blanket under the sink where he slept, and crept out, roused by the noise. 'And you can get rid of that!' Cynthia wept, pointing at him.

Mortimer sat back on his hind legs and started scratching with a *scruff, scruff* sound. Frank, curious, reached out his hand and touched the rough hair. His mother screamed in horror. 'Frank! Don't touch that filthy animal!' Her face was red and her eyes bulged with emotion. She turned on her husband. 'Get rid of it! Tie a brick round its neck and throw it in the canal!' She grabbed Frank's wrist and hauled him away. 'I'm taking Frank and I'm going to my mother's.' She dragged the bewildered Frank to the car, and drove off, leaving Harry alone.

He stood in the doorway and looked at the derelict farm, at the sheds with the sagging corrugated roofs, and the rutted yard in front of the house, and his shoulders drooped. Something cold thrust itself into his hand. He looked down. Mortimer blinked up at him with rheumy eyes. 'I'm sorry, old boy,' Harry said. 'She'll not tolerate you, not at any price.' He gave Mortimer away to a man he met in the pub, an old man who liked to sit in a dark corner and drink beer, and was happy to have a dog as a drinking companion.

Day and night, trucks passed the farm gate on their way to the landfill, their engines throbbing as they laboured up the hill, heavy with their load. They cruised past on their way back, their rusty, high-sided dumpers empty. Harry read the legend on the sides of the trucks: Meadowlands – managing waste for *you*.

Harry walked the bounds of the farm. It consisted of the yard, the farmhouse, the outbuildings and some scrubland that had once been a field. All the rest had vanished under the landfill. There was a wall at the edge of the field, marking the boundary between Harry's land and that of Meadowlands Waste. Water seeped under the wall and trickled into the drainage ditch that was choked with a grey, slimy weed. Nothing grew in the field. Nothing grew anywhere. The land was dead.

He approached Meadowlands Waste. He thought they might like to buy the farm and have more space to dump more waste. The agent's voice was cool as he explained the situation to Harry. Yes, the owners of the site would like to buy the farm. He told Harry the sum they were willing to pay. Harry protested, and the agent smiled. 'Who else will buy it?' he said.

Harry got out his life insurance policy and read it carefully. Then he went to the cupboard under the stairs and took out the shotgun that his uncle had kept illegally for years. It was probably a good thing that, before he took any drastic action, he checked his bank statement to see what funds, if any, he would leave to his family apart from the insurance payout. The overdraft was impressive, but what was even more impressive was the fact that the bank had not paid the insurance premium for the last six months. The policy had lapsed.

It was the end. He could think of nothing else to do.

He looked around the yard. Nothing grew. No birds sang. Nothing could live near the landfill. Except the rats. They seemed to thrive for a while, but then even they died. One of the corpses lay rotting in the yard. Moodily, he turned it over with his foot. A cloud of bluebottles rose from it, their buzzing making a high-pitched, sticky sound. He looked at the heaving mass of maggots that was already infesting the corpse.

It is in moments of true darkness that the real mettle of a man is tested. When life gives you lemons, make lemonade. He saw in front of him, like a vision, the rivers and the canals, the streams and the lakes, the waterways of Britain. And in his vision, he saw ranks of men standing on the river banks and tow paths, rods raised, lines running out into the water, thousands upon thousands. He could see the expanding ripples in the water where the fish had jumped. It was an epiphany.

There *was* something that could live on this land.

Six months later, he drove to his mother-in-law's, his brand new BMW dominating the road. He pulled up outside the house, jumped down from the driver's seat and marched up to the front door. He rapped smartly on the glass.

Cynthia had been peering round the curtains to observe Harry's arrival. She opened the door and looked at her husband with disapproval. 'What have you been getting up to now?' she said.

Under his wife's cold eye, Harry's newly found confidence dwindled. He looked at his feet. 'What you asked me to, dear,' he said. 'Fixing the place up. Providing for you. Please come and see.'

Cynthia stood in thought. Harry was Harry, but her mother was getting on her nerves. And the car was the latest model. 'Alright,' she said, after a moment. They collected Frank from school – it was only a short walk away, but she insisted they take the car – and Harry drove his family back up north.

When they arrived at Meadowsweet Farm, Cynthia stepped out of the car. She looked round, and her eyes narrowed. 'What's that?' she said. She was looking at a new shed, a huge, corrugated iron construction that stood, dark and silent against the evening sky. 'Well?' She eyed her husband narrowly.

The breeze blew towards them, and for a moment, they were enveloped in an appalling stench. 'I'm going nowhere till I know what you've got in there,' she said, folding her arms.

'Magg...mushrooms!' he said. 'Lots of money in mushrooms. White gold. Don't you worry about it, dear. Please come back. And tomorrow, we can go shopping.'

Ten years passed. Frank, at his mother's insistence, had been sent away to school. He didn't like it. It was the kind of school where the boys were supposed to be good at sport, at rowing and rugby and cricket. He was good at maths. But he grew up biddable and well-spoken. His mother was pleased.

On his sixteenth birthday, he came home for the summer so that his father could show him the family business. 'This is how it works, son,' Harry said, proudly. Every morning, trucks came up the lane, but not to Meadowlands Waste plc. Meadowlands Waste had been sued for breaching environmental regulations and had been closed down. The trucks came to Meadowsweet Farm now. They pulled into the yard and dumped their loads into the sheds that stood in the once derelict field. Frank gagged at the smell that rose up.

'Ragmeat,' Harry said, rubbing his hands with satisfaction. 'Where do the farmers get rid of their dead chickens? Their diseased cows and sheep? Easy. They pay me, they bring them here, and my little beauties do the rest. Come on, son.'

He took Frank into the first shed. Frank held his scarf over his nose, and looked at the mound of dead and decaying flesh on the floor. A movement caught his eye. He leaned forward and saw the whole pile was gently heaving. Tentatively, he reached out with his foot and turned it over. He recoiled. It was a white, seething mass.

'My beauties,' his father said. 'My white gold. Now come and meet my queens.'

Frank looked into Harry's shining eyes, and decided that his father must have gone insane some years ago. He caught his breath, apprehension rising up in him as he followed Harry to the door of the next shed. His father pushed it open and Frank looked in. He could see a dim room with walls that were dark and iridescent.

As they stepped through, a shrill chorus filled the air as the walls took flight. Fat bluebottles launched themselves into space and flew madly around in the shadows, their bodies making a tinny noise as they batted against the walls and the roof. Something landed on Frank's cheek, something else on the lids of his swiftly closed eyes. Something explored his lips, something tried to explore his nostril. He blew out through his nose and gripped it, began to open his mouth to breathe, closed it again. He wanted to scream.

'My queens,' his father said proudly. 'Here, Bess! Here!'

Frank looked round in the dim light, blinking his eyes to keep away the questing flies. Bess? Had his father brought a dog in with them? But his father was standing with his hand raised, a hand that slowly vanished under an iridescent glove. 'Good girls,' his father said. 'Good girls.'

* * *

Frank returned to school with his mind made up. His visit home had decided him. He was going to be an accountant. His headmaster, apprised of his plans, looked resigned. He didn't expect his boys to become accountants. He expected them to become captains of industry, to employ accountants, teams of accountants. In one or two cases, they employed so much time of so many accountants that their names appeared in the Sunday papers and they had to take long holidays in certain South American states.

On the other hand... He contemplated the youth in front of him, noting the pale skin that always looked slightly damp. He noted the pink-rimmed eyes, blinking a little as though the light was too bright. He noted the thin, mousy hair. An accountant.

'Very well, Stout,' he said, his voice kind.

But it was just a few weeks into term that Frank was summoned to the headmaster's study again. He edged nervously through the door, and saw to his alarm his mother sitting there, snuffling into a lacy handkerchief.

The headmaster looked up and cleared his throat. 'Ah, Stout,' he said. 'Very bad show. Dreadful news. You must take care of your mother, lad.'

And to Frank's deep and abiding horror, his mother fell on his shoulder with a howl of anguish. 'Frank!' she sobbed. 'My Frankie. My poor, fatherless boy!' From this, Frank gathered that his father had died, but it was some days before he found out the circumstances of his death, suffocated under a delivery of ragmeat as he was checking the welfare of his latest clutch of maggots.

'You must come home with me,' his mother wept. 'You must be the man of the house now.' She looked at the headmaster. 'We'll expect a rebate on this term's fees.'

'Our policy is no remission of fees,' the headmaster said automatically. 'You can take it up with our accountants, if you wish.'

So Frank had maggots thrust upon him.

He remembered his father's pride in his work and he tried to cultivate – if not love, at least respect for the bluebottle, and its offspring. But it was as if they knew that the person who had cared for them was gone. It was as if they knew that no matter how meticulously Frank attended to their welfare, he wasn't a true maggot man. The number and quality of larvae deteriorated. They were smaller. They were less plump and juicy. They weren't so lively as bait, less inclined to wriggle alluringly on the end of a hook, enticing the fish to swallow the barb. Sales began to drop off. Frank proposed to his mother that she sell the maggot farm, and he would take his accountancy exams.

His mother was horrified. 'Sell your father's farm? His life's work? What kind of son are you? Shame on you Frank.'

So the years went by and Frank continued to raise maggots.

One rainy afternoon after the delivery truck had been, he was working on the accounts for Meadowsweet Farm. It was the one task that gave him real pleasure. He was absorbed in the books, when the door opened and a young woman came in. 'Oh,' she said in surprise. She was carrying a heavy box full of cleaning equipment, as well as the old-fashioned vacuum cleaner that his mother had never bothered replacing. 'I'm so sorry. I didn't mean to disturb you.'

Frank leapt to his feet. 'Let me help you with those,' he said. 'You aren't disturbing me,' he added. He realised at once who she was. She was his mother's most recent cleaner. His mother seemed to get through cleaners rather quickly. This one was small and pretty, and she told him that her name was Sheena.

Later that afternoon, when she'd finished her work, she brought him a cup of tea, and seemed inclined to talk. They talked about Frank's exams and about Sheena's career as an actress. She worked as a cleaner because she earned very little money from acting, and wasn't trained to do anything else. 'I wasn't very clever at school,' she confided. She had, however, just been offered a part in the Christmas pantomime at the small theatre in town. 'It could be my big break,' she told him. 'Juliet LeJoy is starring.'

Frank had never heard of Juliet LeJoy, but Sheena seemed excited so he smiled and nodded. He thought that he had never before seen a girl as pretty as Sheena.

She looked at her watch, and her face flushed a beautiful pink. 'Oh, my goodness,' she said. 'Look at the time.' She hurried out. Frank looked at the clock. They'd been talking for an hour.

After that, he looked forward to the days she worked. They got into the habit of having lunch together. Sheena would make sandwiches, and then they would sit at the old farmhouse table where Frank did the accounts, and talk. Frank had never really talked to a girl before. They didn't seem to notice him. Sheena did.

She listened to everything he said with wide-eyed fascination. He even told her about his dreams of becoming an accountant. 'You're so clever,' she sighed.

And in the week before Christmas, she brought some mistletoe to the gloomy farmhouse – Cynthia had decided that they couldn't possibly celebrate Christmas in the years since her husband had died – and held it above Frank's head. She stood on tiptoe, and touched his cheek with her lips. 'See you in the New Year,' she whispered. Frank's face was scarlet, and his head was spinning.

He didn't notice Cynthia watching the exchange from the door of her room.

When the festive season was over, the day came for Sheena's return. Frank lingered over breakfast, then, wanting some activity that would keep him in the house, he set to work putting up some shelves in the kitchen. He was aware of his mother's eyes on him as he wielded the powerful cordless drill.

'It's very inconsiderate of you to make a mess in here today,' she said after a while. 'Mrs Mason isn't coming until Thursday.'

'I'll clear up,' Frank said. He had no intention of leaving the mess for Sheena. Then he realised what his mother had said. 'Who's Mrs Mason?'

His mother lifted her tea cup to her mouth, and drank before she answered. 'You don't make the tea strong enough, Frank. Mrs Mason is our new cleaner. She's starting on Thursday.'

The drill felt heavy in Frank's hands. 'What about Sheena?'

Cynthia's lips thinned. 'I sacked her,' she said.

'You can't sack her.' Frank stepped towards her, his hands held out. 'Please, mother. I love her.' He hadn't realised it before, but as soon as he said it, he knew it was true.

'Love her,' his mother scoffed. 'She was just making up to you because she's after your money. I said so in the letter. Well,' she sipped her tea again, '*you* did. It was one of the letters you signed last week.' She pushed her chair away from the table and stood up.

'Mother! You've got to tell her...'

She ignored him and went to leave the room. Frank reached out to stop her, forgetting that he had the drill in his hands. He flinched as she tried to push past him, and his finger tightened inadvertently on the trigger. The drill howled and his mother shrieked – once.

It is a fact that Frank was probably aware of, but to which he hadn't until that moment given much thought, that the human eyeball does not require something as powerful as a Bosch drill with a masonry bit to penetrate it. A simple hand drill would have sufficed.

'Mother?' he said, apprehensively. He looked at the body on the floor, then he looked at the drill in his hand. He wasn't stupid. He knew how this would look.

As he stood there, frozen, the phone rang. He picked it up. 'Meadowsweet Bait,' he said automatically. It was the delivery firm. They wouldn't be able to bring the truck load of carcasses until the next day. After he had rung off, Frank stood there staring at the wall. He'd killed his mother. Her body was in the kitchen. But he had more important things to deal with. The truck wasn't coming. The maggots would go hungry, and then some of them would die. His father would never have allowed that to happen.

He looked at the phone. He looked at his mother's body. He looked at the maggot shed.

And he had an idea.

The maggot farm was thriving again. Somehow, Frank had become attuned to the bluebottles, and to their larvae. He owed them a debt of gratitude for saving him from considerable embarrassment. Two weeks after his mother's unfortunate accident, he collected the clean, white bones – how strange that his all-powerful mother should really have been so small – and dropped them down the well in the middle of the yard. The run-off from the landfill site had poisoned the well a long time ago, leaving the water toxic and corrosive. He thought it would suit his mother very well.

He decided that he would probably be best advised not to use a cordless drill again – the manufacturers do warn against the possibility of accidents – so he stowed it in his car with a view to getting rid of it some time.

He told himself he was happy. But he was lonely. He missed Sheena. He'd tried phoning her, but she'd put down the phone. He'd sent a letter, but she'd returned it unopened. He needed to talk to her, to explain to her that it hadn't been him that had written to her in such a hurtful way, to tell her that he would think it an honour if she were to accept his hand, and his fortune.

He waited outside her flat, but he didn't have the courage to approach her. He followed her to the theatre, where he saw the huge posters adorning the walls: *Juliet LeJoy in Aladdin! With Bobby Beaver as Widow Twankey!* The names didn't mean anything to him, but he noticed that the show was running until the end of January. He went to the box office at once, and bought a ticket for every night.

That evening, he sat at the front of the dress circle, entranced by the brilliance of the stage. The curtain drew back, the dancers came on and there, tiny and airy and graceful, was Sheena, more beautiful than he had remembered. To Frank, she was the star of the show, the light that illuminated the stage, though in truth, he had to twist in his seat and peer to even see her, because Juliet LeJoy, a strapping woman with yellow hair, seemed always to be between Sheena and the audience, seemed to edge her off the stage, and to cut her few moments of performance short. Frank didn't care. He had seen Sheena again.

After that first night, he went to the best florist in town and ordered the biggest and the most expensive bouquet they could produce. He stood in the shadows outside the stage door that evening, waiting for her to arrive. But when she came, she was with a young man, looking up at him as they walked, listening with that intent, serious expression Frank remembered so well. His heart twisted, and he stepped back into the shadows.

Every evening, it was the same. He would wait with a new bouquet, but even though, after that first evening, Sheena arrived alone, he couldn't screw up the courage to approach her. It was almost the end of January, and the last performance loomed. Frank waited, determined that this time, he would speak to her. But when she arrived, she was on the arm of the young man. He stood there in despair. He'd lost her. He was turning to leave – he couldn't bear to watch her in her last performance – when a car pulled up at the stage door. 'Take it round to my parking space,' the driver ordered the doorman as she got out. 'And don't make a mess of it this time.'

Frank realised it was Juliet LeJoy, the star of the show. She worked with Sheena. She would see Sheena in just a few moments. He cleared his throat. 'Excuse me,' he said.

She raised her eyebrows as she ran her eyes up and down him. 'Yes?' Her voice wasn't friendly.

'I wondered,' Frank said timidly, 'if you would give these flowers to Sheena...' His voice trailed off as he realised his mistake.

'How dare...' she began, then her eyes narrowed as she looked at the bouquet. It was the most expensive the flower shop could provide – roses and maidenhair fern and orchids and lilies. Her eyes studied Frank more closely, looked past him to his brand new Toyota Land Cruiser V6 300 turbo inter-cooler. She gave him a dazzling smile. Her teeth had a porcelain whiteness that reminded him of the sheen on a bluebottle's egg. 'I'll see what I can do,' she said, and took the bouquet into the theatre with her.

Frank sat in his accustomed place, rigid with tension. The music played, the dancers swirled. Sheena glittered in her small part. And then at the end of the show, the cast lined up to take a final bow. Frank could see a stagehand waiting in the wings, carrying a magnificent bouquet, the bouquet that he had bought for Sheena. He watched, not breathing, waiting for Sheena's face to light up when she was presented with the flowers. She would read the card and know that he was there. And when she looked round the theatre, he would bow and she would see him, and after the show when she came out of the stage door, he would step out of the shadows, and...

The stagehand stepped forward. He raised the bouquet, and laid it reverentially in the arms of Juliet LeJoy. She gasped with manufactured pleasure and read the card. Then she looked directly at Frank and blew him a kiss. And at the same time, Sheena looked up and saw him sitting there. She gave him a sad smile that pierced his heart.

Disconsolate, he walked slowly to the stage door, and found Juliet LeJoy waiting for him. 'I'm so sorry,' she said, 'but Sheena was upset about the flowers. She was afraid that her fiancé – did you know she's engaged to be married? – her fiancé would be terribly angry if a man sent her a bouquet like that. So I promised her I would pretend they were for me.'

Frank felt as though his heart had been torn in two.

'You're the man who owns Meadowsweet Farm, aren't you?' Juliet LeJoy went on. 'She told me about you. We could go for a drink, if you like.' Frank, numb with grief, barely heard what she was saying. She climbed into his car, then looked at him with surprised impatience. 'Come on,' she said.

Slowly, he sat behind the wheel. 'Where do you want to go?' he said.

Soon, they were sitting in the plush bar of the only five star hotel in the area. Frank sipped orange juice while Juliet drank something called a Slippery Nipple, and talked.

She told him how famous she was, except people didn't appreciate her any more. She told him how expensive it was to buy the clothes she needed for public appearances, how she needed someone to invest in a show in which she would star.

When they left the hotel, she snuggled up to him and asked him if he would drive her home. He didn't want to, but he didn't seem to have a choice. They drove for a while, then she directed him to park his car in a secluded lane. Frank looked out at the dark landscape. 'You live here?' he said. He couldn't see any houses.

Before he could say anything else, he was seized in a violent embrace. Juliet pressed her lips against his astonished gape, her tongue flopping in his mouth like a netted goldfish. She fell back onto the car seat, and pulled him down on top of her. She seemed to have double the usual complement of hands that found their way through every weak spot the barrier of his clothes presented. 'Frank!' she moaned.

Then she pushed his head down, down below her protuberant chest, below her belt, below... His mouth fell open in panic. He felt a pair of thighs muffle his ears as her heels landed against his shoulders and her calves tightened round the back of his neck. He took a terrified gasp and then he was choking and smothering in a claustrophobic nightmare beyond anything he'd ever imagined.

He was, more literally than he might have realised, going down for the third time, when there was a sudden, shrill whining noise. Juliet jerked violently. The vice around his neck released and he sprang free, gasping for breath and wiping his mouth. He leaped out of the car and was about to escape into the night, when he realised that Juliet was lying very still and very silent. He went back. He averted his eyes and pulled her skirt down over her knees, then looked more closely.

He saw at once what had happened. The drill – the Bosch drill with the masonry bit, the drill with which he had already had one unfortunate accident – was wedged down the side of the seat. Juliet's weight must have been enough to trigger it. It had drilled a neat size 8 hole through the back of her neck, probably a neater hole than Frank would have managed had he been holding the drill himself. It had proved the manufacturer's claims about the robustness of the tool. It had also proved fatal.

Frank drove home in a state of confusion. It was pitch dark by the time he got back to Meadowsweet Farm. He looked at Juliet, still slumped in the seat beside him.

He looked at the maggot shed.

He was just negotiating Juliet out of the car, when he heard a sound. It was like a muffled sob. Cautiously, he pushed Juliet back into the car and closed the door, then peered through the darkness. The sob came again. He followed the sound until he came to his front door. There was someone huddled against it, weeping silently, just the occasional sob escaping to reveal that she was there.

He knew at once who it was. 'Sheena?' he said.

'Frank?' Her voice, quivering with tears, was as soft and beautiful as he remembered. 'I'm going away tomorrow, and I had to see you just once more.'

Slowly, hesitantly, he put his arms round her. He could see the white of her neck glimmering in the darkness as she drooped her head onto his shoulder.

'Sheena, I love you,' he said. And before she could pull away, he told her about his mother's letter, about his attempts to contact her, about the bouquet he'd asked Juliet to give her.

As she listened, Sheena stopped crying. 'Oh, Frank,' she said. 'Juliet was lying. I'm not engaged. She told me you had been waiting for her every night to give her flowers. I saw you drive off with her tonight. I've been so unhappy.'

'You don't need to be,' Frank said gallantly, but he was becoming uncomfortably aware of Juliet as an unwanted third party on the scene. He couldn't bear to lose Sheena now.

'I've been so stupid,' she said. 'I should never have doubted you. And now it's too late.'

'Too late?' he said.

'I've got a job touring the Middle East,' she said. 'I auditioned for a part with the company here. I almost got it, but they gave it to Juliet instead.'

All at once, everything became clear to Frank. 'Don't go,' he said. 'Stay. I have a feeling it's all going to work out.'

She mopped her eyes with a tissue. 'All right, Frank.'

He felt the surge of triumph he'd felt that day before Christmas when she'd held up the mistletoe and kissed his cheek. 'Will you marry me?' he said.

'Oh, Frank, of course I will. But what about your mother?' She looked at him with wide eyes.

'Oh, she's gone away.' Frank had more or less forgotten about his mother. 'You go into the house,' he said. 'I'll just – er – put the car away.'

The disappearance of Juliet LeJoy was a bit of a nine-day-wonder. Her career had been going downhill rapidly. Her agent let it be known that she owed him money – rather a lot of money. A friend, in between expressing her concern and anxiety, expanded on Juliet's earlier career when her foray into artistic film had been – well – artistic. There were videos. For a brief time, Juliet LeJoy was a bigger star than she had been for years, but then newer stories emerged to fill the headlines.

Sheena got a place in the repertory theatre. She wasn't given lead roles – those went to an ex-soap star whose career had taken a downward turn, but whose name could still be relied on to attract a provincial audience.

Sheena moved into the farmhouse. She tore down the heavy paper with which Cynthia had covered the walls, and painted them white. She put vases full of flowers on the tables. She took down all the net curtains that were shutting out the light. The old, dark house was transformed, and Frank and Sheena were happy.

But one day, she came back from the theatre in tears. The ex-soap star was angry because she said that the director favoured Sheena. 'He says he can't afford to offend her,' Sheena wept. 'He's very sorry, but he says I'll have to go.'

Frank patted her absent-mindedly on the shoulder. He'd been a bit worried that morning, as he'd done his rounds.

He'd spent time with the maggots, and he could see that they were – not ailing, but not as content as he would like them to be. He knew that they needed something they weren't getting, and he had been turning the problem over in his mind. And suddenly he had an idea.

'Don't worry, dearest,' he said.

Sheena, surprised by the change in his tone, looked up. 'But it's so hard to get work. I'll have to leave,' she said, her eyes still brimming with tears. 'I'll have to join the tour in the Middle East.'

'Oh, I don't think so.' Frank smiled his reassurance at her. 'But I've got to go out. I won't be long. I need to pick up a food supplement for the…mushrooms.'

The rise to fame of Sheena Stout was legendary. Her picture smiled out from magazine covers, from posters, from celebrity columns in newspapers. 'I've been very lucky. But I couldn't have done it without Frank,' she murmured when she was interviewed by Richard and Judy. In fact, the only thing that marred her story was the trail of mystery and disaster that seemed to dog her co-stars, who had a tendency to vanish without trace in a cloud of ill-feeling and bad debt.

Frank, back home at Meadowsweet Farm, was happy. His wife was successful. His maggots were thriving. Every morning, he went into the sheds and watched the mass of white bodies squirming and growing fat, glowing with health and contentment.

Every day, he went into the shed where the iridescent insects laid the eggs that hatched the white gold. The blue-black bodies would swarm around his head. Sometimes, one of the flies would land on his outstretched fingers and gaze at him with her multi-faceted eyes. She would rub her front legs together, her gauze wings trembling, then she would take off to join the joyous flight of her companions. 'Bess,' he would whisper. He no longer wanted to be an accountant. He knew that he owed them his happiness.

And locked away in the attic was the cordless drill with the masonry bit. Who knew when it might be needed again? After all, every man, even a man as happy as Frank, needs some insurance against misfortune.

It was a quiet afternoon in Heaven. This was not unusual. It's always afternoon in Heaven and, by definition, it's always quiet.

Inspector Gabriel was bored. He was still glad he had gone to Heaven rather than The Other Place, but after his first fifty years of Eternity, he was beginning to learn the truth of the old saying that you could have too much of a good thing. OK, the Big Man had been generous to him. Given him his own precinct, just like he'd had on earth, and put him in charge of solving every crime that happened in Heaven. But, though initially gratifying, the appointment carried with it an in-built contradiction. Indeed, it joined all those other jokes about being a fashion designer in a nudist colony, or trying to make it as a straight actor in New York, or being George W Bush's conscience. There actually wasn't much of a job there.

So Inspector Gabriel had precisely nothing to do. And the same went for his sidekick, Sergeant Uriel. They'd done out the station more or less as they wanted it, though they did have a real problem recapturing in Heaven the essential shabbiness of the working environments they'd been used to on earth. But they lacked cases to work on. They had reached the goal towards which every terrestrial cop aspired. Heaven really was a crime-free zone.

They looked out of their windows – far too clean to have been part of any real-life station – and watched golf. White-clad figures with golden clubs addressed their green balls on the undulating cloudscape. Mostly newcomers – they had to be – who still got a kick out of holes-in-one from every tee.

In the same way, the people sipping vintage nectar on the terrace of St Raphael's Bar had to be recent arrivals. However good the liquor, the fact that in Heaven no one ever got drunk or had a hangover rather took away the point of drinking.

'Do you reckon I should go and check out the back alleys?' suggested the Sergeant. 'See if there's been a murder...? Even a mugging...? Someone making a rude gesture...?'

Inspector Gabriel sighed. 'Uriel, you know full well there aren't any back alleys in Heaven. And no rude gestures either...let alone the more extreme crimes you enumerated.'

'Yeah, I know.' A wistful shake of the head. 'I kinda miss them, you know.'

'You're not the only one.' The Inspector looked out over the vista of perfect white. A moment of silence hung between them before he vocalised an idea that had been brooding inside him for a long time. 'Maybe we should start looking at old cases...'

'How d'you mean, boss?'

'Well, look, we could spend a long time sitting here in Heaven waiting for a new crime to be committed...'

'We could spend Eternity.'

'Right, Uriel. Funny, till you get up here, you never really have a concept of Eternity. I mean, you may kind of get a feeling of it, if you've watched golf...or baseball...or cricket, but up here it's the real deal.'

'Yup,' the Sergeant agreed. 'Eternity's a hell of a long time.' He looked shrewdly across at his boss. 'You mentioned looking at old cases. You mean crimes that happened on earth? Like murders?'

'That's right. Most of the victims end up here, and if you wait long enough most of the suspects will also arrive eventually.'

'Hm.' Sergeant Uriel nodded his grizzled head thoughtfully. 'There is one drawback, though.'

'What's that?'

'Well, we won't get the villains coming up to Heaven. By definition, the actual perps are going to end up in The Other Place, aren't they?'

'Oh, come on, Uriel. You know how many murder investigations end up fingering the wrong guy. People who're capable of getting away with murder down on earth are not going to have too much of a problem blagging their way into Heaven, are they?'

'I guess not. So you're saying there actually are a lot of murderers walking round up here?'

'Of course there are. Well, there's Cain, for a start.'

'The Daddy of all murderers. Yeah, we see plenty of him.'

'Constantly maundering on. Complaining about that Mark on his forehead. And insisting that he was stitched up for the case, that he never laid a finger on Abel.'

Sergeant Uriel let out a harsh laugh. 'Still, you hear that from every villain, don't you? They all claim they're innocent.'

'Yes.' Gabriel gave his white beard a thoughtful rub. 'Mind you, it is odd that he's up here, though, isn't it? I mean, the Bible says he did it. The Word of God. There's never been much doubt that he did. And yet here he is in Heaven, boring everyone to tears by constantly saying he didn't do it. Why? The Big Man doesn't usually make mistakes on that scale.'

'No. I'd always assumed that Cain came up from The Other Place in one of the amnesties. You know, when they redefined the crimes that you had to go to Hell for. I mean, way back everyone who got executed went straight to The

Other Place – never any question about whether they were guilty or not.'

'I heard about that, Uriel. All those poor little Cockney kids who'd stolen handkerchiefs.'

'Right. Well, I figured Cain got a transfer up here as part of one of those amnesties.'

'Yes. Except his crime is still murder. That's about the biggest rap you can take.' There was a gleam of incipient interest in Inspector Gabriel's eye. 'I definitely think there's something odd about it. Something worthy of investigation. If we could prove that Cain was innocent…'

Uriel was catching his boss's enthusiasm, but still felt it his duty to throw a wet blanket over such speculation. 'It'd be a very difficult case.'

'We've cracked difficult cases before. What makes this one so different?'

'It's all a long time ago.'

'A very long time ago. In fact, by definition, about as long ago as it possibly could be.'

'Yeah. Then again, boss, we've got a problem with lack of suspects. We start off with Adam and Eve, then they have kids, who are Cain and Abel. Abel gets killed so he's kind of out of the equation, unless we get into the suicide area…'

'Don't go there.'

'No, I don't want to.'

'I've been thinking about this for a while,' said Gabriel, 'and doing a bit of research. The obvious thing to do, of course, would be to ask Abel, but the funny thing is, nobody up here seems to know where he is. Which is odd. I mean, he wouldn't have gone to The Other Place, would he?'

'Unless he *did* commit suicide.'

The Inspector dismissed the idea with a weary shake of the head. 'I'm sure we'll find him somewhere up here.'

'So, boss, going back...we've just got the three suspects. Cain, who took the rap for it...'

'Not just the rap. He took the Mark too. Don't forget the Mark.'

'Could I? The Mark's the thing he keeps beefing on about. But the fact remains, given our current level of information, we've only got three suspects. Cain, Adam and Eve.'

'And the Serpent. What happened to the Serpent?'

'I don't know, boss. He probably just slipped away.'

'Like a snake in the grass. But he's important, Uriel. I mean, with any list of suspects, the first thing you ask is: who's got form? Adam, Eve – just been created. Cain – just been born. When have they had a chance to mix with bad company?'

'And how do you *find* bad company in Eden?'

'Ah, but remember, they weren't in Eden when it happened. Adam and Eve had been kicked out by the Big Man.'

'For eating the Apple. Yeah, that was a crime. So they've got form too.'

'But not form on the scale that the Serpent has. God recognised him straight away, knew the kind of stuff he got up to. I mean, come on, this guy's Satan! Also, he's in disguise, which is not the kind of behaviour you expect from the average denizen of Paradise. And, second, he was responsible at that time for all the evil in the known world – though, granted, not much of it was known then – but this Satan was still one nasty piece of work. So far as I'm concerned, the Serpent's definitely on the suspect list.'

'And he'd have been clever enough to frame Cain and make him take the rap.'

'Be meat and drink to him, that kind of stuff.'

Sergeant Uriel nodded agreement. 'So what do we do? Go after the Serpent?'

'Call him by his proper name. He's Satan.'

'Aka Lucifer.'

'Yeah, but that was a long time back.'

'OK. So we go after Satan? That's going to involve a trip down to The Other Place.'

'Not necessarily, Uriel. He comes up here for conferences and things, you know, ever since the Big Man got more ecumenical and He started reaching out to embrace other faith groups.'

'Yeah. I'm afraid that still sticks in my craw – the idea of Satan coming up to Heaven.'

'Now you mustn't be old-fashioned. We've got to try and build bridges towards these people. Maybe they aren't so different from us.'

'Huh.' The Sergeant's hunched body language showed how much the idea appealed to him.

'Anyway, Satan's not our first port of call in this investigation.'

'No? So who is?'

'Cain, obviously. As you say, he's always maundering on about how he didn't do it. Now for the first time, we'll actually *listen* to what he's saying. Let's go find him.'

'OK.' Sergeant Uriel eased his massive but weightless bulk up off his white stool. 'And when we talk to him, boss, what...? We use the old Good Cop routine?'

'Do we have any alternative, Uriel?'

* * *

Cain was sitting in a white armchair in the corner of St Raphael's Bar. Alone. He was nearly always alone. His one-track conversation tended to drive people away.

As ever, in front of him stood a bottle of the finest two-thousand-year-old malt whisky, from which he constantly topped off his chalice. The conventional wisdom in Heaven was that, however much you drank, you never got intoxicated. Cain didn't buy that. He reckoned that somewhere in infinity was the magic moment when the alcohol would kick in and do its stuff. He drank like he was determined to find that moment.

The two cops idled up to the bar. They didn't want to make a big thing of their entrance. Inspector Gabriel ordered the first lot of drinks. Even though no payment was involved in St Raphael's Bar, there was a strictly observed protocol as to whose round it was.

Sergeant Uriel asked for a beer. Gabriel ordered it from St Raphael, adding, 'And I'll have an alcohol-free one, thanks.' It didn't make any difference, but it did make for variety.

They stayed leaning against the counter and looked across the bar towards Cain. It was the mid-afternoon lull, but then it always was the mid-afternoon lull in St Raphael's Bar. Knots of newcomers at a few tables enthused about how great it was to be there, how relieved they were not to be at The Other Place and how really nice Heaven was. They all looked white and squeaky clean against the white and gold furniture.

The only bright colour visible in the room was the Mark on Cain's forehead.

The sight would have settled a lot of ancestral arguments amongst biblical commentators and freemasons. The Bible remains tantalisingly unspecific about the nature of 'The

Mark of Cain'. Some authorities maintain that it was the name of God etched across the miscreant's forehead. Others thought that it was dark skin and that Cain was the father of all the world's people of colour. Some rabbinical experts even identified it with leprosy. (And it is also, incidentally, the name of an Australian rock band.)

But all the theorists would have been silenced by the neat red cross tattooed above Cain's eyes.

'I never understood,' said Uriel, 'why he didn't have that removed in C & P.'

'C & P' stood for 'Cleansing and Purification'. It was a service offered to all new souls as soon as they had finished their Pearly Gates paperwork. The nature of the dying process meant that few arrived looking their best, but C & P gave them the chance of a complete makeover and the opportunity to select their 'Heaven Age', the stage of their lives at which they would like to stay for all Eternity.

It was hardly surprising that a lot of souls – particularly women – chose to look a good few decades younger than their death age. Not Gabriel and Uriel, though. They'd opted to stay the way they'd looked just before the car-chase which had brought them up to Heaven – though they'd had their actual injuries tidied up. They reckoned the grizzled look added gravitas to their image as cops.

'I mean,' Uriel went on, 'those C & P boys can do wonders with facial blemishes. And some of the stuff they've done with reassembling organ transplant recipients with their donors…it's just stunning. For them, a little thing like Cain's forehead wouldn't present problems.'

'You're missing the point, Uriel. Cain wants to keep it.'

'Yeah?'

'Sure. Until his innocence is proved, it's part of his identity. And it's a conversation piece. I mean, anyone incautious enough to ask, "What's that Mark on your forehead?"...'

'Gets the full spiel.'

'Exactly. And that's what we're about to do.'

'I mean, how many more times have I got to say this?'

Not many more – please, thought Inspector Gabriel. They'd been talking to Cain for three-quarters of an hour and he'd already said his bit at least a dozen times. Trouble was, the bit he'd said lacked detail. When you stripped away the grievances about the millennia he had spent with a Mark on his forehead, being shunned by all and sundry, Cain's monologue still consisted of just the one assertion: 'I didn't do it.'

Inspector Gabriel tried again. 'Can you be a bit more specific? We have it on good authority that—'

'What authority?'

'The best authority available. The Bible. Holy Writ. The Word of God.'

'Oh, forget that. The Word of God has never been more than just a whitewash job. Public Relations. Spin.'

'According to the Bible,' the Inspector persisted, '"it came to pass, when they were in the field, that Cain rose up against Abel his brother, and slew him."'

'I was never in the damned field!'

'Ah, but you were. Only just before the incident you had "brought of the fruit of the ground an offering unto the Lord."' Gabriel was rather pleased with his logic. 'How could you have got "the fruit of the ground" if you were never in the field?'

'It was a different field! Abel was killed in the field from which he took his offering, "the firstlings of his flock and of the fat thereof." It was a different kind of field, a different kind of farming. I was arable. Abel was "a keeper of sheep". I was just "a tiller of the ground". I never went into his field. I'm allergic to sheep!'

'It doesn't say in the Bible which field Abel was slain in.'

'There's a lot of things about the case that aren't mentioned in the Bible. The guys who wrote the Old Testament, these bozos who claimed to be transcribing the Word of God, all they wanted was everything neat – nice open-and-shut case, no loose ends. "Cain slew Abel," that's easy, isn't it? They'd rather have that than the truth.'

'So what is the truth?'

'I didn't do it!'

Inspector Gabriel had difficulty suppressing his exasperation. 'So why didn't you say that when God challenged you about the murder?'

''Cause I was taken by surprise, that's why. Suddenly He's asking me where Abel is. I don't know, do I? I haven't seen him for a while. We're not that close and, apart from anything else, he always smells of sheep and, like I say, I'm allergic to—'

'Yes, yes, yes. But why didn't you tell God you didn't do it?'

'He didn't give me the chance! He asks me where Abel, my brother is, and I say "I know not: am I my brother's keeper?" And at this stage I don't even know anything's happened to the guy, so why should I be worried? But immediately God's saying that "the voice of thy brother's blood crieth unto me from the ground" and then that I'm "cursed from the earth, which hath opened her mouth to receive thy brother's blood from thy hand". I mean, when do I get the chance to tell my side of the story?'

There was silence. Sergeant Uriel, who'd been feeling a bit left out of the conversation, was the one to break it. 'But you don't have anything else? You haven't got an alibi for the time when the homicide took place?'

'I was in my field. The field where I grow "the fruit of the ground". That's what I do. I'm a tiller.'

Uriel looked bewildered. 'I thought he was a Hun.'

'Who?'

'Attila.'

Inspector Gabriel tactfully intervened. 'Don't worry. We have a slight misunderstanding here. So, Cain, nobody actually saw you in your field at the relevant time? Nobody could stand up in court and give you an alibi?'

A weary shake of the head. 'Only the vegetables.'

'I don't think they're going to be much help. After all this time, maybe the best thing would be,' the Inspector went on, 'for us to have a word with Abel. Except nobody seems to have seen him recently. Do you know where he is, Cain?'

'Oh, don't you start!' And he shouted, 'I know not: am I my brother's keeper?'

'Sorry. I didn't mean to do that.'

'I should bloody hope not.'

'But Cain,' asked Uriel urgently, 'if you don't have an alibi, maybe you saw someone? Someone who might have been the perp? Someone who went into that field with your brother?'

'I tell you, I was nowhere near Abel's field. I didn't see a soul.'

The two cops exchanged looks. The Sergeant's long

experience read the message in his superior's eyes: we've got all we're going to get here, time to move on.

'Yes, well, thank you Cain, this has been—'

'Have you the beginning of an idea what it's like going through life with a thing like this stuck on your forehead? Everyone convinced you're guilty of a crime you didn't commit? It wreaks havoc with your family life, for a start. You know, after I was framed for Abel's death, I went into the Land of Nod, and I knew my wife "and she conceived and bore Enoch... And unto Enoch was born Irad: and Irad begat Mehujael: and Mehujael begat Methusael: and Methusael begat Lamech. And Lamech took unto him two wives: the name of the one was—"'

'Yeah, we get it,' said Inspector Gabriel. 'You have a big family. What exactly is your point?'

'Just that they're all up here and, because I got this Mark on my forehead, none of them ever comes to visit.'

'*Cherchez la femme*,' said the Inspector as they wafted back to the station.

'I'm sorry. I don't speak foreign.'

'"Look for the woman." Old-fashioned bit of advice, but sometimes old-fashioned is good.'

'What, boss? You're suggesting we check out Cain's old lady? The one who conceived and bore Enoch?'

'No, no. We may get to her eventually, but she's not where we go next.'

'Then who?'

'Look, Uriel, Cain and Abel were brothers. Bit of sibling rivalry there I'd say. In fact, if Cain did actually do it, the ultimate sibling rivalry. And who's going to know those two boys best? Who was around all the time they were growing up?'

'Eve? You mean Eve?'

'You bet your life I do.'

Officially, there wasn't any pecking order in Heaven. Everyone was entitled to exactly the same amount of celestial bliss. That was the theory anyway, but some souls, by virtue of the profile they'd had on earth, did get special attention. Gabriel and Uriel were made well aware of that as they entered Eve's eternal home.

The décor was very feminine. Clouds, which are by their nature fluffy, had never been fluffier, and Eve herself moved around in her own nimbus. She had selected for her body image the moment when she first sprang from Adam's rib and, although she was now clothed, the diaphanous white catsuit, through which a fig-leaf *cache-sexe* could be clearly seen, left no ambiguity about the precise definition of her contours. The two detectives could not repress within them a vague stirring which they distantly remembered as lust.

Eve was surrounded by other female souls, similarly dressed. Their main purpose was apparently to worship her, but there seemed little doubt that, if the need arose, they would protect her too.

She was one of the souls whose position in Heaven had undergone radical reassessment. After Cain and Abel, Eve had given birth to Seth. 'And the days of Adam after he had begotten Seth were eight hundred years: and he begat sons and daughters. And all the days that Adam lived were nine hundred and thirty years: and he died.' So, though Eve did slightly predecease her husband, she had had a busy life and, at the time of her death, she was very tired.

And then, when she arrived at the Pearly Gates, there had been a rather unseemly altercation. St Peter, a Judaeo-Christian traditionalist, blamed Eve for Original Sin, and was not about to let in a soul who, to his mind, had corrupted the purity of humankind for all Eternity. The Big Man himself had to intervene before the newcomer was admitted, and for a good few millennia, Eve suffered from a certain amount of misogynistic prejudice.

It was only when Sixties feminists – particularly American ones – started dying that her status changed. The new generation of female souls entering Heaven saw Eve as an icon. Her eating of the Apple and persuading Adam to do the same was no longer a shameful betrayal of the human race; it was now viewed as an act of female empowerment. Eve had resisted the phallocentric dictates of the traditional male establishment and asserted herself as a woman. So far as her newly arrived acolytes were concerned, she could do no wrong. For them, she was an Earth Mother…in every sense.

Uriel may not have been, but Inspector Gabriel was aware of this recent reassessment, and accordingly circumspect as he began his questioning.

'I'm sorry to go into ancient history, Eve…'

'It's not about the Apple again, is it?'

'No, no. Nothing to do with the Apple, I promise.'

'Thank the Lord! I've done so many interviews on that subject that I'm totally Appled out.'

The expression was greeted by a ripple of sycophantic appreciation from her acolytes.

'The Apple won't be mentioned.'

'Good.' She gave Gabriel a shrewd, calculating gaze. 'So does that mean it's sex?'

'No, not even sex.'

She started to look interested. 'There's a novelty. I tell you, the number of times I've had to talk about sex to *OT Magazine* or *Halo*, well, you just wouldn't believe it.'

'No, I want to talk about your kids.'

'Which ones? There were quite a few of them. Remember for over nine hundred years Adam was a serial begetter.'

'It's the first two we're interested in. Cain and Abel.'

'Ah.' Eve looked thoughtful. 'Those boys have a hell of a lot to answer for.'

'Not least giving Jeffrey Archer an idea for an novel,' Sergeant Uriel mumbled.

His boss ignored him. 'The thing is, we all know the official story. As printed in the Bible. I just wondered, Eve, what with you having been on the scene at the time, do you agree with what's written there?'

'It's the Word of God. That was there in the beginning. Holy Writ. Doesn't pay to argue with the Word of God.'

'I wasn't asking you whether it paid.' Inspector Gabriel's voice took on the harder note he'd used to employ in interrogations. It sounded pleasingly nostalgic. 'I was asking whether you agree that Genesis, Chapter Four, is an accurate account of what took place in that field.'

'I was never in the field.'

'No. Cain says he wasn't either.'

'Oh.'

'I mean, when he was growing up, was Cain a truthful kid?'

'Yeah, I did my best to teach all of them the value of honesty.'

'The knowledge of right and wrong?'

'I thought I made it clear, Inspector Gabriel, that the Apple was off-bounds.'

'Oh, sure. Sorry. Listen, Eve, what were Cain and Abel like? What kind of kids? Did they have similar personalities?'

'No way!' She grinned wryly at the recollection. 'No, no, no. Abel was very anal. You know, the way he kept those sheep, all in neat little folds, clearing up after them all the time with a pooper-scooper. Whereas Cain was more laid-back, bit of a slob really. OK, he'd occasionally till the fields, but not like his life depended on it. Tilling – he could take it or leave it.

'I mean, when they presented God with the offerings, that was typical of their characters. Abel got all "the firstlings of his flock" groomed with little bows round their necks "and the fat thereof" in neat little packages. That's Abel all over. But when Cain comes up, well, for a start he's late, and "the fruit of the ground" is a few root vegetables still covered in earth, like they'd just been pulled up that morning, which of course they had.

'So it was no wonder the Big Man went for Abel's offering rather than Cain's...as Abel had planned He would.'

'But did the incident cause dissension between the two boys?'

Eve shrugged. 'Not that I was aware of. Cain knew Abel was always going to be the arse-licker, he was cool with that.'

'And yet, according to the Bible, he still slew his brother.'

Eve looked uncomfortable. 'Yeah, well, he must've had a rush of blood to the head.' She fell back on the old formula. 'It's the Word of God. You can't argue with that.' Her manner became brusque. 'Now I'm afraid I really must get on. Another feminist historical revisionist has just died and we girls are organising a Welcome Party for her at the Pearly Gates.'

'Yeah, just a couple of things before you go…'

'What?' Her patience with him was wearing thin.

'I wondered if you knew where I could find Abel?'

'No one has seen him since he came up here, assuming, that is, he did come up here.'

'Doesn't that seem odd?'

Another shrug from the archetypal shoulders. 'I've found it doesn't do to question too many things that happen up here. The Big Man knows what he's doing. We get very well looked after. Doesn't do to rock the boat. Just trust the Word of God.'

'And what about Adam? Will it be easy for me to find Adam?'

She let out a sardonic chuckle. 'Oh yeah, easy to find him. Probably not so easy to get any sense out of him.'

'Why? What's he—?'

But Inspector Gabriel had had all the time Eve was going to allot him. She looked around at her acolytes. 'Now let's get this party organised.'

Her words were greeted by an enthusiastic simpering of dead American feminists, through which Inspector Gabriel managed to ask, 'One last question. Did Cain have any allergies?'

'What?'

'Was there anything he was allergic to?'

'Oh, we're talking a long time ago now. A long, long time ago. You're asking a lot for me to remember that. I mean, after all those kids…' Eve's heavenly brows wrinkled with the effort of recollection. 'Yeah, maybe there was something, though…'

'Can you remember what?'

'No, I… Oh, just a minute.' A beam of satisfaction spread across the original female face. 'Yeah, there was one thing that used to bring him out in this really nasty rash, not helped of course by his clothes being made of leaves, and there weren't any antihistamines around then or—'

'I'm sorry, I must interrupt you. What was the thing that Cain was allergic to?'

'Sheep,' said Eve.

'It sounds to me like he was telling the truth,' said Sergeant Uriel, suddenly loquacious after taking a backseat during the interviews with Cain and Eve. 'I mean, his own Mom's confirmed Cain had this allergy, so he's not going to go near Abel's field, is he? Not if it's full of sheep.'

'I wouldn't be so sure.' Inspector Gabriel shook his head solemnly. 'I've dealt with enough murderers to know how strong the urge to kill can be. A guy who's set his mind on topping someone is not going to be put off by the thought of getting itchy skin.'

'Maybe, boss, but I'm still having problems seeing Cain as our murderer.'

'Me too. But we don't have any other very convincing scenario, do we? I mean, if only we could prove that Cain had an alibi. But there once again we're up against one of the big problems of the time period we're dealing with.'

'How d'ya mean?'

'It's like with the suspects, Uriel. Not a lot of people

around, either to commit the murder or to give someone an alibi to prove they didn't commit the murder.'

'Yeah. We're back to Cain, Eve and Adam.'

'And the Serpent. Never forget the Serpent, Uriel.'

'I won't.' The Sergeant shrugged hopefully. 'Oh well, maybe we'll get the vital lead from Adam.'

'Maybe. I wonder what Eve meant about it not being easy to get any sense out of him.'

It soon became clear why his former rib had lowered her expectations of coherence from her husband. Adam was seriously old. When he grew up longevity was highly prized, and he got a charge from being the oldest man to have died in the world (though, had he thought about it, he would have received the same accolade by dying at ninety-eight, or forty-three, or seventeen, or one week). So he had selected the moment of death as his Heaven Age...and no one looks their best at nine hundred and thirty.

He was, of course, very well looked after. Some deceased nurses, who'd really got a charge out of their caring profession on earth, were in Seventh Heaven with Adam to look after.

But, as a subject for police interrogation, he left a lot to be desired. All he did was sit in a wheelcloud and chuckle to himself, saying over and over again, 'I'm the Daddy of them all.'

Gabriel and Uriel didn't bother staying with him long.

Back at the station a pall of despondence hung between them as they yet again went through the evidence.

'Every minute I'm getting more convinced of Cain's

innocence,' said the Inspector, 'but I just can't see who else is in the frame.'

'There's still the Serpent.'

'Yes, sure. I checked. Satan's coming up here for an Interfaith Symposium in a couple of weeks. He's giving a paper on "George W Bush and the Religious Wrong." We could probably get a word with him then, but...' Inspector Gabriel's lower lip curled with lack of conviction.

'Why have you suddenly turned against Satan as a suspect? Come on, he's the Prince of Darkness. He's responsible for all the bad things in the world. Slaying one keeper of sheep here or there isn't going to be a big deal to a guy like that.'

'No, but that's why I'm going off him. It's too small a crime. There's no way Satan would bother with killing Abel. Or if he did it, he'd certainly claim the credit.'

'Yeah, but his old boss God had just started His big new idea – Mankind. Satan wants to screw that up, so he kills Abel and makes it look like Cain did it.'

'But if he wanted to destroy Mankind, why did he stop there? Why didn't he slay the other three humans?'

'Erm, well...' Theological debate had never been Sergeant Uriel's strong suit. He'd always been better at splaying hoods across their automobiles and getting them to spill the beans. 'Maybe he slays Abel, because that way he brings evil into the world?'

'He'd already brought evil into the world by making Eve eat the Apple.'

'But...'

'No, no, quiet, Uriel.' Inspector Gabriel scratched at his grizzled brow while he tried to shape his thoughts. 'I think we've got to go right back to the beginning.'

'The beginning of the case?'

'The beginning of the world. What's the first thing that happens in the Bible?'

'"In the beginning God created the heaven and the earth,"' quoted Sergeant Uriel, who had been to Sunday school.

'OK, that's Genesis. But we have another description of the beginning.'

'Do we, boss? Where?'

'First verse of The Gospel According to Saint John. "In the beginning was the Word, and the Word was with God, and the Word was God. The same was in the beginning with God." What does that sound like to you, Uriel?'

'I don't know. It's kinda neatly written.' The Sergeant thought about the words a bit more. 'Sounds kinda like an advertising slogan.'

'Yes.' Gabriel nodded with satisfaction. 'That's exactly what it sounds like. And what did Cain say? "The Word of God has never been more than a whitewash job. Public Relations. Spin."'

'Yeah, but he would say that, wouldn't he? If he was the murderer, he'd say it.'

'But if he wasn't the murderer, why would he say it then?'

'Because, but for the Word of God, he wouldn't have had to go through life with something on his forehead that makes him look like an ambulance.'

Inspector Gabriel tapped a reflective finger against the bridge of his nose. 'That might be the reason. Other possibility is that he said it because it was true...'

'Sorry?'

'That it all was just a whitewash. PR. Spin.'

* * *

Obviously, though there were no secrets in Heaven – that would have gone against the whole spirit of the place – some things weren't particularly advertised. Where the Big Man lived was one of them. The precise location was never defined, for security reasons of course. Though He wouldn't have been at risk from any of the usual denizens of Heaven, there had been considerable slackening of border controls in recent years, and the increase of Cultural Exchange Programmes with The Other Place brought its own hazards.

In the same way, the whole administrative apparatus of Heaven was, well, not overt. This was for no sinister reason. Most people had spent far too much of their time on earth organizing things, and longed for an Eternity which was totally without responsibilities. Too much evidence of the stage management of Heaven would only have brought back tedious memories for them.

But everything was, of course, above board, and totally transparent. Any soul who wished to find out some detail of the celestial management would instantly have been given the information required. It was just that very few people ever bothered to ask.

This was borne in upon Inspector Gabriel when he first began enquiring about The Word. Most of the souls he talked to claimed ignorance of where he'd find it, so he went to ask Raphael, who heard all the heavenly gossip in his bar. But the Saint was uncharacteristically evasive. '"The Word of God?" That's always been around. The "Logos' from the Greek, you know.'

'But you don't know where it actually is?'

Mine Heavenly Host shook his head. 'I've always thought of it more as a metaphysical concept than a concrete one.'

You did get a high class of bar room chat at St Raphael's.

But it was in the bar that Inspector Gabriel found the clue. There was a list of regulations pinned up on the wall. They weren't there because they were likely to be infringed, but for a lot of souls a bar didn't feel like a bar without a list of regulations. So there were a few prohibitions like 'Thou shalt not spit on the floor', 'Thou shalt not wear muddy boots in the bar' and 'Thou shalt put thy drinks on the nectar-mats supplied.' At the bottom of the list, though, as Gabriel pointed out triumphantly to Uriel, was printed: 'A Word of God Publication', followed by an address many clouds away.

It was a huge white tower block, with 'The Word of God' on the tiniest, most discreet gold plate by the front door. The receptionist wore smart business wings and a huge professional smile. 'How can I help you, gentlemen?'

'There's something we want to inquire about the Word of God,' said Inspector Gabriel.

'May I ask what is the nature of your inquiry? Is it Purely Factual, are you looking for an Informed Commentary on the Text, tracing your family history through the Begetting Lists or Challenging the Accuracy of Holy Writ?' Her voice contained no disapproval of any of these possibilities.

'I guess it'd be the last.'

Sergeant Uriel spelled it out. 'Yes, we're Challenging the Accuracy of Holy Writ.'

'Very well,' said the girl, with another omnicompetent smile. 'You'll need to speak to someone in Doctrinal Spin.' She leant forward to the keyboard in front of her. 'Let me see who's free.'

* * *

The man who was free had chosen thirty-five as his Heaven Age. He was neat and punctilious, and his character was reflected in a neat and punctilious office. Pens and papers were laid out on his desk with geometric precision.

'Cain and Abel,' he said. 'Goodness, you are going back a long way.'

'Nearly to the beginning of time. I hope your records go back that far.'

'Don't have any worries on that score,' he said with a patronising laugh. 'Remember, "In the beginning was the Word". These offices have been here right from the start.'

'Even before "God created the heaven and the earth"?' asked Sergeant Uriel.

'Oh yes. Long before that. It was here that the whole department strategy for the creation of the heaven and the earth was devised.'

'So this is where the Big Man did the planning?'

'This is where He was advised on the most appropriate ways of planning, yes. And, incidentally, in these offices we still refer to Him as "God". The "Big Man" initiative was only developed in the last century to make him sound more approachable and user-friendly.'

'OK,' said Gabriel. 'So you're kind of strategic thinkers and advisers to God?'

'That's exactly what we are.'

'Right then, can you tell us the strategic thinking behind the Cain and Abel story?'

The young man pursed his lips unwillingly. 'I won't deny that I'd rather not tell you. My personal view is that some secrets should be kept secret. In the same way, I can't claim to be an enthusiast of all these Interfaith Dialogues with The Other Place.'

'Maybe not, but since the Freedom of Heavenly Information Act, you are obliged to—'

'I am fully aware of my obligations, thank you,' he snapped. 'Yes, the new buzz word in Heaven is transparency. All records are available to whoever wants to see them.'

'And presumably,' said Inspector Gabriel, 'it was God who brought in that policy?'

'Goodness, no, God doesn't bring in any policies. The Think Tanks here at The Word of God recommend policies to Him. In the past those policies have been extremely sensible. But in recent years there has been a younger element recruited here' – his lip curled with distaste – 'who have brought in these modern notions of transparency and accountability. I was always more in favour of keeping some mystery about Heaven. Nothing wrong with a bit of ignorance, you know. But these new, so-called Young Turks have no respect for tradition and keep trying to make God trendy, and I'm afraid to say He listens to them in a way that—'

Inspector Gabriel stemmed this flood of bitchy office politics. 'Can we get back to Cain and Abel, please?'

The young man's lips were tightened as if by a drawstring. 'Very well.' Unwillingly he summoned up a file to his computer screen. 'What precisely do you wish to know?'

'Whether Cain was the perp or not,' Uriel replied.

'You have to set this in context,' said the young man primly. 'The creation of the heaven and the earth and light and the firmament and the waters and the dry land and the seeds and the fruit and the sun and the moon and every living creature after their kind and man was a very considerable achievement – particularly inside a week. But obviously it wasn't perfect. Corners had been cut so inevitably shortcomings were discovered, and in the ensuing weeks and years a certain level of adjustment was required.

'The really big problem was that of good and evil.'

'But I thought that was sorted out in the Garden of Eden. Adam and Eve got the knowledge of good and evil after the Serpent had persuaded her—'

'Inspector Gabriel, will you please let me finish! Having the knowledge of good and evil was not enough. Even outside the Garden of Eden, Adam and Eve's lives were still pretty idyllic. The Think Tanks here reckoned a more vivid demonstration of human evil was required. So a rather brilliant young copywriter had the idea—'

'Copywriter? You have copywriters here?'

'How else do you think the Word of God got written? Of course we have copywriters. Anyway, this rather brilliant young man had the idea of creating a really archetypal act of evil.'

There was an inevitability about it. 'The murder of Abel by Cain.'

'You're ahead of me, Inspector,' the official said sourly. 'Yes. If this murder was recorded in Holy Writ, then it would serve to all mankind as an example of human evil. And we had to get more evil into the world somehow. The people in this building had to look ahead. George W Bush was going to need people to bomb. How can you bomb people unless you can convince other people that they are evil? Paradise – even the paradise that Adam and Eve found after they'd been evicted from Eden – was just a bit too good, not viable in the long term, you know.' He snickered smugly. 'Setting up an apparent murder solved that problem at a stroke.'

'You say an "apparent murder".'

'Yes, and I say that quite deliberately, Inspector.'

'You mean' – Sergeant Uriel pieced things together – 'Abel wasn't actually killed?'

'His death was recorded in Holy Writ. That was all that mattered. There was no need for him to actually die.'

'So Cain didn't do it?'

'No,' the man agreed smugly, 'but everyone thought he did it, so the aim of that rather bright young copywriter was achieved. The world now contained evil, which in the future could provide a justification for…absolutely anything.'

'So what happened to Abel? Adam and Eve and Cain would have noticed if he was still around, wouldn't they?'

'Yes, Inspector. The people here at the Word of God did a deal with him. They offered him an early exit from earth and a good job up here, where he could keep to himself and wouldn't have to mix with all the other riff-raff. Who's going to turn down that kind of package? And all this was the work' – an even more complacent smile spread across his face – 'of one very bright young copywriter.'

'I get it,' said Inspector Gabriel. 'You're that bright young copywriter, aren't you?'

'No,' came the reply. 'I'm Abel.'

The cops were surprised by Cain's reaction to the findings of their investigation. They thought he'd be ecstatic finally to have his innocence proved.

But no, he asked them to keep quiet about the whole business. Take away his claim not to have killed his brother, and he wouldn't have anything to talk about.

Besides, he was getting rather fond of the Mark on his forehead.

Don't give me shit about ghosts.

Things that go bump in the night

The fuck are you kidding?

I've seen enough monsters walking around to give any tough guy nightmares and the sooner they got put in the ground, the better

When I hit sixty, I got out.......my line of work, you kill people for a living, it takes its toll and you know what, it was getting stale, kind of lame, no buzz there no more. Sure, it was a regular gig, I'm not bitching, let's get that clear from the off, I want to whine, you'll know.

But I had the bucks stashed, nice little investment plan and figured, enjoy.

My roots are Irish, I'm not saying it helps to be a Mick in the killing business, we don't have the edge in it, ask the Italians, but I like to think I brought certain poetry to my work, an artist if you will

Truth to tell, and I always tell the truth, I cant abide a liar, give me any scumbag, don't care what he's done, he fronts up, I can cut him some slack but a liar, whoa, don't get me started, the thing is, I was getting slow, the old reflexes were zoning out.

And I just didn't have the taste for it, you got to love what you do, am I right. Don't read me wrong here, you listening. I didn't love *killing*........I'm not some psycho. I relished the details, the planning, and the clean efficiency of despatch.

My Mom was Irish, came over on the boat, got a job as a cleaning lady and then met my old man, all he ever cleaned was his plate. She was from Galway, reared me to stories of The Claddagh, the swans, the old streets of the what used to be a Spanish town and the music, ah the wild mix of bodhrans, uileann pipes, spoons, fiddle, and the keening voice.

Jeez, she'd a grand voice, hear her sing.......Carrickfergus, fuck, that was like a prayer in action. She was real hot on religion, mass every Sunday, confession, the whole nine

Get this, my old man was an atheist, believed in nothing, especially not work, he wasn't violent, just feckless, found a woman who'd pay the freight and let go. When I was 17, big and OK, a little mean, I slung his ass on out, him whining

'Where am I going to go?'

I said

'Try the track, you spend most of your life there anyway.'

My Mom would have taken him back, Irish women, that demented loyalty, but I was running the show and she was real proud of the money I was producing. I heard he got him some other woman in Canarsie, like I give a fuck

Good riddance

I'd done my first job for Mr Dunne, he'd told me

'Kid, I got a guy giving me lots of grief, you got any ideas on that?'

I did

The guy is in the East River

Mr Dunne never asked for details, just handed me a wedge of serious change, said

'You're my boy.'

I was

He used me sparingly, a full year before he had another problem and I took care of that too.

Automobile accident.

Grimaldi's was the place back then and he took me out for dinner there, said, handing me an envelope,

'Get a good suit, we're putting on the Ritz.'

He talked kind of odd but I respected him

The staff there, falling over him and he said

'See kid, this is juice and you.......you're my main supply.'

I was mid bite on the biggest steak I'd ever seen and swallowed it sweet, asked

'Really?'

He was drinking wine, lots of it, I never cared for it, give me a cold one, I'm good, and a nice shot of Jameson to round out the evening, what more do you need? He said

'See, I don't have to do a whole lot now, I hint...you want the kid on your sorry ass and presto, the problem's gone.'

He ate a half mountain of mashed potato, awash in gravy, then said

'You've a dark future ahead of you kid but you need to be real careful.'

I pledged that I would.

And I was

My Mom got sick last year, the cancer, and on her last night, she took off her wedding band, the gold Claddagh, put it on my finger, croaked

'Go to Ireland for me gasun (son)'

I tried to give her back the ring, me heart was torn in a hundred ways and she near screamed

'I worked hard for that piece of gold, you think I'm letting it sit in a box in the cold ground.'

It's on my right hand, the heart pointing out, means I'm on the lookout

I'm not

Women talk

I don't talk

My last job, I don't really like to dwell on, it was before Mr Dunne got his, a two bit loan shark gutted him, left him spilling his mashed potatoes all over East 33rd and Second.

Mr Dunne has summoned me, looked bothered, said

'Frank, I have a real delicate situation.'

I was no longer the kid, had moved too far along for that. He lit a cigar, his face serious, continued

'There's a teenager, seventeen years of age, name of Gerry Kane, he's knocked up my niece and is fond of hitting her, I want him brought to his senses, nothing major, you understand but he has to understand how to behave, you reading me?'

I had thought I was

It went south, badly

I'd given him a few slaps, the way you do and the punk, he pulled a knife

Can you fucking believe it?

A knife.......

On me?

Didn't he know anything

And it got away from me, first time ever, I lost it, big time, they say I scalped him and other stuff

I'm not making excuses, trying me own self or nothing but I'd been doing a lot of speed, you think you can just kill people and get by on the odd brew with a Jameson chaser

Grow up

He had the most amazing blond mop of hair, like Brian Jones before the swimming pool and wait til you hear this, he was seventeen, right? And on his right arm, was the tattoo, *Semper Fi*.........the little bastard, I had my buddy buy the farm in Desert Storm and this piece of shit, this trash, this *nothing*, was wearing it......for fashion?

That section of skin, I threw in a dumpster on Flatbush

The shit hit the fan, naturally and maybe it was just as well that Mr Dunne got diced by the loan shark.

I was finished in the biz.

So, I made my move, liquidised my assets, sold my Mom's house and flew to the West of Ireland

Rented a little cottage in Oranmore, a beautiful village on the outskirts of the city.

There's a little river runs right by my window and get this, you can fish it, got me some nice trout and cooked the suckers me own self.

My cottage looks just like the one in *The Quiet Man* and the locals, they're real friendly, the one place in the world where they love Yanks. They're not too nosy, I go to the local on a Saturday night, buy for the house and they like me a lot, well, they like my dollars

Same difference.

They even try some matchmaking, a widow named Theresa, she comes round after the pub on Sat and I give her a workout, she thinks I'm very quiet but her, she could talk for Ireland, and does

I like to read...you're going to laugh your socks off but I read poetry, that guy Yeats, the fucker had it...sings to me, there's a small bookstore, mainly second hand stuff and they keep any poetry for me.

I'm getting me an education

I was reading....... *A terrible beauty*....

Jeez, like some awful omen that

I had that marked with my Mums memorial card when.......when.......how do I describe the beginning.

I had a log fire going, the book on me lap, and a wee drop of Jameson by my arm when there was a scratching on the door...I figured some stray dog.

I opened the door and no one there, then noticed a small envelope on the step, took it inside, reckoning it was another invite to some local event. Tore the flap and inside was a single sheet of paper with the words..........*Semper Fi*

OK, so it knocked a stir out of me

I'm not going to argue the toss

But I'd been down this road

When I arrived in Ireland, before I got this cottage, I had to stay in Galway, in a hotel, no hardship there, but the city, it was like mini America........Gap, Banana Republic, MacDonalds, all the teenagers talking like hybrid rejects from The O.C.

And in the pubs, on tap, freaking Millers, Bud, Pabst..........the fuck was going on?

And then I saw him, the blond kid, working the stick in a pub on quay St.......the spit of Gerry and he smirked at me.......like he knew.........said

'You're a Yank.....been there......*Dunne that*.......'

Unnerved me, fuck, gave me a shot of the tremors but I was lucky, a local skel, a bottom of the pond dealer, hooked me up to my beloved speed and once I got in that place, I knew what to do

Scalped him

Yeah, see who *Dunne that*?

I have his blond hair in my trunk

And figured that was that

Now this

Who was fucking with me and why

The next Sat night, I'm in the pub and Dolan, the owner, a smarmy schmuck, asks

'You met Gearoid?'

What?

I couldn't even pronounce it, one of those dumb Irish names that you need to be a German with a bad lisp to say, so I went

'Who?'

He smiles, indicates a group of young people drinking, yeah, bottles of Bud, Tequila chasers and I see the Brian Jones look alike, Dolan says

'That's him, he's got his own band.......named Punk.........he's hoping to get to America, you might give him a few pointers.'

I got the fuck out of there, leaving a full pint of Guinness on the counter.

I was back home, draining a double Jameson when Theresa came round, all concern, *Dolan* had told her I took a *turn* and she was fussing, like a freaking hen, the speed was hitting max in my blood and the Jameson was whispering to it, not whispering anything good. I asked

'That nephew of his, Garage...is it?'

She laughed, the dumbass Yank, mutilating the accent, and I tell you, I don't take mocking real good, she said

'Use the English form.'

My teeth were grinding, I could hear them and I near spat

'Gee, I would if you'd share it, is it like a secret or something?'

She shot me a look

Me..............

Shoot me a look?

Was she fucking kidding, you don't give me looks, unless you're packing something more lethal than bad attitude, but then, she changed course, like women do, said

'Gerry, it's Gerry.'

I dropped my glass, Jameson leaking into the rug and she's fussing, searching for a cloth, I roared

'Leave the fucking thing, is that his name, are you jerking my chain?'

She put her hands on her hips, barked

'Don't swear at me mister, my late husband, God rest his soul, he never swore at me and I'm not going to let some........'

I cut her off, demanded

'Why he's here?'

She was thrown, asked

'What........he's on holiday, he has a band he......'

'I know about the fucking band, I asked you why he's here.'

She gathered up her coat and the groceries she'd brought for our meal, said

'Well, I know when I'm not wanted, I'll return when you soften your cough mister.'

After she was gone, I poured some Jameson, chanced another hit of speed, needed to think.......

The kid in Galway, when I'd done him I'd been confused, because when I lifted his sleeve, there was no tattoo, none.

I went to my trunk, unlocked the heavy Yale on it and pushing aside the blond hair, I took out my knife, the blade honed to wafer thin perfection, shouted out loud

'Let em come, I'm so fucking ready.'

Later, I chilled, thinking, I'd over reacted, new country and all, those spuds and the Guinness, that shit knocked you on yer ass.

So I calmed a bit, was even able to read some Yeats, selected a poem at random...........*The Stolen Child*

Fuck, isn't that what the Irish love.......that irony they go on about........I laughed out loud, laughed till the tears ran down my face, the knife sitting snugly in my lap.

Next few days were without incident, but I kept the knife in my jacket, I was easing down a notch but I was getting antsy, I was ready, they could send all the Brian Jones they liked, I'd take em all, see if I wouldn't

Changed pubs though

On the other end of the village, was a more modern place, I preferred the traditional one but what the hell, killers cant be choosers.

Sitting there over my pint, Bushmills as back, the Jameson was obviously not agreeing with me, a tiny hint of speed in me blood, reading the Irish Independent, lots of reports on Iraq, I skipped them.

Then a feature on a new movie about the life of Brian Jones, speculating that he'd been murdered.

A shadow fell across me, I looked up to see Dolan's nephew, sweeping the blond locks out of his eyes.

He was wearing faded flared jeans and a black sweat shirt with the logo

Harvard hurts

Like he'd fucking know?

He asked

'May I join you for a moment?'

His accent had that quasi American uplift, as if

everything terminated in a question, if he asked me about
The Mets, I'd pop him in the goddamned mouth. I said

'Why not.'

He slid onto the stool opposite, never taking his eyes off
me, asked

'Get you a jar?'

Least he hadn't called it a brewski............yet. His
sleeves were rolled down and I couldn't see his arms, his left
wrist had all those multicoloured bands they collect, the
barman brought him over a bottle of Bud, packet of chips,
or crisps as they call them here. No glass, he drank from the
bottle, cool as the hippy choker round his neck. He raised
the bottle, said

'Slainte.'

I raised my pint, said

'That too.'

His mouth had that half smirk going, as if the joke was
known to everyone but me, I asked

'Help you with something?'

He drank noisily, I hate that, all gurgle and no finesse, he
belched then

'Me and me band, we're going Stateside and I was
wondering if you could hook us up with the names of some
hotels in the Village, Like Greenwich Village, we're going to
try for a gig at The Fillmore.'

Good luck

I said

'The internet, your best bet.'

Something dark flitted briefly across his face and he tossed
his hair, said

'I thought you might know someone who, you know,

would open some doors for us?'

He wanted to mind fuck, I'd gone rounds with the best of em and left em in the dumpster,........so I could play........said

'Kid, my age, most people I know, they're dead.'

Didn't faze him, he signalled for another brew, said

'Ah, tis a pity but shure, never mind, t'was worth a shot.'

The speed hit a wave and before I knew it, I asked

'Show me your right arm'

'What?'

I kept my voice steady, said

'You're not deaf, you heard me.'

He stood up, gave me his tough eye, said

'Jaysus, you're not all in it, you need to get a grip buddy.'

He was waving away the barman and the ordered drink, I said

'I'm not your buddy.'

He moved to the counter and joined some gaggle of girls, I could see them glancing over, laughing out loud

Man, jeering, that's all they've got, like that rates on my radar.

I finished my drink, made my way out and grabbed his arm, whispered to him

'Hair today, gone tomorrow.'

I stopped sleeping, I wanted to be ready lest someone leave something at my door, I slugged the Jameson, did some of the speed, read Yeats a lot but he'd stopped talking to me, the music was gone

Must have been a week after, I saw a poster for the band.......Punk, last concert before the American tour

In the local hall.

The way I have it figured, I'll wait in the alley behind the venue, get him on his way out.......... No, better, follow him home and do the business

Then I'll get to examine his arm at leisure

The tattoo's going to be on there, isn't it?

I don't doubt that other blond punks will show up but I'm real easy

The trunk has lots of room

Maybe I'll try another poet, you think?

Murder was done on Court Eleven on the third day of Wimbledon, 1981. Fortunately for the All England Club, it wasn't anything obvious like a strangling or a shooting, but the result was the same for the victim, except that he suffered longer. It took three days for him to die. I can tell you exactly how it happened, because I was one of the ball boys for the match.

When I was thirteen I was taught to be invisible. But before you decide this isn't your kind of story let me promise you it isn't about magic. There's nothing spooky about me. And there was nothing spooky about my instructor, Brigadier Romilly. He was flesh and blood all right and so were the terrified kids who sat at his feet.

'You'll be invisible, every one of you, before I've finished with you,' he said in his parade-ground voice, and we believed him, we third-years from Merton Comprehensive.

A purple scar like a sabre-cut stretched downwards from the edge of the Brigadier's left eye, over his mouth to the point of his chin. He'd grown a bristly ginger moustache over part of it, but we could easily see where the two ends joined. Rumour had it that his face had been slashed by a Mau Mau warrior's machete in the Kenyan terrorist war of the Fifties. We didn't know anything about the Mau Mau, except that the terrorist must have been crazy to tangle with the Brigadier – who grabbed him by the throat and strangled him.

'Don't ever get the idea that you're doing this to be seen. You'll be there, on court with Mr McEnroe and Mr Borg – if I think you're good enough – and no one will notice you, no one. When the game is in play you'll be as still as the net post, and as interesting. For Rule Two of the Laws of Tennis states that the court has certain permanent fixtures like the net and the net posts and the umpire's chair. And the list of permanent fixtures includes you, the ball boys, in your respective places. So you can tell your mothers and fathers and your favourite aunties not to bother to watch. If you're doing your job they won't even notice you.'

To think we'd volunteered for this. By a happy accident of geography ours was one of the schools chosen to provide the ball boys and ball girls for the Championships. 'It's a huge honour,' our headmaster had told us. 'You do it for the prestige of the school. You're on television. You meet the stars, hand them their towels, supply them with the balls, pour their drinks. You can be proud.'

The Brigadier disabused us of all that. 'If any of you are looking for glory, leave at once. Go back to your stuffy classrooms. I don't want your sort in my squad. The people I want are functionaries, not glory-seekers. Do you understand? You will do your job, brilliantly, the way I show you. It's all about timing, self-control and, above all, being invisible.'

The victim was poisoned. Once the poison was in his system there was no antidote. Death was inevitable, and lingering.

So in the next three months we learned to be invisible. And it was damned hard work, I can tell you. I had no idea what it would lead to. You're thinking we murdered the Brigadier? No, he's a survivor. So far as I know, he's still alive and terrifying the staff in a retirement home.

I'm going to tell it as it happened, and we start on the November afternoon in 1980 when my best friend Eddie Pringle and I were on an hour's detention for writing something obscene on Blind Pugh's blackboard. Mr Pugh, poor soul, was our chemistry master. He wasn't really blind, but his sight wasn't the best. He wore thick glasses with prism lenses, and we little monsters took full advantage. Sometimes Nemesis arrived, in the shape of our headmaster, Mr Neames, breezing into the lab, supposedly for a word with Blind Pugh, but in reality to catch us red-handed playing poker behind bits of apparatus or rolling mercury along the bench-tops. Those who escaped with a detention were the lucky ones.

'I've had enough of this crap,' Eddie told me in the detention room. 'I'm up for a job as ball boy.'

'What do you mean – Wimbledon?' I said. 'That's not till next June.'

'They train you. It's every afternoon off school for six months – and legal. No more detentions. All you do is trot around the court picking up balls and chucking them to the players and you get to meet McEnroe and Connors and all those guys. Want to join me?'

It seemed the ideal escape plan, but of course we had to get permission from Nemesis to do it. Eddie and I turned ourselves into model pupils for the rest of term. No messing about. No detentions. Every homework task completed.

'In view of this improvement,' Nemesis informed us, 'I have decided to let you go on the training course.'

But when we met the Brigadier we found we'd tunnelled out of one prison into another. He terrified us. The regime was pitiless, the orders unrelenting.

'First you must learn how to be a permanent fixture. Stand

straight, chest out, shoulders back, thumbs linked behind your back. Now hold it for five minutes. If anyone moves, I put the stopwatch back to zero again.'

Suddenly he threw a ball hard at Eddie and of course he ducked.

'Right,' the Brigadier announced, 'Pringle moved. The hand goes back to zero. You have to learn to be still, Pringle. Last year one of my boys was hit on the ear by a serve from Roscoe Tanner, over a hundred miles per hour, and he didn't flinch.'

We had a full week learning to be permanent fixtures, first standing at the rear of the court and then crouching like petrified sprinters at the sideline, easy targets for the Brigadier to shy at. A couple of the kids dropped out. We all had bruises.

'This is worse than school,' I told Eddie. 'We've got no freedom at all.'

'Right, he's a tyrant. Don't let him grind you down,' Eddie said.

In the second and third weeks we practised retrieving the balls, scampering back to the sidelines and rolling them along the ground to our colleagues or throwing them with one bounce to the Brigadier.

This was to be one of the great years of Wimbledon, with Borg, Connors and McEnroe at the peaks of their careers, challenging for the title. The rivalry would produce one match, a semi-final, that will be remembered for as long as tennis is played. And on an outside court, another, fiercer rivalry would be played out, with a fatal result. The players were not well known, but their backgrounds ensured a clash of ideologies. Jozsef Stanski, from Poland, was to meet Igor

Voronin, a Soviet Russian, on Court Eleven, on the third day of the Championships.

Being an ignorant schoolboy at the time, I didn't appreciate how volatile it was, this match between two players from Eastern Europe. In the previous summer, 1980, the strike in the Gdansk shipyard, followed by widespread strikes throughout Poland, had forced the Communist government to allow independent trade unions. Solidarity – the trade union movement led by Lech Walesa – became a powerful, vocal organisation getting massive international attention. The Polish tennis star, Jozsef Stanski, was an outspoken supporter of Solidarity who criticised the state regime whenever he was interviewed.

The luck of the draw, as they say, had matched Stanski with Voronin, a diehard Soviet Communist, almost certainly a KGB agent. Later, it was alleged that Voronin was a state assassin.

Before all this, the training of the ball boys went on, a totalitarian regime of its own, always efficient, performed to numbers and timed on the stopwatch. There was usually a slogan to sum up whichever phase of ball boy lore we were mastering. 'Show before you throw, Richards, show before you throw, lad.'

No one dared to defy the Brigadier.

The early weeks were on indoor courts. In April, we got outside. We learned everything a ball boy could possibly need to know, how to hold three balls at once, collect a towel, offer a cold drink and dispose of the cup afterwards, stand in front of a player between games without making eye contact. The training didn't miss a trick.

At the end of the month we 'stood' for a club tournament at Queen's. It went well, I thought, until the Brigadier debriefed us. Debriefed? He tore strips off us for over an hour. We'd learnt nothing, he said. The Championships would be a disaster if we got within a mile of them. We were slow, we fumbled, stumbled and forgot to show before the throw. Worse, he saw a couple of us (Eddie and me, to be honest) exchange some words as we crouched either side of the net.

'If any ball boy under my direction so much as moves his lips ever again in the course of a match, I will come onto the court and seal his revolting mouth with packing tape.'

We believed him.

And we persevered. Miraculously the months went by and June arrived, and with it the Championships.

The Brigadier addressed us on the eve of the first day's play and to my amazement, he didn't put the fear of God into me. By his standards, it was a vote of confidence. 'You boys and girls have given me problems enough this year, but you're as ready as you ever will be, and I want you to know I have total confidence in you. When this great tournament is over and the best of you line up on the Centre Court to be presented to Her Royal Highness before she meets the Champion, my pulse will beat faster and my heart will swell with pride, as will each of yours. And one of you, of course, will get a special award as best ball boy – or girl. That's the Championship that counts, you know. Never mind Mr Borg and Miss Navratilova. The real winner will be one of you. The decision will be mine, and you all start tomorrow as equals. In the second week I will draw up a short list. The pick of you, my elite squad, will stand in the finals. I will nominate the winner only when the tournament is over.'

I suppose it had been the severity of the build-up; to me those words were as thrilling and inspiring as King Henry's before the Battle of Agincourt. I wanted to be on Centre Court on that final day. I wanted to be best ball boy. I could see that all the others felt like me, and had the same gleam in their eyes.

I've never felt so nervous as I did at noon that first day, approaching the tall, creeper-covered walls of the All England Club, and passing inside and finding it was already busy with people on the terraces and promenades chatting loudly in accents that would have got you past any security guard in the world. Wimbledon twenty years ago was part of the social season, a blazer and tie occasion, entirely alien to a kid like me from a working class family.

My first match was on an outside court, thanks be to the Brigadier. Men's singles, between a tall Californian and a wiry Frenchman. I marched on court with the other five ball boys and mysteriously my nerves ended the moment the umpire called 'Play.' We were so well-drilled that the training took over. My concentration was absolute. I knew precisely what I had to do. I was a small, invisible part of a well-oiled, perfectly tuned machine, the Rolls Royce of tennis tournaments. Six-three, six-three, six-three to the Californian, and we lined up and marched off again.

I stood in two more matches that first day, and they were equally straightforward in spite of some racquet abuse by one unhappy player whose service wouldn't go in. A ball boy is above all that. At home, exhausted, I slept better than I had for a week.

Day Two was Ladies' Day, when most of the women's first round matches were played. At the end of my second match I lined up for an ice-cream and heard a familiar voice. 'Got overheated in that last one, Richards?'

I turned to face the Brigadier, expecting a rollicking. I wasn't sure if ball boys in uniform were allowed to consume ice-cream.

But the scar twitched into a grin. 'I watched you at work. You're doing a decent job, lad. Not invisible yet, but getting there. Keep it up and you might make Centre Court.'

I can tell you exactly what happened in the Stanski-Voronin match because I was one of the ball boys and my buddy Eddie Pringle was another, and has recently reminded me of it. Neither player was seeded. Stanski had won a five-setter in the first round against a little-known Englishman, and Voronin had been lucky enough to get a bye.

Court Eleven is hardly one of the show courts, and these two weren't well known players, but we still had plenty of swivelling heads following the action.

I'm sure some of the crowd understood that the players were at opposite extremes politically, but I doubt if anyone foresaw the terrible outcome of this clash. They may have noticed the coolness between the players, but that's one of the conventions of sport, particularly in a Grand Slam tournament. You shake hands at the end, but you psych yourself up to beat hell out of your rival first.

Back to the tennis. The first set went narrowly to Voronin, seven-five. I was so absorbed in my ball boy duties that the score almost passed me by. I retrieved the balls and passed them to the players when they needed them. Between games, I helped them to drinks and waited on them, just as we were programmed to do. I rather liked Stanski. His English wasn't up to much, but he made up for it with the occasional nod and even a hint of a smile.

Stanski won the next two sets, six-four, six-three.

Half the time I was at Voronin's end. Being strictly neutral, I treated him with the same courtesy I gave his opponent, but I can't say he was as appreciative. You can tell a lot about players from the way they grab the towel from you or discard a ball they don't fancy serving. The Russian was a hard man, with vicious thoughts in his head.

He secured the next set in a tie-break and took the match to a fifth. The crowd was growing. People from other courts had heard something special was happening. Several long, exciting rallies drew gasps and shrieks.

Voronin had extraordinary eyes like wet pebbles, the irises as black as the pupils. I was drilled to look at him each time I offered him a ball, and his expression never changed. Once or twice when Stanski had some luck with a ball that bounced on the net, Voronin eyeballed him. Terrifying.

The final set exceeded everyone's expectations. Voronin broke Stanski's service in the first game with some amazing passing shots and then held his own in game two. In the third, Stanski served three double faults and missed a simple volley.

'Game to Voronin. Voronin leads by three games to love. Final set.'

When I offered Stanski the water he poured it over his head and covered his face with the towel.

Voronin started game four with an ace. Stanski blocked the next serve and it nicked the cord and just dropped over. He was treated to another eyeballing for that piece of impertinence. Voronin walked slowly back to the line, turned, glared and fired a big serve that was called out. The second was softer and Stanski risked a blinder, a mighty forehand, and succeeded – the first winner he'd made in the set. Fifteen-thirty. Voronin nodded towards my friend Eddie for balls, scowled at one and chucked it aside. Eddie gave him another. He served long. Then foot-faulted. This time the line judge received the eyeballing. Fifteen-forty.

Stanski jigged on his toes. He would never have a better opportunity of breaking back.

The serve from Voronin was cautious. The spin deceived Stanski and the ball flew high. Voronin stood under, waiting to pick it out of the sun and kill it. He connected, but heroically Stanski got the racquet in place at the far end and almost fell into the crowd doing it. The return looked a sitter for the Russian and he steered it cross-court with nonchalance. Somehow Stanski dashed to the right place again. The crowd roared its appreciation.

Voronin chipped the return with a dinky shot that barely cleared the net and brought Stanski sprinting from the back to launch himself into a dive. The ball had bounced and risen through another arc and was inches from the turf when Stanski's racquet slid under it. Miraculously he found enough lift to sneak it over at a near-impossible angle. Voronin netted. Game to Stanski.

Now there was an anxious moment. Stanski's dive had taken him sliding out of court and heavily into the net-post, just a yard from where I was crouching in my set position. He was rubbing his right forearm, green from the skid across the grass, and everyone feared he'd broken a bone. After a delay of a few seconds the umpire asked if he needed medical attention. He shook his head.

Play resumed at three games to one, and it felt as if they'd played a full set already. The fascination of the game of tennis is that a single shot can turn a match. That diving winner of Stanski's was a prime example. He won the next game to love, serving brilliantly, though clearly anxious about his sore arm, which he massaged at every opportunity. Between games the umpire again asked if he needed assistance, but he shook his head.

Voronin was still a break up, and when play resumed after the change of ends he was first on court. He beckoned to me aggressively with his right hand, white with resin. I let him see he wouldn't intimidate me. I was a credit to the Brigadier, showing and throwing with the single bounce, straight to the player.

Stanski marched to the receiving end, twirling his racquet. Voronin hit the first serve too deep. The second spun in, shaved the line and was allowed. Fifteen-love. Stanski took the next two points with fine, looping returns. Then Voronin met a return of serve with a volley that failed to clear the net. Fifteen-forty. The mind-game was being won by Stanski. A feeble serve from the Russian allowed him to close the game.

Three all.

The critical moment was past. Stanski's confidence was high. He wiped his forehead with his wristband, tossed the ball up and served an ace that Bjorn Borg himself would have been incapable of reaching. From that moment, Voronin was doomed. Stanski was nerveless, accurate, domineering. He took the game to love. He dropped only one point in winning the next two. It was over. The crowd was in ecstasy. Voronin walked to the side without shaking hands, slung his racquets into his bag and left the court without waiting for his opponent – which is always regarded as bad form at Wimbledon. Some of the crowd booed him.

Stanski seemed to be taking longer than usual in packing up. He lingered by the net-post looking down, repeatedly dragging his foot across the worn patch of turf and raising dust. Then he bent and picked something up that to me looked like one of the needles my mother used on her sewing-machine. After staring at it for some time he showed it to the umpire, who had descended from his chair. At the same time he pointed to a scratch on his forearm. The umpire nodded indulgently and I heard him promise to speak to the groundsman.

I learned next day that Stanski was ill and had withdrawn from the tournament. It was a disappointment to everyone, because he had seemed to be on a roll and might have put out one of the seeds in a later round.

Two days after, the world of tennis was shocked to learn that Jozsef Stanski had died. He'd been admitted to St Thomas's complaining of weakness, vomiting and a high temperature. His pulse-rate was abnormally high and his lymph glands were swollen. There was an area of hardening under the scratch on his right forearm. In the night, his pulse rose to almost two hundred a minute and his temperature fell sharply. He was taken into intensive care and treated for septicaemia. Tests showed an exceptionally high count of white blood cells. Blood was appearing in his vomit and he was having difficulty in passing water, suggesting damage to the kidneys.

The next day an electrocardiogram indicated further critical problems, this time with the heart. Attempts were made to fit a pacemaker, but he died whilst under the anaesthetic. It was announced that a post-mortem would be held the following day.

I'm bound to admit that these medical details only came to my attention years later, through my interest in the case. At the time it happened, I was wholly taken up with my duties at Wimbledon, programmed by the Brigadier to let nothing distract me. We were soon into the second week and the crowds grew steadily, with most interest on the show courts.

Eddie and I were picked for the men's semi-finals and I had my first experience of the Centre Court in the greatest match ever played at Wimbledon, between Bjorn Borg, the champion for the previous five years, and Jimmy Connors. Borg came back from two sets down, love-six and four-six, to win with a display of skill and guts that finally wore down the seemingly unstoppable Connors. I will go to my grave proud that I had a minor role in that epic.

I'm proud, also, that I was one of the ball boys in the final, though the match lacked passion and didn't quite live up to its promise. John McEnroe deserved his Championship, but we all felt Borg had fired his best shots in the semi.

Like Borg, I was forced to choke back some disappointment that afternoon. I'd secretly hoped to be named best ball boy, but a kid from another school was picked by the Brigadier. My pal Eddie (who wasn't on court for the final) put an arm around my shoulder when it was over. We told each other that the kid had to be a brown-noser and the Brigadier's nephew as well.

I may have heard something later on radio or television about the post-mortem on poor Jozsef Stanski. They concluded he died from blood-poisoning. Samples were sent for further analysis, but the lab couldn't trace the source. At the inquest, a pathologist mentioned the scratch on the arm and said some sharp point had dug quite deep into the flesh. The match umpire gave evidence and spoke of the needle Stanski had picked up. He described the small eye close to the point. Unfortunately the needle had not been seen since the day of the match. In summing up, the coroner said it would not be helpful to speculate about the needle. The match had been played in full view of a large crowd and there was no evidence of anyone attempting to cause Stanski's death.

Huge controversy surrounded the verdict. The international press made a lot of the incident, pointing out that as recently as 1978 a Bulgarian writer, Georgi Markov, a rebel against his Communist government, had been executed in a London street by a tiny poison pellet forced into his thigh, apparently by the tip of an umbrella. The poison used was ricin, a protein derived from the castor oil seed, deadly and in those days almost undetectable in the human bloodstream. He took four days to die, protesting that he was the victim of political assassination. Nobody except his wife took him seriously until after he died. The presence of the poison was only discovered because the pellet was still embedded in a piece of Markov's flesh sent for analysis. If ricin could be injected in a public street using an umbrella, was it so fanciful to suggest Jozsef Stanski was targeted by the KGB and poisoned at Wimbledon two years later?

In Poland, the first months of 1981 had been extremely tense. A new Prime Minister, General Jaruzelski, had taken over and a permanent committee was set up to liaise with Solidarity. Moscow was incensed by this outbreak of liberalism and summoned Jaruzelski and his team to the Kremlin. The Politburo made its anger known. Repression followed. Many trade union activists were beaten up.

The papers noted that Stanski's opponent Voronin had quit Britain by an Aeroflot plane the same evening he had lost. He was unavailable for comment, in spite of strenuous efforts by reporters. The Soviet crackdown on Solidarity was mentioned. It was widely suspected that the KGB had been monitoring Stanski for over a year. He was believed to be acting as a conduit to the free world for Walesa and his organisation. At the end of the year, martial law was imposed in Poland and the leaders of Solidarity were detained and union activity suspended.

Although nothing was announced officially, the press claimed Scotland Yard investigated the assassination theory and kept the file open.

Since the Cold War ended and the Soviet bloc disintegrated, it is hard to think oneself back into the oppression of those days, harder still to believe orders may have been given for one tennis player to execute another at the world's top tournament.

In the years since, I kept an open mind about the incident, troubled to think murder may have happened so close to me. In my mind's eye I can still see Stanski rubbing his arm and reaching for the water I poured.

Then, last April, I had a phone call from Eddie Pringle. I hadn't seen him in almost twenty years. He was coming my way on a trip and wondered if we might meet for a drink.

To be truthful, I wasn't all that keen. I couldn't imagine we had much in common these days. Eddie seemed to sense my reluctance, because he went on to say, 'I wouldn't take up your time if it wasn't important – well, important to me, if not to you. I'm not on the cadge, by the way. I'm asking no favours except for one half-hour of your time.'

How could I refuse?

We arranged to meet in the bar of a local hotel. I told him I have a beard these days and what I would wear, just in case we didn't recognise each other.

I certainly wouldn't have known Eddie if he hadn't come up to me and spoken my name. He was gaunt, hairless and on two sticks.

'Sorry,' he said. 'Chemo. Didn't like to tell you on the phone in case I put you off.'

'I'm the one who should be sorry,' I said. 'Is the treatment doing any good?'

'Not really. I'll be lucky to see the year out. But I'm allowed to drink in moderation. What's yours?'

We found a table. He asked what line of work I'd gone into and I told him I was a journalist.

'Sport?'

'No. Showbiz. I know why you asked,' I said. 'That stint we did as ball boys would have been a useful grounding. No one ever believes I was on court with McEnroe and Borg, so I rarely mention it.'

'I made a big effort to forget,' Eddie said. 'The treatment we got from that Brigadier fellow was shameful.'

'No worse than any military training.'

'Yes, but we were young kids barely into our teens. At that age it amounted to brainwashing.'

'That's a bit strong, Eddie.'

'Think about it,' he said. 'He had us totally under his control. Destroyed any individuality we had. We thought about nothing else but chasing after tennis balls and handing them over in the approved style. It was the peak of everyone's ambition to be the best ball boy. You were as fixated as I was. Don't deny it.'

'True. It became my main ambition.'

'Obsession.'

'OK. Have it your way. Obsession.' I smiled, wanting to lighten the mood a bit.

'You were the hotshot ball boy,' he said. 'You deserved to win.'

'I doubt it. Anyway, I was too absorbed in it all to see how the other kids shaped up.'

'Believe me, you were the best. I couldn't match you for speed or stillness. The need to be invisible he was always on about.'

'I remember that.'

'I believed I was as good as anyone, except you.' Eddie took a long sip of beer and was silent for some time.

I waited. It was obvious some boyhood memory was troubling him.

He cleared his throat nervously. 'Something has been on my mind all these years. It's a burden I can't take with me when I go. I don't have long, and I want to clear my conscience. You remember the match between the Russian and the Pole?'

'Voronin and, er...?'

'Stanski – the one who died. It should never have happened. You're the one who should have died.'

Staring at him, I played the last statement over in my head.

He said, 'You've got to remember the mental state we were in, totally committed to being best boy. It was crazy, but nothing else in the world mattered. I could tell you were better than I was, and you told me yourself that the Brigadier spoke to you after one of your matches on Ladies' Day.'

'Did I?' I said, amazed he still had such a clear recollection.

'He didn't say anything to me. It was obvious you were booked for the final. While you were on the squad, I stood no chance. It sounds like lunacy now, but I was so fired up I had to stop you.'

'How?'

'With poison.'

'Now come on, Eddie. You're not serious.'

But his tone insisted he was. 'If you remember, when we were in the first year, there was a sensational story in the papers about a man, a Bulgarian, who was murdered in London by a pellet the size of a pinhead that contained an almost unknown poison called ricin.'

'Georgi Markov.'

'Yes. We talked about it in chemistry with Blind Pugh. Remember?'

'Vaguely.'

'He said a gram of the stuff was enough to kill thirty-six thousand people and it attacked the red blood cells. It was obtained from the seeds or beans of the castor-oil plant, *Ricinus communis*. They had to be ground up in a pestle and mortar because otherwise the hard seed-coat prevented absorption. Just a few seeds would be enough. Old Pugh told us all this in the belief that castor oil plants are tropical, but he was wrong. They've been grown in this country as border plants ever since Tudor times.'

'You're saying you got hold of some?'

'From a local seedsman, and no health warning. I'm sorry if all this sounds callous. I felt driven at the time. I plotted how to do it, using this.'

Eddie spread his palm and a small piece of metal lay across

it. 'I picked it out of a litter bin after Stanski threw it away. This is the sewing machine needle he found. My murder weapon.'

I said with distaste, 'You were responsible for that?'

'It came from my mother's machine. I ground the needle to a really fine point and made a gelatine capsule containing the poison and filled the eye of the needle with it.'

'What were you going to do with it – stick it into my arm?'

'No. Remember how we were drilled to return to the same spot just behind the tramlines beside the umpire's chair? If you watch tennis, that place gets as worn as the serving area at the back of the court. The ballboys always return to the same spot. My plan was simple. Stick the needle into the turf with the sharp point upwards and you would kneel on it and inject the ricin into your bloodstream. I'm telling you this because I want the truth to come out before I die. I meant to kill you and it went wrong. Stanski dived at a difficult ball and his arm went straight down on the needle.'

'But he went on to win the match.'

'The effects take days to kick in, but there's no antidote. Even if I'd confessed at the time, they couldn't have saved him. It was unforgivable. I was obsessed and it's preyed on my mind ever since.'

'So all that stuff in the papers about Voronin being an assassin...'

'Was rubbish. It was me. If you want to go to the police,' he said, 'I don't mind confessing everything I've told you. I just want the truth to be known before I go. I'm told I have six months at most.'

I was silent, reflecting on what I'd heard, the conflicting

motives that had driven a young boy to kill and a dying man to confess twenty years later.

'Or you could wait until after I've gone. You say you're a journalist. You could write it up and tell it in your own way.'

He left me to make up my own mind.

Eddie died in November.

And you are the first after me to get the full story.

Afternoon slurs into evening. Tony is standing on the balcony, a tab in his hand, staring at the rolling Tyne, the figures in the distance crossing the Millennium Bridge, similar figures on the roof of the Baltic. Inside the flat, Cleo has her legs curled under her, watching a repeat of *Trisha* on the big-screen television. All humanity is there, from the pinch-minded biddies to the shrill and ignorant flabby families airing their grievances at prime time.

Cleo was a Bollywood beauty at seventeen. Eight months later now and her eyes are hollow and black. Her works are sitting out on the coffee table, tin foil moving slightly in the breeze. Tony feels a stab in his lungs, ditches the cigarette over the rail and walks into the living room.

'I'm gonna see Grundy,' he says.

Cleo doesn't say anything. He doesn't expect her to.

'I'm gonna sort this out, Cleo.'

The buzzer sounds and Tony tells Jacko he'll be right down. He grabs his Adidas bag from the bedroom, stops in the doorway before he goes and takes one last look at Cleo.

Somebody'll take care of her.

The sounds of war are loud in Goose's lounge. He's a guy with a pot belly and one leg, sitting in a wheelchair and talking like he's kept the best eight ball for himself. He calls himself Goose because he says he lost the leg at Goose Green in '82. Anyone who's known him longer than a minute knows he lost the leg because he tried to mainline an artery. Nobody mentions it, though. Goose provides gear that's second-to-none. There are too few decent wholesalers in Tyne and Wear, and having a one-legged dealer means he doesn't step on the merchandise so much. That's the way Goose tells it, anyway.

So whoever spends their time with Goose, they have to sit there and hear the crazy bastard's stories from a war that didn't last three months. In the background, Goose keeps a tape of *Tumbledown* playing on the video, and he'll tell you all about the time he put his cock in a dead Argie's mouth and 'hang on a sec, I got a picture of it somewhere...'

'Goose,' says Tony. 'I seen it already.'

'I didn't come or nowt. I'm not sick.'

'Goose, leave it. You know I wouldn't push if time weren't a factor.'

'Nah, I appreciate that, Tone. I appreciate that. You always been up front.'

'Good, 'cause I got a favour to ask off of yez, Goose. Only one I'm gonna ask you, but it's a big one.'

Goose nods to himself, his bottom lip sticking out. 'I heard you had some trouble, like.'

'I ain't bringing the busies to your door, man.'

'I never said that.'

'It's what you're thinking. I got an old score to settle.'

'And this is the favour?'

'This is the favour.'

'Wey,' says Goose. 'You know me, son. You can ask us to do owt you want, long as the cash shouts loud enough to drown out me conscience.'

Tony smiles. 'I'm pretty sure you'll hear nowt but the folding of note, marra.'

* * *

Raw Earth is blasting its 1970 cut of 'Get Ready' as Tony slips into the Mazda. He puts Goose's package on his lap as he gets settled.

'Y'alright?' says Jacko.

'Aye.'

'It's sorted.'

'Aye.'

Tony listens to the music as they pull away from the kerb. It soothes, just like all good soul does. Tony's tried to get Jacko into this, but Jacko's thick as fuck, too hopped up on shite dance to appreciate a good horn section. He doesn't get the dirty-sweet soul of Solomon Burke or Lou Pride. Tony remembers the time he took Cleo to see Pride at The Cluny, up close and sweaty. A tiny stage, it was amazing that his band all managed to fit on it. Especially Pride himself. He wasn't in the Burke league of flabby bastards, but he was heaving around a lot of man that night.

Tony digs out a wrap, dips his thumb and raises it to his nostril. The ache in the back of his neck spikes to a full stab. He wipes his nose, offers the wrap to Jacko. Jacko shakes his head.

'You still sure about this, man?' says Jacko.

Tony looks at his driver, blinks. Jacko's got that face on, the same expression Jacko had the night they burned down Phillie's place on St James Boulevard. He's scared out of his mind. Tony wants to laugh. What the fuck does Jacko have to be scared about?

'Aye,' says Tony. 'I'm still sure about this.'

'Where you gonna go?'

'I can't tell you, you know that.' Tony fiddles with the seat, leans back. 'I don't tell you nowt, you can't tell any other fucker nowt.'

'I'm not gonna grass you up, Tone. Jesus fuckin' Christ, you don't trust us or something?'

'Trust's got nowt to do with it, marra. And I'm not saying you're a fuckin' grass. I'm saving you from yourself is all. You know nowt, you got nowt to grass if things get a bit fuckin' hairy. You know as well as I do, man, morality's circumstantial. You're not playing the martyr for me, no fuckin' way. It's nowt personal.'

'Sounds fuckin' personal.'

'Then get over it, Jack.'

Baby Huey and The Babysitters, 'Listen to Me', cross-fading into 'Change Your Ways' by Willie Kendrick. Jacko throttles Kendrick as he pulls the Mazda into the NCP. They park up, get out, Tony lighting a Regal.

It's a short walk to Grundy's club. It's called Grundys. Kevin Grundy has no imagination. The crowd outside the club couldn't give a fuck what the place is called, though. Saturday night, and the check-shirt brigade is out in force. Tony reckons it looks like they're holding the World Ugly Contest right outside the club, but then this place isn't known for its beautiful people. Studio 54, it ain't.

Inside, they're playing a thumping bassline instead of music, making Tony's heart shake in his chest. Makes him think he's walking on loose stones as he crosses the dance floor, Jacko at his back. He wishes he'd thought to bring Errol. Big fucking Errol, the prize-fighter looking bastard, deep nasty eyes and shoulders as broad as his accent. But Errol was seen in bad company and Tony can't take the chance. Jacko's a streak of piss, he's a runner, but he's arrow-straight and has a talent for survival. Jacko can smell a bad situation like a Sikh's fart, and Tony's glad to have him as an early warning.

Muscle would be a bonus, though.

Right now the only muscle Tony trusts is the one twitching in the back of his neck. He can't be relaxed in Grundy's club. The word is, Kevin Grundy's losing his mind one snort at a time. And one thing Tony's learned, you don't fuck around with a cokehead. Those fuckers know no mercy.

Right now, it's pure Martha Reeves and The Vandellas: '(Love Is Like A) Heatwave'. Sweat glistens on Tony's forehead, runs down and stings his eyes. The DJ mixes in that ubiquitous shite which brings the fat girls out to throw their arses around like the bird in the sweaty-crotch video. One fat girl makes a play for Jacko; he smiles and ducks out of the way, gets slapped by arm fat that'll be a bingo wing in about twenty years' time. The fat girl has an L plate on her lifted-and-separated chest. One glance at the gaggle of women following her onto the dance floor and the smell of a hen night suddenly fills the air like knock-off Estée Lauder. Over at the fluorescent glow of the bar, a gang of short-haired men swig bottled beer.

'This fuckin' place,' says Jacko. 'It's like Butlins on fuckin' mescaline.'

'Aye.'

'Grundy about tonight, you reckon?'

'I know a man who'll know,' says Tony, leading the way to the chill-out room.

Colin's the last lad who should be in a chill-out room. He breathes electricity, his hands flying about like a couple of methed-up doves when he talks. Which he does. A lot. His fingers brush at what little hair he has left on his head, wearing it away, making him look a good thirty years older than he is. He throws numbers in one of the glass and sandstone buildings down by the Quayside. Way he sees it, it's a slow death, but it lets him live at night.

Jacko taps his hands on his knees. Tony waits it out. Colin's been at the wraps since he finished work Friday night, it looks like. He's chewing Extra. The lad needs gum or else he'll chew the inside of his cheek to ribbons.

'Last week, right, last week, we had these gadgies in the office. And they were laying cables for the new network, right, these blokes, these electricians, and I was going to take a piss, right, I was going to the bogs, and I realise that one of these workmen blokes is gonna take a piss, too. And what happens? I hang back, know what I mean? I make out I'm going to the water cooler to get me a cup of water, make out like I'm dead fuckin' thirsty and that. And then I think to myself, what's the fuckin' point in losing me bottle like that? This cunt, he's no fuckin' hardcase, he's no tough lad, why'm I getting my bollocks all shrivelled 'cause of this cunt? So I go in the bathroom and he's in one of the cubicles and y'know, I can *hear him pissing*. Like he's one of them, you know them, the fuckers with the tiny cocks and he's not comfortable pissing at one of the pissers, like he has to sit down and take a piss like a fuckin' bird, right? So I get all boiling and that. And I kick the fuckin' cubicle door. Hard, so it slams right open and there's this gadgie and he's sitting with his trousers round his ankles and it's a good fuckin' job he's sitting down because I think he just shat himself. And I tell him – get this – I tell him, "Nobody's gonna fuckin' believe you..." and I leave him. Can you believe that, man? Can you fuckin' believe that? I am *dangerous*. I am a fuckin' time bomb.'

You're a twat, thinks Tony. You're a twat and I haven't got time for this shite.

'Did you take your piss?' asks Jacko.

'Fuck's this?' says Colin. 'Fuck's the cheeky cunt?'

'Where's Kev the night, Colin?' says Tony.

'He's not in, man. It's Wednesday.'

'It's Saturday,' says Jacko.

'Fuckin' funny cunt, eh? I'd fuckin' batter you, son, I weren't so fuckin' dry,' yells Colin.

'It's Saturday.'

'Fuck do you know? If it's Saturday, he's about. If it's Wednesday, he's at home. Fuck you asking me for? I look like I know what's going on? Now you selling or what?'

'Not tonight, Col.'

'Fuck's the matter with you?'

'I got some business with Grundy.'

'That's *Mister* Grundy, fuckhead, alright? You ain't selling? Really? Fuck's the matter with you, you're not selling? You're always selling.'

Tony gets up. 'I'll have another scout around.'

The gents toilet stinks like a Drew Barrymore movie. Jacko's at the bar. One brush with Colin and he said he needed a drink. Tony splashes cold water on his face, notices the heavy shake in his hands when he lowers them. He can't remember the last time he slept. Above the mirror, someone's scrawled TOON ARMY. The floor throbs under his feet; his head starts to thump in time. The chemicals in his blood start to thicken in his veins like slow-freezing water. Tony reaches into his pocket, does the rest of the wrap.

Blinks. Closes his eyes for a second.

Fuck this. Fuck this noise. Baby Huey: 'There's a thousand people out here, watching me...'

'Can you say Mighty, Mighty?'

He looks at his reflection in the mirror, feels for the package in his jacket.

If this works out, he tells himself, he'll be cool. He'll be fine. Just one step at a time.

Cleo watches Living TV. Movie of the week. Battered wives and alcoholic husbands. Tony wishes life was that simple. Wishes there was a twelve-step programme for what he has to do tonight. Christ, wishes there were ad breaks every fifteen minutes so he could grab a breather, a chance to think straight.

Tony swallows back acid phlegm, screws up the wrap and tosses it into the sink. The reason he stopped doing this shite in the first place, his mind caught in a runaway train of thought, turned in on itself, colliding.

The bang of the toilet door makes him turn. He's ready to deck Colin, the fucker.

But it's Jacko.

'Grundy's here,' he says. 'Says he'll talk to you out back when you're ready.'

Cleo and Grundy, that's how it used to be. Grundy with his ponytail and flapping lips sheened with perpetual spit. Grundy with his tacky club and delusions of grandeur, thinking that a fistful of cash and a couple of bent coppers would make him anything other than the pig-nosed prick he was. Cleo singing, 'Mr Big Stuff, you never gonna get my love...'

Kevin Grundy doesn't have an office anymore. He used to

have one above the club decked out with a *Carlito's Way* vibe. Back then, he fancied himself a kingpin, a drug lord, Tony Montana with a ponytail. Tony remembers the first time they met, he said, 'You know why it's called a ponytail, Kev?'

''Cause it looks like a pony's tail.'

'Nah, it's because when you lift it up, there's always a horse's arse underneath.'

Grundy's lips thinned. No imagination, no sense of humour.

Now Grundy's a silhouette down the end of the alley that runs behind the club. He's smoking a tab by a skip, flicking ash onto the ground. Doing business in an alley like he's ghetto. Tony recognises the big bastard next to him: Errol.

'Y'alright, Tone?' says Grundy.

'I been better, Kev.'

'Aye, looks like it. Who's your muscle?'

Jacko works his mouth.

'You buying, Kev?'

Grundy ignores him, says, 'How's that bird of yours?'

'Cleo's fine.'

'I heard things is all.'

'You got ears, you're gonna hear things. If you're not buying, I'll go, man. I just heard you was in the market.'

Grundy smiles; it looks like someone's taken a Stanley knife to his face. He dumps his tab. 'Aye, Tone, I'm buying. I'm just wondering why you're selling wholesale.'

'This is a one-off. Call it a favour for an old mate.'

'You think?'

'Aye, I think. You're not interested, I'll find someone who is.'

'Way I hear it, you're not doing much business these days.'

Tony can feel Jacko staring at him. Wondering how he's going to play this. Tony wonders if Jacko ever really knew what was going on. 'I'm doing fine, Kev. Business never been better.'

Errol shifts his feet; Tony glares at him. Any information Grundy's got, he's got it from Errol. But fuck it, this deal and Tony's out of here.

Tony hears movement behind him. He hefts Goose's package in his right hand. 'It's a solid weight, Kev. You got the cash?'

Grundy rubs at his nose. 'You know what, Tone? I don't think so. That's from Goose, right?'

Tony doesn't say anything.

'Well, thing is, Goose gave us a call. Telt us what was transpiring here. He's not happy about a bunch of fuckin' things. Mostly he's pissed off 'cause he's losing a valuable customer, but then there's the shite you got in your hand there. It's one thing to lose a customer, right? It's another thing when that customer tries to poison future trade.'

'I don't know what the fuck you're—'

More movement behind him, the scrape of a foot on concrete.

And then there's the smell of burnt hair in Tony's nostrils, the crackle of a stun gun, the flare against his cheek. And Tony's world flashes red, white and blue (how very fuckin' patriotic) before he loses his legs, hits the ground in a shaking heap.

'Man plans, and God laughs his balls off, Tony-son.'

Somewhere in the fog, Tony swears he can hear 'One Toke Over The Line', someone singing loud and off-key. That, and the growl of an engine.

* * *

The night before, Tony finds Cleo on the couch, her legs curled under her. The big-screen television is on, but it's just Teletext. Tony knows something's rotten.

When he tries to get Cleo's attention, he knows what it is.

And he spends the rest of the night with her in his arms. He weeps until his throat is dry.

He talks to her, tells her what he's going to do. Tells her he's giving up the life, tells her he's going to see Goose tomorrow, get him to cut a brick through with arsenic, bleach, fucking strychnine. Punt that brick onto the cunt that got her in the habit in the first place. At worst, let him stamp on it, sell it on and fuck his reputation by killing his customers. At best, and what Tony prays for, Grundy takes a shot himself, feels his veins burn up, his heart explode.

Then, pull a Keyser Soze, ride off into the sunset.

Live the happy ending.

'Antony David Hills...'

They used his Sunday name, his court name. And right then, he knew he was fucked. These were the busies Grundy liked to use. Grundy once said to him, 'I like using coppers, man. They always know where the really good fuckin' spots are, know what I mean?'

They've laid the foundation on the student and key worker accommodation, but there's a development down by City Road that's just started. Tony remembers watching the builders with Jacko, telling him that the students of Northumbria University would be gagging for a decent dealer.

'The world is ours,' he said.

Now Tony can't see anything but grey and black, his eyes swollen shut. The smell of fear and blood in the air, the ammonia stench of his own urine, burning his thigh.

I didn't cry. Least I didn't fuckin' cry.

Underneath him, a wooden pallet's holding him upright, his legs splayed out and twisted in front of him. He whistles when he breathes, air squeaking through the blood crusted around his nose and mouth. He thinks about how he tried not to scream, not to cry, playing the hardcase. The thought makes his face tighten, bringing a wave of pain from freshly opened cuts, a high screeching horn section to the bassline ache of his battered body.

He calls out for Jacko, but the name comes out cracked and low: '*Aggo?*' It kills him to speak, and he knows Jacko's not going to respond. Tony was conscious when the big bastard copper, the one with the stun gun and the girl's laugh, stamped his boot down hard on the back of Jacko's neck, heard that dull crack, a soft thump and smelled Jacko's bowels loosen.

But Tony's not dead. That's where they fucked up. Not so long ago, back when Tony Hills was king of the world, he wouldn't have allowed that to go by. Someone tries to kill you, someone tries to fuck up your business, you show no mercy. You put him in the ground. But these coppers didn't have the nous to finish the job. Which means he's in the clear, out of the city just as long as he heals.

I fuckin' tried, love. I fuckin' tried. At least I did that. Get them back for you. Jack it in, fuckin' throw the life to the wind, get the fuck out of Dodge.

Tony tries to pull himself off the pallet. The ringing in his ears stops, the sound of an engine outside.

'Fuckin' hell,' says a voice, punctuated with a high-pitched giggle. 'Would you look at that?'

The sound of a shovel scraped across concrete, coming closer.

Tony digs his fingers into the ground; it's cold to the touch. His cheeks warm and stinging. Pulling himself away from the voice. A fingernail snaps.

'What d'you want me to do?' says the voice.

I'm sorry, love. I'm so fuckin' sorry.

'Fuck d'you think? *Drop* the bastard...'

A breeze brushes Tony's face. Then a white flash and the world falls.

Man plans, and God laughs.

Aye, that'd be right.

Perhaps it was merely a foolish whim to walk the last mile or two to Canterbury. The idea of driving into the city to find a parking place didn't seem right on the path along which so many pilgrims had passed before him. He wanted to reflect, not to fight twenty-first century traffic. He was over eighty now, but this was his penance, and his own two legs must carry him to it.

Here at the bend of the eastern edge of Harbledown Hill, pilgrims had caught their first glimpse of Canterbury Cathedral, its steeple crowned with a gilt angel. Here they would dismount and fall on their knees to give thanks, for within that cathedral lay their destination, the shrine of St Thomas à Becket.

Murder and religion, he reflected. The passions aroused by both had been linked in the day of Archbishop Thomas as they had been ever since. In the year of 1170 it had taken four knights to strike down Thomas à Becket within his own cathedral, and for the rest of their lives, so legend said, they had wandered the world in penance and misery after their terrible crime.

A night in Canterbury in World War II had changed his life too. He had been a young man in his early twenties when the murders were committed. He, unlike the other two, had lived on. Perhaps that in itself required a penance at the Martyrdom or the site behind the Cathedral altar where Becket's magnificent shrine had once rested. Then Thomas Cromwell had boasted that he would make Henry VIII the richest king of England there had ever been. The Pope's supremacy had been renounced, and Cromwell's men destroyed and looted even this most sacrosanct of memorials.

Before that time, the pilgrims would advance up the steps from the Martyrdom to the Trinity chapel, first to see the golden likeness of the Saint's head, and then to the shrine itself, guarded by iron railings through which only the sick were allowed to enter. The shrine would be invisible as they approached; it was concealed by a wooden canopy suspended from the roof by ropes. At the given moment, the canopy was drawn up, and the shrine itself blazed forth with all its glittering jewels and gold decoration. The largest jewel had been the Regale of France, given by King Louis VII. It was a huge carbuncle, a ruby said to be as large as a hen's egg, which glowed fiery red as the light caught it.

For sixty years the man had forced himself not to think about the night of Sunday 31 May 1942, but now he must do so. It had been sheer greed that brought murder to Canterbury. Did the whole story matter now that the jewel was gone for ever? Yes.

As the music of the great organ of Canterbury Cathedral soared around him, Lieutenant Robert Wayncroft wrestled with his conscience. On Friday after his grandfather's funeral the solicitors had given him the sealed envelope he had expected. His grandfather had been his sole close family relation, and so Robert had been permitted a brief compassionate leave to sort out his affairs. He had inherited the house on Lady Wootton's Green, and Chillingham Place, the Tudor ancestral home near Chilham, now in a sorry state of repair and requisitioned by the army. It was the letter that concerned him most, however, for it contained the details of the closely guarded secret that had been handed on from generation to generation of Wayncrofts: the whereabouts of the Regale of France.

'The blessing of God almighty...' The service was ending, but Robert remained in the cathedral, thinking about what he should do. With Canterbury under constant threat of air raids, the jewel could hardly be safe where it was. Only ill health had prevented his grandfather from moving it, as had happened before when the jewel seemed in danger – not least when Napoleon looked set to invade Kent. That much was clear. What was less clear was what should happen to it after he had found it. Try as he might, the insidious thought of the money that the huge ruby would fetch crept into his mind, and refused to leave. He could do so much with it when the war was over. He could even rebuild Chillingham Place; alternatively he could, his conscience told him, give the money to the church. Then he battled with more personal ways of spending the money. What was the point of the jewel being hidden away when if he sold it to a museum it might be displayed for all to see?

'Only to ensure the safety of the jewel is your duty, Robert, not its future,' his grandfather had made clear in his letter.

Yet this was wartime, Robert argued with God, and there was no sign of the war's ending. The time for old legends was past, this was the twentieth century, and the old faith would never again be restored to Canterbury Cathedral.

He stood up. It was time to leave. He would go to where the jewel lay hidden and take it to safety. That was the first priority.

He glanced around him as he moved out into the aisle, aware of the increased tension in the city streets even though it was still light. Most people would be at home, fearful of air raids in retaliation for last night's RAF bombing raid on Cologne. What better cathedral to aim for than Canterbury? Since April German policy had been to strike at the historic cities of England: so far, Exeter, Bath, Norwich and York. A target as tempting as Canterbury could not be long delayed, and the sooner he fulfilled his mission the better.

Something made him stop. Would he, even now, be followed by someone watching in the dark recesses of the cathedral? He decided to make his way through the Cathedral precincts to the Broad Street exit, and he slipped out of a side door and down the steps to the remains of the old monastery. It was silent here, and despite the daylight, gloomy as he entered the so-called Dark Entry. He paused to listen for any footstep following him, and as he did so he remembered his grandfather telling him that there had been gruesome stories about the Dark Entry passageway even back as far as Henry VIII's reign.

'It was here, Robert, that your ancestor Sir Geoffrey Wayncroft met his death in trying to prevent the theft of the Regale by Cromwell's men.'

As a child Robert had been terrified by the place, imagining that any Wayncroft who walked here might meet a similar fate.

He pulled himself together. He was a soldier, trained to kill if necessary. What if someone *were* following him, someone who remembered his foolish talk on the beaches of Dunkirk two years earlier. The nightmare came back. He had been sitting with two other soldiers, but not from his battalion. They were in the lightly wounded category, waiting, it seemed endlessly, for ships that might with luck return them home across the Channel to England. With the Luftwaffe screaming overhead, minutes ticked by like hours. Family secrets hadn't seemed so important then; lack of food, sleep and the need to communicate with anyone, made him loose-tongued.

'Ever heard of the Regale jewel? It was a huge carbuncle,' he heard himself saying.

'That's what you get on your bum, ain't it?' the private sniggered.

Robert had been furious and it made his tongue the looser. 'It was a ruby as huge as an egg. It hasn't been seen since the sixteenth century – and I'll tell you why. When my grandfather dies, I'll be the heir and know the secret of the hiding place. The Wayncrofts have been guarding it as a sacred duty until the Pope returns to Canterbury.'

'May that be soon, *mon ami*,' said the French lieutenant.

Robert had been too engrossed in the need to bolster his own importance. Now he glanced at the other two men, and saw naked greed on their faces: the Cockney and the Frenchman, Lieutenant Christophe Bonneur and Private Johnnie Wilson.

'And your name is Wayncroft?' asked Bonneur.

'You must have heard of the Wayncrofts of Chillingham Place.' Robert glided smoothly away from the topic of jewels. 'We had to move out, patriotic duty of course in wartime, but we'll go back when the war's over. The old pile's falling down though.' Even then he had thought it was a pity that the family hadn't put the jewel to better use.

To his horror, Christophe had replied casually: 'I've heard of this Regale, *mon ami*. It belongs to France, you know. It was our king Louis VII, who gave it to the shrine.'

Robert had tried to be equally casual. 'He tried very hard *not* to, you mean. He offered a mint of money to the Archbishop in compensation for loss of the jewel, and it was accepted, but the Regale had other ideas. The story is that it simply flew out of his hand and stuck like glue onto the shrine.'

'So our poor king lost money and jewel too,' Christophe laughed. 'That is evidence, is it not, that the jewel belongs to France, not once but twice. Yes?'

Johnnie Wilson, who had been listening quietly, now contributed to the conversation: 'How did you Wayncrofts get it then? Nicked it, did you?'

The nightmare had begun, a nightmare Robert had managed to suppress, until this evening. As he came out into Broad Street, every shadow seemed to hold a threat. It wasn't like him to be jumpy, he told himself, maybe he *was* being followed. He'd go back to the house at Lady Wootton's Green just in case, he decided, and come out later. No one would expect him to leave it so late. It would be safer then. Another hour or two would not matter.

The jewel had waited for over 400 years.

Sir Walter Barbary dismounted at Harbledown, for Canterbury was in sight. He had no penance to perform as pilgrims usually had, only a mission on behalf of his dying monarch. It was cold and raining, and he took refuge in the inn from the November chill, while he made his final decision on what he should do.

'Walter,' Queen Mary had rasped last evening. 'I know you to be a good Catholic and true to our faith, as you are to me. Would you do me one last service?'

He bowed his head. 'Your majesty.' It was well known that the Queen was near her end. She had been slipping in and out of consciousness, and it was rumoured she was dying of a broken heart. She had good cause; the child she longed for had never come, despite all her fierce endeavours she had not completely restored the Pope's supremacy over the English church, and now Calais, England's last foothold in France, was lost.

When he had been summoned to St James's he had guessed it was not merely to give him thanks. Queen Mary had something more in mind.

With an effort the Queen withdrew a shabby velvet pouch from among the cushions of her bed, and handed it to him. It was heavier than he had expected from its size and within seemed to be a large oval stone that felt cold even through the velvet.

'Do not stay to open it, Walter. We may be disturbed. Take this to Canterbury, for me, back to the place from which it was stolen by those rebelling against the true faith. Those who influenced my misguided father.'

Sir Walter did not proffer his own views on the part played by the late King Henry VIII in establishing the new church. It had been, as his daughter Mary knew full well, imposed on England to satisfy his own lusts with the sanctity of a so-called marriage to Anne Bullen – a marriage that had failed to produce the male heir he wanted.

'My father used it as a toy, a huge ring worn on his thumb,' Mary whispered, 'and when he tired of it, he gave it to me to wear in a golden collar. I have done so for his sake but it lies heavy on my conscience. I would have my soul at peace as I face God. When Cromwell's Royal Commission destroyed the shrine of the blessed St Thomas, they stole the Regale and it must be returned.'

'Your majesty,' Walter chose his words carefully, 'despite all you have done to restore England to the guidance of the Holy Father the Pope, the Cathedral might not yet be a fitting place for the Regale. Once more it might be treated as a toy.'

'You are a diplomat, Walter.' Queen Mary smiled with great effort. 'You mean if – *when* – my sister Elizabeth rules, she will bow to no Pope. Walter, you must ensure that the stone is kept safely in Canterbury until the true faith is established there once more.'

He had left for Canterbury immediately. This morning, as he left the inn, news had just arrived that the Queen had died at dawn. By that time, thanks be to God, he was well set on the pilgrims' route to Canterbury. They would have sent to Hatfield for the new Queen and once she entered into London the hunt for the Regale would begin. If he knew Bess Tudor, who had a great liking for jewelled collars, she would waste little time. He must be gone, and gone for ever.

Walter decided to lead his horse for the last mile or two in order that Our Lady might grant him inspiration, for despite his halt at Harbledown, he still could not decide what to do with the jewel. As he neared Canterbury, he could hear the bells ringing – but for no Pope. He knew he could not hand over the jewel, nor keep it for himself, for this would go against his promise to Queen Mary, yet he would instantly be suspect when the jewel was missed. He had no choice. He must fulfil his mission, then ride for Dover and sail overseas for France.

He paused unrecognised at the Cathedral entrance, watching as the dignitaries of Canterbury came to give thanks for the new queen, whether they were sincere or not. One of them was Sir Edward Wayncroft, whom he knew well, and

Walter gave thanks to Our Lady, for surely here was his answer. Sir Edward was of good Catholic family, staunch to the last. It had been his father who had been slain in the passageway trying to prevent the theft of the Regale by Cromwell's men. He would ask Sir Edward to guard the jewel until these rebels and their so-called new religion were swept away.

As twilight came, Robert retraced his steps to the Cathedral, on the grounds that on the remote chance that anyone was *still* following him, the assumption would be that the Regale was hidden there. His stalker – was he real or in his imagination? – might even be amongst those few bowed heads still in the cathedral at this late hour. Involuntarily he glanced over his shoulder. His grandfather's death had been announced in *The Times* as well as in the local newspapers. What if his avid-eyed companions on the beach at Dunkirk had remembered his chance words? He had seen neither of them since, but in theory they could be here, waiting for him to make his move to reclaim the jewel. Would one of those so earnestly praying suddenly rise up and strike him down, as Becket himself had been?

Robert took hold of himself. Of course they would not do so. Even if one of them were waiting for him, he could not be sure whether Robert had the letter, or when he would go in search of the jewel. In any case, he would need to follow Robert to where the jewel lay hidden. His imagination was getting out of control, Robert decided, but nevertheless he would take precautions. He would linger by the steps to the Murder Stone, then walk briskly down the north aisle to the main door – then *past* it. Instead he would stroll up the south aisle, and mount the steps leading to Trinity chapel where was the site of the shrine itself. Yes, that was fitting, since any pursuer would assume the Regale was hidden near there, and would pause there regardless of whether he could still see his quarry. By that time, Robert would have hurried down to the cloister door, and out in the night air.

He breathed it in thankfully as he walked into Burgate Street and then through Butchery Lane and on to the Parade. Robert felt safer now, if only because it was uncommonly light, even for the end of May. There would be no air raids tonight. A man whistled, nothing uncommon in that; a few people hurried towards their homes, that too was natural. A cat howled as he passed the Corn Exchange and came into St George's Street; the sound of Glenn Miller on a wireless drifted down through a blacked-out window.

Briskly, he walked in the twilight past a row of timber-framed buildings. There was a confectioner's, a tobacconist, all very normal – and yet his confidence began to ebb away. It was so very still in the half-light. On such a night he might even pass knights on their way to murder Thomas in the cathedral. The eerie atmosphere was only in his *mind*, Robert told himself, as he passed the grocery store of David Greig. There ahead of him was the tower of St George's church. He was nearly there. He crossed over Canterbury Lane, remembering its bakery shop and how he had loved as a boy to gorge himself on the Chelsea buns. Innocent pleasures in pre-war days, all gone. He sensed a moving shadow behind him; an innocent one perhaps, but it turned him from the church and into the White Lion pub next to it. He would have a pint of beer to steady himself.

'You're lucky, mate,' someone remarked. The bell for last

orders had rung as Robert paid for his order.

'My lucky day.'

In Robert's pocket were his masked torch, gloves, a small hammer and chisel, all he should need for his mission. He drank his pint slowly, wondering whether the door might open and his pursuer enter. What would he do if that happened? Robert firmly quelled the flutters of his heart. No one came in, and Robert departed with his fellow drinkers. Then at last he walked through the Norman tower doorway into St George the Martyr's church.

St George's was an ancient church much extended in Victorian times, and Robert strolled all round it, not yet needing his torch. He strained for the slightest sound, alert to the smallest movement, for he could not begin until he was sure he was alone. Suppose those men had remembered, suppose someone in the solicitor's office had read the letter and resealed it. After all, the solicitor had access to the house and the seal was in his grandfather's desk. Robert steadied himself. This was the solitude and approaching darkness speaking, not common sense. Resolutely he walked to the old doorway that had once led to the belfry staircase. Now it was blocked up, and what better place to hide the jewel? Quickly he looked above the lintel, and for the place behind the plaster where the stonework had been loosened to insert the jewel and only lightly replaced. It was old mortar, and should give easily, the letter had told him.

Swallowing, he built up a small pile of hassocks to stand on, and identified where he must excavate.

Just as his chisel was poised to chip the plaster the silence was shattered. The familiar eerie wailing of the air raid siren was joined almost simultaneously with the shrill sound of

Tug-Boat Annie, the local name for the Canterbury inner warning system. Usually this followed the siren alert to indicate that hostile aircraft were approaching the city; to have it come so hard on the siren's heels was ominous.

What to do? How could he leave now for an air-raid shelter? Feverishly Robert chipped away, almost sobbing with tension, expecting to hear the crash of bombs at any moment. Tug-Boat Annie's three blasts on the steam whistle would be repeated every fifteen minutes until danger was past.

He worked on as the light began to fade more quickly, but as Tug-Boat Annie sounded once more, he realised to his horror he'd made a mistake. He'd chipped off the wrong corner. Again he began his work, trying to control his trembling hands, and was rewarded after five minutes by the sound of the 'all-clear'. The original warning was a mistake, of course it was. No German bombers would be fool enough to come so early, on such a light evening.

It took him another two hours or more before at last sweating with fear and exertion, he managed to prise the stone concealing the pouch out. It fell to the floor with a crash, and the noise resounded throughout the church. He listened, heart in mouth, in case it might attract attention from outside, but there was nothing. Excited now, he put his hand in the hole and pulled out the prize for which he had worked so hard, the canvas pouch, for Sir Walter's velvet covering had been changed several times.

Robert's heart thudded painfully as he held it in the flickering light of his masked torch, for the light inside had now gone. Carefully he balanced the torch on the pile of hassocks and opened it. Within the canvas was another, silken pouch, through which he could feel the chill of a large stone.

Was it fear or excitement that was keeping every nerve taut? Carefully he withdrew the silk covering.

The Regale was in his hand. He held it in the light of the torch and even in that dimness it glowed red, as fiery red as the pilgrims to Becket's shrine had reported long ago. Its beauty confused him, making him once more uncertain of what he would do with it, save that he must take it with him.

'*Bonjour, Robert*!'

For a moment the words did not register. The whisper came from nowhere: it was the voice of conscience, or the voice of St Thomas. But then, with a deadly chill sweeping over him, Robert realised it was human, and that the words were French.

He sensed, then half saw, a black figure in the darkness moving towards him. It was Nemesis, in the form of Christophe Bonneur.

'It's you,' Robert said flatly, some of the terror evaporating. An enemy, even in the darkness, is easier to deal with than the unknown. He began to laugh at the inevitability of fate. 'You remembered? Of course you would.'

'You have found my jewel for me, Robert. *Merci*.'

'*Yours*?' His hackles rose. 'What the devil do you mean?

'*Mais oui, cher ami*. I was intrigued by your so-interesting story on the beach at Dunkirk. All families have legends, my family too. It is said that an ancestor of mine was English but he came to France where he married a French girl and took her name for fear of enemies from England. It is said that Sir Walter left in Canterbury what he should have brought with him to return to the king, the famous Regale carbuncle.'

'It was given by your king to St Thomas's shrine.'

'Against his will, *mon ami*, and you told us in your interesting story that the Regale was returned to Canterbury on condition the true faith was restored. It never was and so is ours again by right.'

'It was given into the safe-keeping of my family.' Robert's mind was numb. Desperately he tried to size up his situation.

'*Non*, it is to be returned to its rightful owner.'

Robert regained the power of logical thought. 'And will you restore it to the crown of France?' he sneered.

Christophe laughed. 'There is no crown to receive it, and France is under German occupation. Never fear, I will keep the Regale until happier times. Would you return it to St Thomas if I left it with you?'

'That would be against my duty,' Robert prevaricated.

'But there is a Catholic church in Canterbury, a mere stone's throw away. Why not surrender the Regale to its priest?'

'What I do with it is my concern,' Robert snapped. The ruby seemed to glow warmly in his pocket where he had put it for safety, as if it were telling him that it too had a voice in this discussion. Perhaps it did, for in the sudden silence that fell, Robert heard the sound of aircraft. A long way off – no need for concern.

Or so he thought, until the siren alert wailed out, and once again Tug-Boat Annie's three blasts. Through the windows the sudden light in the sky confirmed Canterbury was the target, as flares were dropped by German aircraft.

Christophe laughed as though nothing had happened. 'So you will not hand me the Regale – and I have no qualms in telling you, *mon frère*, that the public coffers of France will know nothing of either.'

'You speak,' Robert managed to say evenly, 'as if it were in your pocket, not mine.'

'It soon will be, my friend. Or shall we share it amicably?'

'Never.'

Christophe sighed. 'Your British SOE has given me excellent training in silent methods of killing. If you refuse to give it to me, I shall have practice as well as theory before they drop me into occupied France.'

Robert quickly debated his options. He was strong enough, and a trained soldier, but he was unarmed, save for his tools which would make uncertain weapons. If this Frenchie was right about his training, Robert would stand little chance against him, unless he could take him by surprise. He estimated they were about three yards apart, although it was hard to tell in the dark. If he could knock Christophe off balance he stood a chance of escaping with the Regale while the Frenchman recovered. The tower door was close, though not quite near enough to make a run for it without first distracting Christophe. But how to take him by surprise? Robert slid his hand into his pocket and realised there was only one way. It was a risky one, but with the aid of his torch it might be possible.

He inched the stone out of his pocket, making no sudden movement, and flung it straight at where Christophe's face must be.

He hit truer than he had dared hope, according to the Frenchman's howl of pain as the carbuncle took him full in the face. In a flash, Robert was at his feet, scrabbling on the floor for the stone as Christophe, blood streaming from his face, dropped to the floor to clutch at him.

'*A la mort*, Englishman,' he hissed.

Where was the Regale? Sobbing, Robert tried to tear off the clutching hands, and just as the first crash of bombs came in the distance, he saw the ruby. Christophe wrenched his hand away and stretched it out to where it lay. But another hand reached towards it, a hand whose owner had been hidden in the darkness listening. But it was Robert, having scrambled to his feet again, who grasped it first – until Christophe tripped him, sending him crashing to the floor again. Murderous hands round his neck made him loosen his hold on the stone.

'Ta very much. Thanks, mate.' There was a whisper, as the hands round his neck fell away, the words were almost drowned by the crash of bombs on Canterbury's ancient city. The explosions were almost overhead now.

Two of the men escaped, the other lay dead even before the bomb hit St George's church.

Private Johnnie Wilson paused briefly in Canterbury Lane. The heavy bombers were screaming overhead, and more and more arriving. Was anyone following him from the church? He looked back past the White Lion to the church. It was time to get the hell out of here and find a shelter, if no one was following him.

But there was. A moving shape lit by the flames in the sky was coming out of the doorway. He took to his heels, all thoughts of a shelter gone. He was nearly at Butchery Lane by the time the bombs demolished half of St George's Street behind him.

The blast knocked him to the ground and stunned him; he was choking on the dust when he came to. Tug-Boat Annie was sounding, there was the noise of bombs falling and the roar of more aircraft coming in. He picked himself up and stumbled onwards, with falling masonry and fires from the incendiaries all around him. There was a split second of eerie silence, and then he could hear screams.

Was he still being followed? If so, who by? The Englishman or the Frenchman? He'd seen the Frenchie at Canterbury station, and as he had read the report of Wayncroft's death in the local rag, Johnnie had guessed exactly what he was doing here.

Now he was in a hell like no artillery barrage he'd ever been through. He stayed right where he was in the middle of the road, as buildings crumbled like card houses. Where he was standing seemed relatively untouched, but St George's Street behind him was an inferno.

Johnnie lost all sense of time, listening only to the bomb explosions. Rose Lane area seemed to have copped it badly, and the whole city was lit up by flame, smoke and flares. Canterbury was disappearing. The road behind him was like the old pictures of Passchendaele. Where there had been pubs, shops and the old gateway to Whitefriars monastery were now only piles of rubble and smoke. He could hear the clang of fire engine bells, but no all clear yet. The barrage was still going on.

St George's church had been hit, but the tower was still standing, and its clock still sticking out like a yardarm. *And there was someone coming after him.* Automatically Johnnie took to his heels, his ears deafened by the blast. He couldn't even think about that stone in his pocket.

'You all right, mate?' An air raid warden caught his arm as he stumbled on.

'Yeah. I'll give you a hand,' Johnnie replied. But he didn't. He had a bit of a limp, a godalmighty bruise from a lump of stone or something, but nothing too bad. Even so, it was like running in a nightmare; his legs wouldn't move as quick as he wanted, and all the time his pursuer was gaining on him. Where should he go? Johnnie hesitated for a moment.

Then he knew the answer. Over there he could see the cathedral, still standing proud, lit up by flame. Bits of it must have been hit judging by the smoke, but the cathedral looked mainly intact. Johnnie was not a God-follower, but he knew now what he had to do. He had to get into that cathedral. It was like St Thomas was waiting for him.

People were coming out onto the streets, even though the all clear had not yet gone, emerging to see the ruins of their city, or their houses, and to help where they could, though the raid was not yet over. Johnnie staggered through the gateway to the cathedral grounds, glancing back to see if he were still being followed. He bloody well was, though by whom he couldn't tell. He had to get into that cathedral and quick. But they wouldn't let him.

The fire fighters and wardens stopped him, the officious twits. 'Not in there, mate,' said one smugly. 'Don't know if it's safe yet.'

Breathless, terrified, Johnnie remembered his battalion being brought to a service here, and that there was a door into the cloisters from the place where old Thomas à Becket met his Maker. He rushed round to the north side of the Cathedral, scrambling his way into the cloisters. No bombs here, and he ran for the door into the cathedral – only to find it shut. Sobbing with fear, he turned left, for there was no way back.

At the far end was another door, but in the corner of his eye he caught a glimpse of a man running to cut him off from this exit. Everywhere was noise and the smell of smoke, which was billowing out into the cloister. With relief he realised that what he'd taken to be a window was in fact the entrance to a passageway between two buildings.

Or had been two buildings. The one he passed was more or less intact but the further one, he saw as he reached the passageway, was a pile of smoking, smouldering rubble behind the cloister wall. It had been a library by the looks of the charred paper and leather, but there was little left save part of the far wall.

He could hear his pursuer behind him as he stumbled over the debris that had spilled into the passageway. In seconds he would be upon him, and Johnnie realised this was going to be as near as he could get to St Thomas. He reached the end of the passageway, clambering over the piles of smouldering rubble into what had once been a Cathedral building.

He took the Regale from his pocket, and felt his pursuer's hot breath and then his hands round his neck – just as Tug-Boat Annie sounded once more. For a split second they both looked up – to see part of the remaining masonry of the wall by their side about to collapse upon them. With his free arm and last ounce of strength, Johnnie tore himself free and threw the Regale into the fiery rubble of the library.

'Here you are, Tom,' he shouted. 'If you can't have it, no one else is bleedin' going to.'

After sixty years there were no traces here now of that terrible night of the blitz in 1942. The tower, fully restored, was all that was left of St George's church, its clock still projecting from it as though to remind the passer-by that this church could not be defeated by time. Much of St George's had fallen in that night and what was left had been demolished save for this tower. A casualty had been found within it, so he had read: a soldier gone in there to pray. Apart from this tower there was nothing to recognise – or fear – in St George's Street or its church.

He had come to pay penance to St Thomas for the night that had changed his life for ever, a penance for being alive, when morally there was little difference between the three of them. He was a murderer, no doubt of that, though he'd had good reason. Yet the knights that had murdered Becket had believed that too, and they had ended their days reviled and hated by all men. Johnnie Wilson had given the ruby back to St Thomas just as he was pushed under that falling wall. He hadn't meant to kill him, he was just crazed out of his mind. And after all, Johnnie Wilson was a murderer. He had knifed a man to get the stone away from him.

Nevertheless Johnnie had redeemed himself. He had given the jewel back to St Thomas – and through his action redeemed his killer, so he was twice blessed. That final shout of Johnnie's had changed his life. He had devoted his life to the good of others. Just as the knights who murdered Becket went on pilgrimage to the Holy Land, he had taken aid and food wherever it was needed in the world, and when too old for that had returned to run a well-known charity.

It wasn't quite enough. He paid his entrance fee and walked into the Cathedral to the place of Becket's martyrdom.

There, to the great astonishment of the tourists around him, Robert Wayncroft fell to his knees in penitence.

The crash of breaking glass made Maggie flinch. It always had ever since the Blitz.

'Don't worry, Mrs Cross,' said the woman from Number 23, 'it's only Phoebe dropping her tumbler. Look, Colin's picking up the bits.'

At the far end of the long table, with its red checked cloth and pretty flowers, one of Number 23's sons was reassuring five-year-old Phoebe from next door.

'He's only fourteen,' said Number 23 proudly. (Maggie couldn't remember any of the names of these young people who spent fortunes buying houses in her street.) 'But as tall as me already.'

'Yes,' Maggie said, wishing her eyesight was better. But she could tell he was taking trouble with the little girl.

'Have another sandwich,' Number 23 said, 'or a cake.'

Maggie took a small brown sandwich with smoked salmon in it. 'Thank you,' she said. 'This is nice. We never had parties like this in the old days. Not even when the war ended.'

'You must have been here longer than anyone else. When did you first come?'

'I was born in your house. My dad was a coal heaver.' Maggie tried not to smile at the thought. 'But it wasn't grand like you've made it with the conservatory and all that. I moved in to 46 when I married Alf.'

'Isn't that wonderful?' said Number 23. She wasn't nearly as snooty as she seemed at first. 'But it makes what happened to you even worse. I was so glad when I saw you safely back from your sister's and out and about in the street again. And even more when I heard you were coming today.'

'I wouldn't have missed it for the world,' Maggie said. 'You've all been so good to me since Hallowe'en.'

A faint blush spread in Number 23's cheeks. She must have been remembering the days when they'd all talked about 'Mad Maggie' and the 'old witch in Number 46, who never weeds her front garden'. Funny how being so frightened could make you a heroine, Maggie thought.

'I wasn't sure I could ever come back,' she said. 'Not till you all sent that card to my sister's and invited me to the party.'

'We were so shocked by what happened to you. Those louts could've burned the house down.'

'I know.' Maggie always tried not to think about it. For weeks after Hallowe'en, she hadn't been able to sleep, and she'd spent her days hiding behind her curtains in case they came back. She'd always hated Hallowe'en and the trick-or-treating children. But it had never been as bad as last year. She shivered now, in spite of the sun and the kindness all around her.

First she'd had raw eggs thrown by a group of teenage girls who thought she hadn't given them enough, so she didn't answer the door to the next lot. They put flour through her letterbox to punish her, and it turned the eggs into a terrible mess. The arthritis was so bad she couldn't bend down to clean it up. Not wanting more flour, she did answer the door the third time and saw two big figures in horror masks. One of them looked as if he'd drawn a bat on his hand. It was only when she peered more closely that Maggie saw it was just a birthmark.

She was angry by then, so she told them what Hallowe'en

really meant and how they should be praying for the souls of the dead, not scaring old ladies and demanding money with menaces.

Then she shut the door on them and their greediness.

Someone filled up her teacup and asked if she needed another cushion.

'No thank you, dear,' she said, glad of the respite from her memories. 'I'm very comfortable.'

If she shut her eyes, she could still hear the hiss from outside the door as the trick-or-treaters lit their firework, and the bang as it fell onto her mat, shooting out sparks and flames. If it hadn't been for her heavy winter coat, hanging ready on the peg by the door, she'd never have been able to put them out. Number 23 was right: she could have burned to death.

'You've been so brave,' she said now.

Suddenly Maggie remembered her name. 'It's kind of you to say so, Sarah,' she said. 'And I'm having a lovely time today.'

One of the young men from the far end of the street had a guitar and was playing a folk song Maggie recognised. She began to hum in tune. Lots of the others joined in.

Everyone was smiling at her. They'd welcomed her like royalty and made her feel safe again. Tonight she could go to bed happy.

'I think you made those awful boys from the council flats really ashamed of themselves,' Sarah said when the song ended. They've never given any trouble since. We all owe you so much, Mrs Cross.'

'Thank you, dear. I'm getting a bit tired now. And the sun's very bright. I'd like to go home.'

'Shall I come with you? Just to make sure you don't fall?'

'Don't you move. I'm sure your Colin would help me, and he's already on his feet.' She beckoned.

A minute later the boy was standing beside her, smiling gravely, and asking if she wanted him to help her off her chair.

'No, thank you. Just to walk with me over the potholes in case I trip.'

'Of course, Mrs Cross.' He kept a steady hand under her elbow, then waited patiently while she looked for her door-key at the bottom of her big bag. When she'd opened the door, he smiled, showing off his brilliant white teeth. 'Will you be all right now?' 'Yes. I want to give you something.'

'No, no, please,' he said. 'It was nothing.'

'It's advice. There's no point disguising yourself with a mask at Hallowe'en if you let everybody see that birthmark on your right hand.'

'I... Mrs Cross, you... I...' Now his face was bright red, and there were tears welling in his eyes. 'What are you going to do?' 'I'm not sure, yet.' She found herself smiling at him, no longer scared of any memories. 'It's funny how seeing other people frightened makes you feel strong, isn't it, Colin?'

An Ellie Hardwick, Architect, Mystery

I knew I shouldn't be doing this. It was against all the firm's safety rules to enter a deserted church, at dusk, alone.

I was due to inspect the place the next day anyway, in the morning sunshine and the comforting presence of Ben Crabtree, the county of Suffolk's best ancient buildings contractor. So why couldn't I wait? Why was I creeping, ankle-deep in rotting wilton, along the aisle, jumping at every owl hoot and mouse rustle, torch in one hand, mobile phone in the other and the firm's hard hat on my head?

I'm a romantic, I suppose, and I love old buildings in all their different moods. I'd come to catch what might well be the grace notes of the splendour of All Souls, adrift in the fields outside the village of Crowden. It would be my five-year survey tomorrow that would sign the death warrant for this once-lovely building. It had been disused for years and the grants for money, never generous enough, had finally run out. The fabric was considered dangerous and it was inevitable that the bulldozers would roll. The only people vocal in its support were the Bat Group.

'But the pipistrelles!' they shrieked. 'They're a protected species! Their habitat must not be demolished!'

'I've nothing against bats but I'd like to slap a closing order on their support groups!' I'd said to my boss when he handed me the church file with a warning. 'The Barmy Bat Army! That chairman of theirs! Lady What's 'Er Name...'

'Frampton,' supplied Charles. 'Lucinda Frampton.'

'Yes. Well, the lady gave me a very bad time over Mendlesett Church last year. I don't fancy another encounter just yet.'

'Oh, I don't know,' said Charles vaguely. 'I suppose the bats are worth saving. Never seen it myself but they do say the twilight flight of bats out of the church tower is one of the sights of Suffolk. They were still firmly in place when the last quinquennial inspection was done. Byam did it. Now *he* seemed to get on all right with the lovely Lucinda.' Charles rolled his eyes in a meaningful way. 'They spent quite some time observing the habits of our leather-winged friends in remote church towers all over the country, I seem to remember.'

'Byam? Byam who? Or should I say who Byam?'

'Ah... He left a couple of years before you arrived. Byam Somersham. Good architect...but... Anyway, he left the country soon after this bit of work. Went to Spain...or was it Portugal?'

I'd been passing on the main road on the way home from a job in Norfolk and had suddenly caught sight of the tower of All Souls silhouetted against a darkening blood-red sky, streaked with saffron. One of those vivid late-summer sunsets we get just after harvesting. I couldn't resist. 'I'll just poke my head inside,' I told myself, turning into the driveway to the church. 'Might be in time to witness the twilight flight of the pipistrelles.' I watched the shadows lengthen under the stand of ancient oaks which gathered protectively, still wearing their dark leaf canopy, around the secluded stones but no bats flew out to greet me.

And here I was, giving in to temptation and enjoying the guilty frisson of going against all common sense and Charles's firm rules. I paused to sit on the back row of pews to say a silent prayer for the building as I always did and then went on down the aisle, sorrowful for the poor condition of the fabric, the boarded-up windows, the cracked masonry, the water stains running down the plastered walls.

And then I heard it. A trickle of sound at first, growing louder and more insistent: the chirping, twittering, agitated noise that bats make when they're about to take off. I decided to find out where they were roosting. If I was quick enough, I might actually see them emerge from their holes in the rafters or window dressings. I hurried silently back down the nave to the bell tower. The door was swinging open. Checking the state of the staircase with my torch, I was relieved to see that this bit of fabric at least had been replaced since the Middle Ages. It was of stout steel. Not pretty, but a tug and a kick convinced me it was firm. I began to climb. I planned to go as far as the first floor but no further than that. Too risky. Up on the platform, the noise of the bats was louder. Would the light of my torch disturb them? I shone it anyway over the floor. Stout oak floorboards, complete, and no holes down which I might stick a foot. There were hundreds of bats tuning up in the woodwork all around me and, I guessed, in the very top floor above my head, thousands more. Not too late, then.

I shone the torch upwards from my feet. No staircase to the top floor. A very old oak ladder reached upwards to the trapdoor giving access to the bell tower. I ran the beam along it to check its condition. There was no chance I would climb that tonight but if it was obviously rickety I would ask Ben to bring a ladder with him tomorrow and impress him with my forethought.

Looking up, I became aware of a darker shadow amongst the shadows of the raftered roof. As I watched, it moved gently with a sudden gust of wind through a broken pane.

I leaned against the ladder to steady myself, unable to look away.

Above my head a huge black shape was suspended, life-sized, vampire-like. A stiff cape flapped in another gust. With a mew of fear audible even over the noise of the bats, I held my torch in both hands, lighting up the horror dangling above my head. Life-sized, yes, because this thing had once been human and alive. Legs and feet hung from the cloak, arms reached upwards, truncated, caught under the heavy trapdoor. I forced myself to light the face. This was no pallid, bloodstained Dracula mask of horror films but – no less terrifying to me – I saw leathery features which might have lain, undiscovered for millennia, in an Egyptian sarcophagus or been hauled, as brown as the envelope earth, from the depths of a peat bog.

I gulped and, as people do when frightened out of their wits, I said something very silly, just to hear the human sound of my own voice. 'Byam? Byam Somersham? Could that possibly be you?'

At that moment, with a rush and a high-pitched whirring, the whole population of bats poured from holes in every part of the tower. They surged into the air, zipping and diving past me, and I flapped at them in panic, groping my way back to the head of the stairs. I was grateful to hear the clang of my boots on steel treads as I scrambled down. I ran out to my Golf and, still shaking, dialled up a number on my mobile phone.

'Inspector Jennings? I wonder if you remember me? It's

Ellie Hardwick here. I'm at All Souls' Church near Crowden and something awful's happened!'

Richard Jennings of the Eastern Counties CID groaned. 'I'm just going off duty and I don't think I want hear this. What *is* it with you and churches? Oh, go on, then...'

He listened silently as I burbled on, ending dramatically with, '... Inspector...it's every architect's nightmare – getting themselves caught up in one of those trapdoors! In a deserted church...no one to hear you scream...your phone's in your pocket and you can't get to it...' And, with an increasing hysteria I didn't like to hear: 'And you know no one's going to come near the building for another five years! It's Byam, isn't it? Byam Somersham?'

'Calm down and I'll get straight out to you,' said Jennings. 'Don't move from your car! Have you got a flask of coffee in there? Good. Keep some for me. Ten minutes.'

Cocooned in the lights of my car with an up-beat jazz album playing and the windows fogging over with coffee fumes, I managed to get my teeth to unclench and my hands to stop trembling by the time the police car drew up. The Inspector was by himself. He slid into the passenger seat, a large, masculine presence, took my cup from me and drained my coffee. He listened again to my story, nodding quietly.

Finally, 'I've been on the phone with headquarters on the way here,' he said. 'Spoke to someone in Missing Persons. Your bloke Somersham was reported to them nearly five years ago. By his wife. But then she had to withdraw the notice because he turned up in Spain.' He paused for a moment, thoughtful. 'His car was found abandoned near Stansted airport. And he sent her a postcard on her birthday from Barcelona. He's sent one every year since he went off. CID checked. Date stamped in Spain. Certified husband's handwriting. A constable was actually on hand at the letter box to intercept one on delivery. At the lady's request. So that was that. No case. We'll have to look further. Floating cloak, you say, on the body? Ecclesiastical gear? What's the odds that a vicar's gone missing lately, wearing one of those what-do-you-call-ems?'

'Surplice? No, it's much shorter than that. Like...an old-fashioned policeman's cape...'

'Eh? Good Lord!' said Jennings.

The Inspector's torch was more powerful than mine but I stayed as close to him as I could without inviting comment.

'You don't have to do this, you know,' he said when we reached the ladder. 'Leave it to me.'

'I'm coming with you,' I said and began to climb after him. 'Don't worry. I won't touch anything I haven't already touched.'

We stood together gazing in silence at the corpse. The brighter light of the police torch revealed further horrors. Now I saw that the dead face was even more appalling than I'd guessed from my first startled look. It didn't have the dreamy, at-rest quality of a bog-burial or a Pharaoh: the eyes had been picked out long ago by the carrion crows that haunted the fields around and accusing black holes were trained down on us; the shoulders were stained with trailing white patches of pigeon droppings. It had the macabre force of medieval execution, the look of a body left to rot away on a gibbet.

And that was odd, I thought.

And not the only odd detail. 'Look at his shoes,' I whispered. 'Under all that dust those are smart shoes, practically unworn. He didn't walk three miles in those. He drove here. So, if this is Byam, who took his car to the airport and why didn't they come forward when he disappeared?' I shuddered at the implication.

Jennings put an arm protectively around my shoulders and I didn't shrug it away. I'd noticed that, in spite of his strength, the arm was quivering. I think he was glad of my company.

Half an hour later several urgent phone calls had produced a squad of professionals and I had lost the Inspector to the well-oiled police machine as it took over, reducing the gothic horror of the setting to an arc-lamp-illuminated, plastic-taped, sanitised crime scene.

He paused by my car to say, 'You can go home now, Ellie, and I'll take your statement in the morning. Probably no more than a grisly accident we think but I'll call by your office at – say – nine? You'll have to put off your survey for while, of course. Oh, your first guess was right, by the way. His hard hat's abandoned in the upper tower…wallet in his pocket had his driving licence and cards in it… It *was* Byam Somersham.'

By the time Ben Crabtree arrived to pick me up at the office I'd spent an hour studying the Crowden file. Richard Jennings had given me his automatic 'just leave it to the experts' speech but I was hardly listening. And in this field I counted myself an expert anyway. Ben hurried in, stunned and excited in equal measures by the brief outline I'd given him on the phone. After a few minutes of, 'Corst, blast! Who'd ever a thought it? So the old devil got his comeuppance! That trap's lined with ten pound lead, did you know that, Ellie? Accident waiting to happen! Poor old sod, though…awful way to go…' we settled down, file open on the desk, coffee mugs at elbow, to a gossipy discussion of the dead architect and his work. Strangely, Ben had most to say about the man himself.

His broad honest Suffolk face clouded and he looked at me shiftily. 'Don't want to speak ill of the dead but...he were right lot of no good, yon chap, Ellie. Fair architect – no denying *that* – but no good to the firm or any firm for that matter. We all said it when he went off – "Good riddance!"'

'That's a bit harsh, Ben? Why do you say that? Oh, come on, you can't leave it there!'

'Not to be trusted with the...er...female clients, shall I say?' he finally confided.

'Really! Attractive man was he?'

'Oh, yes, I'll say. Even *I* could see it!'

This was quite an admission from the aggressively masculine Ben. And as far as he was prepared to go. Suffolk people are nothing if not discreet and unjudgemental and I was going to hear no more gossip from Ben.

Not so with Charles though. Hurrying through the office at that moment, he hesitated, picking up his bag. 'Attractive, you say? Byam? Good looking bloke but it was his manner more than anything. He'd look at a woman – very long eyelashes he had, I remember – as if she was the only woman in the world and, do you know, at that moment he very likely thought so... And he could make 'em laugh. He'd have made *you* laugh, Ellie. You'd be surprised how many female clients suddenly decided to splash out on an extension so long as *he* was the architect in charge! I must say – he certainly brought the work in!'

Charles carried on, oblivious of our disapproval, 'Vain bloke though! Lord, how the man fancied himself! Snappy dresser and always wore a suit to work. But that cloak! Used to whisk about in it something sickening! He thought it made him dashing – and the trouble is – it damned well did! While the rest of us were muddling about on mucky sites in plastic Andy-Pandy suits for protection, he'd be swishing about looking like some sort of superhero. The blokes on site used to laugh but the women loved it because he could carry it off! Anyway, whatever he did, it worked.'

He looked thoughtful for a moment and added, 'No...they don't make them like that anymore.'

'Sounds like a species we can well do without,' I said crisply. 'He had a wife hereabouts, didn't he?'

'Catherine. Poor Catherine. Lovely Catherine. Still lives in the village. No one could understand why she put up with him and his goings-on. But she always maintained he'd come back. Showed everyone postcards she got from him in Spain every year. "It's just a question of time," she says. "He's working out there. He'll be back when he's made his reputation." Not that she couldn't have done well for herself, either. She'd had a bloke in the background for years. Gentleman-farmer type. Scott. Have you heard of him?'

I nodded. Handsome, middle-aged and perpetually broke, Tony Scott was quite a figure in the village. A single man since his divorce, he was rumoured to be paying out large alimony bills. I'd never connected him with the artistic Catherine Somersham with her eyes always dreamily on the middle distance. I'd seen her at village street fairs, I'd even bought one of her paintings, but had never met her.

Charles went off with a cheery, 'Say hello to the Plod for me...sorry I can't stay, but it's you they want to see, Ellie.'

Ben and I turned to the quinquennial survey typed and filed

and I raised a question that had occurred to me even while gazing at the leathery corpse. 'Look, I don't know much about the state of dead bodies and no doubt the pathologist will have answers but, Ben, how do you think it could have been preserved like that for five years? Didn't putrefaction occur? You were the appointed builder at the time, I see. Can you remember what the weather was like that summer?'

Ben's jaw dropped and he began to stir excitedly. 'That were hot. Days and days of heat. Best harvest for years, they say. And the autumn, the same. Do you think he might have been...well...kippered? Swinging about up there like an Orford smokie?'

'Could be. We'll ask Jennings when he arrives. But something else puzzled me, Ben... I'd have expected the body to have...um...fallen apart...been eaten by insects. Wouldn't you?'

Ben considered for a moment. 'Look on page one, there should be something about pre-existing conditions...there – look.'

His splayed thumb indicated a paragraph and I read, '...extensive anti-infestation treatment carried out on all woodwork...insecticidal fluids...' Mmm... Heavy duty stuff. And the tower was sprayed. Small space – Byam prudently says he put the inspection off for a couple of days to allow the fumes to dissipate. I see. Are you thinking that any winged creatures that might have been interested in a body would have been knocked cold by the treatment?'

'It's possible, I'd have thought.'

There was a screech of gravel outside and Jennings strode into his office. He looked refreshed this morning and as brisk and bright as I remembered. He'd never met Ben before and I introduced the men, explaining the builder's role in the Byam Somersham saga.

'...So, accidental death is what it seems to have been. A cracked skull caused instant death. He didn't suffer, Ellie,' the Inspector was concerned to tell me. 'It looks as though he was coming down from the upper bell tower (though what the hell he was doing up there when the survey job was complete, I've no idea), missed his footing on the ladder and dropped the trap he was holding up over his head. It crashed down – did you known it was lead-lined? – of course you did – sorry. It bashed in the back and top of his head...here...' He picked up a file and demonstrated on Ben's head. 'Killed him at once and trapped his arms which were still extended over the lip of the hole.'

'We were wondering why the body didn't disintegrate and drop?' I said tentatively. 'In fact we've had some ideas.'

'To start with the most obvious thing – his suit was of very good quality, a light summer fabric but strong enough to sustain the weight of his body until...well, until we found it. To go on – we think putrefaction didn't occur because of the exceptional weather...'

'All those hot harvest days and it was well ventilated up there. Not one of those louvred windows is intact. "Kippered" is what Ben's saying.'

'Right. Yes. Well done.' He fished about in his briefcase and produced an email print-out. 'Forensic entomologists – that's grub experts to you – are a bit puzzled though,' he said. 'This is just a preliminary statement – work could take days – but they're not able to find a great deal...'

'Ah. We think we can help you there!' Ben and I exchanged smug looks.

* * *

After Ben left, Jennings 'you'd better call me Richard', stayed on for a second cup of coffee. There was an uneasiness about him and I sensed that he still had questions. He didn't know whether to grill me in his role of interrogator or chat to me as a helpful assistant so I made it easy for him by launching into a few questions of my own.

'What was he doing up there when the report was finished and had been handed in for typing? Look here. Charles is very old-fashioned and doesn't yet quite trust modern technology. Oh, it's all on computer but he keeps the original dictated tapes just in case. Someone told him a bolt of lightning can have a dire effect on your hard-drive, since when it's been belt and braces.' I showed him a plastic bag which had been filed next to the document. I took out the small Dictaphone cassette it contained. 'I've checked it and you should perhaps have this but it's nothing more than the architect's survey. This is what may be important.' I peeled the small pink post-it note from the back of the cassette. 'It says "Bats! A.S. Ch. 8 p.m." He'd forgotten to inspect the bat accommodation. No reference to it in the body of the report. I think he probably went back as an afterthought to check up on the colony.'

'A.S.?'

'All Souls, the name of the church.'

'Of course, I'd better take those. Yes, thanks, Ellie. This all begins to fall into place. Except...'

'Those postcards to his wife? He can't have sent them. Who did? Is Catherine lying? What's going on?'

Jennings looked uncomfortable. 'I called on the widow last night and broke the news. She seemed distressed and horrified, I'd say. She stuck to her story about the cards...she keeps them in a row on her mantelpiece... And, as the authenticity was corroborated by the police – what can I say? It's all a bit awkward.'

Carefully, I said, 'I was thinking that, on behalf of the firm, I'd go along to see Catherine and express our condolences. A bunch of flowers, perhaps... What do you think, Richard?'

He grinned. 'I think that would be a good idea, Ellie. She teaches art at the local college. You'll probably find you have a lot in common.'

He turned to me as he left, his hand on the doorknob. 'Oh, if you get into a girlie chat with her, you might ask how she's going to spend the two hundred grand.'

'The two hundred grand?'

'Life insurance policy. She'd kept up the payments on her husband's life.' He paused and added thoughtfully, 'I always think it should be called a "death insurance policy", don't you?'

Catherine Somersham's greeting when she answered the door to the Old Mill House (conversion by Byam, I guessed) was warm. She even knew my name. I stood uncertainly on the doorstep, almost hidden by a generous armful of white arum lilies.

'Come in! It is Ellie Hardwick, isn't it? You work with Charles? I'm just making some tea, will you have one? I won't say "Oh, you shouldn't have,"' she said gracefully, taking the lilies, 'because these are my favourites! Flowers *are* a sort of consolation, you know. And consolation is, even after five years, much needed.'

While she went to put them in water I cast an eye around the living room and began to relax. I find anything minimal bleak and soulless and this room was the very opposite of minimal. It defied any label – I doubt Catherine was the kind of woman who cared about style – and she would probably have laughed if I'd suggested 'bohemian-chic'. It looked as though she had just collected into the room everything she admired or found comfortable. White sofas covered in coarse linen, wooden floors with Scandinavian rugs scattered over, books spilling over from shelves no longer equal to the task of housing them, white walls and everywhere, paintings, not all her own.

The conversation was surprisingly easy and led on from my genuine and enthusiastic comments on the painting I'd bought at the previous year's village art festival. She invited me to look at the other pictures on the walls and, while on my feet, I took the opportunity of strolling to the fireplace and admiring a bronze turn-of-the-century figure of a little dancer on the mantelpiece.

'No! It can't be a Degas, I know that! But it's the next best thing!'

'It's my great-grandmother.'

'She sculpted this?'

'Oh, no, sorry! She was the model. My great-grandfather did it,' she smiled. I replaced it carefully, then hastily began picking up the pile of postcards my manoeuvrings had scattered.

'Oh, dear!' I said in tones of mock horror. 'I wouldn't have taken you for an admirer of modern architecture... Spanish is it?... Yes, these two are in Barcelona – a couple of Gaudí's best...then the Guggenheim Museum? The Sant Jordi Sports Palace? Not my favourite!'

'Nor mine,' she said easily. 'You can look at them if you want to. They're postcards Byam wrote.' She chewed her bottom lip for a moment, started to say something, sighed and then took the plunge. 'Ellie, I don't know what to do! Oh, do you mind my laying this on you? You'll wonder what on earth you've walked into!'

I made encouraging noises and she went on haltingly, 'I've been fooling the police and now they know it. That nice Inspector who came last night saw straight through the rubbish I was telling him. I'm not a good liar and I think he's pretty smart. What on earth can I say to them? I think they might be going to arrest me.'

'It's never a bad idea to tell the truth. That Inspector you saw...Jennings?...he's halfway human. He would listen. I could give you his number if you like. Er...if it would help to rehearse it, see how it comes out, I'd gladly listen.'

I put on my receptive face. Not difficult as I was eager to hear and she responded by launching into her story.

'Five years ago when Byam disappeared I was left in limbo. Not a word. No note. He'd told me he was due some leave and he was going off for a few days by himself.' She glanced at me, her expression one of mixed defiance and shame. 'He did that occasionally. It was a price I paid...not happily but with a certain resignation, I suppose. But this time, none of the local ladies he'd had an affair with had gone missing in a companionable way.'

I looked at her, startled by her cold rationality.

Misinterpreting this she said hastily, 'Oh, *you* weren't... surely you...?'

'I never met the man,' I said firmly. 'I've only been working in the village three years.'

She took a photograph from a table and handed it to me. 'Meet him now,' she said quietly.

Even from the photograph the quality of the man leapt out. Not classically handsome, I thought, but I'd have turned in the street to look at him and speculate. Humorous, clever and interested is what he looked. It made last night's horror even more of an obscenity.

She took the photograph from me and sat holding it in her lap while she continued. 'Shortly after he went off I had a very good reason to insist that he was still alive at least. I didn't want to be a widow and I didn't want to get a divorce. Two years before, we'd had a holiday in Spain and he'd bought and written out some postcards to friends and family and, as usual, he handed them to me to do the donkeywork – "Here, Cath, you'll remember the addresses. You can finish these off." Well, I rebelled. I didn't bother. They just came back home with us in the luggage. When I wanted to prove he was still alive, I remembered them. I took five or six of them over to a place I know in Spain and paid the hotel manager to post them to me on a given date, one a year. I put each of them in a typed envelope. The police believed me because – well, why wouldn't they? I was saying what they wanted to hear. They must have been expecting me to try to prove he was *dead* because of the life insurance policy. But I needed my husband *alive*. For personal reasons.'

I was about to encourage her to enlarge on this when a Range Rover tore down the drive and parked in front of the house. A florid-faced man got out and hurried straight in. I noted with distaste that he had a bottle of champagne in the capacious pocket of his waxed jacket.

'Cathy! Cathy! Have you seen the news? Accidental death is what they're saying. Oh, who's this? Didn't realise you had company.' He looked around in a stagy way for my car.

'I walked. I work in the village.'

Catherine performed the introductions. 'My neighbour, Tony Scott.'

He stood glaring at me, willing me to leave. He was too large for the room, he'd left muddy prints on the shining floor, he smelled of diesel and he frightened me.

'Pleased to have met you Mr Scott,' I lied with a sweet smile, 'but I must dash. Oh! Before I go! Nearly forgot, Catherine! The name of that new hairdresser...I like to support local initiatives, don't you?' I confided as I scribbled. 'Ask for Ricardo at Hairtique,' and added his mobile number.

Catherine smiled and nodded. 'Quite right, Ellie. Thank you for coming. I'll take your advice,' she said.

'It's so obvious why she's been deceiving people like that,' I said to Richard over a pint in the Angel that night. 'That Scott won't take no for an answer. She's been doing a Penelope.'

'A what?'

'Odysseus's wife! Repelling suitors by insisting her old man's still alive. Just taking an awfully long time to get back from the Trojan War. Penelope promised to marry one of the brigands who were after her fortune as soon as she'd finished a bit of weaving she was doing. But at night she used to creep down and unpick what she'd done in the daytime. Delaying tactics! Spun it out for years! Catherine's house must be worth a bob or two and now you tell me she's due to get a large sum from the insurance company. Tony's well known to be a bit short of cash...well – there you are. He's been putting pressure on her. Won't take no for an answer. You know the type. He's worried, Richard. He's a ball of pent-up violence. You're not to go near him.' I stopped abruptly and bit my lip.

'I'll be sure to keep my styling scissors ready in my back pocket,' he grinned.

'You'll just have to forgive her. All she's done is waste police time, isn't it?'

'I'll forgive your new friend if you'll do something for me,' he said mysteriously. 'Would you mind presenting yourself back at the scene tomorrow morning? Something I want to check on.'

'Never had the Law at my feet before.' I almost giggled with nerves at the sight of Richard's body, face down, on the dusty floor of the tower.

'Get on with it, Ellie,' he grumbled. 'My helmet's conveniently over there in the corner, you've coshed me on the head with one of those planks that litter the floor. I'm dead. Now pull me towards the trapdoor.'

'Ankles or knees, Richard?'

'Take your pick.'

I tugged him by the ankles and to my surprise his body moved easily with the grains of the boards to the hatch. Gingerly I climbed halfway down the ladder and pulled him after me. When I'd got him balanced with the weight of his upper body still bearing on the lip of the hole, steadying him firmly against the oak structure, I reached up and grasped the handle on the flap of the trapdoor which I'd propped open with a piece of planking on either side.

'I could do it Richard!' I gasped. 'If I push out one of the props and then the other, tugging you as it gives way, you're a dead man! Would be if you weren't already!'

He surged back to life and carefully moved the door out of reach.

'It could be done!' he said with satisfaction. 'And if *you* can do it, a 5' 4" female, anyone can. Let's get out of here, shall we?'

We went out into the sunshine and I flapped a hand at his jacket front, covered in dust and worse. He looked at it with interest.

'Probably splinters of oak floor boarding in there as well,' he said. 'Just like the ones we found down the front of Byam's cloak. We know he'd arranged a meeting up here with someone. Had he lured some female up here with romantic intent? "Come up and experience the twilight flight with me?"' he purred. He studied his jacket. 'Nice roll in the pigeon droppings? Amatory activity witnessed by a million swooping bats? Not the place *I'd* choose for an assignation.'

'Wouldn't work for me either,' I agreed. 'Have you thought, Richard, someone could have lured Byam here? He (could be she) sets up a meeting, gets someone to drop him off here, climbs the tower and kills him, leaves him dangling. He takes the keys from Byam's pocket and drives the car to the airport car park. With everyone's eyes on Spain, no one's going to look in a deserted church lost among the cornfields. He'd finished the job anyway and, according to his schedule, was supposed to be going on holiday.'

'The killer knew that the body would be found sooner or later but you could reasonably expect a body exposed like that to be judged a nasty accident as – for the moment – it *is*,' said Richard. 'And to show your faith in his survival and your innocence, you keep up the payments on his insurance policy and by waiting patiently – you know he'll be discovered in five years at the outside – you come into a tidy sum of money – and five years' rebate probably.

They're in it together! Catherine and Scott.'

'Hold on! I'm not so sure,' I objected. I was remembering the way Catherine had held her husband's photograph. Protectively. Lovingly. 'We're missing something here. Take me back to the office will you, Richard? There may be something in Byam's work records that throws up some information. Let's find out what else our local Don Giovanni was busy with.'

Charles was out on a job when we got back and we settled down with the dusty ledger from five years earlier which recorded the hours spent by each architect on each of his jobs. I pointed out Byam's record. It seemed he had quite a full programme. Ongoing repairs at five churches besides the quinquennial on All Souls. He had, typically, spent half a day at each, usually mornings. His afternoons had been spent on domestic projects: he'd been working on extensions to two private houses. In the record, one was named as 'Moat Farm Extns.' The other 'The Limes Extns.' Both were common names hereabouts.

'Out-of-county contractors, I see, on both so no use asking Ben for his insights,' said Richard.

I remembered the cutting comment Charles had made about the ladies who ordered extensions and I wondered. I shared my suspicions with Richard.

'Names,' he said. 'How do we correlate these jobs with names of clients?'

'We look in the back. That's where Liz wrote down the accounts and payments before it all went on computer.'

We tracked down the two extension jobs and looked at the names of the clients.

'But isn't this...?' Richard started to say, recognising one of them. 'Oh, Good Lord! You don't imagine...? Surely not...?'

I stared at the page for a moment, taking in the meaning of the scene we had uncovered and, in an unthinking gesture of appalled rejection, I slammed the ledger shut.

'We can't leave it there,' said Richard. 'However much you might want to. But at the moment, all we've got is the suspicion of a scenario that could possibly have led to murder. It's not much. How can we find out more without committing ourselves?'

'I think I know how. Look at the dates. The work was started a year before Byam died. This lady was spinning it out? "While you're here, Byam, you might as well look at..." We get a lot of that. Can you imagine? It would have been under way by Christmas six years ago. I'll get the album.'

Every year Charles threw a party in mid-December for staff and clients and anyone who'd been involved with the firm in the past year. He enjoyed going around photographing the junketing and faithfully stuck his shots in an album. It was well thumbed. I leafed back to the Christmas in question. Byam's last. Faces, familiar and unfamiliar, smiled happily or drunkenly at the camera.

'Look at this one, Ellie,' Richard murmured. 'Says it all really, don't you think?'

Byam was standing with his arm around a dark and flamboyantly good-looking woman. He was grinning at the photographer and waving a glass around. The woman was paying no attention to the man behind the camera; she only had eyes for Byam. I was a stranger to both of them but the relationship was clear. It seemed to be clear also to the man standing to the right of the pair, some feet away. He was not smiling. Head lowered, he was showing all the aggression and pent-up anger of a tormented bull. An anger directed straight at the unconcerned Byam.

Richard put a hand down the centre of the photograph, covering up the partying crowd in the background and concealing all but the two main players. The effect was astonishing. Revealed was a crime about to happen. 'Murderer and victim, would you say? I think Byam extended himself a little too far on this occasion,' said Richard. 'Husband sees wife the victim of a serial cuckolder...perhaps she's threatened to leave him and go off with the glamorous architect...so what does he do? Makes an appointment with the scallywag in a remote place and engineers his disappearance.'

'It didn't work, you know,' I added slowly. 'All in vain. The lady left her husband anyway, shortly after. He lives by himself.'

'A tragedy for all of them then. Makes you want to just slam the trapdoor back and cover the whole thing over,' said Richard surprisingly.

We sat together in silence, each assessing the evidence, hunting for a flaw, neither of us ready to take the next step. 'Oh, who's this?' said Richard, annoyed. 'Someone's just drawn up in a van. You've got a visitor.'

'It's Ben. You met him yesterday morning. I'm sure he can shed some light on this,' I said. 'Want me to leave?'

'You just stay put!'

Ben came striding in with his usual sunny confidence and stopped as he took in the books and the album open in front of us. Richard rose to his feet.

'Ah! The Christmas party book,' Ben said and he sat down in Richard's vacated chair to look at the photographs. 'You'll have figured it out then?' he added prosaically. His calloused forefinger gently traced the face of the dark-haired girl. 'You never met her, Ellie. Rachel. She was always too good for me. I knew that.' He swallowed and growled, 'She deserved better, but not him. No, never *him*! I couldn't stand by and watch her break her heart over that no-good poser. If he'd loved her back I don't think I'd have bothered.'

Richard stood uncertainly by. He seemed to be waiting for me to say something.

'You rang and arranged to meet him at the tower, Ben? Mentioning some problem with the bats?' I suggested. 'The contractor,' I explained for Richard's benefit. 'Just about the only person in the world the architect would have agreed to see at that late hour at the end of a job. You got one of your blokes to drop you off and after you'd...afterwards...you drove off in Byam's car.'

'Story came out that he'd gone off to Spain. Broke my Rachel's heart. She didn't blame me. Why would she? – I never let on. But she pined for him. Never laughed again. Not like that.' He looked again with pain at the photograph. 'Nothing I could do. Seemed I'd killed her as well, in a way. She packed her bags and went off.'

Seeing Richard's shoulders tense he added wryly, 'Oh, nothing sinister! You'll find her at her mother's in Stowmarket. Well, shall we go, then? I always expected it would come out. But I reckoned I had five years. Five years to try to get her back. No chance now.'

He turned to me, tears glazing his eyes. 'Wouldn't be sorry to hear that damned church had been demolished. Was looking forward to swinging a half-ton ball at it myself! Let me know, Ellie, would you, when you've done the deed?'

'No change,' Neil said. A redundant statement. He smiled to himself ruefully. Charlton nodded. Placed a hand on one of Aimee's. Squeezed. He looked to the heart monitor, and back down the corridor to the crowded wards, to the windows full of darkness and rain. To Aimee's brother and his lover. Felt his eyes burning. Looked away again before he gave way beneath the weight of it all.

'Time for coffee,' Neil said with too much forced levity in his voice.

'Leave me here,' Charlton said. 'You go.'

Neil was shaking his head. 'Coffee and a smoke then. On me.'

'No. I'll stay here.'

'*Up.*'

Charlton felt his fist close. Blood rushing in his head. He closed his eyes.

A darkness waited for him there, one he was reluctant to admit. It was the dark of rage, of wanting retribution for what was done, the dark that was pacing him day and night wherever he went. It refused to be outrun, outdistanced; it waited for him to wake in the morning, it hindered his sleep at night.

He got up.

'It's my fault,' Charlton said as he closed his hands around the cup. 'My fault.'

'Bollocks,' Neil said quickly, too quickly. John looked up from scratching at the Formica surface on the table. Smiled. 'Bollocks,' Neil said again, quietly this time. 'This has *nothing* to do with you. You can't protect people twenty-four seven. This shit just happens. It's a fucking harsh thing to sit with but it's true. There's no point in feeling guilty. It's not going to help her, and you know it.'

'Why your fault?' John enquired quietly.

Charlton could feel his jaw clenching. Tension rising in him. *Christ, he had no fucking control any more.* 'A white woman with a black man?'

'Oh, bull*shit*. It was just some—'

John raised a hand. Placed it over Neil's to placate him. There were families glancing up whenever Neil raised his voice. They only wanted this to be a haven from the problems *out there*. Just somewhere to drink their coffee and smoke their cigarettes; to stare out of the window at their own darkness looking back at them.

Neil saw all of this in John's eyes, Charlton realised. It was the kind of closeness that came with time and intimacy. Had he shared that with Aimee? He couldn't decide. Her absence kept making him remember her differently, made him soften the edges perhaps. But it was nothing they'd not have been able to iron out, given time. Just the residue of past relationships, old wounds and recriminations that she hadn't felt able to speak about. All he'd got were the scars they left on her, both actual and otherwise; the rough edges that he'd not been given the time or opportunity to smooth away.

Rage again. Boiling in him. Every time it was a struggle to keep it down. He'd known from the get go that once he and Aimee had developed into an item that certain types of people would have a problem with the idea. Even members of his own family. The only answer he felt was just to *get on with it*; fuck everyone else. Living your life according to other people's expectations was no life at all. But now he wasn't so sure. He had no idea if this was guilt or something else. Just a feeling for the sake of feeling.

Charlton hung his head and smoothed a hand across his brow. He had to stay calm. He couldn't afford to explode. His emotions were a roller coaster crashing from uncontrolled rage to uncontrolled grief. He needed to retain some semblance of control.

Intellectually he knew Neil was telling him the truth. There was no proof the attack had been anything other than some sick fucks getting their kicks at Aimee's expense. But his heart and gut told him different. His chest cavity was filled with broken glass and each beat of his heart ground the ache in deeper; compounded the fear and guilt.

He *was* to blame. No matter how he looked at it, it was his fucking fault. He'd promised to protect Aimee, sworn he'd never allow her to be hurt again.

He had failed. And worse, he had lied.

The noise of the chair slamming over on the tiles cut the room's murmured conversations off like a gunshot. Charlton felt frowns and hostile scowls lash his back as he pushed through the swing doors and fled down the corridor. He ignored them. He could feel the darkness growing inside him; alienating him from everyone. He didn't know how to stop it or if he even *wanted* to.

The rain splashed over him as he escaped the confines of the hospital. Above him the evening blossom of fireworks lit the sky. He ran through the hospital car park, the falling water blinding him. He needed distance in order to think. And used the movement in order not to.

* * *

When Charlton stopped and came back to himself he was standing on the lawn in front of Aimee's flat, blankly staring at the darkened windows. His clothes were soaked through. He was cold and wet, but his head was clear. The fury that had driven him from the hospital had momentarily abated, sunk once more into the depths. Charlton slumped, sagging, suddenly weary without the adrenaline rush of his rage. Wide-eyed he stared at the sky. *Shit*, he thought, *what've I done?* He shook his head, despondent, finding no easy answer in the heavens. He shivered and looked back at the flat before him. The blocky edifice was dark, the windows along the face darker still. It was late. Time he went home. He needed sleep.

He raised his eyes one last time to the third floor window that was Aimee's bedroom and flinched, starting at the sudden blaze of light. The window was no longer a blind pool of shadow. It shone with warmth and colour. 'Aimee?' he asked, his voice little more than a sigh. Charlton frowned. *What the—? Was someone in Aimee's flat?* Anger flared, flooding his brain with hot molten fury. *Someone was in Aimee's fucking flat!*

With a bang, Charlton flung open the glass outer door and, before the noise had cleared from the stairway, pounded up the two short flights. At Aimee's front door he pulled her spare keys from his sodden jeans and scraped them over the metal lock plate, haste making his fingers clumsy. He twisted and pushed simultaneously, crashing into the hallway, the door banging against the wall and tearing the keys from his hand. Charlton bulled into the unlit living area, a snarl plastered across his face. A growl rumbled in his throat. God help whosoever was in the flat, because Charlton wouldn't – he couldn't help himself. If there was someone fucking with

Aimee's stuff, he'd kill them. So help him God, he'd fucking kill them!

The bedroom door was ajar. Light filtered through the gap. Movement. A shadow. Charlton crossed the distance and kicked open the door. 'Right, you fuckers!' he screamed, spittle flying from his lips. Hands fisted and ready.

No one. The room was unoccupied, just as it should be.

Charlton spun around and searched the remaining rooms, slapping the walls to light the flat, switches digging into his palms. Living room. Bathroom. Kitchenette. There was no one. The only presence he felt was the fading ghost of Aimee.

The scent of her perfume lingered in the bedroom, floating up from pillow and sheets, wafting from her wardrobe when he threw open the door. On the bedside cabinet Harry Potter lay discarded, unfinished, her place marked with a slip of paper. Cosmetics were haphazardly scattered on bathroom shelves, a crumpled tissue forgotten on the vanity unit beneath. Silken, spun gold threads were caught between the bristles of her brush. A cushion sagged and shaped by wear in the living room. Aimee's outline imprinted upon the sofa from countless evenings sat before the television. The jewelled shell of a CD lay discarded on the hi-fi, hinting at her last mood. A cup stained with stale dregs of tea on the end table.

Like a marionette with cut strings Charlton folded down onto the sofa. Visions of Aimee flashing through his memory like slides through a projector. Each remembrance more painful than the last, until grief broke in him and he cradled his head in his hands, his chest hitching as the sobs tore him apart.

He couldn't stop here. It was too painful. Aimee's absence was too palpable. And he knew from bitter experience that his own flat would be little better.

Everywhere he looked he saw Aimee.

The projector clicked in his head. The slideshow changed. The pictures cast upon the screen were no longer the Aimee that was. No longer the tall and willowy Aimee with the long blonde hair that seemed to shine from within; with the robin's-egg blue eyes that changed with her mood, one minute pale green, the next lightest blue. No longer the beautiful, trembling, loving, hopeful woman he had fallen for. Now the slideshow was all the ravaged and broken Aimee. Raped and beaten so brutally her skin had turned the colour of rotten fruit. Bones broken. Skin torn, stripped, grazed and cut in a million places. New, far worse scars layered on top of the old, faded, almost forgotten ones. His beautiful Aimee lost in the darkness of a coma. Lost in a darkness that would be with her even after the drugs were washed from her system.

His own darkness welled up from within Charlton and swamped him. Like a wave it rushed through him, smothering the pain, banking the hate. It was a darkness that demanded.

Thrusting himself up from the sofa, Charlton left the flat. He slammed the door behind him and headed down the stairs. Feeling sorry for himself did no one any good. The motherfuckers that had blinded Aimee, that had cut out her tongue and punctured her eardrums, that had carved signals of hate upon her chest, they would all pay. Three times three. An eye for a fucking eye.

He wanted to know how Neil stayed so fucking calm. He was her brother for God's sake. Neil should be out there hunting those scumbags down with him.

He's got John to think about. Charlton stopped. He was breathing hard. The chill air and the steadily increasing rain cooled him down. Had Neil been right? Did shit just happen?

Was it really nothing to do with him? Or had his philosophy of *fuck 'em, who cares, it's our life* been to blame? Was he really *so* blameless? No. It had to be his fault. *If she'd been going out with a white bloke this would never have happened.*

Round and round. Up and down. Charlton felt like he was going mad. He needed to sort his fucking head out. He needed some place to chill.

Pulling his mobile from his jacket, Charlton dialled up Neil and John's number. Ear pressed to the thin plastic he listened to the phone trill, counting the number of rings. Was it too late? Perhaps he shouldn't call—

'It's me, Charlton. I...' He didn't know what to say. What the hell was he doing ringing these guys? They had enough on their plate without mollycoddling him.

'You OK?' John asked the silence. Wide-awake now. 'CK, you there? You OK?'

In the background Neil asked a question. The words were muffled, lost across the distances, but the concern was clear as a bell. Charlton felt his throat threatening to close around his voice and hurriedly choked out his request. 'Can I crash at your place? I...' He couldn't finish.

'Sure. What's happened? Are you OK?' John asked.

Charlton couldn't answer, his throat was too tight; it clicked whenever he swallowed, too dry to work. No moisture left. He heard John's voice, tinny in the background. He heard the phone exchanged. 'Charlton, it's Neil. What's up? Are you OK?'

'I'm fine. I just can't...I just need a place to stay. For tonight?'

'Where are you? You OK to get here?' Neil asked. Then without pause, 'Look, get a cab. I'll cover the cost, OK? It's not a problem. We'll see you in a bit, yeah?'

There was no hesitancy in Neil's voice. Like Aimee, his door was always open. It made Charlton's chest tighten. 'Thanks, Neil. I'm... Well, I'm sorry about this evening, you know, at the hospital? I didn't mean to go storming off like some—'

'It's forgotten,' Neil interjected, cutting Charlton off. 'Just come home. OK? Just come home.'

They'd made up the spare bed for him by the time he arrived. Neil and John sat him down, trying to work the edges out of him. But he was having none of it. He couldn't decide why this was; he felt as if he were outside of himself, incapable of any kind of stillness. There was no placating him. But he could suddenly see with cold clarity the distance between good and bad. It seemed that there were no greys left in the world. *Pick a side*. His head was fucked.

'Have a drink,' Neil was saying, disappearing into the kitchen. 'There's some vodka somewhere...'

'Just *sit* for a while,' John said. He sat on the table opposite Charlton; his eyes set with concern, frustration at not being able to get through. 'This is not doing anyone any good.'

'I thought I saw someone,' Charlton said as Neil reappeared with half a bottle of Smirnoff, and some glasses, which he placed in between the three of them. 'In Aimee's place.'

'Aimee's?' Neil said, a note of concern rising in his voice.

'But it was empty,' Charlton said disconsolately. 'No one fucking there. Ridiculous. I'm seeing things now.'

Neil had emptied the vodka into the tumblers. 'We're all at our wits' end, mate. Drink up, eh? To Aimee?' He raised his glass and an eyebrow, hoping for affirmation from the others.

* * *

He didn't think he'd sleep but when he put his head down in the dark, shivering despite the radiators creaking with warmth throughout Neil and John's flat, he succumbed quickly. In the dream Aimee called to him and, without any conscious volition, Charlton found himself following. She led him barefoot into the city, her hair flying into her face and hiding her eyes whenever she glanced back at Charlton to beckon him on, urging him to keep up as he stumbled and tripped in somnambulistic haste, unable to close the distance between them.

The city surrounded Charlton, vacant but for the birds flooding the sky. They arced across his vision, seemingly trapped in a perpetual loop. Like a moment spliced together that never ended. He had followed Aimee once before and knew what came next.

Tears ran down his face as Aimee pressed herself in and out of the shadows cast by the cathedral and back into darkness through the gates out onto Colmore Row.

She guided him across the road, past the empty façades that housed an office and a bank, and turned to wait at the mouth of the deserted alleyway, the piece of the loop where her three attackers stood, ready to enact, without remorse or regret, scenes that would haunt him time and time again. Aimee stepped into the alley and her eyes dragged Charlton in with her, forcing him to bear witness to the atrocities her attackers performed, seeking out his eyes at all times as he watched helplessly, unable to look away, recording the detail of their crimes to ensure punishment was just.

Ben MacKay dodged a solitary car, the Queensway slick under his Adidas as he crossed the road, Hurst Street at his back. The chill wind cut through the cheap denim of his jacket, prickling and puckering his flesh like a fear he felt at the flat. He'd just had to get out; score something to get him through the night, let him sleep without the nightmare. There was no way he could spend another minute in that flea-infested shit hole the council had stuck him with, not without a little smack or blow to take the edge off. The bloody place freaked him out. Ever since Lewis had got done in, the walls had seemed too thin. He could hear the old farts next door whispering about him, their voices scratching and scraping at his mind, making him paranoid. He kept seeing shadows at the edge of his vision, no matter how many lights he left burning; fleeting movement that made his heart race and the breath snag in his throat.

Last night he'd dreamt about the girl they'd done and woken up screaming like a baby. He'd been convinced she stood in the room with him, looming over his prone body as he thrashed in his sweat-soaked bed. They'd only meant to scare her, have a bit of fun. Teach her a lesson for shacking up with a nig-nog. It just got out of hand, that's all, and now he couldn't sleep for thinking what they'd done. He'd spent the rest of the night in his living room, curled up on the threadbare and sagging sofa, eyes burned raw by the hundred-watt glare of the ceiling light. He would not admit it to Webb, or anyone else for that matter, but he was scared. Shit scared. His nerves were frayed, close to breaking; lack of sleep and too much shit taking their toll. He'd not been able to relax for over a week now. Way too jumpy. He felt hunted. Haunted.

Stepping onto the pavement Mack increased his pace, nervously glancing behind him as he turned the corner onto Hill Street, past what used to be the Albany Hotel. He thought he'd heard the slap of footsteps lapping at his own, but the dim sodium revealed nothing more sinister than light and shadow. Another car rounded the traffic island, a taxi taking some late-night revellers home, the starry headlights flashing through the drizzle and hurting his eyes.

Mack faced forward, shaking his head as he hurried along. He really had to get a grip. Webb would beat the crap out of him if he ever let on he was freaked this bad. Webb didn't approve of Mack's habit at the best of times. Sure, he had a reason for needing a fix, what with the girl and then Lewis being killed and all. Not that there was any link. The pigs reckoned Lewis had just fucked with the wrong people. He'd always been a psycho. Still, Webb would kick his arse if he found out about Mack being so shit scared he needed a little something just to turn out the lights.

A bent and discarded Coke can rang out on the pavement, clattering at his heels, and making him jump just as he stepped off the kerb at St George's House to cross Station Street. 'Shit!' he cried out, suddenly breathless and panting. He swung around, his heart beating in his throat. But the street was empty of life.

Must have been the wind, he thought, stepping out of the road and crossing to the edge of the pavement, craning his neck in an attempt to see back around the Albany's corner. Nothing. There was no one in sight.

Mack swallowed, his throat suddenly dry. He wrapped his arms around himself, holding tight. He glanced across the road at The Crown, wishing the bar was open. He could've really done with a drink right about now: a couple of pints of lager, maybe a whiskey chaser to warm him up. Anything to calm him down. He knew he couldn't carry on like this. The strain of holding it all together was too much. He was literally jumping at shadows. Holding back tears, Mack threw a last glance over his shoulder at the way he'd come, then turned and shuffled on up Hill Street.

Fuck this shit, he thought. He couldn't let anyone see him acting like this: like a big girl's blouse. He hawked and spat into the gutter, straightening up from the hunched posture he'd adopted, disgusted with being such a fucking poof. He had to pull himself together.

Pausing to light a Benson's, his hand cupped around the lighter's flame to shield it from the rain, Mack once more heard pursuing footsteps and his shakily reconstructed mask of arrogant belligerence crumbled. He spun around, the unlit fag dropping from his lip, a scream locked tight into his suddenly hitching chest. Eyes wide, pupils dilated, he scanned the street. There was no one. The street was still deserted.

Shaking uncontrollably, his breath coming in shallow gasps, rasping icily through his teeth, Mack backed up. This time he was certain he had heard the click-clack of heels from behind. He *hadn't* imagined it. Not this time. Someone was definitely following him. *Fucking* with him. His jacket scraped along the rough brickwork on his right, the noise startling him and making him cry out as he stumbled along.

Please leave me alone, he silently pleaded, terror bubbling just beneath the surface, pushing icy beads of sweat from his pores. *Just leave me the fuck alo—*

Mack felt a hand slide across his mouth, blocking his airway. Then an arm snaked around his throat and dragged him backward into the recess of an old abandoned emergency exit. He felt the first blow strike his head and his legs crumpled. His vision wavered, black motes flapping at the periphery like crows. Pain exploded through his face as it smashed into the concrete. Lightning flashes of agony went off his skull. Blood poured from his nose, choking him. He could feel a flap of skin hanging down from his forehead and imagined the cold gleam of bone glinting through the rain.

Gagging, Mack spat out a tooth and attempted to raise his arms. If he could get to his feet, fight back, he might have a chance. A kick cracked his ribs and knocked him down. Pain lanced through him, bright and sharp. It hurt to breathe. He couldn't move. Another hard punch, a cheekbone shattered. His head whipped sideways, tearing his scalp on the rough brickwork. Blood swam across his eyes. Another blow. And another. And another. Mack twitched and whimpered amidst the stink of piss. A kick lifted him. Another caught his head. Blinding agony as his eye disgorged from the socket like a bloody oyster. The rain of blows registering less and less as darkness clawed at his senses. The last thing Mack felt was the crunch of his spine, then death claimed him and he felt no more.

When he woke Charlton felt the hard surface beneath him. Not the bed he'd fallen asleep in. Panic rose inside him as he felt something flutter against his face. A leaf. He sprung to his feet as if stung. He was in the square surrounding St Philip's Cathedral.

The phone roused him. He reached into his jacket pocket. Stared at it for a moment, not really registering the caller on the display. Distracted. The leaves were still blowing around him. The sound of early morning traffic sluicing through the rain. His clothes were sodden and stained. 'Neil,' he said. Nothing else. His mind was a blank.

The generosity had finally gone from Neil's voice. 'Where the fuck are you?'

Charlton closed his eyes. He was too tired for this. 'Town. When did I leave?'

There was a moment while Neil gathered himself. He was a man unused to bursts of temper. 'I didn't realise you *had*, you daft bastard. Came in this morning and you'd gone.'

'Too much to drink, I daresay,' Charlton said. He felt adrift. That distance again. Getting wider. Like looking at the remains of the world through the wrong end of a telescope.

'Two measures of Smirnoff?' Neil said. 'Not fucking likely.'

'Neil—'

'*Listen*. There's only so far you can go until you start alienating people,' Neil said, his voice quieter now, more controlled. 'And the rope is *fraying*, my friend. Don't let this change who you are.'

There were sirens somewhere in the city. A cacophony of them. Neil's voice was diminishing. Charlton stood, felt the wind leafing through him. Ambulances. Police too. Something big. He couldn't think about that when all it did was remind him of Aimee. It was nothing to do with him. Forget it.

'Look, I'm *sorry*, alright. Neil? I need to sort this out myself. I'm fucked over this,' he admitted. But the line had gone quiet as the sirens diminished. Neil?'

'Charlton,' Neil said. 'I'll call you back, alright?'

Charlton couldn't decide what he could hear in Neil's voice. 'What? What is it?' he asked.

There was a pause. Then Neil said: 'The police are here.'

They had all three of them in separate interview rooms by afternoon. Left them alone with the grilled window high above head height; the screwed down table; the uniform green paintwork; the tape recorders, both video and audio.

Charlton couldn't move. There was a weight inside him now that wouldn't be dislodged. *Bring it on*, he thought, *I don't give a shit*. What, after all, was there left to lose? He could hear the bustle of activity in the police station above him, in adjoining rooms. He wondered if they were interviewing them all in turn: John first, then Neil, then himself. Comparing answers, trying to find a chink in the armour. But their armour was *innocence*, surely to Christ. They couldn't pin anything on them if there was no guilt to be found. That kind of bullshit only happened in TV, in cinema.

By the time the investigating officer arrived with a young female DC, Charlton was asleep, spark out, his head on the table. However inhospitable this room was, it was a sight more comfortable than a park bench. He felt female hands rousing him and he started awake suddenly, the blood roaring in his ears. 'Rough night, Mr Keen?' the DI asked. The necessary stiffness in the man's voice instantly raised Charlton's hackles. He felt the chair complain and give as he leaned back into it. No good. Too many kinks to work out.

'*Every* night is a rough night at the moment.'

'I daresay. DC Allen, would you mind terribly getting Mr Keen here a cup of our delightful coffee?' To Charlton he said without a trace of humour in his voice, 'Black, I take it?'

Charlton felt a sudden rush of vertigo. Had to shake away the feeling that this old man who looked too much like Ernie Wise, but with a cross to bear, was trying to goad him, to get him as edgy as possible before the interview began.

DC Allen turned on her heels and the DI watched her go, his eyes trailing from her shoes to her black tights to her rear end. Charlton watched him watching. Old school policing.

Perfect. He felt heat in his extremities. Adrenaline pumping.

With the formalities dispensed with and the tape recorder set, the DI introduced himself as John Rose. Charlton stared from the file between them to the man's hard expressionless face. He tried to will a vacancy into his eyes. Clasped his hands between his knees. Heard *Bring me Sunshine* in his head, but it didn't help.

'First I'd like to know your whereabouts last night, Mr Keen. Could you give me an outline of your movements from the beginning of the previous evening after you left the hospital?'

The DC returned with a polystyrene cup of coffee. Set it down in front of Charlton and seated herself beside Rose. Her face was as blank as Charlton was willing his to be. He touched the cup. Watched the coffee steam. Could feel their eyes on his face.

'I found myself at Aimee's flat after I left the hospital—'

'*Found* yourself?' Rose interrupted. 'Had you not intended to return there? Do you often find yourself simply stumbling from one location to the next?'

Charlton found himself sighing through his nose. His jaw clenching. *You smug cunt.* 'I was disorientated. Confused.' Charlton paused. 'Perhaps unconsciously it felt like the safest place to go.' If he expected any sympathy, neither of the faces on the opposite side of the table offered any. He suddenly felt afraid of where this might be going.

'Did you let yourself into Ms Williams' flat?'

Charlton saw the third floor window, awash with light. He saw himself rushing up the stairs, fumbling with the keys to Aimee's flat, bursting into each room in turn, finding nothing. No one. Just the ghost of Aimee's presence in her things, the way her life used to be lived. 'Yes,' he said. 'I thought perhaps someone might be inside.'

'Who? An intruder?'

'I don't know. Whoever attacked Aimee perhaps.'

'But there was no one?'

'No.'

'Just you.'

'Yes,' Charlton said, and fixed Rose with his eyes, hearing the implication in the man's tone. The DI stared him back down. There was an extraordinary stillness in Rose's eyes that left Charlton cold. There was no wedding ring on his finger, he noticed, for reasons he couldn't dwell on. This was a man who lived for the job, was changed incrementally by it over the years. The thought chilled Charlton. *Changing. Don't let this change you.*

Rose wanted to know, was he there long? What time did he leave? What did he do next? How would he describe his state of mind at the time? Charlton tried to keep a lid on the anger rising inside him. *Just answer the questions*, he thought. *They have nothing on you.* 'And afterwards,' Rose continued after referring to his notes, 'after you'd returned to Ms Williams' brother's home, what did you do?'

'We had a drink. The three of us.'

'Mr Williams, his *partner* Mr Saunders, and yourself?'

Charlton ignored Rose's tone when he said *partner*. 'Yes. The three of us.'

Rose snorted. Sat forward. 'Hardly the time to be drinking socially was it Mr Keen?'

Charlton gripped the hard plastic of the chair. 'I think it was *exactly* the time to be drinking socially. Neil thought it'd ease all of our nerves.'

'So you were saying your nerves were frayed. You were at your wits' end?'

'Yes,' Charlton said, adding quickly, 'but not the way you're implying. My girlfriend was beaten within an inch of her life, and even though the culprit is still out there, you see fit to waste your time badgering innocent people.'

'No need to get agitated, Mr Keen,' the DC piped up, her eyes wary. Her body was tensed, as if she expected Charlton to lunge at Rose. Perhaps it happened a lot. 'We aren't implying anything,' she added. 'We're simply trying to ascertain a clear picture of the last few days.'

Charlton sat back but Rose wasn't finished. 'But you hadn't been there long before you left again, had you Mr Keen? Where did you go upon departing?'

Charlton began to speak but then hesitated. Where *had* he gone? All he remembered was the dream of Aimee, guiding him to the scene of the crime, to watch helplessly as the loop continued. Unable to avert his gaze. A *dream*. So. What to say? The words felt wrong. Felt like a lie before he had them on his tongue and out. 'Walking. I walked into the city. I felt trapped indoors. I had to be out and about.'

He felt Rose's eyes searching his face. He tried to maintain eye contact but the lie wouldn't let him. But if Rose was aware of the deception, then his next question betrayed nothing. 'And you woke *where* exactly this morning, Mr Keen?'

'St Philip's Cathedral,' Charlton said, glad momentarily to be certain of something. He'd told Neil the same thing this morning and Neil would have said as much in his interview.

'On a bench,' Rose said. 'And you don't remember how you got there?'

'I must have been tired. No buses home, so I slept there.'

'No money for a taxi home?'

'I'd had a drink. I was tired. I wasn't thinking clearly,' Charlton said, exasperated.

Rose raised his eyebrows. Exchanged glances with DC Allen while Charlton sipped at his coffee. 'So you couldn't accurately describe your whereabouts from the hours of, say, four a.m. to six a.m.?'

Charlton sighed. 'No. Probably not.'

'And we wouldn't find incriminating evidence on your clothes, now would we, Mr Keen?'

But before Charlton could reply, Rose changed tack suddenly. Turned over a loose leaf of paper in his file on the table between them. 'Do you know this man?' He pushed a black and white photograph towards Charlton.

The face in the arrest picture rang no bells. He looked like an addict. A druggie. Hollowed out. Cheekbones you could cut yourself on. Hair unwashed and ragged, starting to fall out. Eyes that looked used.

Charlton shook his head, saw Rose watching his reaction to the face. 'No. Never saw him before in my life.' Shook his head again. 'Sorry,' he said heavily.

'What about this man?' A second picture. Skinhead, stubble growing in like grain on the photo. Hard eyes.

'No.'

Rose retrieved the pictures and closed the file on them. He looked disappointed. Then he yawned. Rubbed at his neck. There was an uncomfortable lull. The DC was not about to open her mouth again so the silence lingered. Rose tapped at the file, seemingly lost in thought. Charlton pulled at the edges of the cup, concentrating solely on his nails and the polystyrene sliding beneath them.

'One last question,' Rose said finally, his face troubled. He placed a palm flat on the file, then looked challengingly at Charlton.

Charlton waited, his hand frozen on the cup.

Afterwards, the walls couldn't contain him. He paced his flat like a wounded animal. Picked objects up and looked at them, hardly recognising them: the dish that held the seashells that Aimee had collected one wet morning in Bournemouth before he woke; the dog-eared John Updike paperback that he'd begun weeks ago and that had gone untouched since Aimee's attack; the plates on the drainer from the last meal they'd shared together; the pictures of them at Neil and John's last party, both of them too pissed to conceal their affections so late in the evening. How could an *event* reduce a life so? How could the loss of one person be enough to diminish the spark of another?

Charlton felt the familiar swirl of vertigo pluck at him. Pulling him off centre. The darkness rising. He felt sick. Nauseated. White noise hissed through his head. Deafening. Was this letting go?

Carl Webb. That name felt like a scar on his mind.

Questions were demanding answers he was unable to provide. He wanted to scream at the injustice of it all, to weep it all away. His sinuses burned from all the unshed tears evaporated by the anger raging inside. His gut was a seething cauldron of bubbling hate for a man he didn't even know.

Carl Webb. How could he not have known about Carl Webb?

That was a question. That was *the* question. The *one final question*, and it had almost undone Charlton. Over and over it replayed in his head. The interview. The questions. Rose's innuendos and insinuations, poorly concealed barbs ripping at Charlton's mind, scarring it, permanently etching a name into the creases and fold, burning a single name into his psyche like a brand; the acid marking him for life.

'One final question,' Rose had said. 'One final question,' daring Charlton to rise to the bait. Waiting him out. 'One final question. Do you know a *gentleman* by the name of Carl Webb?'

The name had meant nothing. Charlton had resignedly shaken his head, just wanting it to be over. 'No,' he said.

'No?' Rose asked. 'I am surprised.' Rose had looked anything but as he'd stared at Charlton. 'Strange, that,' he continued after a beat, 'because I've been led to believe Ms Williams knew *him* quite well. *Intimately*, in fact. It also seems Mr Webb used to knock Ms Williams about. Not know anything about that either, do you, Mr Keen? Not something you like as well, now is it?'

The jet engine roar of Charlton's rage drowned the remainder of the interview out. Charlton had no idea how he managed to stop himself flying apart and answer Rose's questions that, no, he didn't know any Carl Webb, and, *no*, it wasn't something he liked. *How fucking dare he?!*

The thought of what Rose had been implying made Charlton's blood boil. Rose was nothing more than a dirty old bastard. He *knew* nothing. Probably thought Aimee got what she deserved for going out with a darkie. The racist fuck!

Why hadn't Aimee told him about Webb? Why protect the fucking scumbag? All Charlton had known was her last boyfriend had hurt her. Hit her. He didn't know the bastard had put Aimee in the fucking hospital. She should have told him. What did she think he'd do? Didn't she trust him? Didn't she...

No. That wasn't it. It was just too painful. Bad memories. Aimee always said the past was history and the present was what counted. She'd just wanted to forget, move on, Charlton knew that. But why the fuck didn't she tell him? Why hadn't *Neil* told him? He must have known about—

Neil! The phone creaked in Charlton's fist as he pressed the receiver to his ear, listening to it ring at the other end of the line. *Where the hell are they? Come on. Answer the phone. Answer the damn phone.*

'Hello?'

'Neil. It's Charlton—'

'Where'd you run off to, you daft bastard?' Neil asked, cutting Charlton off before he could start. 'We need to talk.'

'Too fucking right we do. Why didn't you tell me?'

'Tell you what? When? Look, we need to—'

'About fucking Carl Webb,' Charlton shouted, ignoring Neil's confusion and concern. 'About Aimee.'

'Charlton. Listen, calm down.' Charlton could hear the strain in Neil's voice. 'We need to talk about the police. About Rose.'

'I don't care about Rose. I want to know about—'

'For fuck's sake,' Neil exploded. 'They're trying to fit you up. They think you—'

'Carl Webb.' Charlton snarled the name, once more overriding Neil. Nothing else mattered. He had to know.

There was a moment of silence on the line as Neil reined in his fraying temper. 'He's a Nazi prick, mate,' Neil finally answered, voice quiet. 'You *know* this. This is old ground, for

Christ's sake. Forget him. You've got more important things to worry about.'

'He did it, didn't he?' Charlton said, numbly. His voice so soft Neil almost didn't catch it.

'What? Charlton? Charlton?'

The phone dropped from Charlton's suddenly nerveless fingers and clattered on the glass tabletop. Forgotten, Neil's voice was a distant, insectile buzzing from the handset's speaker. Charlton pulled the residential directory from the shelf beneath the telephone table and opened it. Finding the address he sought he moved woodenly down the short hall to the front door. Behind his eyes it all played out for him. the projector in his head clicked from one slide to another, fitting the pieces together. It all made a horrible kind of sense: Carl Webb, Aimee's Nazi ex, left behind for a black man; the swastika carved into Aimee's chest, raw and bloody; the motiveless, meaningless attack; the police, Rose's questions. Everything made sense.

With the front door to his flat open, Charlton paused in the doorway, his mind still reeling from the shock of discovery. He swayed. He couldn't seem to catch his breath. His balance was off. He seemed to be vibrating, suppressed energy shaking him from head to toe. Something in him wanted to let go, relinquish his hold and just float away, give in to the darkness.

The flat was down a side street off the Hagley Road. It sat above a dingy, rundown newsagent's. The shop's roughcast exterior flaked and stained. The unwashed display windows were dark and sightless, begrimed with dirt from the road. Discarded sweet wrappers, cigarette packs and torn front pages, forgotten already, huddled in the shop's doorway to escape the chill wind. A gated stairway at the side, lock broken, bulbs smashed, led up to Webb's flat.

The steep steps were litter choked and filthy as Charlton edged up them. Someone had smeared dog shit over Webb's walls and broken glass crunched under his boots. The claustrophobic space crowded him, suffocating, damp and reeking. In the gloom Charlton could just make out the tags and obscene cartoons that decorated the walls beyond the stain of shit. All around him were neon-coloured swirls of abuse, crowned at the summit of the staircase by a badly spray-painted swastika. Clearly Webb was already a marked man.

The darkness that had paced Charlton from the first moment he had heard what had happened to Aimee, finally, fully caught up with him. His mind went blank.

Charlton raced across the small landing that opened out before him, the space only fractionally wider than the staircase preceding it. He couldn't discern any light from inside. Charlton closed his hand around the corroded knob and twisted, but the door was locked. He banged on it. 'Hey!' he shouted, pounding on the wood with his fist. 'Open the door, you piece of shit!'

From inside he heard muffled thuds, the sound of a rat in a cage. 'Leave me alone you cunt! Just fucking leave me alone!'

Charlton hesitated. Did Webb know he was coming? He could hear fear in the man's voice. He sounded like a man who'd been under siege for days.

'Webb! You let me the fuck in or I swear I'll kick this fucking door down!'

'Fuck off! You've had your pound of flesh already. Isn't

240   SIMON AVERY & IAN FAULKNER

that good enough for you? You're a fucking maniac, you are!'

That was *enough*. He'd had his fill of people treating him like they *knew* him. How could they when he scarcely recognised himself these days? Charlton stepped back and rammed his shoulder into the door. It gave a little, the wood creaking under the impact, but refused to open. He raised his foot and kicked out. Wood cracked. He kicked again. And again. The wood splintered at the fifth blow, the cheap lock ripping free of the frame. The door slammed open and Charlton rushed into the flat, into the darkness.

The police found him on his knees in the living room, hunched over the body. Blood on his hands, on the carpet, on the walls. They took him outside, pushed him roughly into the back of the squad car. He pressed his forehead against the metal grille, until one of the officers told him to sit back. There was a vacancy burrowing itself into his gut, an absence of feeling. He heard the officers murmuring, could see the lights flickering in the street as a crowd of onlookers gathered. Staring at them he felt divorced from it all. *Us and them*.

He thought of being returned to the interview room and of Rose, and closed his eyes. Just darkness. Floating in darkness. *This* was how it felt to cross the threshold.

As the crowd parted to let the car pull away he felt the spark of something inside, and realised it was Aimee, standing in her flat, lying beside him, leading him through the city, and into Webb's flat. He'd carried her like a burden and like a light at the end of some impossibly long tunnel. A spark. Flickering in the darkness. He willed it to go out.

* * *

'How long do you wait?' *How many times do you ask yourself?*

'I don't know, love. You'll just know when it's time.'

'It's just such a huge decision. How do you decide?'

John didn't know of course; how could he? How could anyone?

Finally they talked themselves there. They'd stayed up all night, drinking cheap Australian wine, then had sex that Neil felt symbolised everything and nothing. Hung over and unshaven the following morning, he and John had brushed hands in the waiting room, stared at the vacant faces, then squinted at the sunlight that lanced through the doctor's office. Voiced the decision that Neil felt might change him forever. He'd felt rooted to the chair, as if gravity was forcing him down. Tying him to the Earth for his troubles.

There were forms to be signed and dated. Too many. John was a constant presence beside him; the rock that Neil swam to, clung to. When it was done, the day suddenly grew overcast and the doctor's office felt impossibly small. Neil closed a hand over his face while the doctor stepped outside.

That afternoon they turned off the machines almost ceremonially. It felt like closing a book that Neil wasn't yet done with. The room felt weighted down with silence. Neil buried his face in John's hair and wondered what there was to feel next, what there would be to feel in a week, a month, a year. He realised he was holding his breath on behalf of Aimee. But he couldn't let go.

He spoke to Charlton the following day on the phone. The conversation was terse, the silences intractable. How could he *know* this man any more?

'She was always there,' Charlton said. 'In the flat. In the

street. In Webb's room. Always there.' He sounded inconsolable.

'She's gone now,' Neil said. 'At peace, I suppose.'

But wherever Charlton had gone, Neil couldn't follow. Had it happened to John, would he feel differently? Who knew? Charlton wasn't still denying he'd known anything about Carl Webb before the attack. But witnesses had placed him at Webb's flat *days* before. It only went to show how deeply losing Aimee had affected Charlton. Perhaps he had always been a coiled spring, violence waiting to happen. Had Aimee been his only comfort? His control?

He spoke about leaving, about floating into darkness, and with every word, Neil only felt more lost. Rooted to the spot. He was glad to be done with the call.

The day they sentenced Charlton for the murders of Darren Lewis, Benjamin MacKay and Carl Adam Webb, they flew to Italy for a week. John had surprised him with the tickets. Promised him sex, sun and culture but not necessarily in that order. And somewhere miles above the ground, Neil looked out at the clouds and realised that he was still holding his breath. Aimee's breath.

He breathed out.

'It'll be simple,' Mary urged me. 'What better legacy can I leave you than escape from that man?'

It's hard to resist the deathbed wishes of a dearly loved older sister, particularly when they echo your own deep felt urges. I mulled them over as I sat in the dispiriting little cell that was all the NHS could afford for its psychotherapists, watching the doctor dig out my notes. A fairly thick file now. My previous therapist had had the decency to mug up on my problems beforehand. I found this physical reminder of all I'd said – or, more accurately, not said – particularly unnerving. I was supposed to be here for a free and frank dialogue, so I told him so.

'Exactly! That's why I'm doing it: just to get you to communicate with me.' His anxious eyes shone in his thin face: he always looked so concerned for me, though he might simply have been worrying about the effect on his life of his student debts. 'Unless and until you bring out into the open the terrible thing that happened to you, I can't possibly help you.'

'It didn't *happen* to me,' I said. 'Everyone says it was *done* to me. Quite different. And I can't survive if I think about it. It's one thing to be denied the prospect of ever having a normal sexual relationship, let alone having all my hopes of children completely destroyed. It's quite another to talk about my feelings towards the man who—' I stopped.

'Please. Try to go on.'

I shook my head firmly.

'The ostrich technique never works,' he pleaded.

If that was true, it was a pity. Because that was precisely what I wanted to do: bury my head in the sand and not come up, even for breath. Ever.

My sister's suggestion was a modified version of this. She wanted me to take her place. Oh, not literally. Not in her sick bed in the hospice. Though I would have done if I could. At thirty-six, she had so much to live for; I, though two years her junior, had so very, very little now. Outside, the early daffodils and narcissi planted to cheer people in her situation bobbed in the pale sun. I doubt if she could even see them by now. She, who'd always loved her garden, her organic vegetable plot, even her compost heap, as if they were children, was denied even that solace.

'It won't take much to change the name on the death certificate from Mary to Margaret. Not with Dr Terry's handwriting. It's lucky we had such unimaginative parents, isn't it?' A rictus contracted her face. I knew it was meant for a smile. 'So then you're officially dead. You testify to a solicitor that you want to change your name by deed poll – oh, some whim of mine – and you sell your house and move into mine. You become me, miraculously in remission. You're pale and thin enough these days, goodness knows, to look as if you've been very ill. Come on, we've pretended to be each other often enough in the past. None of our boyfriends could ever tell our voices apart on the phone. But the moment you can, you sell my house. And move again. Cover your tracks. I want to make sure that both Margaret and Mary Lovett have completely disappeared from the face of the earth. Maybe he'll send a friend to heaven to look there – and seek him in the other place himself! Oh, Margaret, do you remember the last time we saw *Hamlet* together...'

We talked actors and acting till I thought she'd drifted back into what passed for sleep those days. But suddenly her hand fluttered onto my wrist, her urgent grasp surprisingly fierce. 'Remember what he said in court. As they took him down.'

I shook my head.

'Oh, Margaret – surely you remember the expression on his face. He meant it. He'll hunt you down as soon as he's out.'

No, it was all mercifully hidden, behind that nice thick curtain of amnesia.

'In that case, you'll just have to trust me,' she said. 'And next time you come, bring your National Trust booklet and a road map. We'll decide where you're going to move to. It'll be ever such fun.'

Whatever else I might or might not do, I couldn't deny her such a simple pleasure, when she had so few others left. I obeyed.

I thought she'd abandoned her weird notion because for the next few days we talked not about where I might move to, but simply about the places we'd been. Bleak East Anglia for Felbrigg and Blickling; the affluent South for Bodiam and Sissinghurst; the West Country of our family holidays for Lanhydrock and Cotehele. But there were some places she'd never managed to reach, and her face would cloud as she drowsed off.

One day, just after I'd left her and was at home making a lonely cup of tea, the hospice called me. Mary had lapsed into a coma and was not expected to live. Leaving the tea where it was, I got into the still warm car.

Her doctor was writing notes as I rushed into reception. How anyone could ever decipher such a scrawl goodness knew. He caught me looking at it and flushed with embarrassed amusement. 'I know. One day I'll learn proper calligraphy. Now, Margaret, your sister was very worried about something. She got very agitated. So I promised to give you a message. It didn't mean anything to me. It may not to you.'

Bother messages. I wanted to be with her as long as she breathed.

He called after me, 'We've given her the maximum medication. You'll find her very quiet and peaceful now. There's not long to go.'

I darted into her room. The doctor had been right. It was only a short vigil. She who'd been such a fighter seemed glad to give up now.

As I was leaving, to my shame more exhausted than upset, the doctor stopped me. 'You never asked me what the message was. She said, "Start at Dunstanburgh." That's all. "Start at Dunstanburgh."'

I shook my head. No, it didn't make any sense at all. After Mary's death, nothing did. Zombie-like, I simply carried out her last requests.

Lovely as Northumberland was, it was too bleak for me, and I felt my Midlands accent made me much too noticeable. But I stuck it out in my rented cottage, getting work temping as and when I could: we'd both got secretarial qualifications. Meanwhile, the house I'd actually bought near Oxford was getting more and more valuable as prices in the M4 Corridor ballooned. The solitary existence enabled me to grow into my new identity and to develop a side of Mary I'd never really appreciated – her green fingers. If she could turn a tip into a garden so could I. But she'd never had to contend with the late frosts and icy winds from the North Sea. My neighbours tutted with sympathy at the skeletal little remains of herbs and lavenders I'd so optimistically planted, and recommended hardier species for next year. But there wouldn't be a next year. I'd do as Mary had told me – a quick flit. One autumn day I was there, the next I was battling with an early blizzard down the A1(M).

Not to Oxford, though. I'd sold that house at such a profit I managed to afford a bijou flat in that most anonymous of places, London's Docklands. I'd make my balconies – yes, I had two, one west, one south facing – testaments to the joys of container gardening. There wouldn't have been time for more, quite honestly, as I'd landed a full-time job in the City, earning silly money for looking efficient and being thin, two things I did quite well. Officially I was PA to some man in red braces. In fact, I spent most of my time sobering him up. Without ever even sailing near the wind of insider trading, I learned enough about shares to acquire a portfolio, bits and pieces of which I was constantly selling; in six months I'd made enough from my job, my shares and the rocketing values of the flat to be glad to escape from the pigeons which turned my little gardens from Eden into a grey and white patchwork. Maybe I should have kept the flat – the views up and across the Thames to Greenwich were an unfailing delight to a provincial woman like me – but I could see that slowly but inexorably the property boom was slowing. So I bought two places, one near Carcassonne, the other in Cheshire. Mary would have loved Little Moreton Hall and Erddig, but would probably have turned her nose up at the industrial wonders of Quarry Bank Mill. Mary? I mean, my late sister Margaret, of course.

The West Midlands; the East Midlands. Each time I moved I made a bit more profit, enough to try the Cotswolds again. There was so much to see there I stayed long enough to become a mature student at Oxford Brooks University, and become a qualified teacher. A new job and then a promotion took me to schools in different locations – Herefordshire and Hampshire. And then I moved to Dorset, where we'd always planned to see Max Gate and Verities, as headmistress of a village school. On paper the village was called Wheelbarrow Town. In fact it was a disorganised jumble of cottages sprawling along a common on one side and deep fertile valley the other, and no one ever called it anything except Wilberton.

However hard they had to work these days, teachers earned a decent salary, and I was able to outbid affluent city types wanting a holiday home for three weeks a year. I wanted my neglected Georgian rectory, just beyond the village boundary, for far more than that. I wanted it to live in for ever and ever, enough to sell the cottage in France to raise the funds to buy it and restore the roof and the garden walls.

Secure in my latest existence, and comfortable in the weight and odd grey hairs of a woman in her mid-forties, at last I could allow myself to become part of the community I'd settled in. I joined things like the gardening society, tried hard to ring church bells and started a music club, hiring a minibus to take us into Bournemouth for symphony concerts. My school, once a run-down building with outside lavatories and depressed staff, benefited from an anonymous donation (the remains of the Carcassonne fund, of course) which built a new main block with not just lavatories but a computer room and a gym. Soon parents were queuing up to enrol their children. The Secretary of State for Education came down in person to congratulate us on our academic and sporting success. We were headline news on not just local but national TV.

The strange thing was that the happier I became, the more I started to get mysterious dreams. Nothing more than frightening fragments at first. I'd wake sweating with fear, impelled to check all my windows were locked. In the cold light of day I cursed myself for a fool, but nonetheless got my intruder alarm system upgraded. The young man installing it looked bemused – there was nothing of any value in the house.

'No,' I smiled. 'All my gold is in the garden. Look.' I pointed to the sea of daffodils in the orchard. I might have been waving to my sister.

For the first time I felt able to try my hand at truly organic vegetables. Friends from the gardening society had got me started on a compost heap as soon as I moved in. There was enough room in the garden for a couple of modern converters, too, the sort you turn regularly to oxygenate the humus. Now they advised me on how to plant my cabbages and beans. Double digging and lots of lime for the former, they said. As for the latter, I'd long suspected there was more to it than simply popping beans into pots and transplanting them so they'd grow up rickety poles. I was right: I had to dig a deep trench – at least eighteen inches was the kindliest recommendation, though some insisted on nearer three feet – and fill the bottom with rich compost. Then I was to put in a layer of crumpled newspaper, then a layer of bonemeal and finally more compost. I was to soak the lot thoroughly before replacing the earth. I may have pulled a face but I knew I had to do it: this crop wasn't for me,

Marion Lovage, but for a woman I'd loved years ago called Mary Lovett. Poor Mary. I might once have become her, but now I seemed to be outgrowing her. There were certainly many days when I was simply too busy at school to think of her. And she'd certainly not had the ambition that had driven me to find this sort of identity.

Or the reason that lay behind my moves. My nightmares lasted longer each time. Any time now I'd recall the incident that had set all this in train.

By now my screams woke me. I went so far as to get my GP to make me an appointment with a psychotherapist. The NHS being what it was, it would be weeks before he could see me.

While I waited, I immersed myself in work, both for the school and in the garden. A bright day in the Easter holidays told me the time had come. This was the day of the trench. Then I'd lime the cabbage patch.

Because the ground had long since lain fallow, one of my gardener friends had lent me a pickaxe, but I soon set it aside in the long grass. A few minutes with the spade showed that I was working friable loam. It probably didn't need all the enrichment I'd provided, but once I'd set my hand to the plough, as it were, there was no turning back. The trench grew with reassuring speed, deeper, wider, longer. When I'd refilled it and all the soil had settled, I'd make a strong wooden frame like my neighbours', one lasting for many years and many crops of beans all as long as your arm. Yes, it was hard work. But I was very fit after a winter of digging and barrowing and enjoyed every minute. I was sweating hard in the noonday sun when I heard the footsteps on the gravel path. It was that sound that finally broke all my nightmares.

I was back in that quiet suburban cemetery, taking a shortcut on a warm summer's night because the last bus had broken down and it would be quicker to walk home than to wait for the replacement. The footsteps had been swift. In my silly summer shoes I couldn't run, but toppled headlong onto a Victorian grave.

> Sacred to the memory of Thomas Parkinson, JP
> Born 1815
> Taken to the bosom of our Lord, 1877
> And to his dearly beloved wife,
> Anna, 1820 – 1840,
> And his second wife,
> Elizabeth Jane,
> Mother of
> Herbert, both taken to a better place in 1842
> IN THEE WE TRUST

Goodness knew how many times I read it, learning it by heart, as you can see, much as I doubted the sentiment, anything to take my mind off what that man was doing to me. And then he flung me over onto my back, and started all over again. That was his mistake. He let me see his face. And his tattoos. And his cold, hard eyes.

His eyes were still hard but burning hot as he turned in court when they went to take him down – life, for aggravated rape – and pointed to me. 'I'll be even with you for this. When I get out I'll finish the job. I'll kill you.'

The face before me now had aged as much as mine had, but where mine was tanned and healthy, his was pale, with the sort of pallor that brought Mary to my mind. Prison pallor.

His eyes were cold again. His tattoos moved as the muscles under them shifted: he was taking a firmer grip on his weapon of choice, an empty bottle. Then it had been beer, now it was wine. He said nothing. He didn't need to. Fuddled as he might be with the wine, his intention was all too obvious.

As before, I screamed. As before, he laughed. This time he added, 'You can holler all you like. Place in the wilds like this – who's to hear?'

'The neighbours—' I blustered.

'No neighbours for miles, are there? And you don't suppose I exactly advertised my presence. I've got a nice little alibi already set up. So you might as well face it. I'm going to finish what I started all those years ago before you had me sent down.'

The headmistress in me spoke. 'I don't know who you are or what you're talking about. And how can you have a perfect alibi?'

He snorted with laughter. 'That stately home down the road—'

'Yes. Verities—'

'I got one of those timed tickets. Went in with the second party. Slipped out. No one will admit to having missed me – too bloody proud of their security.'

'Your family – friends—'

'You're joking!'

Yes, he looked as if he'd been sleeping rough.

'How did you find me?' I took a step back.

'Easy: you were on the bloody box, weren't you?'

With every word he'd inched nearer. And I inched further back. But not straight back. I drifted sideways, towards the grass. Resigned, I said, 'Let's get it over with then, shall we?'

* * *

The bean row looked remarkably professional. I could be proud of myself. It ran true and straight, with strong posts at each end supporting well-seasoned branches for the young plants to climb. George, the gardening club friend who'd lent me the pickaxe, awarded me ten out of ten when he came to collect his property.

He raised an eyebrow when I presented him with a new one. I'd bought it at the same time as I'd bought a new load of lime.

'It wasn't quite up to the job of breaking up those old greenhouse foundations,' I laughed, pointing at the mess of brick ends. Had I really checked if I'd got all the hair and bloodstains from the original one? And, in case I hadn't, taken it with me to a head-teachers' conference in Derbyshire, and en route dropped the pieces in a landfill site? Surely I must have dreamt it. And why had I needed more lime? What had I spread the first lot on, if not on the garden? It wasn't the sort of thing you spread in bean trenches, not unless you wanted something to rot down quickly.

'You'd need a contractor for that,' George protested. 'I know you women claim you can do everything, but you have to draw the line somewhere.'

He was right. I did. I knew I'd have to stop all this racketing around the country, and put down roots at last. I had to stay here for as long as I lived. Probably I was relieved, but after so many years on the move, I might get itchy feet, and what then? No, I couldn't trust anyone else to look after my house and garden, that was sure, and I certainly couldn't put it on the market, ever. Not in my lifetime.

My decision made, I phoned the doctor to cancel the psychotherapy appointment. I'd managed to resolve my problems, I said. Finally. I'd faced the cause of my fears, just like it said in the self-help books, and dealt with it.

I didn't add that there was one matter I couldn't resolve. I couldn't ever fancy any of the beans. I might have buried the past, but eating it was another matter.

Monday 3rd January

It was cold, very cold, pleasantly, reassuringly cold, for this was January of the year, still within the twelve days of Christmas and was, as normally so, cold, as cold as the man could wish it to be, as cold as he recalled it being in his childhood. It was the period of snow and ice and biting easterlies, of the weather that folk would complain about. But in the last few years the winters had been mild, too mild, unhealthily mild, more like a prolonged autumn than a proper winter. No good, hard, prolonged frost which killed off all the sickly fauna and flora, and occasionally, tragically a few aged and sickly humans as well, but then, the man thought, that was the nature of winter, it was how things should be in this part of the world, and this winter was like the winter of old. Not as long lasting perhaps, but the cold snap had lasted for a few days now, ice formed on ponds, householders worried about burst pipes, black ice caused car accidents, the air was cold to breathe for the first time in a very long time. The man walked with his dog on Askham Bogs, the ground beneath his feet was reassuringly frozen underfoot. His dog, as all dogs are, was unhappy in the heat, but this weather suited him admirably, and the man himself, wrapped up against the cold, felt a sense of reassurance as he surveyed the frost, Christmas card-like scene, for this was exactly, exactly how it should be in Yorkshire during the winter. It was in Askham Bogs that the man, the dog walker, met another man who did not complain about the weather. The second man was dead.

The dog walker first saw the man when he was still some distance away, his heart thumped in his chest at the sight, a pit seemed to open in his stomach with such suddenness that it felt like he had been punched. Hard. For the second man was certainly dead, even from that distance, he was dead, ill clad for the weather and lying face down. It was, then, still only eight a.m. and the dog walker thought he knew what had happened, a youth, out partying, for this was the season to be merry, had taken too much alcohol, decided to walk home, become hypothermic and had begun to wander in a daze, finally collapsing to sleep his last sleep in the midst of lonely Askham Bogs. The dog walker turned to the other man, for life might not yet be extinct, his dog too seemed to sense the urgency and trotted beside his owner. But the urgency was wasted. Upon closer inspection, the man lying on the cold, cold ground beneath a cold blue sky, was dead. Clad only in a shirt and denims and the sort of shoes joggers wear, he was clearly deceased, his arm already rising in rigor. He was youthful, the man saw a pleasant looking blond-haired youth of about twenty summers. A life cut short, tragically short. The man plunged his hand into his pocket and took out his mobile phone and noticed his dog's reaction with interest: the dog, knowing death, curled up on the ground some distance from the body but looking at it intently. The man phoned the three nines '…very dead, I'd say,' he said. 'Life is not threatened…not any more.'

The man pocketed his mobile and, calling his dog, he walked away from the body towards Tadcaster Road to await the police vehicle, and the ambulance. He was standing on the pavement of Tadcaster Road when the police vehicle arrived, followed by the ambulance. They would have been dispatched separately but had clearly 'met' each other on the traffic-free, pre-rush hour roads.

'Oh, he's dead alright,' the man said to the youthful looking constable and the equally youthful looking ambulance crew, both female. 'I'm a doctor in general practice...life is extinct...you can't see him from here, but that direction,' he indicated a route about 90° from the road, 'follow your nose, you'll see him...fine looking young man. At least he was.'

'Happens every winter,' the constable said with a cynicism which the man thought was beyond the constable's years. 'A youth, male or female, gets a skinful of alcohol, a walk home turns out to be not the walk they planned. I knew there'd be a death in this cold snap...just knew it.'

'Strange place to walk...'

'Sorry, sir? What do you mean?' The constable took out his notebook. 'Can I have your name by the way?'

'Clark, Jeremy, Dr...' He gave an address in the nearby Bishopthorpe estate.

'What do I mean? Well, like you I assumed this to be a tragedy, a young man with too much alcohol gets disorientated, but look where he is...he is wearing only denims and a shirt...you'll see that when you view the body. Where did he come from and where was he going that he might end up in Askham Bogs?'

'That's a point, sir.'

'It was freezing last night. If he left the nearest houses, which are where I live, he would have succumbed to the cold long before he reached the centre of the bogs, he probably wouldn't even have left the house in such an ill-clad manner.'

'Ah...' The constable gazed towards the bogs, trees clad in

a white frost, hoarfrost on the grass, a blue sky above.

'Just a thought,' Dr Clark said, 'but it may be prudent to treat this death as suspicious until you know otherwise.'

The constable reached for his collar-mounted radio, he pressed the send button. 'PC 347 to control.'

'Control receiving,' the radio crackled.

'Location...opposite Askham Bogs on Tadcaster Road, ambulance crew already in attendance...death confirmed by member of the public who is medically qualified...death may be suspicious, CID attendance requested.'

'Control...understood...out.'

'Well, I will leave it with you.' Dr Clark shook his dog's lead. 'We must be off. My surgery starts at eight a.m.'

George Hennessey looked down at the youth as the SOCO camera flashed. Like the dog walker who had found the body, Hennessey was struck by the boy's youthfulness and his good looks. Not a person who would have any difficulty in attracting the girls, he thought, but he was now stiff with death. Soon his parents will be weeping. Dr Mann, turban-headed, smartly dressed, approached Hennessey.

'Life is pronounced extinct at 08.34, Chief Inspector,' Mann said.

'08.34.' Hennessey noted the time in his notebook. 'I'm sorry to have to drag you out here so early when a medical man has already pronounced death but procedures have to be followed.'

'That's perfectly alright, Chief Inspector,' the police surgeon smiled. 'It is my job, I am honoured to do it.'

'Thank you,' Hennessey smiled.

'I can find no evidence to suggest the death is suspicious

from a medical point of view,' Dr Mann said, 'no injuries, for example, but I do take the point that it's a long way and a strange way to have walked by himself, especially so ill-clad.'

'Noted,' Hennessey replied.

'But whatever, he can be removed to York City Hospital for the post-mortem if you feel one ought to be performed.'

'I'd be happier,' Hennessey said softly. 'Both yourself and the gentleman who found him are medical men, both of you are of the opinion that this is a long way for him to come by himself from the nearest house. I'd be happier to have a thorough examination of this young corpse.'

The Scene of Crime Officer's camera flashed again.

'The body is that of a well nourished male of approximately twenty years of age.' Dr Louise D'Acre spoke for the benefit of a microphone which was attached to an aluminium angle-poise arm which in turn was attached to the ceiling of the pathology laboratory directly above the dissecting table. The body of the youth lay face up on the table with a standard white towel placed over his coyly termed 'private parts'. 'There is no sign of outward injury...but I think you are right to be suspicious of this death, Chief Inspector.'

'Oh?' Hennessey, observing for the police, stood at the edge of the laboratory.

'Yes...you see this area of darkened skin, here down his left side?'

'Yes...'

'That is hypostasis, it's caused by blood settling according to gravity. It meant he was placed on his left side at death or shortly after and remained in the position for at least twelve hours. It takes that length of time for blood to solidify after the heart has stopped beating. Now...if the young man was found laying face down, as I believe he was...'

'He was.'

'Well, in that case it means he died elsewhere and was moved after his death.'

'That is suspicious.' Hennessey raised an eyebrow and glanced at Paul Fry, the mortuary attendant who returned the glance with a smile and a shrug of his shoulders. Hennessey had time for Paul Fry, he had always found the short, rotund mortuary attendant to be a man of warmth and good humour, unlike many, nay, most, other mortuary attendants that Hennessey had met. He had often wondered whether such dour men are drawn to the job because it has some macabre appeal for them or whether the job makes them sour, cynical, and humourless. But here was Paul Fry, who radiated like sunlight in this room of death and tragedy. 'That and the fact he was so ill clad for the weather.'

'Any identification?'

'No...nothing in his pockets...a till receipt...and a credit card receipt slip which we can trace him from, if it is his, but no wallet or similar. The till receipt is from a supermarket...seems to have bought food and cleaning materials...the sort of shopping a young man who lived alone would buy, so we don't think he lives at home.'

'I see... I think you're right to think that. A young man who buys cleaning materials is a young man who lives alone.'

'We'll see,' Hennessey smiled.

'Oh, take it from me.' Louise D'Acre also smiled, but avoided eye contact.

'He has a small callous on his right middle finger, a classic writer's callous ... a lump where the pen lodges. He was right-handed and wrote with a pen as much as or in preference to a word processor.'

'A student?'

'Possibly…but whatever, he used a pen a great deal. Now this is interesting…' Dr D'Acre peered at the right shoulder of the dead youth.

'What have you found?'

'Come and see…'

Hennessey, dressed in the same green coveralls as D'Acre and Paul Fry, walked slowly to the dissecting table.

'There,' Dr D'Acre said. 'You see that?'

'It's like a small mole.'

'It's a puncture point. It's caused by being injected quite roughly with a hypodermic needle, jabbed more than injected…and without the benefit of an antiseptic wipe beforehand. Druggies are covered with them but this is the only one…high up on the right shoulder…and the callous on his right middle finger tells us he was right-handed…it suggests…strongly so, that he was injected rather than injected himself. Even if he was ambidextrous, he would have difficulty injecting himself there with his left hand…even with a small syringe.'

'I can see that…' Hennessey mimicked the motion of injecting himself on his upper right shoulder. 'He'd be more likely to put the thing into his forearm, as drug takers do.'

'Mr Fry,' Dr D'Acre turned to the mortuary attendant, 'can you get a photograph of this please. Place a ruler beside it, we'll need a scale.' Dr D'Acre and Hennessey stepped back to allow Paul Fry access to the right shoulder. 'It's recent too,' D'Acre said as the camera flashed, 'very recent, twenty-four hours…possibly less. I'll trawl for traces of poison, see what we find…with a corpse as recent as this, traces of light toxins will still be in the bloodstream and long bones.' She thanked Paul Fry as he stepped away, having taken three close-up photographs of the puncture point. She took a scalpel and placed it on the stomach of the deceased as Hennessey returned to the edge of the room.

'I won't disturb the face...' She explained, 'He will have relatives who will doubtless be asked to identify him...but if you can't trace the relatives, I will remove the jaw...and take a cast of his lower dentures. He can be identified by dental records, if you can find his dentist.'

'Understood,' Hennessey said, though he knew the procedure well, having used it many times. If the police believe they know the identity of a deceased and can find out who his or her dentist was, then dental records will confirm or refute their suspicions. Very useful in the event of much decomposed or completely skeletal remains being found.

Dr D'Acre drew the scalpel over the stomach, dividing the flesh with three incisions in the shape of an inverted 'Y'. It was, Hennessey believed, called a 'standard mid-line incision'.

'Curiouser and curiouser,' Dr D'Acre said.

'What have you found?'

'Well he had no food for at least 48 hours before he died. And he looks well nourished and the supermarket receipt indicates that he was eating.'

'Strange...'

'Well, that's your department, not mine, but I would have to say he was kept against his will and then filled full of something. He died lying on his left side and was carried out to where he was found. I'll send samples of blood and tissue to the forensic laboratory at Wetherby...you'll get the results tomorrow.'

* * *

Afternoon, Monday 3rd January

'Sounds like Charlie.' The young woman in the red T-shirt which advertised an alcoholic soft drink, a so-called 'alcopop', pondered the description given to her by Detective Sergeant Yellich.

'Charlie?' Yellich glanced along the bar, the three other young women all wore the same style figure-hugging T-shirt. That brand of 'alcopop' was clearly being promoted.

'Charlie Pimlott.' The woman pulled a pint for a customer who limped up to the bar as if she knew which drink he wanted. 'He comes in here a lot...near daily...hasn't been in for the last day or two.'

'You give cash back, love?'

'Yes, up to fifty pounds...customers prefer to use the bar than go to a cash dispenser, they charge a fee, a pub doesn't. If they ask for fifty pounds they get fifty. If they draw out fifty pounds from a machine a further five pounds is debited from their account. The fifty pounds is credited to the pub's account and they receive the cash. They use it to buy drink.'

'I see... Charles Pimlot does that?'

'Yes, a lot.'

'What can you tell me about him?'

'Charlie...not much really.'

Yellich glanced around him. The Elm Tree was a dark dive, patronised by some very 'iffy' looking customers. It was still early, many seats were still vacant.

'He came in during happy hour, from three p.m. to seven...fifty pence off selected beers. Couldn't have much cash...only drank cheap beer. At seven p.m. when the price went up to normal, he'd turn and find the exit. Gabrielle is the one to ask.'

'Gabrielle?'

'Girl over there...' The barmaid nodded towards a worryingly thin-looking woman with dark, greying hair who stood alone at the bar in front of a pint of lager. 'They were mates.'

Yellich thanked the barmaid and sidled along the bar and stood next to the woman identified as 'Gabrielle'. He showed his ID. 'I'd like to ask you a few questions.'

'About?' Gabrielle had a soft voice. She wore a long, dark blue skirt and layers of dark coloured clothing above her waist. She emitted an air of low esteem bordering on depression, so thought Yellich.

'A young man called Charles Pimlott?'

'Charlie? Not seen him for a day or two.'

'What is he to you?'

'Friends. Drinking friends. I'm a lot older than he is...there was nothing between us.'

'You are?'

'Gabrielle Ingham.' She raised her glass to her lips and drank deeply, like a man. 'I do this during happy hour and then go home for a vodka or two...or three...I get through a bottle a day.' She fumbled for a cigarette and lit it with a bright orange disposable lighter. 'So what has Charlie done to make the police interested in him?'

'Nothing. He's dead.'

Gabrielle Ingham's knees buckled slightly, she clutched the bar and steadied herself. Yellich took her elbow but she shrugged him off.

'So you knew him?' Yellich continued after a pause.

'Aye...he lived with me once... I mean he rented a room off me, gave me a bit of rent.'

'Did he work?'

'Employed? No...but work, yes.' Gabrielle Ingham drew deeply on the nail. 'He wanted to be a writer...of fiction...was at university reading law, said it was too tame, wanted to write...what did he say? "Tell it like it is fiction"..."life as it is on the streets"...that sort of thing...that's how I got to know him. He started to come into the Elm... I mean, you can see what a dive it is, full of alcoholics like me...ex cons...some real ducking and diving going on...some students who live in rented houses rather than in halls of residence... Charlie came in here looking for "copy" as he called it.' Gabrielle Ingham's voice was not just soft, but almost musical. Yellich thought that words tumbled from her mouth in a melodious manner. He thought that near derelict as she appeared to be, she had clearly been in receipt of an education and had fallen from grace to become a barfly at the Elm, and had probably fallen a considerable distance.

'I warned him...but did he listen?'

'Warned him?'

'He was asking questions of the wrong people...this pub may be for lowlifes like me, but there's contacts to be had if you want them. The Elm is a conduit to some very dangerous people.'

Conduit. Again Yellich had the impression that Gabrielle Ingham had had an education and had fallen a long way from somewhere to have fetched up in The Elm.

'There are some dangerous people in this small city. He was wanting to talk to them for his book. What was it he said he wanted? Copy...that was it.' She took another drink of her lager, gulping it like a sailor would. 'I mean, you don't do that...not to these guys...these guys are seriously heavy.'

Yellich groaned. The naivety of youth, as with the youngster who went to Northern Ireland to try to make sense of the 'troubles' for himself so he could better understand them, went hitchhiking round the province...eventually got into the wrong car and was later found by the roadside with a bullet in his head. Not only did he do that, but he did that when in possession of an English accent. Fatal. 'Do you know to whom he was talking?'

Gabrielle Ingham shook her head, vigorously.

'Is it dangerous for you to talk?'

'Yes. They know you're a cop...I could get a kicking if they think I'm giving you information...not from anyone here...but word will get to where word will get to...a lot of tourists visit York...they never see this side of the railway line.'

'You've had an education, I think?' Yellich couldn't resist the question.

'I'm a nurse...a staff nurse...well, I have the qualifications...right now I am unemployed, on sickness benefit...long term. I won't work again. I sold my house and pay rent now...released a lot of money for this,' she tapped the side of her beer glass, 'and these.' She tapped the packet of cigarettes. 'I'm on the way out, 45 years old, so I want to make it as smooth as possible. Tuberculosis,' she said matter of factly. 'Used to be called consumption...seems a more accurate name to me...folk would visit spas to take "the cure" knowing there was no cure...just remission now and again.'

Yellich nodded sympathetically. He had heard that the disease had re-emerged in the late twentieth century and had taken a toehold by the beginning of the 21st century. Not yet of epidemic proportions, but a toehold nonetheless. 'What specifically was Charlie Pimlott asking about?'

'The drug culture...the heroin trade. I mean, you don't ask questions of those people.'

'I see.'

'Where can I reach you?'

'Micklegate Bar Police Station. Do you have information?'

'Might do. I have done little of use in my life, and if I am to be planted soon, I think I'd like to do at least one good thing. And Charles was a nice lad...he didn't deserve to be murdered so young, even if he did invite it by his stupidity.'

'If it is Charlie. No positive ID yet.'

'Well his family live in the south, in the outer London area, somewhere in the Home Counties...the university will have his home address.'

'Where did he live?'

'Above the greengrocers on the corner of this street. There is a small flat above the shop, they rent it out. Charlie took the tenancy a few weeks ago...immersing himself in the street to get authentic detail for his book. So if I do have information, who do I ask for?'

'Yellich, DS Yellich.'

'I'll remember that name. We'll have to meet some place, can't meet here and I can't be seen walking into the police station...I'll be a watched woman for a few weeks now. I don't want my face carved or my ribs kicked to pieces. And that's the least I can expect.'

'Understood.'

Yellich left The Elm and walked down the street, pulling his collar up as protection against the chill easterly. A slight drizzle fell. The street was typical Holgate...narrow, lined with soot blackened terraces, where washing would be strung across the street on a good drying day...not, as Gabrielle Ingham said, the York the tourists visit. Yellich came to the greengrocers. He entered it. The greengrocer was a healthy looking man who seemed to love fresh vegetables. His younger female assistant also looked healthy amid the carrots and potatoes and the mushrooms. Yellich had the impression that they were an item, not just proprietor and assistant, but man and wife...lovers at the very least.

'How can I help you, sir?' the man smiled.

'By letting me look at the flat I understand you let out, the one above the shop.'

'Police?'

'Yes.' Yellich showed his ID.

'If the lad's in trouble, I know nothing of it. I told him I want no drugs, I don't even let the room to smokers, but he seemed alright.'

'He's not in any trouble. If he is who we think he is, he's dead.'

The man jolted...glanced at the young woman, who gasped. Then he recovered his composure. 'I'll get the spare key.' He left the counter and returned a few minutes later with two keys strung onto a Volkswagen key fob. 'The entrance is at the rear of the shop...round the corner, down the alley...metal staircase...careful of the staircase; it's slippery in the wet.'

'Chaos. Violence. Something happened here,' Yellich said to himself as he stepped across the threshold, not requiring the keys because the door of the flat was standing ajar. Inside the flat was a scene of destruction, of smashed furniture, of upturned tables and lamp stands. Yellich reached into his pocket and took out his mobile. He phoned DCI Hennessey. 'Better get here, boss. If this is the youth's flat, his name was Charles Pimlott and he didn't go without a struggle.'

'He definitely didn't, did he?' Hennessey looked round the small bedsit. The signs of struggle were everywhere as if what fight had taken place in the flat had spilled into every corner of every room, bed on its side in the bedroom, plates smashed in the small kitchen. A photograph on the mantelpiece showed a picture of a young man and woman side by side somewhere in the sun. The young man in the photograph was clearly the same young man who had been found earlier that day lying face down in the frost in Askham Bogs. A name on a Social Security card, also on the mantelpiece, was that of Charles Pimlott. 'His home address will be here somewhere. I'll contact his parents when I find it.'

'Believed to come from the south,' Yellich said. 'I'll search for it once SOCO have finished.' A camera flashed. A second SOCO officer dusted for prints with a small squirrel hair brush. 'There are no witnesses that I can find. Had a chat with the greengrocer who lets the flat...all he could say is that it must have happened one evening or one Sunday day time. He lives elsewhere in the city and doesn't check on the flat, calls just once a week for his rent. The post was behind the door...the earliest postmark was four days ago, 31st December...no delivery on New Year's day...so it happened sometime before New Year's day, if he received something in the post each day.'

'Big "if", Yellich,' Hennessey growled. 'I don't think we'll pin the time of this attack by the post.'

'No, boss…just musing. Found someone in the local pub. I think she has information…but she's frightened. But she also seems angry about something. I'll be surprised if she doesn't contact us, Gabrielle Ingham, by name.'

Morning, Tuesday 4th January

It never got easier. It was the walk with the next of kin, the clutching, trembling hope against hope attitude, the drawing back of the curtain, the wailing, the sobbing as the person lying behind the glass, dressed in bandages and by some trick of light and shade, looking as if they are floating peacefully in space, is recognised as their own. In this particular case, Yellich found it easier than most, but it was still hard. The Pimlotts revealed themselves to be of the English middle class, there was a brief gasp, a slight sob, but beyond that, their emotions were contained.

'It is our son,' Mr Pimlott said.

Yellich nodded and the curtain was drawn shut.

'How did he die?' Mr Pimlott had a trim moustache, suit, he carried an overcoat and trilby.

'We believe he was murdered.' Yellich spoke softly.

'How?' Mrs Pimlott turned to him, she was sombrely dressed in a blue two piece.

'He was injected with heroin. We found out just this morning…the toxicology report revealed a massive amount in his system.'

'But he was such a clean living boy…' Mrs Pimlott's words trailed off.

'There is no indication that he was a user,' Yellich said. 'The indication is that he was injected against his will. Did he tell you anything at all about what he was doing?'

'No…he gave up his university course. I wanted him to follow me into the law…but he left…he was doing something, he had a project he was working on but he didn't tell us what.'

'It was as if he was going to surprise us with some achievement.' Mrs Pimlott's voice was shaky. 'Can we go back to the hotel, dear?'

'Yes.' Mr Pimlott squeezed his wife's hand. He turned to Yellich. 'We drove up yesterday evening, booked into an hotel…as you can imagine we didn't get a great deal of sleep. We'll have a nap and then drive home. You don't need us for anything else?'

'No…thank you.'

Yellich walked the walls of the medieval city back to Micklegate Bar Police Station. He signed in and checked his pigeonhole. There was a message from Gabrielle Ingham. She had phoned requesting him to meet her at the Rose and Crown pub in Selby (opposite the Abbey), read the note. Yellich looked at the constable at the enquiry desk whose initials were on the note. 'How did she sound…drunk?'

'No, sir. Well, if anything, she was frightened. She phoned from the railway station, I heard the public address system in the background. That's York Station…I know Selby…there isn't a P.A. system at the station there. Train information is by way of a television screen.'

'Good for you,' Yellich smiled. 'It's that sort of observation and local knowledge that gets results. I'll go and meet her.'

Yellich walked to his office and recorded in the file on Charlie Pimlott that his identity had now been confirmed by his parents. He then drove out of York across flat landscape the short twenty minute drive to Selby. He parked his car in the railway station car park in the shadow of the Abbey and located the Rose and Crown. It was, he found, quite different to The Elm...carpets...a soft, quiet hotel-like atmosphere, bar staff in smart uniform of white shirts and black waistcoats. Gabrielle Ingham, dressed in the same long skirt she had worn the day previous and in the same black jacket, sat at a table in the corner. She smoked a cigarette, a pint of beer, half consumed, stood in front of her. She smiled at Yellich who sat next to her.

'I wasn't followed,' she said. 'I wouldn't be here if I was followed. They don't rate me much anyway. I'm a slush...not a real threat.'

'They?'

'Baruch's boys.'

'You're not involved with them!'

'Not me... I'm just a soak, a barfly, but I see things... Baruch's moving into Holgate.'

'Bit downmarket for him...from what we know, he supplies cocaine to the county set and ecstasy to the clubbers. I've never seen him.'

'No one has. They say his house is like the Tower of London...wire...guards...dogs...he's a frightened man. He's moving heroin into Holgate.'

'Really?'

'He's selling it to the youth. Remember the pub yesterday?'

'Yes.'

'Did you see two guys at the end of the bar...one with a beard, the other clean shaven?'

'Didn't notice them.'

'Well, they're always there... Sydney Jarvis and Henry Cooke. They were *the* villains in Holgate, selling cannabis and some duty free tobacco, playing at it really. Anyway, recently they were told that they were now working for Baruch...and they were moving heroin. They're out of their depths, they are scared. I mean, I am scared, but not like they must be.'

'So, what happened?'

'What exactly, I don't know...but Charlie Pimlott was asking questions, like I told you...this didn't come from me, right? I won't make a statement or give evidence.'

'OK.'

'But you should talk to Cooke and Jarvis. I overheard something...they had something to do with Charlie's murder...on Baruch's orders.'

'Understood.'

'That's all you're getting from me...and don't follow me out.' Gabrielle Ingham stood. 'I may not have been followed, but Baruch's people are everywhere...seriously, everywhere.'

Both men looked nervous. Very nervous indeed. When they were placed in separate cells at Micklegate Bar Police Station, they looked even more nervous.

'We can hold you for twelve hours without charging you,' Hennessey said to Cooke. 'I'll come back and see you in ten hours' time...so wait here and decide what you want to do...just you and your thoughts. You work for yourself or you work against yourself. We'll listen to you if you want to talk to us before your mate. I'm now going to see him and say the same thing to him. Remember, Baruch will know you've been lifted by now.' Hennessey left the cell and the door was clanged shut.

* * *

Tuesday evening

'If I tell you, I'm dead.'

'If you don't tell us you're dead. Baruch won't take any risks, he'll have you silenced anyway. You and your mate both.'

'He's not that much of a mate.' Henry Cooke stroked his beard nervously.

'Well, he may well drop you in it. We haven't talked to him yet.'

'I never wanted it to go this far.'

'No one ever does.'

'But you don't mess with Baruch...never seen him, but if he gives the word, someone dies...he hides away...if he goes out he's chauffeur-driven in a car with tinted glass. He can see out but you can't see in.'

'We know. We've wanted Mr Baruch for a long time.'

'But I've seen him.'

'Do you want a lawyer present?'

'No, this is off the record, the less people that know what I am saying, the better.'

'It can't stay off the record.'

'You won't get Jarvis to testify, Baruch's got something to hold over him...he's got family in Holgate. One word from Baruch and they'll all disappear. But I haven't...Baruch's got nothing to hold over me.'

'Keep talking.'

'I want witness protection...new name...new identity.'

'Only if you are a witness, if you murdered him or were part of the crime, you won't qualify...and you have to stand up in court and testify.'

'Baruch murdered the boy.'

'Go on.'

'He heard the boy was asking questions...he had him brought to his house, Baruch is totally paranoid. Anyway, me and Jarvis were told to come to Baruch's house out in the Vale of York...the boy was there...he'd been starved of food for three days to make him talk. Baruch was certain the boy knew all about his operation, but the boy knew nothing. When we got there, he was tied to a chair...a wooden upright chair...putting his fingerprints all over it. Like he was leaving you guys a present.'

'Really?' Hennessey turned to Yellich who raised his eyebrows.

'Then Baruch produced a syringe...and said to me and Jarvis "this is what I do if I don't like someone" and jabbed it into the boy's arm. Then we were driven away. Didn't know what happened to the boy until yesterday.'

'Better get out there,' Hennessey said. 'Go in force...if we can lift Charlie Pimlott's fingerprints from the chair...with the statement, that will convict him. He's slipped up.'

'Only if he hasn't sent in the cleaners.' Yellich stood. 'We'd better move quickly.'

Ten months later Hennessey and Yellich sat in silence as a scarlet clad judge sentenced Thomas Alfred Baruch, aged 33, to life imprisonment for the murder of Charlie Pimlott, and twelve years' imprisonment for the possession of a quantity of cocaine with intent to supply. Both sentences to run concurrently.

After giving evidence at the trial at York Crown Court, Henry Cooke was ushered away in a police vehicle to begin a new life in a new location with a new identity. He lived from then on with the knowledge that from his prison cell Thomas Baruch had put a one million pound price tag on his head.

A scream quivered out from Lady's rooms upstairs, followed by soft thumps of bare feet running. My Master sighed.

'Sounds as if they've found another one. Or a dozen.'

Eyes didn't glance away from the man on the stone-flagged floor.

'It's a strange business, investigating a man's murder in a world full of frogs,' he said.

There were two of them in the hot white room, Master and Eyes. Or three, if you counted Baker, who was dead on his back on the floor with a knife in his chest. Or four, if you counted myself, who is not usually counted. Or several dozen if you counted the frogs, which was not easy to do since Master was striding up and down all the time, making them scatter from under his feet. As I watched, one of them hopped onto Baker's forehead, blinked a few times and hopped off again.

'Where do they all come from?' Master said.

He was more disturbed than I'd ever seen him, forehead beaded with sweat, voice unsteady.

'From the river,' I could have told him. 'From a thick bubble of water with a black dot inside.'

But I said nothing, because I must not speak to the Master or to anybody else above me (which is very nearly everybody in the world) without being spoken to first. I could have told him too that the bakery – with only a few dozen frogs – was nowhere near as full of them as the rest of the house because they loved shade and coolness. They were clustered so thickly under the palm trees in the courtyard that they looked like the trees' own shadows made flesh. Every now and then, as

Master paced and Eyes looked down at the body with his hands beside his back, more screams would drift in from the kitchens, the laundry rooms, the granary, the storerooms. Brooms were thumping and swishing in the background as the overseers tried to make the slaves stem the tide, but it was like attempting to hold back the Nile itself.

'I believe the priests are working on it,' said Eyes, still looking down at the body of Baker.

Eyes seemed unworried by the frogs. I liked him for that. Eyes was an important man. Probably I should never breathe the air in the same room with a man so important. In fact, I was trying to breathe as little and as shallowly as possible, so as not to take up any air he might need and show lack of respect. I always did that if I happened to be with Master, who is Pharaoh's Bread Steward, and from the way Master behaved I knew Eyes outranked him by several steps. Eyes was not as imposing as Master to look at, being thin and lower than average height, but there was a great stillness about him.

'How was the body discovered?' he asked.

His voice was deep for a small man's and smooth as water just before it plunges over a cataract. Master nodded towards me.

'Woodboy found him.'

'When?'

'He'd just come back with the wood, soon after sunrise. He informed the guard, who sent word up to me. Naturally, I sent a messenger running to Pharaoh's household at once, but unhappily...'

Master stopped and his face went red.

'It was some time before anybody would take any notice of

the messenger, on account of the frogs,' Eyes said, politely passing over the fact that Master might have come within a breath of criticising Pharaoh's household. 'Does the boy always come with the wood at the same time?'

'Yes. Woodboy's duty is to bring bundles of wood up from the river and put them to dry in the sun, ready to fire the ovens. He must be at the river before daylight to get the best wood before the boys from the other households.'

Master was good at his work and knew the routines of everybody in the household. He made it all sound orderly, as if it were simply a matter of strolling along the river edge, selecting here a branch and there a log. He'd never seen the woodboys fighting each other for the wood, bodies black against red sunrise reflected in red water, doubly black from the mud. Serious fights they are, that leave shoulders dislocated, noses bleeding, sometimes boys drowned because to go back to your household with no wood, or only a bundle of twigs and dead rushes, means a beating. I am seldom beaten. Master is good at his work and I am good at mine.

'Has the boy reason to come inside the bakery?'

'Yes. When he has brought back the day's first bundle, he must carry the dried wood from three days ago inside and pile it beside the oven.'

'And that's what he was doing when he found Baker's body?'

'Yes.'

Eyes glanced at the neat pile of dry wood beside the oven. The oven was almost cold now, just a few ashes glowing. On the other side of the courtyard, Baker's deputy would be hurrying the slaves to fire up the oven in the old bakery, kept in reserve for emergencies such as this. Come frogs or murder, Pharaoh must have his bread.

'He stacked it there after finding Baker's body?'

'Yes.'

But Master blinked and looked uneasy. Although that was exactly what I had done – come frogs or murder, wood must be tidily stacked – Master had no way of knowing this.

'Very calm of him,' said Eyes.

And he looked at me as if he meant to draw the insides from me with that one look. I should have lowered my eyes, but sensed that he didn't want that, so stared straight back at him.

'You saw, I suppose, the knife sticking out of his chest?'

I nodded.

'It's the knife used for opening flour sacks,' Master said, annoyed that I should be addressed directly rather than through him. 'Baker usually left it on the edge of the kneading trough over there.'

Our eyes went to the stone trough, full of a plump cushion of risen dough. Normally by this time of the morning it would have been turned into sweet-smelling discs of bread, under the supervision of the man now lying on the floor. He was beginning to stink.

'Were you frightened when you found him?' Eyes said to me.

Either he was unaware of Master's annoyance or had decided to disregard it. I nodded again, hoping that was the answer he wanted. The true answer was that I felt very little, because my head was too full of the wonder of the frogs.

* * *

They came just before the sun rose. As I went down to the river I met the advance guard of them, hopping up to the city. When I came to the water, the mud was restless round my bare feet, then it became a whole sheet of frogs, moving slowly but purposefully up the bank, frogs up and down the river, as far as the eye could see. I shouted for the joy of them. I've liked frogs as long as I can remember. There is no picture in my mind of father, mother, brother or sister. As far as I know I never had any of them and might have grown out of Nile mud, with feet ready for wading and hands ready for grabbing wood. Yet I can remember as clearly as sunlight my first frog. I must have been quite small at the time, possibly crawling, because the frog seemed large and on a level with me. We stared at each other and I was aware of a great wisdom and gentleness. As I grew, I found out more about them. There were tiny frogs, so small that they could sit on the nail of my little finger and still have space round them. I thought I should like to see a mother giving birth to these small frogs and watched for many years before I found out the truth. When I puzzled it out at last – that the black dots inside the bubbles took on life and became strange little fish and the fish grew legs and hopped on land – I laughed and turned somersaults from sheer delight. The priests in our temples have their signs and wonders and understand the will of the Sun God. The Israelites have their great conjurer who, they say, can strike water from bare rocks and turn a stick into a serpent. But did any of them, priest or conjurer, ever do a marvel like this one? So when the world turned to frogs and I was there to see it, perhaps I did not care as much as I should have done for the death of a man who in life had done me nothing but hurt. Before blaming me for that, consider the comparison between Baker and a frog, any frog.

* * *

One, a frog is sleek and pleasant to the eye. I have seen many thousands of frogs, but never one which is fat or greasy. Baker was both. Two, a frog smells cleanly of water. Baker, even in life, smelt bad. Three, a frog is temperate and regular in its habits. Once a year it mates, as is necessary. Baker was forever bothering the servants and slave girls. Four, a frog is peaceable and harms nothing but flies. Baker was always pinching, kicking and slapping his workers, usually without reason. Five, a frog is the calmest of creatures. Baker had a foul tongue and a worse temper. Six, a frog is honest. Baker cheated Master and we all knew it. Seven, a frog speaks no evil of other frogs. Baker was a tale-bearer. I mourned for the frogs being crushed under the beating brooms of the slaves, but not for Baker.

'Had Baker any enemies in your household?' Eyes said to Master.

'None that I know of.'

I looked at the floor, pitying Master. If he'd said yes, most people disliked him – which he surely knew was the truth – he would be admitting to Pharaoh's representative that the household was less than harmonious and that would have shamed us all. When I glanced up again I thought Eyes looked annoyed. But then, it was his own fault for asking the question.

'Of course,' Master said, 'it may have been an enemy from outside.'

'Hardly likely, is it? I suppose you keep good guards.'

Yes, Eyes was certainly annoyed.

'My guards are personally selected and trained,' Master said stiffly.

'So would hardly let in a stranger.'

Master said nothing. Eyes thought for a while, hand to his chin.

'I must speak to members of your household.'

'Certainly. If you would care to come and drink a pomegranate juice in my rooms, we'll send for whoever you please.'

'I prefer to go my own way. I should be grateful if you'd let your people know that I have your authority to ask questions.'

'Certainly. Oh certainly.'

Eyes was merely being polite. A man with Pharaoh's authority behind him didn't need Master's. He walked to the door and turned.

'Are those the women's apartments overhead?'

'Yes. My wife's personal maids and some of the laundresses.'

'They are the most likely to have heard anything that happened. Would you kindly let your wife know that I should like to talk to some of them?'

'Yes. I'm afraid my wife is an invalid or I'm sure she...'

Master's voice trailed away. He looked more wretched than at any time since the body had been discovered.

'I'm sure the Lady won't object to my asking her maids a few questions. If you could arrange for me to do it in a room reasonably free of frogs it might save us some more screaming.'

He walked out. Master looked down at Baker's body.

'What am I supposed to do about this?'

I knew he didn't expect me to answer. He sent me to call one of the guards, to watch over Baker while he decided. I took myself off, joined twenty or so frogs sitting quietly in a shady corner of the courtyard and thought about Lady's personal maids, especially Lily.

Most of the maids are beautiful, but Lily is the best of them. She has a kind nature too. One evening, when she came down as usual to fetch Lady's bricks from the oven, she saw my ear was bitten from a fight with the red boy from the scribe's household.

'It's nothing,' I said.

I was ashamed that the bite made me ugly in her eyes. She wrapped the two bricks in the cloths she'd brought with her and carried them upstairs. Soon she was down again, with a pot of ointment.

'Sit there,' she said.

I sat against the wall while she smoothed the ointment on my ear with her white fingers. It was as cool as Nile mud in the early morning and smelt of jasmine. Next evening she touched my ear very gently.

'It is better?'

'It is better.'

She reminds me of a frog, not in looks, only that so many of the good things about her are froglike. Her skin is smooth and she smells clean. She moves silently and without fuss. She watches everything with her wide brown eyes but says little. She harms nobody and never bears tales or says unkind things about the other maids, though some of them are cruel to her because they envy her. So, on Lily's account, I wondered what Eyes wanted with Lady's maids.

* * *

I heard Master in the courtyard, giving orders to one of the slaves.

'You are to take a broom and stand at the doorway of the blue room. If the frogs try to go in you must beat them away. A very important person is inside and must not be disturbed.'

When Master walked away I slipped out to the courtyard and found the slave in tears. I asked him what was wrong. He was no more than a child and addressed even me with respect.

'Oh sir, I am so scared of the frogs, I don't know what to do.'

'You are a great baby,' I said. 'Still, I shall take pity on you and do your duty for you.'

I grabbed the broom from him and took up my post by the door to the blue room, a pleasant place where Master sometimes sits after his evening meal. A curtain woven from rushes hung over the doorway, but didn't quite stretch to the sides, so I was able to see in quite easily. Eyes was sitting on a stone bench by the wall with one of the maids standing in front of him. She had her back to me, but from the width of her hips and the coarseness of her hair I knew she was the one they called Parrot. Her voice was quieter than usual as she spoke to Eyes.

'Yes, Excellency, we sleep above the bakery. I heard nothing last night.'

'When did you last see Baker alive?'

'At noon yesterday. He was standing in the doorway to the bakery with Tallyman, counting in the flour sacks.'

'How long have you served your Lady?'

'Four years, Excellency. I have been here longer than any of her other maids.'

'So you know the household well?'

'Yes, Excellency.'

'To your knowledge, did Baker have any enemies in the household?'

'It is a well-run household, Excellency. We do our best to work harmoniously together for Master and Lady.'

Eyes tapped his foot impatiently, disturbing a frog that had been sitting quietly beside it.

'Please, let's take all that for granted. Did Baker have any enemies?'

A little silence. I couldn't see Parrot's face, but knew from the way Eyes' expression changed that she'd looked some kind of a message at him.

'He did?'

'It isn't my place to bear tales, Excellency.'

'Oh, but it is.' His voice had gone very cold. 'It is your duty, and everybody else's duty in this household, to tell me all they know about Baker's death. I ask you a third time, did Baker have any enemies?'

'She was very angry with him.'

Parrot said the words as if savouring a sweet pomegranate pip.

'Who?'

'Lily.'

Three frogs had arrived at the threshold. I banged the broom down, beside them but not on them, so that they hopped away. After they'd gone, I gave two or three more bangs. It was my only way of protesting, though my whole body was twitching with the urge to push the curtain aside, rush in and shout at Eyes: 'Don't listen to her, Excellency. She is an evil, lying bitch, jealous because Master takes Lily to his bed instead of her.' Unthinkable. The sky would fall if a woodboy spoke uninvited to the Eyes of Pharaoh. Through the rush of blood in my ears, I made myself listen.

'Lily being?'

'One of the other maids. She only came here last year.'

'And you say she was angry with Baker?'

'She told us she'd slapped his face.'

'Told who?'

'Me and the other maids.'

'When?'

'Yesterday evening, after we'd put Lady to bed.'

Eyes leaned forward.

'Tell me exactly what she said.'

'One of the other girls noticed that she'd been crying and wanted to know why. Lily said when she went down to the bakery to get Lady's bricks—'

'Bricks?'

'Lady suffers from pains in her side. When Baker has finished baking bread for the day, he puts two bricks in the oven. By evening, when the oven has cooled, they're just warm. We wrap them in clean cloths and put them in the bed beside her. It gives her some comfort.'

'I see. Was it always Lily who went down for them?'

'Usually. That evening, she said Baker had been waiting and caught hold of her when she went in. According to her, he wanted her to lie with him there and then on the bread table.'

'Had she been accustomed to lie with him?'

I banged with the broom again, though no frogs were near. I wanted to shout, 'No, of course she hadn't. Lily is a clean girl and would lie with nobody but Master.'

Parrot shrugged her shoulders.

'Answer me,' Eyes snapped at her.

'I don't know, Excellency.'

But the tone of her voice said something else.

'In any event, I take it that she refused to lie with him yesterday evening.'

'So she said. She said he tried to force her and she slapped his face, picked up the bricks and ran out.'

'Slapped his face, that was all?'

'All she said she did, yes.'

Eyes sighed.

'You may go for now. You are strictly forbidden to talk about this conversation to anybody else. Send Lily to me.'

As Parrot pushed her way out through the curtain I brought the broom crashing down within a hair's breadth of her squashy flat foot. She jumped, squawked and called me a bad name.

'Master's orders,' I said.

No sooner had Parrot gone than Master himself arrived, so hot and harassed he didn't seem to notice that I'd taken the child's place on frog duty. He pushed the curtain aside and went a little way into the room.

'Is everything in order, Excellency?'

Eyes looked at him, like a man turning a question over in his mind. Master's shoulders went tight.

'Yes, thank you. Tell me, did Baker have any particular friends in the household?'

'Friends?' The word seemed to puzzle Master. 'I don't think so.'

'Or any person he worked with particularly?'

'The bakery slaves, of course. Of his own rank, only

Tallyman. They must be together several times a day because of accounting for the flour and the loaves.'

'How is the accounting carried out?'

Master took a deep breath and his shoulders relaxed. This was something he understood.

'In the morning, Tallyman has the flour sacks for the day brought out of the store. They are weighed and carried over to the bakery. Tallyman records them on his sticks and Baker makes...made...a mark on another stick to record that he'd received them. When the bread is baked, Tallyman counts the loaves and sends the allocation to Pharaoh's household.'

Eyes looked at him. Master grew nervous again.

'I hope there has been no short-falling in Pharaoh's bread.'

'As far as I know, everything is in order.'

There, for once, Master was wrong though I couldn't say so. Pharaoh's household would get its daily allocation, but there was a short-falling in Master's own household that we all felt in the pit of our stomachs. Over the past few moons, the loaves of the servants and slaves had been growing smaller and smaller so that we were hungry most of the time and the sound of rumbling guts vibrated through the place like an animal growling in its sleep. We couldn't complain, but it made for general bad temper.

'Send Tallyman to me,' Eyes said. 'If the girl Lily arrives, tell her to wait outside.'

Master's head jerked back at Lily's name. I thought he was going to protest but he said only, 'Yes, Excellency.'

I expected him to send a slave for Tallyman but he went across to the storerooms himself, walking like a man giddy from fever.

* * *

Tallyman arrived some time afterwards, an unrestful kind of man, sallow of skin and thin as a dried rush, with a nervous way of moving his mouth as if always munching on something not very nourishing.

'I am sorry if I am late, Excellency. We were trying to get the frogs out of the cellars.'

Eyes gave him a cool look, but Tallyman babbled on.

'Nobody's seen the like of them, cellars knee deep in the filthy things, crawling over each other. People are saying it is a curse on us, Excellency, that we've displeased the gods. Do you think it's a curse?'

The frogs or Baker's death must have unsettled him badly, putting a question to a person so far above him in rank. Eyes frowned.

'We should leave these matters to Pharaoh and the priests. I sent for you to talk about bread, and particularly your duties with Baker.'

'Yes, Excellency.'

Tallyman's account for the first part of his day was almost word for word the same as Master's.

'So when the trays of loaves went to Pharaoh's household, was that the last you saw of Baker for the day?'

'No, Excellency. The empty trays must be counted back. The slaves bring them from Pharaoh's household every evening. I count them and return them to Baker, and Baker must notch the stick to record that he has received them.'

'In the evening?'

'Yes. The time before sunset.'

'And you did that yesterday evening?'

'Yes.'

'And Baker was alive?'

'Yes. He notched the stick. I can bring it if...'

'That won't be necessary. Was there anything unusual about Baker yesterday evening?'

'What do you mean, Excellency?'

'Did he seem scared or angry?'

'No.'

'Did he speak of having an enemy?'

'No.'

'So things were in every way as normal?'

'Yes. He was kneading the dough when I came in, quite as normal. He counted the trays, notched the stick. We spoke for a while.'

'What about?'

'One of the trays had been damaged by a slave's carelessness. He wanted to make sure he wouldn't be blamed for it.'

'So an entirely routine conversation?'

'Yes.'

'And you left him still kneading dough?'

'As I recall, Excellency, he finished kneading it while I was there. I remember him washing his hands at the water jar while we were speaking. The light was going by then.'

'And the dough would stay in the kneading trough till morning?'

'Yes.'

'And his knife on the edge of the trough?'

'I think so, yes.'

'Did you see Baker after that?'

'No. The next thing I knew was somebody shouting in the morning that Baker was dead.'

* * *

A soft step beside me and the smell of fresh river water round green rushes. Lily had arrived. Her brown eyes were wide and scared.

'Eyes of Pharaoh has sent for me. Is he in there?'

I told her that Tallyman was with him. Her little feet quivered on the ground from fear. I wanted to stroke her hair, like calming a frightened animal. All I could do was let my hand touch hers, so lightly that it might have been accidental. Then we had to move apart as Tallyman came through the curtain, blowing out his cheeks from relief at leaving the presence of Eyes.

'I should go in now?' Lily said.

She went through the curtain. A frog was sitting on the threshold, quite still, not trying to go anywhere. I squatted down beside it, to see and hear better.

'I believe you were angry with Baker last night,' Eyes said.

The tone of his voice was not unkind, but from the way she flinched he might as well have hit her.

'Speak up, please. Yes or no?'

'Yes.'

'Why?'

She was ashamed to tell him, though it was no fault of hers. He didn't become angry with her – not quite – just let her see that he might become angry if she didn't answer. He had the story from her, much as Parrot had told it, but without the malice and with things much worse against Baker. She'd gone in, not expecting to find him there. He'd hidden behind the oven, come out suddenly and tried to force her backwards onto the bread table, only she'd struggled free, hit him and run out.

'Only hit him?' Eyes said.

'Only hit him, Excellency. My hand on his cheek.'

'Not a knife in his chest?'

'I had no knife.'

'Did you not see the knife on the side of the kneading trough?'

'I don't remember one.'

'It was evening when you struck him?'

'Just before we helped Lady to bed, yes.'

'He was dead by the time the sun rose.'

'Yes.'

'So he died between evening and sunrise?'

'Yes.'

'Do you know of anybody who saw him alive after you struck him and ran out of the bakery?'

'No.'

Her voice was no more than the first stirring of the morning breeze among the reeds. I might have walked into the room then and said untruthfully that I'd seen Baker alive later, only there was a little commotion behind me in the courtyard. I turned and saw two big slaves carrying a chair between poles, another slave holding a sunshade over the person sitting in the chair. I hardly recognised her at first because it was so long since any of us had seen her outside her own rooms and she'd grown so thin and fine-drawn. Lady. The slaves brought her right up to where I was standing and set the chair gently down.

'Is my maid Lily inside with him?' she said, speaking directly to me as if I were somebody of consequence. Her voice was husky, but firm.

I nodded, not daring to speak to her.

'Take me inside,' she said to the front slave.

The slave with the sunshade and I held the curtain aside for them.

* * *

Eyes stood up as the slaves set her chair down in front of him.

'I apologise a thousand times for intruding on your work, Excellency,' Lady said. 'But I have something important to say to you about the killing of Baker. You will permit me to send my maid away for a while?'

He nodded and took his seat again on the bench. She told Lily to wait in the women's rooms until she was sent for again. Lily walked past me, eyes straight ahead. The chair slaves followed her and squatted in the dust in the shade of the wall. I kept my hand on the curtain, desperate to hear what Lady was going to tell him and full of fear for Lily. Lady would surely know about her and Master.

'It's about Lily,' Lady said.

Sure she was going to carry on the bad work Parrot had begun, I was too scared even to bang my broom.

'Lily is a good girl,' she said. 'A good, obedient girl.'

From the expression of Eyes, I knew that he'd heard about Master and Lily and was as surprised as I was. He simply nodded again.

'Is it true that you suspect her of killing Baker?'

He didn't answer at first, as if weighing up whether to trust her.

'She has admitted hitting him,' he said.

'And told you why?'

'Yes.'

'She is speaking the truth. She came to me straight after it had happened, distressed and crying.'

'With respect, she would have been distressed if she had killed him.'

'She had no blood on her hands or clothes.'

'She might have returned to do it later in the night.'

'No, she was with me all night, from the time she came to me crying to when the first of the frogs arrived in the morning.'

'I don't doubt your word, Lady, but can you be sure of that? She might have crept out while you were asleep.'

'I sleep very little, and more lightly than a dragonfly. Besides, waking or sleeping, I should know if Lily left the room. I keep her with me whenever I can because she soothes me and is more gentle than all my maids.'

When I heard that, I wished I could run into the room and kiss Lady's thin white feet in their gilded sandals. Eyes frowned.

'Lady, I hope your Lily is not guilty. Nevertheless, a crime has been committed against a servant of Pharaoh. It can't go unpunished.'

'Baker was a false servant,' she said. There was an edge of anger to her voice. 'He defrauded the household, everybody knows that.'

'Everybody?'

'I have nothing to do all day but listen to the servants' talk. Believe me, I know everything that goes on.'

'Everything? Do you know then who killed him?'

'No, but I know it can't have been Lily.'

He sat for a while, looking at the floor. When he spoke, his voice was sad.

'Lady, you have done me the honour to come to me and I accept that the girl Lily was with you all night. Still, she was the last person I know of to see Baker alive. Hands may be washed and clothes may be changed. I must do my duty.'

'And have Lily put to death?'

'The guilty person must die.'

'Lily is not guilty.'

Another silence. He sighed.

'Lady, will you have the kindness to go back to your rooms and tell Lily to come to me in the bakery.'

'Where the body is?'

'Where the body is.'

I thought at first she was going to refuse. I was willing her to refuse. But at last she clapped her hands and the chair slaves came running in and carried her away. Her face was like stone.

Soon afterwards Eyes came out, deep in thought. He took a few steps past me and turned back.

'What are you doing here, Woodboy?'

'Keeping the frogs away, Excellency.'

'I was about to send for you. Follow me to the bakery.'

I followed him across the outer courtyard. Slaves scooping up crushed frogs or chivvying live ones looked at him sideways and some of them made the sign to turn away evil, keeping it small so as not to attract attention. But they needn't have worried because he walked head down, not looking round. When he stopped suddenly, halfway to the bakery, I almost ran into him.

'Go to your Master and tell him to come to...'

It showed how lost in thought he was that he'd almost given me an impossible order. How could I tell Master to come and go? He changed it.

'Go to Tallyman and tell him to give my respects to your Master and ask him to meet me in the bakery. Tallyman is to come as well.'

I ran to find Tallyman. He was in his office by the storerooms, making signs on a clay tablet. He growled at me when he heard the message.

'You must have muddled it. Why should he want Master there of all places?'

I didn't contradict him, just went on repeating what Eyes had said. In the end he groaned, put on his sandals and went to do as he was told, saying to me in passing that I could expect a beating if I'd got it wrong. I went and waited by the door to the bakery. Lily arrived first, looking so alone and scared that I risked touching her hand as she passed. She looked up at me, eyes full of tears, then bowed her head and went inside. Master came next, with Tallyman hurrying after him. Once they'd gone in, I moved to the little store chamber just inside the doorway. They were all three of them standing by the oven, with Baker on the floor, covered now with a white sheet. The place smelt of him and of sour dough. Eyes stood by the kneading trough.

'The important question is when Baker died,' he said. His voice was calm and quiet. 'We know from Tallyman that at the hour before sunset he had finished kneading his dough and had left it in the kneading trough here.'

He gestured towards the dough. It had risen like a mass of white fungus to fill the trough. Because it had been standing much longer than usual there was a crust on it, but at some places the dough underneath had broken through the crust in paler bulges. It seemed a sinister thing, like another body.

'We know too, from the maid Lily, that sometime later in the evening, she struck him. She says he was alive when she left.'

I couldn't bear to look at Lily, so kept my eyes on the

dough. A frog hopped on top of it and stared at me.

'At first light, Woodboy found him dead and raised the alarm.' He glanced in my direction. 'You had better come in, Woodboy. You are a witness too.'

I went in, shame-faced. Master and Tallyman glared at me. Eyes went on as if nothing had happened.

'As you see, Baker had not started making up the dough into loaves. I assume he would usually do that as soon as it was light enough.'

'Yes, soon after dawn,' Master said.

'So at some time between the evening when Lily struck him and when the light came back in the morning, somebody plunged his own knife into his chest.'

Master was looking at Lily, his eyes sad. I wanted to shout at him, 'Save her. Lady your wife tried to, and she had less cause than you.' He did nothing. I looked back at the dough. There was something sticking out from it, caught between the risen dough and the side of the trough. It looked like a piece of rush or leaf.

'We must also ask ourselves whether anybody besides Lily had cause to be angry with Baker,' Eyes said.

It was the wrong colour for a leaf, the wrong shape for a piece of rush. I moved quietly towards the trough. The frog blinked and hopped down behind it. The little noise it made was enough to make Eyes look my way.

'What is it, Woodboy?'

I touched the thing that was neither leaf nor rush, but something finer and softer than either. I looked up at Eyes, straight into his face.

'What have you found there, boy?'

He was beside me, almost as quick as a frog himself. With my eyes, I signalled to him to touch the thing. He touched it and frowned.

'A frog's foot. Turn the dough over. Tallyman, help him.'

It was below Tallyman's rank to do it, but he had no choice. Together we pulled the heavy cushion of dough towards us, hauled it over and flipped it back into the trough, with a glubbing noise like Nile mud. Master made a sound of disgust.

'Everywhere.'

There were three of them, two crushed as flat as sandal soles, the other nearly so. They were stuck to what had been the lower surface of the dough and was now the uppermost. Eyes turned to me.

'Woodboy, when did the frogs start coming up?'

'They'd already started when I went to the river before dawn, Excellency. I saw some tens of them on the paths as I went down to the river, hundreds as I came back.'

'That's what the priests tell us too,' Eyes said. 'The first frogs came into the houses in the hour before dawn.'

We all stared at the squashed frogs.

'So what do these three dead frogs tell us?' Eyes said.

Nobody answered. He looked at me.

'Well, Woodboy?'

'That the dough was taken out of the trough and put back again in the hour before dawn or after.'

I should have felt scared, saying so many words in front of Master, but there was something about Eyes that gave me courage. It seemed to have the same effect on Tallyman, because he gave an opinion unasked.

'Some frogs are around all the time.'

'Indeed, yes. It is just possible, though unlikely, in the normal course of events, that a frog might happen to be in the trough when Baker kneaded his dough there. But three? Not possible. Therefore we must assume that the dough was lifted out of the trough and thrown back in again with enough force to crush the frogs in the hour before sunrise or afterwards.'

'It couldn't have been afterwards,' Master said. 'Baker was dead by then and a guard on the door.'

'In the hour before sunrise, then.'

'When Lily was with my wife,' Master said.

His voice was full of relief, only I wished he'd spoken before, when things looked so black for Lily. She gave a little sob of relief and almost fell over. Eyes put out a hand to steady her and helped her sit down on one of the flour sacks. I had to look very hard at the dough and the crushed frogs to stop myself running to her. The dough round them was flat and quite fresh looking, as if it had been cut with a knife.

'What are you looking at now, Woodboy?'

Eyes seemed to notice every move I made. I gestured towards the cut surface, not able to put into words what I was thinking. He came past me, touched the dough.

'Cut. In the hour before sunrise, the dough was taken out of the trough, a piece was cut off it and the rest was thrown back into the trough with some force.'

'And in that same hour, Baker was killed,' Master said.

'Quite probably with the same knife. Since I can see no traces of blood on the dough, we may assume that the dough was cut first and Baker killed afterwards. Can you find any connection?'

He looked at Master.

'If somebody were stealing part of the dough...?' Master said.

Master looked at Tallyman. Eyes nodded.

'Exactly. Let us imagine the scene. Baker comes in, just before it's light. He sees somebody hacking away a great lump of dough. Perhaps he has reason to suspect it has happened before and is keeping watch. He challenges the thief.'

Tallyman's face had turned whiter than the dough. Eyes went on speaking in the same calm voice.

'The thief already has the knife in his hand for cutting the dough. He knew the knife would be there where it always was, on the edge of the kneading trough. He had no need to bring one with him. That suggests a man who knows the routine of the bakery well, wouldn't you say?'

He was looking straight at Tallyman now. Tallyman stared at the floor, but that was no use because Baker was lying there under his sheet. Then Tallyman screamed. I'd only heard such a scream once in my life before and that was from a woodboy caught in a crocodile's jaws. Tallyman was screaming because the white cloth over Baker was rising and falling, as if the man were breathing again in gulping, irregular breaths.

'It was your idea,' Tallyman screeched at Baker's corpse. 'It was your idea all along.'

He was still screaming when a frog hopped from under the sheet and out of the door. He went on screaming when the guards came to drag him away.

The frogs stayed with us all the rest of that day and night. But by next morning, as I walked to the river before sunrise, they were streaming back again. It was like being carried on a moving carpet of frogs. I was sorry for the many that had been killed and especially for the two crushed by the dough. Yes, only two. The third that had been less squashed revived after all and hopped away. I was the only one to see it because Eyes, Lily and Master had left the bakery by then. Master was cast down because he should have known that Tallyman and Baker had been cheating him day after day for many moons, selling part of Pharaoh's dough every morning to a baker who kept a wretched little oven just outside the walls. Then, Eyes suggested, there'd been quarrels between the two of them over the division of the money. We could have told him that, all of the slaves and boys, but nobody asked us.

There is a new Tallyman now and a new Baker. Every evening, when Lily comes down for the warm bricks, I make sure I'm there to give them to her. She thanks me and sometimes lets her hand touch mine. As for the frogs, people say what a relief it is that they've gone. They still discuss why they chose to come that day and if they will come again. Some people say the Israelites' conjurer sent them as a sign to Pharaoh, but the priests say not. All I know is that the frogs have not gone at all. They're where they always were, in the mud by the river, living their own quiet magic. Which is a blessing in itself, because what would the world be without frogs?

The Old Man was huffing and puffing, but for once it was a physical thing and not a litany of complaint about how people do things these days and not like they used to. This time the complaining was not his, it was Mama's.

'Use it or lose it,' she said to him. And so now here he was whirling the pedals of a so-called bicycle. But how could it be a bicycle if it didn't go anywhere? Huh!

And, for that matter, what was the 'it' he might *lose* if he didn't do all this going nowhere? Mama spelled it out with talk, talk, talk, but now he couldn't remember. Just that it was because he rested sometimes when he climbed the stairs to the flat. Two flights, that climb. Twenty-eight steps, plus a few more at the doorway. So now and then he turned into Angelo and Gina's kitchen halfway up and sat in a chair. So what? You get a little tired, you sit, plus they were his son and daughter-in-law, who might be home, or their children, or the others. Sitting in a chair doesn't mean you're about to fall over and die, God help you. If it did, who'd be left standing? Huh!

And so what, he watched more television now? What else was it for? And was there a law? Only now, it seemed, there was. Mama couldn't prohibit, but after an hour, or half an hour, she could start to talk at him. And not stop. 'Do this. Do that. Do *something*.'

So maybe that *was* it. In the family business there was less and less something for him to do, him, the *head* of the family, no matter who ran the day-to-day. All of a sudden it's not like he founded the Lunghi Detective Agency and taught them everything they knew. All of a sudden it's not like he can observe and follow and record and *detect* anymore. No wonder he gained a few pounds. What else should he do?

'You want to work more? Show them how fit you are,' Mama said. 'Get rid of some inches.'

'What, become shorter? I'll do that anyway, getting older.'

'Don't be stupid.' And she turned away.

Now he was stupid, too, with everything else?

But, in the end, he did what she wanted because she was delicate and would get upset if he didn't. So here he was. Thursday in the second week of it, at the YMCA gym. On a so-called bike that went nowhere. Soon on a so-called treadmill that had nothing to tread. How many of them here knew from grapes? Huh!

'And after a few weeks,' the Y's Guru Mick said, 'I'll start you on some weights. You're really going to hate me then.'

I should have to wait till then? the Old Man thought. Guru Mick, with his big muscles, took him into a little room and did a 'personal evaluation' and gave a 'personal programme.' All smiles and calling him 'buddy' and saying 'I'm going to be your exercise guru.' Huh!

The Old Man wiped his face with a towel and saw he had seven more minutes of going nowhere.

'I'm so worried about Papa,' Mama said to her daughter-in-law over plates of salad at lunch time. 'So much he sits.'

Midday meetings for lunch were unusual, and today it seemed to Gina that Mama had sought her out because something was on her mind. 'Well, Papa's not as young as he used to be,' Gina said. 'He's entitled to some rest.'

Mama put down her fork. 'It's not entitlement, Gina. It's prison. He hates it.'

'I thought he liked watching TV.' Gina tried to remember the programmes her father-in-law had mentioned at the dinner table. There were the police and detective shows to be pulled to pieces, but wasn't there also some words and numbers game each day in the afternoon? She couldn't pull back its name.

'What he *wants* to do is work.' Mama held up her hands. 'I know, I know. I asked for less for him, but too much less is not enough. I wouldn't interfere, Gina, God knows, but if you and Angelo have cases he could help with then he'd be happy, I'd be happy. Some surveillance without cars, maybe. Or shoplifters, or even serving papers. Anything.'

'If that's what you want, Mama.' Gina pursed her lips and reviewed what was on the agency's agenda at the moment. Other than the routine work for solicitors, there was an industrial, but would *that* be appropriate?

'Meanwhile all he can think to do is go to the gym, that's how desperate he is,' Mama said.

'Papa goes to the *gym*?'

'To be doing, not sitting. He started at the YMCA last week on Monday, so eleven days now. He's determined to lose a few inches, to show you and Angelo how fit he still is. This inch-losing is good for the health too. He should be rewarded for effort, I think. Don't you?'

'Are you waiting for a treadmill?'

The Old Man turned to the voice to find it belonged to one of those musclemen. 'What?'

'The one on the end is free.'

'I'm watching this runner, this red vest,' the Old Man said.

The muscleman looked at the runner the Old Man pointed at.

Red Vest was pounding away on a treadmill in front of them.

'You see that?' the Old Man said. 'How his heels kick out sideways?'

The man looked at the runner on the treadmill.

'Kicking out doesn't go forward. This Red Vest can be as fit as he likes, but in a race he'd lose inches. More if it's longer.'

'Oh.' The man frowned. 'So...you're not waiting for a treadmill, then?'

This muscleman wanted a machine, not an education. The Old Man waved him to it and turned back to Red Vest. The kicking out was extremely pronounced. It even looked uncomfortable, like he could twist his ankles with the kicking.

How old was this Red Vest? Older than David, the Old Man's grandson, but how much? Fifteen? Maybe twenty? Young enough to learn? To correct his ways? Perhaps, if he really wanted to.

The Old Man's running days were long gone, but he'd done enough on tracks and across the foothills of his youth. And then he found himself thinking of the great Emilio Lunghi, who won a silver medal running in the Olympics of 1908, beating the German, Braun, but losing to the American, Sheppard, in the 800 metres. Not a relative, this Emilio, but a famous namesake. And if he had found only a few more inches...

'Did he steal *your* mobile too?'

This time the questioner was a young woman. A girl, only. Was *everybody* so young now? Maybe the age of Maria, his granddaughter, this one. But who can tell these days? 'What?'

'I saw you watching that bastard on the treadmill.'

'He's a bastard?' The Old Man glanced with sympathy at Red Vest.

'He stole my mobile phone.'

'He *stole* it?' Now no sympathy. The Old Man had little sympathy to spare for thieves.

'I was on Saracen Street talking to my brother and *that* bastard came up behind me and pulled my arm down from my ear, grabbed the phone out of my hand and ran away with it.'

'How long ago was this stealing?'

'Monday. Then I came in here to train on Tuesday, and there he was. I couldn't believe it. He was running on a treadmill, just like today.'

'And this phone stealer, did he give it back?'

'Did he, hell. He just laughed in my face and said he never did it and he could prove it. But he *did* do it. He absolutely did.' The look on the young woman's face was one of pure hatred.

The Old Man considered what he'd been told about the theft. She was talking. The bastard came up behind her...
'You didn't see him coming, so you saw him going?' he asked.

'Not his face. He had on a green waterproof with a hood.'

'So...?' The Old Man spread his hands. At home, in the family, at a meal like they would have tonight, everyone would know he was asking for elucidation with the gesture, for explanation. But this young girl just looked from one hand to the other, so he spelled it out. 'You didn't see his face yet you're sure you know it's him? How can this be?'

'Look at the way he runs,' the young woman said. 'See how he kicks out his heels?'

'"Dishing" they call it, in horses,' the Old Man said at the dinner table. 'Jane told me.'

'Horses?' Salvatore said. 'Did I miss something?'

Thursday night was one of three times a week that the

Lunghis made an effort to eat together. This time even Salvatore, Mama and the Old Man's eldest child were there. He was the only member of the immediate family who did not live in the family's connected properties on Walcot Street.

'This girl, this Jane, she rides horses. So she recognised the stealer by his gait.'

'Dishing? Well, who wants another *dish* of curry?' This was Rosetta, the youngest of the senior Lunghis' three children. She cooked on Thursdays, often her trademark curry. 'I'm getting up anyway. Papa?'

Normally the Old Man complained that curry wasn't Italian, and then ate more. But today the three hands that went up for seconds did not include his.

Angelo, the younger son who ran the family business, tapped the side of his cheek as he tried to digest his father's story. 'Am I understanding right, Papa? You're telling us because you want us to take this Jane as some kind of client?'

'It's injustice this thief can dish at the YMCA with impunity,' the Old Man said. 'He dished on Tuesday the day after he stole the poor girl's phone, and laughed in her face. Then today he dishes again, right in front of her.'

'But a *client*, Papa? Is she paying?'

'She has no money to pay,' the Old Man said. 'She's a dropout, to work with horses, though she builds strength in the gym to be a jockey one day.'

'So...*not* paying?' Angelo said.

'What did I just say? Huh!'

There was a silence at the table to mark the moment. This was because it was unprecedented for the Old Man to suggest that the agency work without a paying client. He could have invented, 'Show me the money,' it was so unprecedented.

Angelo looked around the table, catching the eyes of each of the adults. 'For myself,' he said, 'I'm happy to see if we can help. But, Papa, I never thought I'd hear *you* say we should take on work for free.'

'You can think too much about money,' the Old Man said. 'More than a certain amount, who needs more?'

All their lives the Lunghi siblings had listened to their father ask, 'Who's paying?' For him the answer had never before been, 'Us.'

When dinner was over and the dishes dealt with, the middle generation of Lunghis retired to the living room. Angelo brought a bottle of wine.

'What's with Papa?' Salvatore asked for them all. 'I never in my life thought I'd hear about him going to a *gym*.'

Rosetta said, 'He didn't want seconds, and it wasn't because Mama nagged him.'

Angelo said, 'He wants us to work for free.'

Gina, who could have pulled the strands together, kept quiet while the others talked. Maybe they would work it out for themselves.

'It sounds like he's been to the Y every day since Monday last week,' Salvatore said. 'Did it sound that way to you?'

'Maybe he's trying to lose weight, and get fit,' Rosetta said. 'But why now?'

'He wants us to work for free,' Angelo said.

There was a pause.

Gina said, 'Do any of you mind working for free on this?'

No one did.

'So let's think about the case. *Is* there anything we can do?'

'For horsey Jane?' Salvatore said. 'Lots of kids have their phones stolen, don't they?'

'Lots,' Rosetta said.

'What do the thieves do with the phones they steal? Make phone calls?'

'They sell them on to foreign countries.'

'Really, Rose?'

'Places where there aren't so many phones or so many high-tech ones. But there's a market here too. They replace the SIM card and clean them out with a computer so they can be resold as legitimate second-hand.' Rosetta only rarely participated actively in investigations, but she was the family's accountant and expert on things technical.

'So,' Salvatore said, 'this dishing thief will be selling to a middle-man. We could crack a whole ring here.'

'For free?' Angelo's voice was faint.

'But you can see why the police aren't interested yet,' Rosetta said. 'How do you convince a jury with identification evidence that's from the back and just because of the way somebody runs?'

'If she's a pretty girl,' Salvatore said, 'if she bats her eyelashes, she could convince a jury.'

'You and pretty girls,' Rosetta said. Salvatore's success with pretty girls was the stuff of family legend. Rosetta's bad luck with men was legend too.

'It would never come to trial without a lot more evidence,' Gina said.

'And that's where we come in, is it?' Salvatore asked. 'I guess I could make some time.'

'Wouldn't it be better,' Gina said, 'to think about what Papa could do to find more evidence?'

Salvatore and Rosetta studied Gina as they considered this. Gina turned to her husband and pointed a finger as he was about to open his mouth. 'Angelo, if you say "For free?" one more time, I'm going to hit you.'

'You heard them,' the Old Man said. 'All they think is money. Huh!'

'That's not what I heard,' Mama said. 'You want your blanket in that chair?'

'What am I, a dog, with a blanket?'

'I just asked. You might be cold. Sometimes you're cold.'

'All right, all right. I'll be cold. I'll have the blanket and be a dog if that makes you happy. Woof woof.'

Mama passed the Old Man the blanket he usually kept in his lap while watching television at night. 'What *I* heard,' she said, 'was that they agreed it was OK to work for this Jane for free.'

'Who needs agreeing? Can they stop me if I want to do something for injustice?' He patted the blanket into place. 'Where is the pointer? Do you see the pointer?'

Mama looked around for the TV remote. 'You want to do it for this Jane all by yourself, or do you want help?'

The Old Man considered. 'Help, of the right kind...could help.'

'What kind is right?'

'When they don't think they always know better than I do. No do this, do that.'

'There it is.' Mama pointed to the remote control device on the table beside him.

'Thank you. Thank you.' He pushed a button. The television burst into life. 'Huh! So loud. Why is it always so loud?'

'So make it quiet.'

The Old Man muted the sound. 'It's like with mobile phones themselves. People always shout. Is that the way people are now? Everybody shouts?'

'Maybe they're all deaf from loud music.' Mama picked up her knitting.

'I'll be deaf, if I don't watch out.' He turned the sound back on. 'So loud! Huh!'

In the morning Gina went upstairs after the children left for school.

The Old Man was surprised to see her. 'Look at this, Mama. We have a visitor today.' He looked at his wrist. 'Shouldn't you be in the office, Gina?'

'So charming you are,' Mama said. 'Tea for you, Gina? Or coffee?'

'No thanks. I *am* here on business.'

The Old Man frowned. 'What business that's not in the office?'

'After you and Mama came back up last night, we all talked about the mobile phone thief.'

'*After?*' the Old Man said. 'Huh!'

'We wondered what your plan is.'

'My plan?'

'It's your case. We all want to help if you'll tell us what to do.'

'So how did it go?' Angelo asked when Gina came back downstairs and crossed over to the office.

'He's going to talk with Charlie. See for himself what the police position is. All Horsey Jane told him was that they weren't interested.'

Angelo nodded. 'There could be more to it.'

'Even if they're not ready to raid the YMCA gym, I'd have thought the police would be interested that a thief has been identified.'

'If one has.'

'Meaning?'

'If you were a police officer, how much weight could you give to an identification from the back of how somebody runs?'

Charlie, a computer officer at Bath's Manvers Street police station, rose to greet the Old Man when he was ushered in. 'Welcome to crime central, Mr Lunghi. We don't see enough of you.'

'More help you need?' The murder of Charlie's father was the only murder case the Lunghi family had ever investigated. It was the Old Man who solved it.

'I was thinking more that we don't see enough of you socially, but if you have something in the way of business that you'd like to share...'

'I have a thief,' the Old Man said, 'but I don't want to share. You can have him all.'

The Old Man sat and told Charlie about the phone-thief who dished when he ran.

'What's the victim's name?' Charlie asked when the story was done.

'Jane Winchester.'

'Let me look up who she talked to.' Charlie turned to his computer.

'*This* is your computer?' the Old Man said. 'This little thing?'

'Yes. Why?'

'Boxes I thought they were. Screens with big tubes at the back and no room on a desk for anything else.'

'Technology moves on, Mr L.'

While Charlie studied his flat monitor the Old Man considered technology. Getting fit in the gym was one thing, but the modern technology, he could use some of that too, to show his effectiveness.

Charlie said, 'We get a lot of phone thefts in Bath, you know, because of all the students and tourists we have. And your Jane Winchester...' Click, click, click. 'She talked with D.C. Potter. But the officer in charge...' More buttons. Keys, they called them. The Old Man knew *that* much. '...is D.S. Joseph. Let me just check whether she's in the station.' Charlie picked up the phone.

'You're back,' Mama said.

'I'm back. I'm also front and side-by-side.' The Old Man felt jaunty because he'd learned things he didn't know before. He dropped his jacket on a chair. 'I'll go out again in a few minutes.'

Mama didn't know why this precluded his hanging the garment on a hook, but she rode with it in the circumstances. 'Of course,' she said. 'You're working.'

'I'm working,' the Old Man said, 'but—'

'But maybe you'd like a cup of tea?'

'Good idea. I'll take a minute off.' In an instant he was at his place at the small table in their kitchen.

'You saw Charlie?'

'And he found a detective for me. Not the one in charge of the case but the underling, the one who talked with the Jane when she reported the disher's theft in the first place.' The Old Man thought for a moment, then got up to

314 MICHAEL Z LEWIN

retrieve his notebook from a jacket pocket.

While she filled the kettle and put teabags in two cups, Mama decided not to point out how much easier getting the notebook out would have been had the jacket been hanging. These were delicate times and needed discretion.

'This so-called detective,' the Old Man said when he was in place at the table. 'This Potter. You wouldn't believe. He wouldn't detect sugar in a biscuit.'

'You want a biscuit?'

'Twist my arm.'

'So you didn't like Potter the detective. What did he say?' Mama got out the Rich Teas.

'He said the Jane was stupid, expecting an arrest from a thief running away. But I say it doesn't take stupid to recognise from the back and from the feet. It takes clever.'

'So Potter wasn't interested.'

'He thought the Jane wasted his time. But I say he wastes my time.'

'And what did Charlie say?'

The Old Man looked up with a pleased expression. 'Charlie said that if I believed the Jane, then chances were she should be believed.'

Good for Charlie, Mama thought. Perhaps she could cook something for him.

'And he said he would get together information about phone thefts over the last year. I should expect a call.'

'So now you sit here by the telephone?'

'Now? Now I wait for my tea. But then I go to the gym.'

'Good,' Mama said. '*Good*. Mustn't let all this work get in the way of the fitness.'

* * *

But when he got to the YMCA, the Old Man did not change clothes or begin his warm-up routine. First he checked to see if the red vested disher was on a treadmill. He wasn't, so the Old Man sought out Guru Mick.

'How you doing, buddy?' Guru Mick said.

'I need to know about one of your members,' the Old Man said. 'When he comes in, who he is.'

'That sort of thing is confidential, buddy. Sorry.'

'It's to help my grandson, David. David wants muscles. He thinks he's too spindly for the girls.'

'Well we can certainly help him with that,' Guru Mick said.

'But the boy is so shy. He wants to come when there's someone closer to his age. Another boy, or young man. One who runs. One who uses a treadmill, say.'

'Oh yes?'

'Yesterday there was one who was perfect.' The Old Man pointed. 'On that treadmill. He wore a red vest.'

'I don't remember exactly who you mean, buddy.'

'About eleven in the morning. You can't look?' The Old Man gestured to the gym computer. 'Find out when he comes in, if it's regular. I can come then too, ask for a name myself. That's confidential enough, isn't it?'

There was a payphone in the reception area of the YMCA. The Old Man fiddled with change, then got help from the bearded man at the desk. It was all a palaver. This must be why so many people talked into mobile phones all the time. Everywhere you saw them. And they were ringing if they weren't already talking. A noise, a nuisance. But, still, to be able to make a call without palaver...

The number he called was the one he'd been given by Jane

316 MICHAEL Z LEWIN

Winchester. But he got a machine instead. 'I want to meet about the disher,' he told the Jane's machine. 'I want to tell you what I've learned so far. Talk about what to do. Can you come to Walcot Street between four and five? I'll be there.' And he left the address, but it was for the family flat, not the agency office. Who would want to interrupt Gina or Angelo in the office?

The Old Man was waiting in the lower kitchen when David came home from school. 'Hi Grandpa.'

'David, you're home.'

David dropped his school bag on the floor and opened the refrigerator. But then he looked back. 'Do you want me to call Mum?'

'No. No. I'm just waiting.'

David took out the bowls of curry and of rice left over from the night before. He got a clean plate from the dishwasher but then turned to his grandfather. 'I'm hungry.'

'So eat.'

'You want some?'

The Old Man looked at his watch, which read quarter to four. 'Why not? A taste.'

David dished out servings onto each of two plates. While the first was in the microwave he found cutlery.

'Thank you,' the Old Man said, when his grandson brought the steaming plate to him.

'You're welcome,' David said. 'I've been all day in the kitchen trying to get it just right.'

The Old Man mixed up the curry with the rice and took a forkful. He blew on it. Not pasta, not Italian, but not bad. Huh!

They ate for a while in silence. Then David said, 'Did you get tired on the way upstairs, Grandpa?'

'That's not me anymore.'

'It isn't?'

'Now I go to the gym and get aerobic and strong. Maybe you will too.'

'The *gym*? Me?'

'There's something wrong with all those healthy exercises? Huh! Your generation is obese from sitting around.'

'I'm not obese,' David said.

'You *look* thin, but inside who knows? All those hours you sit at your computer...'

'I do PE at school.'

'And tell me, this PE, do you go running, by any chance?'

Horsey Jane rang the downstairs bell just after four-thirty. David answered the door. The fact that she was pretty, and short, left him momentarily speechless. She also looked younger than he'd expected if she was out of school and working with horses.

Jane tilted her head. 'Do I have the right place?'

'If your name is Jane Winchester you do.'

David led her up to the kitchen where the Old Man was rinsing his plate. 'Ah, Jane.'

'Hi, Mr Lunghi.'

'Too late for curry but sit. You want some tea? I'm having tea.'

'Tea would be nice. Thanks.' She sat.

'David, make us some tea, will you? Jane, this is my grandson, David.'

'Me David, you Jane,' David said.

Jane blinked, then finally smiled.

David turned to the kettle, his face flushing.

'I want to report on your case,' the Old Man said.

'Have you found out something?'

The Old Man paused a moment for effect. 'Only that I think I know who this disher is.'

'It can't hurt for me to see who was in the gym at eleven,' Guru Mick had said. 'How old did you say the guy on the treadmill was?'

The Old Man watched as Guru Mick clicked through various screens, cross-referencing members who were fifteen to twenty-five with those who were male and in the gym the previous day at eleven.

It was all too fast for the Old Man to read a single thing on a single screen. He tried, but failed. Did these computer people have special computer eyes? Was that part of high-tech? Was there an operation for it, maybe? Huh!

Click click click.

The Old Man's gaze wandered around the room and stopped with a woman on an exercise bike. Why did they face such bikes at the walls with the backs to the room? Did they know what they made the people on them look like? If Mama came here she would change such things in a minute. Huh!

'OK,' Guru Mick said, 'we're down to three. Tell me, buddy, what build did the guy you're trying to find have?'

'Build?'

'Body shape.'

'He was...normal.'

'So not *big*.'

'Not muscles like you, or fat like the woman on the bike.'

'So that,' Guru Mick said, 'rules out Lennie and...' More clicks. 'And it rules out Darren.' Clicks and a flourish. 'Oh I know him.'

'You do?'

'Quiet lad. Three, four times a week. Yeah, a runner.' Guru Mick turned to the Old Man. 'Now, you do know, Mr Lunghi, that because of the Data Protection Act I can't tell you *any* of the information we have stored here.'

'I know.'

'But I've just noticed that one of the water coolers needs a new bottle. That will take me a couple of minutes.' Guru Mick walked away.

'Alistair Balson,' the Old Man said.

'Alistair Balson...' Jane shook her head. 'Never heard of him.'

'You don't know the name, but why should you? His address I have as well, and that he comes in Tuesday and Thursday. Other days too, but not so regular. And the time can be ten-thirty like yesterday or later.'

'What are you going to do, Grandpa?' David asked. 'Confront him at the gym on Tuesday morning?'

The Old Man wagged his finger at David. 'Confront is what this Jane already did and he laughed. The police don't laugh, but they say Jane's identification is not enough. What we need is new evidence.'

David was getting excited. 'We could wait till he's in the gym and then, when he comes out, I could walk along in front of him and put my phone up to my ear like I'm talking on it and see if he tries to snatch it – only I'll have it on a cord. It would be like a sting.'

'Or a string,' the Old Man said. 'But with a string all we have is another his word against ours.' He looked at Jane. 'This Balson runs fast?'

'Yes.'

'And he does train at it, even though he loses seconds. So we won't catch him by running after. But...' He held up a finger.

'What, Grandpa?'

'We could catch him a different way.'

'Surveillance can be really boring,' David said as he walked Jane down the stairs to the street. 'I know. I've done a lot of it.'

'Really?'

'What with it being a family business and all. I'm older and more experienced than my years.'

Although Jane didn't react, David thought she looked interested, maybe even impressed. But just as they neared the front door, it burst open and Marie pushed past them both. Then she stopped and turned. 'Who's the girlie, maggot-face? Not your *girlie*friend?' Chuckling, Marie ran up the stairs, leaving her blushing brother and the family's puzzled pro bono client to look after her.

'Who's *that?*' Jane asked.

'My half-witted sister. A sad story really.'

After dinner the Old Man came downstairs to find Gina and Rosetta in the kitchen. 'Ah, Rose,' he said. 'Just the person.'

The women exchanged glances. 'What can I do for you, Papa?' Rosetta said.

'I want to check out some high tech.'

'Check it out?'

'For use, on the Jane case. I need mobile phones, two. And camcorder, one. The agency has them, yes?'

'We have them...' Rosetta said looking at Gina.

'Good.' He waited.

'What's the camcorder for, Papa?' Rosetta said.

'For camcording, of course. Huh!'

'I mean, what will you be taking images of?'

'I don't understand what's so hard. Do you keep me waiting or do I get my equipment?'

'Come on through to my office, Papa,' Rosetta said. 'Let me show you what we have.'

The Old Man sat in his chair reading an instruction book. Mama knitted as she watched him. 'What?' he said.

'Nothing.'

Click, click, click...

However, eventually he said, 'When will you be done?'

'With what?'

He waved a hand. '*That.*'

'This pullover?'

'Your knitting. Whatever it is.'

Mama considered. 'Probably in about ten days I'll be finished.' This was not what her husband was asking, which she knew full well.

The Old Man returned to the booklet, his glasses, the camera. He turned the camera upside down. Then he turned it over. He sighed. He sighed again.

Mama took pity on him and put down her knitting. She pulled a chair up close. 'It's a camera. You use cameras. What's so hard?'

'This camera takes videos.'

'It does?'

'It saves a camcorder and is smaller and easier, Rosetta said. She showed me, but I don't quite remember up the stairs.'

'You want to go back down?'

'If I wanted to go down, I would go down. Huh!'

Mama considered the camera. Then she saw there was a second. 'Two cameras you have?'

'One is for David.'

'David?'

'Tomorrow we go out.'

'And does he already know how to use his camera?'

The Old Man shrugged. Then, 'You think I should get him up here?'

If anyone in the family could work out how to operate something with a battery, it was David. Mama picked up her knitting. 'Can't hurt,' she said. Click, click, click.

Because it was a Saturday David was able to leave the house early without anybody asking where he was going. He found his grandfather waiting, as agreed, in the café on Walcot Street, Doolally's. 'Hi, Grandpa.'

'Have you had breakfast?' the Old Man said. 'You want to order something?' But he had already risen from his chair.

They walked to the steps that lead from Walcot Street up to the Crescent Paragon. More steps up even than to the flat, but the Old Man climbed them with comparative ease. Clear improvement, and after only ten days. But by the time they were climbing Lansdown Hill he felt the strain. Without saying anything, he slowed down.

Without saying anything, David slowed too.

It was more than half an hour before they got to Upper Hedgemead Road. The address for Alistair Balson was a two storey house in a terrace of six.

'So that's where he lives, Grandpa?'

'It doesn't look like flats, this house,' the Old Man said, 'but you should go up to the door to confirm.'

'*I* should?'

'He's seen me at the gym, this Balson. He might remember. If you get caught say you're looking for your dog. He's lost. Poor Rover.'

David hesitated.

'Or your cat. Go. I'll be...' The Old Man saw a bench across the street where Lower Hedgemead Road split off from Upper to form the north boundary of Hedgemead Park. 'I'll be on the bench.' He crossed the street, leaving David to gaze at Balson's building.

The bench turned out to be in a good position. They could keep watch on Balson's door in comparative comfort, if they were in for a long wait. The day was not too hot or cold, and was impossible to tell. And who knew if he would come or go or when.

The problem with this Balson was that the Old Man was by no means sure of recognising him. Unless he was running away, of course. That image was clear for him. Like with Jane.

The police were stupid not to accept her identification. Perhaps when the case was resolved he could have a word with Charlie, or other officers, and convince them. Maybe it would lead to a whole new branch of forensic science. The gaits of suspects. The cops could make them run away. That the suspects wouldn't mind. Huh!

David was beaming when he rejoined his grandfather. 'It *is* flats. *And* Balson lives in the basement. There are three bells and the bottom one says, "Balson and Coates: Cyberlocity."'

'Cyberlocity? What is this Cyberlocity?'

David shook his head. 'Maybe some internet business?'

The Old Man gazed across the street, taking in the whole row of buildings. Not what *he'd* call suitable for dividing into flats. Or for locating a business. He shook his head, but said nothing. Who'd have thought when he began to buy property in Walcot Street that the area would become commercial and fashionable?

'Grandpa?'

'What?'

'If it's flats, how will we know who to follow if someone comes out?'

'A young man.' The Old Man looked at David. 'Older than you, but not so much. How many can there be in one house?'

David looked at the house. It wasn't large but if all three flats were let to students...

'A young man comes out,' the Old Man said, 'and what you do is chase him. Shout, say he owes you money. When he runs away I can identify him.'

But in the event they were half-lucky. Less than an hour after they settled themselves on the bench, two young men came out of the house. Both were dressed in clothes that could be appropriate for the gym, but the clincher was that they came up a flight of stairs from below ground level rather than through the building's front door. They could only be coming from the basement flat of Balson and Coates.

'I didn't realise the stairs were used,' David said.

As he said it, the young men pushed bushy branches out of their way and unlocked a chain on the gate to the stairwell.

'Whatever,' the Old Man said. 'These two we follow.'

David rose. 'Do you know which is Balson?'

The Old Man squinted at the pair as they relocked the gate. Could he recall hair colour, build…? But from the distance the two young men looked about the same. All he recalled was the red vest, but both these suspects wore green waterproof jackets. So he said, 'If they split up, we take one each. But this is background surveillance remember, with cameras.'

David had already taken a picture of the young men. He'd taken pictures of several things as he passed time on the bench with his grandfather.

'No risks,' the Old Man said. 'Even if we have the luck and see our Balson steal a dozen phones, we don't interfere. That's why we have the cameras. That's why we have the phones to keep in touch.'

The walk back down the hill was much easier than the walk up, and not just because of the slope. Adrenaline was flowing now. Both David and the Old Man felt it.

At the bottom of Lansdown Road the suspects crossed the street. Then, at the corner of George and Broad, they touched fists and separated. One maybe-Balson went right, toward Milsom Street, pulling up the hood of his green jacket. The other headed a few steps down Broad and turned into the newsagent's there.

The Old Man pointed for David to take the first of the two. David grinned and lifted the camera suspended from his neck to show that it was ready for action. He gave a wave and headed down George Street past the Royal York Hotel.

David's camera reminded the Old Man to get his out too, and turn it on. Position it to be handy to take a picture. Just point and push the button. Not like the old days, with light meter and focus. Pictures were easy now with the high tech. And digital – though always you used your fingers, so it was an odd name for them to choose. Plus there was the video feature so who needed a camcorder?

The Old Man moved to the door of the newsagent's, ready to go in. But instead he had to stand back and make way as his maybe-Balson came out with a *Chronicle*. This maybe-Balson turned toward town and didn't even say thank you. Huh!

But then, only a couple of shops down the street, the young man turned left into an alley. The Old Man followed, though he already knew what the shortcut led to. The entrance of the YMCA.

David felt simultaneously obvious and invisible as he followed his maybe-Balson. If the guy had *any* awareness of the people around him as he turned down Milsom Street, he'd *have* to know that David was tailing him. But at the same time there were tons of young people out on the pavements – it *was* a Saturday in Bath, after all, and Milsom Street was famous for shopping. So why should anyone single him out?

'Hey, Davy!'

What? What? 'What?'

'I said hello.' The speaker was Linzi, a girl from school. One of Marie's friends.

'Hi, hi, Linzi.'

'What are you up to, little man? Hey, *look* at me when I'm talking to you.'

'Sorry, sorry. But I'm working.' David strained to find his maybe-Balson down the street.

Linzi was not tiny in any case, but seeing that David was looking past her, she moved to obstruct his view. 'You. *Working*? At what?'

David moved again and was able to see that his suspect had also stopped walking. Maybe-Balson appeared to be making a call. 'You know what our family does,' David said to Linzi. 'I'm working on a case with my grandfather. I'm sorry. Really I am. But I have to go.' He stepped past the surprised girl.

But then David stopped. Linzi *was* Gwenny Morton's older sister, and Gwenny was *fit*. *And* she laughed at his joke in maths on Friday. He turned back to Linzi, trying to think of some additional way to save the situation. He wouldn't want Linzi telling Gwenny something to make her think badly of him.

But Linzi now had her phone out and was dialling. When she saw David look back at her she waved it at him. 'I'm calling Marie. I'm going to tell her you were *so rude*.' She turned her back.

David was stricken. He twisted to find his maybe-Balson, who was still nearby, talking to someone. Then back to Linzi. But finally he decided that Linzi must be sacrificed. He was at work, after all.

* * *

The Old Man followed his own maybe-Balson through the YMCA's automatic doors, and down the stairs that led to the Health and Fitness Studio. He watched as the young man presented his membership card to the gym's scanner and it was beeped in. Then the maybe-Balson went to the locker board and took the key to locker 41. He left his card in the slot on the board that matched it, and headed for the changing rooms.

The Old Man felt a hand on his shoulder. He turned and found Guru Mick. 'How you doin', buddy?'

'Me? Doing?'

'Not working out today?'

'Uh, no.'

'So what can we do for you?' Guru Mick touched the camera hanging from the Old Man's neck. 'Taking pictures of us? So your grandson can see what it's like here?'

'That's it.'

'Wouldn't it be easier to bring him in?'

'You might not be here for him to see.'

'So, you want a picture of me?'

'Who else?' the Old Man said. 'Plus, my wife, who sent me here to become a muscleman. She should see who makes it happen.'

Guru Mick stepped back and struck a pose.

The Old Man lifted the camera, pointed it at Guru Mick, and clicked the button.

The flash attracted attention from the staff and members nearby. 'Come on!' Guru Mick called. 'Get in a picture.'

The Old Man watched in silence as a tableau of sweat, muscles and Lycra posed itself before him. Then, just as it was all about ready, a young man emerged from the changing rooms. He was wearing a red vest.

'Hey, Alistair,' Guru Mick called. 'Get into the picture!'

Alistair hesitated but Guru Mick dragged him to a position at the front of the group. 'On your knees, buddy.'

Alistair knelt.

'Now,' Guru Mick said, 'everybody say "cheese". Or is that not what you say in Italy, Mr L?'

'We say *formaggio*,' the Old Man said, his spirits suddenly high. He was about to have a picture of red vest Alistair's face. He couldn't have asked for better from this visit to the gym.

'*Formaggio*,' Guru Mick said. 'On three, then, everybody. Ready? One. Two...'

Click.

David was absolutely stricken. 'I am *so* sorry, Linzi.'

'Why are *you* sorry, David Lunghi? *You* didn't steal my phone – that perv did.' She wrinkled her face and glanced up the slope in the direction the thief had run.

David's eyes followed hers. The thief was gone. David lowered his camera.

'My dad is going to be *so* pissed off,' Linzi said. 'He tells me and tells me to be careful when I use it.' She shook her head. 'It was a birthday present.'

David couldn't think how to explain it all to her. Besides, his mind was on what he'd just witnessed.

'Although I must say,' Linzi said, turning her eyes on him, 'it didn't help that while I was trying to get through to Marie you were taking my picture.'

'It was a video.'

'You were *videoing* me?'

'Not you. It was—'

'I *know* when there's a camera pointed at me, David Lunghi. So do you secretly *looove* me? Is that it? Because *I* thought it was our Gwenny you fancy. *She* certainly thinks so. She told me all about the way you look at her during maths, how you're always offering to help her. What was it you wanted to *help* her with, little Davy?' Linzi laughed.

For all that he could tell Linzi's laughter was because she was upset, David felt his face flush like a beacon. 'Maybe...' he said. 'Well, I mean it's possible, maybe... I might be able to get it back for you.'

'Get what back?' Linzi frowned. 'My phone? How the hell could you do that?' She waved a hand behind her. 'He's gone. *It's* gone. I'm toast.'

'Well, the thing is, did you happen to notice the way he ran?'

'You are *so* weird.'

And then David's mobile phone began to ring. For Linzi that was just rubbing her nose in her loss. She turned away in a huff.

'Hello?' David said.

'David,' the Old Man said, 'you'll never believe.'

'Me too, Grandpa.'

'I have a picture, of the face.'

David frowned. 'Whose face?'

'Alistair Balson. He posed for my camera.'

'Where, Grandpa? Where are you?'

'The YMCA gym.'

'He's there *now*?' David tried to figure out how that could be. The YMCA was not far, and there *was* an alleyway shortcut, past the Vintage to Vogue second-hand clothes shop, but still...

'How else do I take a picture? Of course he's here, ever since I followed him.'

'Grandpa, are you saying that the guy *you* followed is Alistair Balson?'

'Is something wrong with your ears? I just said. Huh!'

'Because, Grandpa, I'm on Milsom Street.'

'Good. Not far.'

'And I've just seen *my* Balson steal a phone.'

'Your Balson stole?'

'And he ran away, Grandpa. And he was dishing as he ran. I've never seen *anybody* run like that before.'

David and his grandfather stood together, watching the treadmills. 'You see?' the Old Man said. 'You see how he runs?'

'Yes,' David said.

'This one knocks his knees but he's no disher.'

'My Balson was definitely the disher,' David said.

The Old Man nodded in agreement. When David arrived at the gym he'd played the short video he'd made with his digital camera. The whole thing was only about thirty seconds, and some of it was blurry from the excitement of reacting to a theft that was happening before his very eyes. But for four or five seconds David had caught images of the fleeing thief that were clear enough to confirm the weird style of running.

'So what do we do now, Grandpa?' David asked as they watched the gym Alistair Balson.

'Guru Mick called this knock-knee Alistair, but not Balson. Could there be two Alistairs?'

'Good thought,' David said.

The Old Man considered. Then he said, 'Come,' and he led

David away from the treadmills to the locker board. He took out the card that was slotted beneath the hook marked 41. 'Huh!'

'What, Grandpa?'

'Look for yourself.'

David looked. It was the membership card for 'Jeremy Coates'. 'Grandpa?'

'Yet Guru Mick calls this runner, "Alistair."'

It took a few minutes to prise Guru Mick away from a blonde who was doing lat pulldowns. When they did, he greeted David with enthusiasm. 'So this is your grandson, Mr L? Hi, buddy. Want to put a few muscles on? Impress the girls?' Guru Mick patted David on a shoulder.

The idea of building muscles struck David silent momentarily.

'Shy, eh?' Guru Mick said. 'Your grandpa told me about that.'

The Old Man said, 'For now, it's something else we're here for.'

'What's that, Mr L?'

'The red vest on that treadmill.' The Old Man pointed across the gym. 'You called him Alistair.'

'Yeah, Alistair...Balson.' Guru Mick's face lit up. 'Oh, right. Alistair Balson is the name we found yesterday, isn't it?' He looked at David. 'A gym pal for you, buddy.'

'It's the name,' the Old Man said, 'but not the same person. Because at his locker he leaves the card of somebody else.' The Old Man showed Guru Mick the card he had taken from the slot for locker 41.

'But I know Alistair's a member,' Guru Mick said. 'I

processed his membership myself.' He looked at the card. 'Jeremy Coates. Well, Jeremy's a member too. They came in together.' He looked across the gym to where the red vested runner was knocking his knees on a treadmill. He scratched his head. 'He's using Alistair's card?'

From his silence, David suddenly burst into life. 'I've got it, Grandpa. I've got it!'

Saturday night was not usually a meal at which the whole of the Lunghi family gathered, but Mama was so proud that she summoned everyone and made this Saturday an exception. Even Salvatore came, although later he had a date with a model.

Over pizzas from Bottelino's Gina, Angelo and Rosetta sat rapt as Mama drew out the story that led to the arrests that had followed David's deduction. Even Marie paid attention.

'So from the YMCA you went where?' Mama said.

'To the police station,' David said. 'And from there they took us along when they went to the flat in Upper Hedgemead Road.'

'We were the only ones who could identify,' the Old Man said. 'Since these police don't identify from running, no matter how you explain it to them.'

'But they made us stay in a car while they raided the flat,' David said.

'And how many arrests from your work on the Jane case?' Mama asked rhetorically, and with pride.

'Two, Grandma,' David said. 'Alistair Balson and Jeremy Coates.' He glanced at his grandfather. 'Balson was the disher. Coates knocked his knees.'

'Two arrests so far,' the Old Man said. 'But they'll talk,

these phone thieves. They'll implicate the people they sell the phones on to.'

'They were raising money for equipment,' David said. 'They had a band.'

'Cyber… elastic, or something,' the Old Man said. 'Huh! They've never heard of work for money?'

'*My* men know about work,' Mama said. 'Good work.'

'So did the police recover the phone that started all this?' Rosetta asked.

'Not Jane's,' the Old Man said.

'But four others,' David said. He glanced at Marie. 'Including Linzi's. She won't get it back right away, but she will eventually.'

'And I bet you want to be the one to ring and tell her,' Marie said.

David flushed. 'She was very upset. It's a matter of common courtesy, really.'

'Pity about the pimple on your nose, little David. Gwenny won't be impressed by that.'

David felt his nose. Marie laughed. Mama asked, 'Who is this Gwenny?'

'Nobody,' David said.

'*You're* the nobody,' Marie said.

'Hush, Marie,' Gina said. 'It's been a good day. David and his grandfather did well.'

'So tell me about the gym,' Salvatore said, looking to his father. 'These thieves each trained at the gym, but used the other's membership card when they went?'

'Their idea was it would give an alibi,' the Old Man said. 'Suppose someone thinks he recognises a thief who runs away. With the card scanned at the YMCA, the thief can say, "I was at the gym when your phone was stolen." He can say, "I can prove it." That's what the disher said to Jane.'

'The computer at the Y shows whose card was scanned and the time,' David said. 'But there's no way to tell whether you're scanning in your *own* card.'

'They go to the gym, these thieves,' the Old Man said. 'They always wear red vests. So who can tell this one rather than that one among so many exercising people?'

'Hardly cast iron,' Angelo said.

'But when they were stealing they wore jackets with hoods,' David said. 'That would make it harder for someone to see a face anyway.'

'It ends up one person's word against another's,' the Old Man said, 'and then the computer alibi could make the difference. Who would prosecute? Who would convict without other evidence?'

'Plus,' David said, 'when one was out stealing, the other was running on the treadmill, to keep in training for running away.'

Angelo scratched his head. 'But they never figured somebody would identify the way they *ran*. Well…Well done, Papa.'

'And well done the Jane,' the Old Man said. 'She did it first.'

'And well done David, who got it on the camera,' Rosetta said.

'So, little Davy,' Marie said, 'you going to call Jane too? Tell her the good news?'

David flushed more deeply than ever. 'Well, it really would be no more than common courtesy.'

Kevin Wignall
Retrospective

There was more death and misery in this room than was fit for any civilised place. Mutilated bodies, the diseased and the starving, the fearful and the grief-stricken; and all those empty eyes, the haunted and expressionless faces – it was all here, and it was all his.

Tomorrow night, the Dorchester Street Gallery would open its doors and the celebrities and art world players would get their vicarious thrills as they socialised and flirted and exchanged business cards over wine and morsels amid the horror of his life's work.

Most of his life's work, at any rate; the landscape photographs of recent years had been shunted off into one small side gallery. He didn't mind that, either, conscious of the fact that the landscapes hadn't earned him this retrospective.

When people thought of Jonathan Hoyle, they thought of the images that had been used to fill both the two large gallery spaces and the big fat accompanying catalogue. For nearly twenty years, he'd produced these iconic photographs of the world's war zones and he suspected he was alone in seeing what he'd done. Far from exposing the truth, he'd reduced human tragedy to the level of pornography, or worse, for pornographers were at least honest.

He heard a noise behind him and turned to see the young gallery assistant approaching. Her name was Sophie, he thought, and she looked pretty and mousy in the moneyed way of gallery assistants. If he were a different type of photographer, he'd be trying to seduce her into sitting for him.

'Having a final look around, Mr Hoyle?'

He wasn't sure how to respond, so he said, 'Please, call me Jon.'

'Thank you.' She blushed, and again, he thought maybe he should move from his current obsession to the landscape of the female body. 'It's a bit cheeky of me, I know, but do you think you could sign my copy of the catalogue?'

He looked at the catalogue in her hand and his thoughts crumbled into dust. There was the dead Palestinian boy whose picture had once appeared on newspaper front pages the world over. The gallery had offered him a choice of two photographs for the cover and he'd opted for this one without a second thought, but it still depressed him to see it.

'Of course.' He took the catalogue and the pen she proffered. 'It's Sophie, isn't it?' She nodded and he wrote a simple inscription, thanking her for all her help.

She studied it, apparently happy with the personal touch, then looked at the cover and said, 'It's such a beautiful picture, incredibly moving.' She looked up at him again and said, 'Why did you stop... I mean, why didn't you take any more war photographs after this one?'

He sighed. These questions would always haunt him. The life he'd lived, the person he'd been, out there on the ragged edges of the world, it would always get in the way of the simpler things. You're a pretty girl, he wanted to say, I'd like to go for a drink with you and talk about art, and I'd like to see you naked. But she was right, the Palestinian boy had been the last.

'I stopped because I'd finally captured the truth; there was nothing left to say after that.'

She smiled, uncertain, as if she feared he might be teasing her. 'But your photographs are *all* about the truth.'

'Are they?' She didn't know how to respond. 'Goodnight, Sophie, I'll see you tomorrow evening.' He drifted toward the door, enigma intact, almost self-satisfied.

It was already dark and there was a cold wind picking up, but he decided to walk back to the hotel, wanting to clear his head out there on the streets. As he stepped outside though, he was faced with a black Range Rover, tinted windows, a young guy in a suit waiting by one of the rear doors.

'Evening, Mr Hoyle. Your car.' He was Australian, like most of the people keeping London's service economy afloat. The guy opened the door in readiness for him.

Jon was about to tell him that he felt like walking, but stopped himself and said, 'My car? No one ordered a car for me.'

If he'd had a moment longer he might have figured that the guy's suit was a little too expensive to suggest a chauffeur. He didn't have time though. Before he'd even finished speaking, the guy had produced a gun from somewhere, a silencer already attached. He was pointing it at Jon, but holding it in a casual, almost non-threatening way.

'Get in the car, mate. I don't wanna have to kill you here, but I will.'

The thought of running had died even before it was fully formed. He remembered seeing that French journalist getting shot in Somalia, remembered how sudden and arbitrary it had been – one minute talking to the soldiers, the next crumpled in the dust, oozing blood. There was no running, and he felt bad because, right at this moment, he couldn't remember that French journalist's name, even though he'd drunk with him a couple of times.

Jon got in the back of the Range Rover and the young guy got in after him, closing the door.

'OK, let's go.' Another guy was in the driving seat but it was soon clear the car belonged to the gunman. They lurched forward, nearly clipping another parked car, and the Australian said, 'Mate, if you scratch my bloody paintwork!' He turned to Jon then and said, 'Gotta blindfold you.' He put the blindfold on, tying it behind Jon's head, surprisingly gentle. 'How's that feel?'

'OK, I suppose, under the circumstances.'

'Yeah, sorry about that. The name's Dan, Dan Borowski.' Bizarrely, Jon felt him take his hand and shake it like he was introducing himself to a blind man. And it was bizarre mainly because he knew this was it; whoever they were, they were going to kill him.

I don't wanna have to kill you here, that's what the guy had said, and he'd given his full name, which meant he saw no danger because he was talking to a dead man. He couldn't help but be amused by the irony of it, that he'd travelled unscathed through every impression of hell the world had to offer, only to die in London.

'You're gonna kill me.'

He waited for the voice, and when it came it was a little regretful. 'Yeah. Client wants to meet you first, but your number's up. I'm sorry.'

'Why? I mean, why does he want me dead?'

'Didn't say.' His tone was casual again. 'Gotta be something to do with your work though, don't you think?'

Jon nodded. He was surprised how calm he felt. He wondered if experienced pilots felt like this when their planes finally took a nosedive, if they serenely embraced the void, knowing they'd defied it too long already.

Jon didn't want pain, but he could imagine this guy, Dan, making it easy for him anyway; he was clearly a professional killer, not like some of the monstrous amateurs he'd seen parading around in their makeshift uniforms. He didn't want to die either, but he'd tap-danced around death for so long, he could hardly complain now as it reached out to rest its hand upon his shoulder.

He was curious though, trying to think which aspect of his work had angered someone so much that, even now, a few years after he'd stopped being a war photographer, they were still determined to kill him for it. It couldn't be for offending some cause or other.

He could only imagine this being a personal bitterness, the result of a photograph that had so intruded on someone else's grief or suffering that this seemed a justifiable retribution. That ruled out the landscapes, but not much else.

He supposed a lot of the people who knew and loved the subjects of his photographs would have killed him if they'd had the means. The fact that this person clearly had been able to hire a contract killer perhaps narrowed it down a little further. It made the Balkans, the Middle East and Central America more likely as the source. It hardly mattered though; whoever it was, whichever photograph, they were striking a blow for all the unknown families.

'You *are* a contract killer, I take it.'

'Among other things,' said Dan.

Jon was already getting attuned to having no visuals to fall back on, and although Dan had fallen silent again, he could sense that he had more to say. Sure enough, after a couple more beats, a stop at traffic lights, a left turn, Dan spoke again.

'You know, in a way, you and I are a lot alike. Our jobs, anyway.'

Jon laughed and said, 'I'm cynical about the work I do, but that's a bit rich. I photograph death. In a strange way, I think I sanitise it, but at least I can hold my hands up and say I've never caused it.'

There was a slight pause, during which Jon realised he'd talked in the present tense, even though it was a while now since he'd photographed the overspill of war. Dan seemed fixed on something else, the distraction audible in his voice as he said, 'I'm picking up some negative vibes here, like you're dismissing the work you've produced. I've gotta tell you, Jon, you're wrong about that. You're a great photographer, and it's a document of our times, good or bad.'

'Well, we'll have to agree to differ on that.'

'No way!' He laughed as if they were old friends disagreeing over favourite teams or dream dates. 'Seriously, I'm such a fan of your work. I've even got the book of landscapes. It was one of the reasons I agreed to this job.'

It was Jon's turn to laugh. 'You agreed to kill me for money because you're such a fan of my work! Well thanks, I'm touched.'

Another pause, and Dan's response was subdued, even a little hurt. 'The contract would have gone to someone else, anyway. I took the job because I wanted to meet you, and I wanted to make sure it was done right.'

He couldn't ignore the final point because it was what he'd hoped for, that he wouldn't let him suffer. And maybe another man, certainly one in another profession, wouldn't have looked at his own killer's intentions in quite the same way, but Jon *was* touched by the sentiment now that he thought about it.

'Thanks, Dan. I do appreciate that, and I know if it hadn't been you, it would have been someone else.'

'Yeah, it's too bad.'

'You didn't say how we were similar.'

He was relaxed again, almost cheery as he said, 'I just meant the way we go into areas, not just geographical areas, you know, areas of the human condition that most people don't ever experience. We drop in, I do what I've been paid to do, you get your picture, and we're back out again, onto the next little screw-up.'

'I still don't see it. From my point of view, you're part of the problem. I may not be part of the solution, but at least I'm letting the world know what's really happening.'

Dan laughed and said, 'See, we're already getting somewhere; you're looking at your own work in a more positive light.' The car stopped and the engine was turned off. For the first time, Jon felt a nervous twitching in his stomach. 'We're here.'

Dan helped him out of the car, a brief reminder of the cold night air, a coldness he wanted to savour, to fill his lungs with it like he was about to swim underwater for a long time. They walked through a door and it was still cold but no longer fresh, then up several flights of stone steps.

At the top, they walked through another door and then Dan took off the blindfold. They were in a large loft which looked as if it had only recently stopped being used as a factory or workspace. No doubt its next reincarnation would be as a couple of fabulous apartments, and neither of the new owners would ever imagine that it had been the scene of an execution.

There were two chairs in the middle of the floor, facing

each other, a few yards apart. He noticed too, over to one side, what looked like a picture under a sheet, resting against a pillar. Jon wondered if that was it, the evidence of his crime, the photograph that had cost him his life.

He'd seen that happen to other photographers, their determination to get the ultimate shot drawing them too far into the open. It felt now like a stray bullet had hit him sometime in the last twenty years, the day he'd taken that picture, whatever it was, and ever since, he'd simply been waiting to fall.

'Take a seat. We shouldn't have to wait long.'

'Will you do it here?' Dan looked around the room as if weighing up its suitability. He nodded. Jon pointed at the picture under the sheet. 'Is that the photograph under there? Is that why he wants me dead?'

'I don't know, but you'll find out soon enough. Best you just sit down.'

Dan sat on one of the chairs so Jon took the other. He took a good look at Dan now. He looked young but he was probably thirty, maybe older, good looking in that healthy Australian way, and his face was familiar somehow, but then, Jon had seen so many faces in his life, they all ended up looking a little familiar.

Suddenly, he thought of the blindfold. He had no idea which part of London they were in, though they hadn't driven far. But if he was definitely to be killed, he couldn't understand why he'd had to be blindfolded.

'Does this guy definitely want me dead? There's no way out of it?'

Dan shook his head regretfully and said, 'Why do you ask?'

'The blindfold. If he definitely wants me dead, I can't

understand why I had to be blindfolded.'

'He's just really cautious. And he doesn't know that when I bring someone in, they stay in.'

'How much is he paying you?'

Dan smiled and offered the briefest shake of his head. He stared at Jon for a while then, still smiling, intrigued, and finally said, 'I don't suppose you recognise me?'

'Your face is vaguely familiar, but I don't know where from.'

'You took my picture once.' He could see the look of surprise on Jon's face and waited for it to sink in before adding, 'Not only that – it's in the exhibition.'

'I... I don't remember.'

'Yes you do. Near the Congo-Rwandan border. You were taking pictures of the refugees escaping the fighting. Remember, there were thousands of them, just this silent broken river of people pouring over the border. I walked past you, didn't think anything of it. Then I see the picture, all those refugees walking towards the camera, me walking away from it.'

Jon shook his head, astonished, because he did remember now. He'd been taking shots for an hour or more, never quite feeling he'd captured what he was after. Then a Western soldier had walked past him in black combats, heavily armed but still looking suicidally ill-equipped for where he was heading, a war zone of mind-altering barbarity. That was his picture, another one which had been dubbed iconic.

And the amazing thing was, he'd seen him again, five days later, back in the hotel. He'd recognised him just from his easy confident gait, from his build, the cut of his hair. Jon had asked someone who he was and he'd been told he was a mercenary, that he'd gone in for the German government and brought out some aid workers who'd been taken by the guerrillas. It had always intrigued him, that a man could walk so casually into hell and still come back.

'You saved those German aid workers.'

Dan shrugged and said, 'I saved three of them. One had already been killed by the time I got there. Another died on the way out.'

'I've always wondered about that. Weren't you scared at all, going in there, knowing what was happening?'

'No,' he said, smiling dismissively.

'I've been to some pretty freaky places, but I would have been scared going in there.'

'That's because you only had a camera. I was armed; I knew I could handle it. I didn't know I could get them out alive, I was nervous about that, but I knew I could handle a few drug-crazed guerrillas.'

'So you're not just a contract killer.'

'No, like I said, I do all kinds of stuff. But don't paint me like Mother Teresa – I got paid more for bringing those people out of the jungle than you probably got paid in five years.'

'At least you brought them out. You saved someone; it's more than I ever did.'

'It wasn't your job to save people.'

'It wasn't my job, but it was my duty as a human being. I used to look at some of these people and think they were savages, and yet I'd watch people dying and worry about things like light and exposure.' Dan was shaking his head, the blanket disagreement of a true fan. 'Tell me something, if you'd been in the jungle and stumbled across those hostages, would you have left them there to die? It wouldn't have been your job to save them, no payment, but would you?'

'Yeah, I probably would have had a go.'

'That's the difference, Dan. You may be a cold-blooded killer, but you're still human. I never saved anyone.'

Dan seemed to turn it over for a few seconds and then said, 'You know, certain times of year, if a croc finds a baby turtle on the river bank, it'll scoop it up in its mouth, take it down to the water and let it go. See, they're programmed to help newly hatched crocs, so they just help anything small that's moving toward the water. Six months later, that croc, he'll still kill that turtle.'

Jon wondered if that was true, but was struck then by something else. 'I don't follow. What's your point?'

Dan laughed and said, 'I have absolutely no bloody idea!'

Jon laughed too and then they were both silenced as the street door down below opened and closed and heavy steps worked laboriously toward them. Jon expected to feel nervous again, but if anything, their conversation had left him even more prepared. Maybe the nerves would come again later, but with any luck, he wouldn't have too long to think about it.

Dan stood up now, but gestured for Jon to stay where he was, and as if the approaching man were already in earshot, he said quietly, 'You know, if there'd been any other way...'

'Don't. And I'm glad I met you, too. I was always curious about the guy in that photograph.'

Dan nodded and walked over to the door as it opened and a heavy-set guy in his fifties walked in. He was balding, wearing an expensive grey suit, an open collar. At first, Jon had him down as an Eastern European, but he quickly realised the guy was an Arab.

The guy looked across, a mixture of disdain and satisfaction, but spoke to Dan for a minute or two in hushed tones. Their conversation seemed relaxed, as if they were filling each other in on what had happened recently, and when it was over, Dan nodded and left.

The client walked across the room without looking at him, picked up the picture under its sheet and placed it on the chair facing Jon. He walked around the chair and stood behind it, finally allowing himself to make eye contact.

'You are Jonathan Hoyle.' His voice was deep, the accent giving it an added gravitas. 'May I call you Jonathan?'

'People call me Jon.'

He gave a little nod and said, 'So, Jon, do you know anyone called Nabil?' Jon shook his head. 'It's my name. I am Nabil. It was also my son's name. I know you don't have children, so I also know that you don't understand what it is to lose a child. And I know you don't understand what it is for your dead child's photograph to be made into a piece of art, bought and sold, put on the covers of books. I know you don't understand any of this.' There was no anger in his words; they were no more than statements of fact. And Jon couldn't question them so he remained silent. 'That is what I know about you. And this is what I know about me. I know that killing you tonight will not bring my son back and will not ease my pain. Indeed, the pain may become worse because your death will bring even more interest to your work, but still, I must insist on your death. First, I want you to look again at my son's photograph, knowing his name, knowing...'

He stopped, suddenly overcome, and took a deep breath. Jon lowered his gaze slightly, not wanting to stare at this man who was still so visibly torn by grief. He heard the sheet being pulled away, saw it drop to the floor, and a part of him didn't want to look up, because he had a feeling he knew which picture it would be, and the memory of it was already making him feel sick.

'Look at my son, Mr Hoyle. Jon, look at my son.'

He looked up. There was the print of the Palestinian boy, blown-up life-size. His name had been Nabil and he'd been fourteen years old and now Jon could think of no good reason why he shouldn't die tonight.

The boy's father wasn't crying but he had the look of a man who had no more tears left, a man who'd been beaten by life and was spent. Jon thought of all the times over the last four years that this man had chanced upon that picture and had the wound torn afresh.

Jon knew something of that, because he'd experienced it too. He'd seen the picture pulled from image libraries and used to illustrate newspaper and magazine stories – no context, no explanation, just a cynical, exploitative pathos.

He'd been fêted for that photograph; and yet, as ambivalent as he'd been about it, as much as its appearance had made jagged shards of his memory, he'd never once given thought to the boy's family. He could see it now, of course, how they'd probably come to hate him even more than the unknown Israeli soldier whose bullet had killed Nabil that day in Gaza.

'Do you have anything to say?'

'That was the last photograph I ever took in a war zone.'

Nabil laughed a little, incredulous as he said, 'That's not much of a defence.'

'I don't have any defence. It isn't right for you to kill me, but I can make no sound argument for sparing me. If it means anything, if it offers any comfort, I'm sorry.'

Nabil nodded once, almost like a bow of his head. Jon wanted it over with now, he wanted Dan to come back into the room and end it, but Nabil looked contemplative, as if he was still dwelling upon something and wanted to ask another question. He suddenly became grim and determined though, and started toward the door.

Jon felt his stomach tighten into a spasm, his blood spinning out of control with adrenaline, a mixture of fear and of self-loathing, knowing that it was wrong to leave it like this, without at least telling him the truth. 'Nabil.' Nabil stopped and turned to look at him. Jon felt ashamed because he knew it looked like he was stalling, and he wasn't; his nerves were for something else, for the things he wanted to say for the first time. He wanted to offer this man something more than a trite apology, and he wanted to get something off his own conscience before he died. 'Before you call Dan back in, I want to tell you something about the day your son died. It won't change anything, but I want to tell you anyway.'

Nabil's expression was unyielding, but he walked back toward the chair and stood a few paces behind it. 'Go on.'

Jon took a couple of deep breaths, looked at the photograph again, then at Nabil. 'I took a lot of good photographs that day, and in the days before. You remember how volatile it was at that time, almost like there was something unstable in the air.'

'I remember.'

'So I was there, and there were Palestinian boys, young men, throwing stones at an Israeli patrol. I saw your son.'

Nabil prickled defensively and said, 'Yet you have no pictures of him throwing stones.'

'Because he wasn't throwing stones. Like a lot of people those days, he was just trying to get from one place to another without getting caught up in it. He didn't look scared, he just looked like a kid who was used to it, confident, almost carefree.' He looked at the photograph in front of him and wished, as he had many times, that he'd captured that carefree face as a counterpoint. 'I wasn't even wasting film at that point. Stone throwing, that was just becoming routine. Then someone started firing on the soldiers and one of them got hit. They fired back and one of the stone throwers took a bullet in the shoulder. I got some good pictures of his friends helping him, this hive of activity and this dazed, strangely calm kid in the middle of it all. There were a couple of other photographers with me. And within another ten minutes it was all over. I was walking away on my own when I saw blood on the floor. I walked around the corner, into the yard of a house that had been bombed the week before, and I saw the body lying there. I recognised him right away, the kid I'd seen earlier. I guessed he'd been hit by a stray bullet, had managed to drag himself into the yard. He looked so young, and all the clichés were there – he looked peaceful, his face angelic, and the only thing that went through my mind at that moment, was that I knew this photograph would make front pages all around the world. I took it, just one shot, and I knew I'd got it, the bloody hole in the side of his chest, the angelic face. I felt satisfied. I'm ashamed to say that, but I did, I felt like I'd found that day's star prize. And then the strangest thing happened. I kept looking through the lens, looking at his face, and I just knew something wasn't right, somehow. It took a moment, but I saw it in the end.' He got up out of his chair and walked toward the picture. Nabil glanced at the door, as if ready to shout, but Jon kept his course. He picked up the picture and turned it for Nabil to see. 'This is the truest photograph I ever took, and it's a fake. It shows a dead Palestinian boy, your son, but when this photograph was taken, the boy wasn't dead.'

Nabil looked at him, surprised and yet wary, as if suspecting an attempt to earn his forgiveness. Jon didn't want that though, and wasn't even sure whether it was in this Nabil's power to grant it. He wanted only to tell the truth of how this photograph had been taken.

'Remember, I told you this won't change anything. The circumstances matter to me, but it doesn't change a thing.'

'Please, continue.'

Jon nodded and said, 'I knelt down beside him and checked for a pulse, but I didn't need to. As soon as my hand touched his neck, his eyes opened, and he started to mutter something, very quietly, like he was afraid we'd be overheard. I knew he was really bad.' Jon shook his head, the memory of his own helplessness briefly overpowering him again. 'I just didn't know what to do, and in the distance I could hear the Israeli armoured cars and I thought, if I could just get out to them, they'd have a medic with them, or there might be an ambulance. I put my camera down and I went to leave, but he grabbed my arm and I couldn't understand what he was saying but I could see it in his face, that he didn't want me to go, and I knew he was dying and there was nothing I could do. The injury was bad. He'd lost a lot of blood. And he looked so alone – I'd never noticed that before. So I just held his hand and I looked at him. I was muttering back to him, telling him I was still there.' Jon could feel tears in his eyes, but they weren't stacked up enough to run down onto his cheeks, and he didn't want them to because he didn't want any sympathy. 'I couldn't save him. All the horrors I've witnessed, all the death and mutilation, but I didn't know how to save that boy.'

Nabil was staring at him blankly, overcome with the onslaught of new information about his son's death.

'You stayed with him? Till he died?'

'It wasn't long after that. It was almost like he'd been waiting for someone to find him, so that he didn't die alone. And he didn't die alone, I gave him that much, but another person could have saved him, I'm sure of it. That's why I stopped being a war photographer.'

'Because you watched my son die?'

'I've seen plenty of kids die. No, it was because I had the illusion of detachment snatched away from me, and once you've lost that, you never get it back.' Jon put the picture back on the chair and took one last look at it. He was glad it was over. 'You can call Dan in now. I'm ready.'

Without looking at him, Nabil walked across to the door and opened it. Jon could see Dan sitting on the top step outside. He jumped up and by the time he came into the room, his gun was already in his hand. It would be quick, Jon told himself, and it would be done.

Dan looked at Nabil, surprised that he was still there, and said, 'Wouldn't you prefer to leave first?'

'No, but there's no need for the gun. You can take him back.'

Dan shrugged, expressing no emotional response, no disappointment, no relief, and said simply, 'You do realise this doesn't change anything?'

He was talking about the fee and Nabil nodded and said,

'Of course, and I'm sorry if I've wasted your time.'

'Time's never wasted,' said Dan, smiling.

Nabil finally looked at Jon again. 'It's some comfort that you were with my son in his final moments, but that isn't why I'm sparing you. I was determined to kill the man who took that picture because I knew he had absolutely no understanding of what he'd done by taking it. I was wrong. I see now, you did understand.'

'That once, I understood. But there are thousands of mothers and fathers out there to whom I could offer no answers, none at all.'

The grieving father in front of him said no more. He offered Jon his hand, and when he shook it, he was surprised to find his own palm clammy and Nabil's dry as parchment. Nabil must have given some slight signal then, because Dan touched Jon on the elbow and the two of them left.

He looked back before descending the stairs. Nabil was sitting in the chair he'd occupied himself, and he was staring at the picture of his son, broken, the universe refusing to reform itself around him. Jon wished he could go back in there and say something else to comfort him, but he'd already given him everything he had.

The driver had gone, and Dan drove back with Jon in the passenger seat. He still didn't recognise this part of London. At first neither of them spoke, but after a few minutes, Dan said, 'What the bloody hell happened back there?'

'I don't know.' Jon tried to think back, but all he could think of was Dan coming in with his gun already drawn, then his insistence on getting his fee. 'You would have killed me, wouldn't you? I mean, you wouldn't have given it a second thought.'

'Of course. But I thought I explained all of that. I wouldn't have been killing *you*, Jonathan Hoyle, I just would have been hitting a target.'

Jon smiled. He could imagine this guy being completely untroubled by what he did, sleeping well, walking lightly through the world. He'd been like that himself once, and maybe Dan's moment would also come, but he doubted it somehow.

He'd killed people, he'd saved people, he'd inhabited the same world as Jon, and on at least one occasion, they'd even crossed paths. But Dan Borowski was a natural in that world, someone who wore death easily and saw it for what it was.

No doubt if Dan had found the young Nabil dying in the ruins, he'd have known what to do. If the boy could have been saved, Dan would have left him and gone for help. If he couldn't, Dan would have stayed with him, just as Jon had, but when it was all done, he'd have left it behind.

'When you were talking earlier, about our jobs being similar, you missed something.'

Dan glanced over, casually curious, and said, 'What's that?'

'The need to detach what you're doing from the individual on the end of it – your target, my subject.'

Dan nodded, and at first it didn't look like he'd respond further, but then he said, 'I wonder how many people around the world have died since I picked you up earlier. Hundreds? Thousands? It doesn't matter. None of those lives matter to us. If I'd killed you tonight, the vast majority of the world's population wouldn't have even known about it. If I die tomorrow, it won't matter to anyone. So you see, it's just not worth thinking about. I live well, and that's enough for me. Should be enough for you too.'

Jon nodded, even though he felt like he needed a few minutes to work out what Dan had just said – on first pass, it wasn't much clearer than the crocodile story. Then he realised that they'd turned into Dorchester Street and a moment later Dan had pulled up outside the gallery.

'Oh, God, sorry mate, I've brought you back to the gallery. I'll take you to the hotel.'

'No, this is fine, really. After everything that's happened, I could use the fresh air.'

Dan laughed and said, 'I bet!' He looked serious then as he added, 'It's been a pleasure, Jon, and for what it's worth, I think you handled yourself really bloody well. Not many people would've stayed calm like that.'

'I had nothing to lose.' He smiled and said, 'So long, Dan.'

'You take care now.'

Jon got out of the car and watched as Dan pulled away. He heard his name then and turned to see Sophie coming out of the gallery, her coat on, bag over her shoulder, catalogue under one arm. She managed to lock the door without putting anything on the floor, then walked over to him.

'Hi, what are you still doing here?'

'Long story. I was somewhere else, and then I got dropped off here by mistake.' She smiled, showing interest, the slightly awkward way people did when they felt they had to be interested but weren't really. 'Sorry, don't let me keep you. I'm sure you wanna get home.'

'No, it's fine. I don't have anything to rush back for.' Maybe he needed to go back to photographing people in some form or other because it seemed he'd read her completely wrong.

'Well, I'm only heading back to the hotel – would you like to come back for dinner?'

She looked staggered, maybe even suspecting he wasn't serious, as she said, 'I'd love to, but do you mind? The general word is that you don't care for company.'

'I never used to.'

They started to walk and he couldn't help but smile. A contract killer named Dan Borowski had shot him in the head this evening, a death he'd accepted, even embraced – from now on, everything else was a gift.

'It is so obvious who killed poor Brother Síoda that it worries me.'

Sister Fidelma stared in bewilderment at the woebegone expression of the usually smiling, cherubic features of Abbot Laisran.

'I do not understand you, Laisran,' she told her old mentor, pausing in the act of sipping her mulled wine. She was sitting in front of a blazing fire in the hearth of the abbot's chamber in the great Abbey of Durrow. On the adjacent side of the fireplace, Abbot Laisran sat in his chair, his wine left abandoned on the carved oak table by his side. He was staring moodily into the leaping flames.

'Something worries me about the simplicity of this matter. There are some things in life that appear so simple that you get a strange feeling about them. You question whether things can be so simple and, sure enough, you often find that they are so simple because they have been made to appear simple. In this case, everything fits together so flawlessly that I question it.'

Fidelma drew a heavy sigh. She had only just arrived at Durrow to bring a Psalter, a book of Latin psalms written by her brother, Colgú, King of Cashel, as a gift for the abbot. But she had found her old friend Abbot Laisran in a preoccupied frame of mind. A member of his community had been murdered and the culprit had been easily identified as another member. Yet it was unusual to see Laisran so worried. Fidelma had known him since she was a little girl and it was he who had persuaded her to take up the study of *Anruth*, one degree below that of *Ollamh*, the highest rank of learning, it had been Laisran who had advised her to join a religious community on being accepted as a *dálaigh*, an advocate of the Brehon Court. He had felt that this would give her more opportunities in life.

Usually, Abbot Laisran was full of jollity and good humour. Anxiety did not sit well on his features for he was a short, rotund, red-faced man. He had been born with that rare gift of humour and a sense that the world was there to provide enjoyment to those who inhabited it. Now he appeared like a man on whose shoulders the entire troubles of the world rested.

'Perhaps you had better tell me all about it,' Fidelma invited. 'I might be able to give some advice.'

Laisran raised his head and there was a new expression of hope in his eyes.

'Any help you can give, Fidelma...truly, the facts are, as I say, lucid enough. But there is just something about them...' He paused and then shrugged. 'I'd be more than grateful to have your opinion.'

Fidelma smiled reassuringly.

'Then let us begin to hear some of these lucid facts.'

'Two days ago, Brother Síoda was found stabbed to death in his cell. He had been stabbed several times in the heart.'

'Who found him and when?'

'He had not appeared at morning prayers. So my steward, Brother Cruinn, went along to his cell to find out whether he was ill. Brother Síoda lay murdered on his bloodstained bed.'

Fidelma waited while the abbot paused, as if to gather his thoughts.

'We have, in the abbey, a young woman called Sister

Scáthach. She is very young. She joined us as a child because, so her parents told us, she heard things. Sounds in her head. Whispers. About a month ago, our physician became anxious about her state of health. She had become...' He paused as if trying to think of the right word. 'She believed she was hearing voices instructing her.'

Fidelma raised her eyebrows slightly in surprise.

Abbot Laisran saw the movement and grimaced.

'She has always been what one might call eccentric but the eccentricity has grown so that her behaviour has become bizarre. A month ago I placed her in a cell and asked one of the apothecary's assistants, Sister Sláine, to watch over her. Soon after Brother Síoda was found, the steward and I went to Sister Scáthach's cell. The door was always locked. It was a precaution we had recently adopted. Usually the key is hanging on a hook outside the door. But the key was on the inside and the door was locked. A bloodstained robe was found in her cell and a knife. The knife, too, was bloodstained. It was obvious that Sister Scáthach was guilty of this crime.'

Abbot Laisran stood up and went to a chest. He removed a knife whose blade was discoloured with dried blood. Then he drew forth a robe. It was clear that it had been stained in blood.

'Poor Brother Síoda,' murmured Laisran. 'His penetrated heart must have poured blood over the girl's clothing.'

Fidelma barely glanced at the robes.

'The first question I have to ask is why would you and the steward go straight from the murdered man's cell to that of Sister Scáthach?' she demanded.

Abbot Laisran compressed his lips for a moment.

'Because only the day before the murder Sister Scáthach had prophesied his death and the manner of it.

'She made the pronouncement only twelve hours before his body was discovered, saying that he would die by having his heart ripped out.'

Fidelma folded her hands before her, gazing thoughtfully into the fire.

'She was violent then? You say you had her placed in a locked cell with a Sister to look after her?'

'But she was never violent before the murder,' affirmed the abbot.

'Yet she was confined to her cell?'

'A precaution, as I say. During these last four weeks she began to make violent prophecies. Saying voices instructed her to do so.'

'Violent prophecies but you say that she was not violent?' Fidelma's tone was sceptical.

'It is difficult to explain,' confessed Abbot Laisran. 'The words were violent but she was not. She was a gentle girl but she claimed that the shadows from the Otherworld gave her instructions; they told her to foretell the doom of the world, its destruction by fire and flood when mountains would be hurled into the sea and the seas rise up and engulf the land.'

Fidelma pursed her lips cynically.

'Such prophecies have been common since the dawn of time,' she observed.

'Such prophecies have alarmed the community here, Fidelma,' admonished Abbot Laisran. 'It was as much for her sake that I suggested Sister Sláine make sure that Sister Scáthach was secured in her cell each night and kept an eye upon each day.'

'Do you mean that you feared members of the community would harm Sister Scáthach rather than she harm members of the community?' queried Fidelma.

The abbot inclined his head.

'Some of these predictions were violent in the extreme, aimed at one or two particular members of the community, foretelling their doom, casting them into the everlasting hellfire.'

'You say that during the month she has been so confined, the pronouncements grew more violent.'

'The more she was constrained the more extreme the pronouncements became,' confessed the abbot.

'And she made just such a pronouncement against Brother Síoda? That is why you and your steward made the immediate link to Sister Scáthach?'

'It was.'

'Why did she attack Brother Síoda?' she asked. 'How well did she know him?'

'As far as I am aware, she did not know him at all. Yet when she made her prophecy, Brother Síoda told me that she seemed to know secrets about him that he thought no other person knew. He was greatly alarmed and said he would lock himself in that night so that no one could enter.'

'So his cell door was locked when your steward went there after he had failed to attend morning prayers?'

Abbot Laisran shook his head.

'When Brother Cruinn went to Síoda's cell, he found that the door was shut but not locked. The key was on the floor inside his cell...this is the frightening thing...there were bloodstains on the key.'

'And you tell me that you found a bloodstained robe and

the murder weapon in Sister Scáthach's cell?'

'We did,' agreed the abbot. 'Brother Cruinn and I.'

'What did Sister Scáthach have to say to the charge?'

'This is just it, Fidelma. She was bewildered. I know when people are lying or pretending. She was just bewildered. But then she accepted the charge meekly.'

Fidelma frowned.

'I don't understand.'

'Sister Scáthach simply replied that she was a conduit for the voices from the Otherworld. The shadows themselves must have punished Brother Síoda as they had told her they would. She said that they must have entered her corporeal form and used it as an instrument to kill him but she had no knowledge of the fact, no memory of being disturbed that night.'

Fidelma shook her head.

'She sounds a very sick person.'

'Then you don't believe in shadows from the Otherworld?'

'I believe in the Otherworld and our transition from this one to that but…I think that those who repose in the Otherworld have more to do than to try to return to this one to murder people. I have investigated several similar matters where shadows of the Otherworld have been blamed for crimes. Never have I found such claims to be true. There is always a human agency at work.'

Abbot Laisran shrugged.

'So we must accept that the girl is guilty?'

'Let me hear more. Who was this Brother Síoda?'

'A young man. He worked in the abbey fields. A strong man. A farmer really, not really one fitted in mind for the religious life.' Abbot Laisran paused and smiled. 'I'm told that he was a bit of a rascal before he joined us. A seducer of women.'

'How long had he been with you?'

'A year, perhaps a little more.'

'And he was well behaved during this time? Or did his tendency as a rascal, as you describe it, continue?'

Abbot Laisran shrugged.

'No complaints were brought to me and yet I had reason to think that he had not fully departed from his old ways. There was nothing specific but I noticed the way some of the younger *religieuses* behaved when they were near him. Smiling, nudging each other...you know the sort of thing?'

'How was this prophecy of Brother Síoda's death delivered?' she replied, ignoring his rhetorical question.

'It was at the midday mealtime. Sister Scáthach had been quiet for some days and so, instead of eating alone in her cell, Sister Sláine brought her to the refectory. Brother Síoda was sitting nearby and hardly had Sister Scáthach been brought into the hall than she pointed a finger at Brother Síoda and proclaimed her threat so that everyone in the refectory could hear it.'

'Do you know what words she used?'

'I had my steward note them down. She cried out: "Beware, vile fornicator for the day of reckoning is at hand. You, who have seduced and betrayed, will now face the settlement. Your heart will be torn out. Gormflaith and her baby will be avenged. Prepare yourself. For the shadows of the Otherworld have spoken. They await you." That was what she said before she was taken back to her cell.'

Fidelma nodded thoughtfully.

'You said something about her having known facts about

Brother Síoda's life that he thought no one else knew?'

'Indeed. Brother Síoda came to me in a fearful state and said that Scáthach could not have known about Gormflaith and her child.'

'Gormflaith and her child? Who were they?'

'Apparently, so Brother Síoda told me, Gormflaith was the first girl he had ever seduced when he was a youth. She was fourteen and became pregnant with his child but died giving birth. The baby, too, died.'

'Ah!' Fidelma leant forward with sudden interest. 'And you say that Brother Síoda and Sister Scáthach did not know one another? How then did she recognise him in the refectory?'

Abbot Laisran paused for a moment.

'Brother Síoda told me that he had never spoken to her but of course he had seen her in the refectory and she must have seen him.'

'But if no words ever passed between them who told her about his past life?'

Abbot Laisran's expression was grim.

'Brother Síoda told me that there was no way that she could have known. Maybe the voices she heard were genuine?'

Fidelma looked amused.

'I think I would rather check out whether Brother Síoda had told someone else or whether there was someone from his village here who knew about his past life.'

'Brother Síoda was from Mag Luirg, one of the Uí Ailello. No one here would know from whence he came or have any connection with the Kingdom of Connacht. I can vouch for that.'

'My theory is that when you subtract the impossible, you

will find your answers in the possible. Clearly, Brother Síoda passed on this information somehow. I do not believe that wraiths whispered this information.'

Abbot Laisran was silent.

'Let us hear about Sister Sláine,' she continued. 'What made you choose her to look after the girl?'

'Because she worked in the apothecary and had some understanding of those who were of bizarre humours.'

'How long had she been looking after Sister Scáthach?'

'About a full month.'

'And how had the girl's behaviour been during that time?'

'For the first week it seemed better. Then it became worse. More violent, more assertive. Then it became quiet again. That was when we allowed Sister Scáthach to go to the refectory.'

'The day before the murder?'

'The day before the murder,' he confirmed.

'And Sister Sláine slept in the next cell to the girl?'

'She did.'

'And on that night?'

'Especially on that night of her threat to Síoda.'

'And the key was always hung on a hook outside the cell so that there was no way Sister Scáthach could have reached it?'

When Abbot Laisran confirmed this, Fidelma sighed deeply.

'I think that I'd better have a word with Sister Scáthach and also with Sister Sláine.'

Fidelma chose to see Sister Scáthach first. She was surprised by her appearance as she entered the gloomy cell that the girl inhabited. The girl was no more than sixteen or seventeen years old, thin with pale skin. She looked as though she had not slept for days, large dark areas of skin showed under her eyes that were black, wide and staring. The features were almost cadaverous, as if the skin was tightly drawn over the bones.

She did not look up as Fidelma and Laisran entered. She sat on the edge of her bed, hands clasped between her knees, gazing intently at the floor. She appeared more like a lost waif than a killer.

'Well, Scáthach,' Fidelma began gently, sitting next to the girl, much to the surprise of Laisran who remained standing by the door, 'I hear that you are possessed of exceptional powers.'

The girl started at the sound of her voice and then shook her head.

'Powers? It is not a gift but a curse that attends me.'

'You have a gift of prophecy.'

'A gift that I would willingly return to whoever cursed me with it.'

'Tell me about it.'

'They say that I killed Brother Síoda. I did not know the man. But if they tell me that it was so then it must be so.'

'You remember nothing of the event?'

'Nothing at all. So far as I am aware, I went to bed, fell asleep and was only awoken when the steward and the abbot came into my cell to confront me.'

'Do you remember prophesying his death in the refectory?'

The girl nodded quickly.

'That I do remember. But I simply repeated what the voice told me to say.'

'The voice?'

'The voice of the shadow from the Otherworld. It attends

me at night and wakes me if I slumber. It tells me what I should say and when. Then the next morning I repeat the message as the shadows instruct me.'

'You hear this voice...or voices...at night?'

The girl nodded.

'It comes to you here in your cell?' pressed Fidelma. 'Nowhere else?'

'The whispering is at night when I am in my cell,' confirmed the girl.

'And it was this voice that instructed you to prophesy Brother Síoda's death? It told you to speak directly to him? Did it also tell you to mention Gormflaith and her baby?'

The girl nodded in answer to all her questions.

'How long have you heard such voices?'

'I am told that it has been so since I was a little girl.'

'What sort of voices?'

'Well, at first the sounds were more like the whisperings of the sea. We lived by the sea and so I was not troubled at first for the sounds of the sea have always been a constant companion. The sounds were disturbing but gentle, kind sounds. They came to me more in my head, soft and sighing. Then they increased. Sometimes I could not stand it. My parents said they were voices from the Otherworld. A sign from God. They brought me here. The abbey treated me well but the sounds increased. I was placed here to be looked after by Sister Sláine.'

'I hear that these voices have become very strident of late.'

'They became more articulate. I am not responsible for what they tell me to say or how they tell me to say it,' the girl added as if on the defensive.

'Of course not,' Fidelma agreed. 'But it seems there was a

change. The voice became stronger. When did this change occur?'

'When I came here to this cell. The voice became distinct. It spoke in words that I could understand.'

'You mention voices in the plural and singular. How many voices spoke to you?'

The girl thought carefully.

'Well, I can identify one.'

'Male or female?'

'Impossible to tell. It was all one whispering sound.'

'How did it become so manifest?'

'It was as if I woke up and they were whispering in a corner of the room.' The girl smiled. 'The first and second time it happened, I lit a candle and peered around the cell but there was no one there. Eventually I realised that as strong as the voices were they must be in my head. I resigned myself to being the messenger on their behalf.'

'And the voice instructed you to do what?'

'It told me to stand in the refectory and pronounce their messages of doom.'

Abbot Laisran leant forward in a confiding fashion.

'Sometimes these messages were of violence against the whole community and at other times violence against individuals. But it was the one against Brother Síoda that was the most specific and named events.'

Fidelma nodded. She had not taken her eyes from the girl's face.

'Why do you believe this voice came from the Otherworld?'

The girl regarded her with a puzzled frown.

'Where else would it be from? I am a good Christian and say my prayers at night. But still the voice haunts me.'

'Have you heard it since the warning you were to deliver to Brother Síoda?'

The girl shook her head.

'Not in the same specific way.'

'Then in what way?'

'It has gone back to the same whispering inconsistency, the sound of the sea.'

Fidelma glanced around the cell.

'Is this the place where you usually have your bed?'

The girl looked surprised for a moment.

'This is were I normally sleep.'

Fidelma was examining the walls of the cell with keen eyes.

'Who occupied the cells on either side?'

'On that side is Sister Sláine who looks after this poor girl. To the other side is the chamber occupied by Brother Cruinn, my steward.'

'But there is a floor above this one?'

'The chamber immediately above this is occupied by Brother Torchán, our gardener.'

Fidelma turned to the lock on the door of the cell.

Abbot Laisran saw her peering at the keyhole.

'Her cell was locked and the key on the inside when Brother Cruinn and I came to this cell after Brother Síoda had been found.'

Fidelma nodded absently.

'That is the one puzzling aspect,' she admitted.

Abbot Laisran looked puzzled.

'I would have thought it tied everything together. It is the proof that only Scáthach could have brought the weapon and robe into her cell and therefore she is the culprit.'

Fidelma did not answer.

'How far is Brother Síoda's cell from here?'

'At the far end of this corridor.'

'From the condition of the robe that you showed me, there must have been a trail of blood from Brother Síoda's cell to this one?'

'Perhaps the corridor had been cleaned,' he suggested. 'One of the duties of our community is to clean the corridors each morning.'

'And they cleaned it without reporting traces of blood to you?' Fidelma was clearly unimpressed by the attempted explanation. She rose and glanced at the girl with a smile.

'Don't worry, Sister Scáthach. I think that you are innocent of Brother Síoda's death.' She turned from the cell, followed by a deeply bewildered Abbot Laisran.

'Let us see Sister Sláine now.'

At the next cell, Sister Sláine greeted them with a nervous bob of her head.

Fidelma entered and glanced along the stone wall that separated the cell from that of Sister Scáthach. Then she turned to Sister Sláine who was about twenty-one or -two, an attractive looking girl.

'Brother Síoda was a handsome man, wasn't he?' she asked without preamble.

The girl started in surprise. A blush tinged her cheeks.

'I suppose he was.'

'He had an eye for the ladies. I presumed that you were in love with him, weren't you?'

The girl's chin came up defiantly.

'Who told you?'

'It was a guess,' Fidelma admitted with a soft smile. 'But since you have admitted it, let us proceed. Do you believe in these voices that Sister Scáthach hears?'

'Of course not. She's mad and has now proved her madness.'

'Do you not find it strange that this madness has only manifested itself since she was moved into this cell next to you?'

The girl's cheeks suddenly suffused with crimson.

'Are you implying that…?'

'Answer my question,' snapped Fidelma, cutting her short.

The girl blinked at her cold voice. Then, seeing that Abbot Laisran was not interfering, she said, 'Madness can alter, it can grow worse…it is a coincidence that she became worse after Abbot Laisran asked me to look after her. Just a coincidence.'

'I am told that you work for the apothecary and look after sick people? In your experience, have you ever heard of a condition among people where they have a permanent hissing, or whistling in the ears?'

Sister Sláine nodded slowly.

'Of course. Many people have such a condition. Sometimes they hardly notice it while others are plagued by it and almost driven to madness. That is what we thought was wrong with Sister Scáthach when she first came to our notice.'

'Only at first?' queried Fidelma.

'Until she started to claim that she heard voices being articulated…words that formed distinct messages which, she also claimed, were from the shadows of the Otherworld.'

'Did Brother Síoda ever tell you about his affair with Gormflaith and his child?' Fidelma changed the subject so abruptly that the girl blinked. It was clear from her reaction that Fidelma had hit on the truth.

'Better speak the truth now for it will become harder later,' Fidelma advised.

Sister Sláine was silent for a moment, her eyes narrowed as she tried to penetrate behind Fidelma's inquisitive scrutiny.

'If you must know, I was in love with Síoda. We planned to leave here soon to find a farmstead where we could begin a new life together. We had no secrets from one another.'

Fidelma smiled softly and nodded.

'So he did tell you?'

'Of course. He wanted to tell me all about his past life. He told me of this unfortunate girl and her baby. He was very young and foolish at the time. He was a penitent and sought forgiveness. That's why he came here.'

'So when you heard Sister Scáthach denounce him in the refectory, naming Gormflaith and relating her death and that of her child, what exactly did you think?'

'Do you mean, about how she came upon that knowledge?'

'Exactly. Where did you think Sister Scáthach obtained such knowledge if not from her messages from the Otherworld?'

Sister Sláine pursed her lips.

'As soon as I had taken Sister Scáthach back to her cell and locked her in, I went to find Brother Síoda. He was scared. I thought at first that he had told her or someone else apart from me. He swore that he had not. He was so scared that he went to see Abbot Laisran...'

'Did you question Sister Scáthach?'

The girl laughed.

'Little good that did. She simply said it was the voices. She had most people believing her.'

'But you did not?'

'Not even in the madness she is suffering can one make up such specific information. I can only believe that Síoda lied to me...'

Her eyes suddenly glazed and she fell silent as if in some deep thought.

'Cloistered in this abbey, and a *conhospitae*, a mixed house, there must be many opportunities for relationships to develop between the sexes?' Fidelma observed.

'There is no rule against it,' returned the girl. 'Those advocating celibacy and abstinence have not yet taken over this abbey. We still live a natural life here. But Síoda never mixed with the mad one, never with Scáthach.'

'But you have had more than one affair here?' Fidelma asked innocently.

'Brother Síoda was my first and only love,' snapped the girl in anger.

Fidelma raised her eyebrows.

'No others?'

The girl's expression was pugnacious.

'None.'

'You had no close friends among the other members of the community?'

'I do not get on with women, if that is what you mean.'

'It isn't. But it is useful to know. How about male friends?'

'I've told you, I don't...'

Abbot Laisran coughed in embarrassment.

'I had always thought that you and Brother Torchán were friends.'

Sister Sláine blushed.

'I get on well with Brother Torchán,' she admitted defensively.

Fidelma suddenly rose and glanced along the wall once more, before turning with a smile to the girl.

'You've been most helpful,' she said abruptly, turning for the door.

Outside in the corridor, Abbot Laisran was regarding her with a puzzled expression.

'What now?' he demanded. 'I would have thought that you wanted to develop the question of her relationships?'

'We shall go and see Brother Torchán,' she said firmly.

Brother Torchán was out in the garden and had to be sent for so Fidelma could interview him in his cell. He was a thickset, muscular young man whose whole being spoke of a life spent in the open.

'Well, Brother, what do you think of Sister Scáthach?'

The burly gardener shook his head sadly.

'I grieve for her as I grieve for Brother Síoda. I knew Brother Síoda slightly but the girl not at all. I doubt if I have seen her more than a half a dozen times and never spoken to her but once. By all accounts, she was clearly demented.'

'What do you think about her being driven to murder by voices from the Otherworld?'

'It is clear that she must be placed in the care of a combination of priests and physicians to drive away the evil that has compelled her.'

'So you think that she is guilty of the murder?'

'Can there be any other explanation?' asked the gardener in surprise.

'You know Sister Sláine, of course. I am told she is a special friend of yours.'

'Special? I would like to think so. We often talk together. We came from the same village.'

'Has she ever discussed Sister Scáthach with you?'

Brother Torchán shifted uneasily. He looked suspiciously at Fidelma.

'Once or twice. When the abbot first asked her to look after Sister Scáthach, it was thought that it was simply a case of what the apothecaries call tinnitus. She heard sounds in her ears. But then Sláine said that the girl had become clearly demented saying that she was being woken up by the sound of voices giving her messages and urging her to do things.'

'Did you know that Sláine was having an affair with Síoda?' Fidelma suddenly said sharply.

Torchán coloured and, after a brief hesitation, nodded.

'It was deeper than an affair. She told me that they planned to leave the abbey and set up home together. It is not forbidden by rule, you know.'

'How did you feel about that?'

Brother Torchán shrugged.

'So long as Síoda treated her right, it had little to do with me.'

'But you were her friend.'

'I was a friend and advised her when she wanted advice. She is the kind of girl that attracts men. Sometimes the wrong men. She attracted Brother Síoda.'

'Was Brother Síoda the wrong man?'

'I thought so.'

'Did she ever repeat to you anything Brother Síoda told her?'

Torchán lowered his eyes.

'You mean about Gormflaith and the child? Sister Sláine is not gifted with the wisdom of silence. She told me various pieces of gossip. Oh...' he hesitated. 'I have never spoken to Scáthach, if that is what you mean.'

'But, if Sláine told you, then she might well have told others?'

'I do not mean to imply that she gossiped to anyone. There was only Brother Cruinn and myself whom she normally confided in.'

'Brother Cruinn, the steward, was also her friend?'

'I think that he would have liked to have been something more until Brother Síoda took her fancy.'

Fidelma smiled tightly.

'That will be all, Torchán.'

There was silence as Abbot Laisran followed Fidelma down the stone steps to the floor below. Fidelma led the way back to Sister Scáthach's cell, paused and then pointed to the next door.

'And this is Brother Cruinn's cell?'

Abbot Laisran nodded.

Brother Cruinn, the steward of the abbey, was a thin, sallow man in his mid-twenties. He greeted Fidelma with a polite smile of welcome.

'A sad business, a sad business,' he said. 'The matter of Sister Scáthach. I presume that is the reason for your wishing to see me?'

'It is,' agreed Fidelma easily.

'Of course, of course; a poor, demented girl. I have suggested to the abbot here that he should send to Ferna to summon the bishop. I believe that there is some exorcism ritual with which he is acquainted. That may help. We have lost a good man in Brother Síoda.'

Fidelma sat down unbidden in the single chair that occupied the cell.

'You were going to lose Brother Síoda anyway,' she said dryly.

Brother Cruinn's face was an example of perfect self-control.

'I do not believe I follow you, Sister,' he said softly.

'You were also losing Sister Sláine. How did you feel about that?'

Brother Cruinn's eyes narrowed but he said nothing.

'You loved her. You hated it when she and Brother Síoda became lovers.'

Brother Cruinn was looking appalled at Abbot Laisran as if appealing for help.

Abbot Laisran wisely made no comment. He had witnessed too many of Fidelma's interrogations to know when not to interfere.

'It must have been tearing you apart,' went on Fidelma calmly. 'But instead you hid your feelings. You pretended to remain a friend, simply a friend to Sister Sláine. You listened carefully while she gossiped about her lover and especially when she confided what he had told her about his first affair and the baby.'

'This is ridiculous!' snapped Brother Cruinn.

'Is it?' replied Fidelma as if pondering the question. 'What a godsend it was when poor Sister Scáthach was put into the next cell to you. Sister Scáthach was an unfortunate girl who was suffering, not from imagined whispering voices from the Otherworld, but from an advanced case of the sensation of noises in the ears. It is not an uncommon affliction but some cases are worse than others. As a little child, when it developed, silly folk – her parents – told her that the whistling and hissing sounds were the voice of lost souls in the

Otherworld trying to communicate with her and thus she was blessed.

'Her parents brought her here. She probably noticed the affliction the more in these conditions than she had when living by the sea where the whispering was not so intrusive. Worried by the worsening symptoms, on the advice of the apothecary, Abbot Laisran placed her in the cell with Sister Sláine, who knew something of the condition, to look after her.'

Fidelma paused, eyes suddenly hardening on him.

'That was your opportunity, eh, Brother Cruinn? A chance to be rid of Brother Síoda and with no questions asked. A strangely demented young woman who was compelled by voices from another world to do so would murder him.'

'You are mad,' muttered Brother Cruinn.

Fidelma smiled.

'Madness can only be used as an excuse once. This is all logical. It was your voice that kept awakening poor Sister Scáthach and giving her these messages which made her behave so. At first you told her to proclaim some general messages. That would cause people to accept her madness, as they saw it. Then, having had her generally accepted as mad, you gave her the message to prepare for Síoda's death.'

She walked to the head of his bed, her eye having observed what she had been seeing. She reached forward and withdrew from the wall a piece of loose stone. It revealed a small aperture, no more than a few fingers wide and high.

'Abbot Laisran, go into the corridor and unlock Sister Scáthach's door but do not open it nor enter. Wait outside.'

Puzzled, the abbot obeyed her.

Fidelma waited and then bent down to the hole.

'Scáthach! Scáthach! Can you hear me, Scáthach? All is now well. You will hear the voices no more. Go to the door and open it. Outside you will find Abbot Laisran. Tell him that all is now well. The voices are gone.'

She rose up and faced Brother Cruinn, whose dark eyes were narrowed and angry.

A moment later they heard the door of the next cell open and a girl's voice speaking with Abbot Laisran.

The abbot returned moments later.

'She came to the door and told me that the voices were gone and all was well.'

Fidelma smiled thinly.

'Even as I told her to do so. Just as that poor influenced girl did what you told her to, Brother Cruinn. This hole goes through the wall into her cell and acts like a conduit for the voice.'

'I did not tell her to stab Brother Síoda in the heart,' he said defensively.

'Of course not. She did not stab anyone. You did that.'

'Ridiculous! The bloodstained robes and weapon were in her cell...'

'Placed there by you.'

'The door was locked and the key was inside. That shows that only she could have committed the murder.'

Abbot Laisran sighed.

'It's true, Fidelma. I went with Brother Cruinn myself to Sister Scáthach's cell door. I told you, the key was not on the hook outside her door but inside her cell and the door was locked. I said before, only she could have taken the knife and robe inside and locked herself in.'

'When you saw that the key was not hanging on the hook

outside the door, Laisran, then did you try to open the door?'
Fidelma asked innocently.

'We did.'

'No, did *you* try to open the door?' snapped Fidelma with
emphasis.

Abbot Laisran looked blank for a moment.

'Brother Cruinn tried the door and pronounced it locked.
He then took his master keys, which he held as steward, and
unlocked the door. He had to wriggle the key around in the
lock. When the door was open the key was on the floor on the
inside. We found it there.'

Fidelma grinned.

'Where Brother Cruinn had placed it. Have Cruinn secured
and I will tell you how he did it later.'

After Brother Cruinn was taken away by attendants
summoned by Abbot Laisran, Fidelma returned to his
chamber to finish her interrupted mulled wine and to stretch
herself before the fire.

'I'm not sure how you resolved this matter,' Abbot Laisran
finally said, as he stacked another log on the fire.

'It was the matter of the key that made me realise that
Brother Cruinn had done this. Exactly how and, more
importantly, why, I did not know at first. I realised as soon as
Sister Scáthach told me how she was awoken by the
whispering voice at night that it must have come from one of
the three neighbouring cells. When she showed me where she
slept, I realised from where the voice had come. Brother
Cruinn was the whispering in the night. No one else could
physically have done it. He also had easy access to Brother
Síoda's locked cell because he held the master keys. The
problem was what had he to gain from Brother Síoda's death?

Well, now we know the answer – it was an act of jealousy, hoping to eliminate Brother Síoda so that he could pursue his desire for Sister Sláine. That he was able to convince you that the cell door was locked and that he was actually unlocking it, was child's play. An illusion in which you thought that Sister Scáthach had locked herself in her cell. Brother Cruinn had placed the key on the floor when he planted the incriminating evidence of the bloodstained weapon and robe.

'In fact, the door was not locked at all. Brother Cruinn had taken the robe to protect his clothing from the blood when he killed Síoda. He therefore allowed no blood to fall when he came along the corridor with the robe and knife to where Sister Scáthach lay in her exhausted sleep. Remember that she was exhausted by the continuous times he had woken her with his whispering voice. He left the incriminating evidence, left the key on the floor and closed the door. In the morning, he could go through the pantomime of opening the door, claiming it had been locked from the inside. Wickedness coupled with cleverness but our friend Brother Cruinn was a little too clever.'

'But to fathom this mystery, you first had to come to the conclusion that Sister Scáthach was innocent,' pointed out the abbot.

'Poor Scáthach! It is her parents who should be put on trial for filling her susceptible mind with this myth about Otherworld voices when she is suffering from a physical disability. The fact was Scáthach could not have known about Gormflaith. She was told. If one discounts voices from the Otherworld, then it was by a human agency. The question was who was that agency and what was the motive for this evil charade.'

Abbot Laisran gazed at her in astonishment.

'I never cease to be amazed at your astute mind, Fidelma. Without you, poor Sister Scáthach might have stood condemned.'

'On the contrary, Abbot Laisran, without you and your suspicion that things were a little too cut and dried, we should never even have questioned the guilt or innocence of the poor girl at all.'

A *three day holiday*. Banks sat down at the breakfast table and made some notes on a lined pad. If he was doomed to spend Christmas alone this year, he was going to do it in style. For Christmas Eve, Alastair Sims' *A Christmas Carol*, black and white version, of course. For Christmas Day, *Love, Actually*. Mostly it was a load of crap, no doubt about that, but it was worth it for Bill Nighy, and Keira Knightley was always worth watching. For Boxing Day, *David Copperfield*, the one with the Harry Potter actor in it, because it had helped him through a nasty hangover one Boxing Day a few years ago, and thus are traditions born.

Music was more problematic. Bach's *Christmas Oratorio* and Handel's *Messiah*, naturally. Both were on his iPod and could be played through his main sound system. But some years ago, he had made a Christmas compilation tape of all his favourite songs, from Bing's 'White Christmas' to Elvis's 'Santa Claus is Back in Town' and 'Blue Christmas', The Pretenders' '2000 Miles' and Roland Kirk's 'We Free Kings'. Unfortunately, that had gone up in flames along with the rest of his music collection. Which meant a quick trip to HMV in Eastvale that afternoon to pick up a few seasonal CDs so he could make a playlist. He had to go to Marks and Spencer's, anyway, for his frozen turkey dinner, so he might as well drop in at HMV while he was in the Swainsdale Centre. As for wine, he still had a more than decent selection from his brother's cellar – including some fine Amarone, Chianti Classico, Clarets and Burgundies – which would certainly get him through the next three days without any pain. Luckily, he

had bought and given out all his Christmas presents earlier –
what few there were: money for Tracy, a Fairport Convention
box-set for Brian, chocolates and magazine subscriptions for
his parents, and a silver and jet bracelet for Annie Cabbot.

Banks put his writing pad aside and reached for his coffee
mug. Beside it sat a pristine copy of Sebastian Faulks's *Human
Traces*, which he fully intended to read over the holidays.
There should be plenty of peace and quiet. Brian was with his
band in Europe and wouldn't be able to get home in time.
Tracy was spending Christmas with her mother Sandra,
stepdad Sean and baby Sinead, and Annie was heading home
to the artists' colony in St Ives, where they would all no doubt
be having a good weep over *A Junkie's Christmas*, which,
Annie had told him, was a Christmas staple among her
father's crowd. He had seen it once, himself, and he had to
admit that it wasn't bad, but it hadn't become a tradition with
him.

All in all, then, this Christmas was beginning to feel like
something to be got through with liberal doses of wine and
music. Even the weather was refusing to cooperate. The white
Christmas everyone had been hoping for since a tentative
sprinkle in late November had not materialised, though the
optimists at the meteorological centre were keeping their
options open. At the moment, though, it was uniformly grey
and wet in Yorkshire. The only good thing that could be said
for it was that it wasn't cold. Far from it. Down south people
were sitting outside at Soho cafés and playing golf in the
suburbs. Banks wondered if he should have gone away, taken
a holiday. Paris. Rome. Madrid. A stranger in a strange city.
Even London would have been better than this. Maybe he
could still catch a last minute flight.

But he knew he wasn't going anywhere. He sipped some strong coffee and told himself not to be so maudlin. Christmas was a notoriously dangerous time of year. It was when people got depressed and gave in to their deepest fears, when all their failures, regrets and disappointments came back to haunt them. Was he going to let himself give in to that, become a statistic?

He decided to go into town now and get his last minute shopping over with before it got really busy. Just before he left, though, his phone rang. Banks picked up the receiver.

'Sir? It's DC Jackman.'

'Yes, Winsome. What's the problem?'

'I'm really sorry to disturb you at home, sir, but we've got a bit of a problem.'

'What is it?' Banks asked. Despite having to spend Christmas alone, he had been looking forward to a few days away from the Western Area Headquarters, if only to relax and unwind after a particularly difficult year. But perhaps that wasn't to be.

'Missing person, sir.'

'Can't someone else handle it?'

'It needs someone senior, sir, and DI Cabbot's on her way to Cornwall.'

'Who's missing?'

'A woman by the name of Brenda Mercer. Forty-two years old.'

'How long?'

'Overnight.'

'Any reason to think there's been foul play?'

'Not really.'

'Who reported her missing?'

'The husband.'

'Why did he leave it until this morning?'

'He didn't. He reported it at 6pm yesterday evening. We've been looking into it. But you know how it is with missing persons, sir, unless it's a kid. It was very early days. Usually they turn up, or you find a simple explanation quickly enough.'

'But not in this case?'

'No, sir. The husband's getting frantic. Difficult. Demanding to see someone higher up. And he's got the daughter and her husband in tow now. They're not making life any easier. I've only just managed to get rid of them by promising I'd get someone in authority to come and talk to them.'

'All right,' Banks said, with a sigh. 'Hang on. I'll be right in.'

Major Crimes and CID personnel were thin on the ground at Western Area Headquarters that Christmas Eve, and DC Winsome Jackman was the one who had drawn the short straw. She didn't mind, though. She couldn't afford to visit her parents in Jamaica, and she had politely passed up a Christmas dinner invitation from a fellow member of the potholing club, who had been pursuing her for some time now, so she had no real plans for the holidays. She hadn't expected it to be particularly busy in Major Crimes. Most Christmas incidents were domestic and, as such, they were dealt with by the officers on patrol. Even criminals, it seemed, took a bit of time off for turkey and Christmas pud. But a missing person case could turn nasty very quickly, especially if she had been missing for two days now.

While she was waiting for Banks, Winsome went through the paperwork again. There wasn't much other than the husband's report and statement, but that gave her the basics. When David Mercer got home from work on 23rd December at around 6 p.m., he was surprised to find his wife not home. Surprised because she was always home and always had his dinner waiting for him. He worked in the administration offices of the Swainsdale Shopping Centre, and his hours were fairly regular. A neighbour had seen Mrs Mercer walking down the street where she lived on the Leaside Estate at about a quarter past four that afternoon. She was alone and was wearing a beige overcoat and carrying a scuffed brown leather bag, the kind with a shoulder-strap. She was heading in the direction of the main road, and the neighbour assumed she was going to catch a bus. She knew that Mrs Mercer didn't drive. She said hello, but said that Mrs Mercer hadn't seemed to hear her, had seemed a bit 'lost in her own world.'

Police had questioned the bus drivers on the route, but none of them recalled seeing anyone matching the description. Uniformed officers also questioned taxi drivers and got the same response. All Mrs Mercer's relatives had been contacted, and none had any idea where she was. Winsome was beginning to think it was possible, then, that someone had picked Mrs Mercer up on the main road, possibly by arrangement, and that she didn't want to be found. The alternative, that she had been somehow abducted, didn't bear thinking about, at least not until all other possible avenues had been exhausted.

Winsome had not been especially impressed by David Mercer – he was the sort of pushy, aggressive white male she had seen far too much of over the past few years, puffed up with self-importance, acting as if everyone else were a mere lackey to meet his demands, especially if she happened to be black and female. But she tried not to let personal impressions interfere with her reasoning. Even so, there was something about Mercer's tone, something that didn't quite ring true. She made a note to mention it to Banks.

The house was a modern Georgian-style semi with a bay window, stone cladding and neatly kept garden, and when Banks rang the doorbell, Winsome beside him, David Mercer opened it so quickly he might have been standing right behind it. He led Banks and Winsome into a cluttered but clean front room, where a young woman sat on the sofa wringing her hands and a whippet-thin man in an expensive, out-of-date suit paced the floor. A tall Christmas tree stood in one corner, covered with ornaments and lights. On the floor were a number of brightly wrapped presents and one ornament, a tiny pair of ice skates, which seemed to have fallen off. The radio was playing Christmas music faintly in the background.

'Have you heard anything?' David Mercer asked.

'Nothing yet,' Banks answered. 'But, if I may, I'd like to ask you a few more questions.'

'We've already told everything to her,' he said, gesturing in Winsome's direction.

'I know,' said Banks. 'And DC Jackman has discussed it with me. But I still have a few questions.'

'Don't you think you should be out there on the streets searching for her?' said the whippet-thin man, who was also turning prematurely bald.

Banks turned to face him slowly. 'And you are?'

He puffed out what little chest he had. 'Claude Mainwaring, solicitor. I'm Mr Mercer's son-in-law.'

'Well, Mr Mainwaring,' said Banks, 'it's not normally my job, as a detective chief inspector, to get out on the streets looking for people. In fact, it's not even my job to pay house calls asking questions, but as it's nearly Christmas, and as Mr Mercer here is worried about his wife, I thought I might bend the rules just a little. And believe me, there are already more than enough people out there trying to find Mrs Mercer.'

Mainwaring grunted as if were unsatisfied with the answer, then he sat down next to his wife. Banks turned to David Mercer, who finally bade him and Winsome to sit, too. 'Mr Mercer,' Banks asked, thinking of the doubts that Winsome had voiced on their way over, 'can you think of anywhere your wife might have gone?'

'Nowhere,' said Mercer. 'That's why I called you lot.'

'Was there any reason why your wife might have gone away?'

'None at all,' said Mercer, just a beat too quickly for Banks's liking.

'She wasn't unhappy about anything?'

'Not that I know of, no.'

'Everything was fine between the two of you?'

'Now, look here!' Mainwaring got to his feet.

'Sit down and be quiet, Mr Mainwaring,' Banks said as gently as he could. 'You're not in court now, and you're not helping. I'll get to you later.' He turned back to Mercer and ignored the slighted solicitor. 'Had you noticed any difference in her behaviour before she left, any changes of mood or anything?'

'No,' said Mercer. 'Like I said, everything was quite

normal. May I ask what you're getting at?'

'I'm not getting at anything,' Banks said. 'These are all questions that have to be asked in cases such as these.'

'Cases such as these?'

'Missing persons.'

'Oh God,' cried the daughter. 'I can't believe it. Mother a missing person.'

She used the same tone as she might have used to say 'homeless person', Banks thought, as if she were somehow embarrassed by her mother's going missing. He quickly chided himself for being so uncharitable. It was Christmas, after all, and no matter how self-important and self-obsessed these people seemed to be, they *were* worried about Brenda Mercer. He could only do his best to help them. He just wished they would stop getting in his way.

'Has she ever done anything like this before?' Banks asked.

'Never,' said David Mercer. 'Brenda is one of the most stable and reliable people you could ever wish to meet.'

'Does she have any close friends?'

'The family means everything to her.'

'Might she have met someone? Someone she could confide in?'

Mercer seemed puzzled. 'I don't know what you mean. Confide? What would Brenda have to confide? And if she did, why would she confide in someone else rather than in me? No, it doesn't make sense.'

'People do, you know, sometimes.'

'Not Brenda.'

This was going nowhere fast, Banks thought, seeing what Winsome had meant. 'Do you have any theories about where she might have gone?'

'Something's happened to her. Someone's abducted her, obviously. I can't see any other explanation.'

'Why do you say that?'

'It stands to reason, doesn't it? She'd never do anything so irresponsible and selfish as to mess up all our Christmas plans and cause us so much fuss and worry.'

'But these things, abductions and the like, are much rarer than you imagine,' said Banks. 'In most cases, missing persons are found healthy and safe.'

Mainwaring snorted in the background. 'And the longer you take to find her, the less likely she is to be healthy and safe,' he said.

Banks ignored him and carried on talking to David Mercer. 'Did you and your wife have any arguments recently?' he asked.

'Arguments? No, not really.'

'Anything that might upset her, cause her to want to disappear.'

'No.'

'Do you know if she has any male friends?' Banks knew he was treading on dangerous ground now, but he had to ask.

'If you're insinuating that she's run off with someone,' Mercer said, 'then you're barking up the wrong tree. Brenda would never do that to me. Or to Janet,' he added, glancing over at the daughter.

Banks had never expected his wife Sandra to run off with another man, either, but she had done. No sense in labouring the point, though. If anything like that had happened, the Mercers would be the last people to tell him, assuming that they even knew themselves. But if Brenda had no close friends, then there was no one else he could question who might be able to tell him more about her. All in all, it was beginning to seem like a tougher job than he had imagined.

'We'll keep you posted,' he said, then he and Winsome headed back to the station.

Unfortunately, most people were far too absorbed in their Christmas plans – meals, family visits, last minute shopping, church events and what have you – to pay as much attention to local news stories as they did the rest of the time, and even that wasn't much. As Banks and Winsome whiled away the afternoon at Western Area Headquarters, uniformed police officers went from house to house asking questions and searched the wintry Dales landscape in an ever-widening circle, but nothing came to light.

Banks remembered, just before the shops closed, that he had things to buy, so he dashed over to the Swainsdale Centre. Of course, by closing time on Christmas Eve it was bedlam, and everyone was impatient and bad-tempered. He queued to pay for his turkey dinner because he would have had nothing else to eat otherwise, but just one glance at the crowds in HMV made him decide to forgo the Christmas music for this year, relying on what he had already and what he could catch on the radio.

By six o'clock he was back at home, and the men and women on duty at the police station had strict instructions to ring him if anything concerning Brenda Mercer came up.

But nothing did.

Banks warmed his leftover lamb curry and washed it down with a cold beer. After he'd finished the dishes, he made a start on *Human Traces*, then he opened a bottle of claret and took it with him into the TV room. There, he slid the shiny

DVD of *A Christmas Carol* into the player, poured himself a healthy glass and settled back. He always enjoyed spotting the bit where you could see the cameraman reflected in the mirror when Scrooge examines himself on Christmas morning, and he found Alastair Sims's over-the-top excitement at seeing the world anew as infectious and uplifting as ever. Even so, as he took himself up to bed around midnight, he still had a thought to spare for Brenda Mercer, and it kept him awake far longer than he would have liked.

The first possible lead came early on Christmas morning, when Banks was eating a soft-boiled egg for breakfast and listening to a King's College Choir concert on the radio. Winsome rang to tell him that someone had seen a woman resembling Mrs Mercer in a rather dazed state wandering through the village of Swainshead shortly after dawn. The description matched, down to the coat and shoulder-bag, so Banks finished his breakfast and headed out.

The sky was still like iron, but the temperature had dropped overnight, and Banks thought he sniffed a hint of snow in the air. As he drove down the dale, he glanced at the hillsides, all in shades of grey, their peaks obscured by low-lying cloud. Here and there a silver stream meandered down the slope, glittering in the weak light. Whatever was wrong with Brenda Mercer, Banks thought, she must be freezing if she had been sleeping rough for two nights now.

Before he got to Swainshead, he received another call on his mobile, again from Winsome. This time she told him that a local train driver had seen a woman walking aimlessly along the tracks over the Swainshead Viaduct. When Banks arrived there, Winsome was already waiting on the western side along with a couple of uniformed officers in their patrol cars, engines running so they could stay warm. The huge viaduct stretched for about a quarter of a mile across the broad valley, carrying the main line up to Carlisle and beyond, into Scotland, and its twenty or more great arches framed picture-postcard views of the hills beyond.

'She's up there, sir,' said Winsome, pointing as Banks got out of the car. Way above him, more than a hundred feet up, a tiny figure in brown perched on the edge of the viaduct wall.

'Jesus Christ,' said Banks. 'Has anyone called to stop the trains? Anything roaring by her right now could give her the fright of her life, and it's a long way down.'

'It's been done,' said Winsome.

'Right,' said Banks. 'At the risk of stating the obvious, I think we'd better get someone who knows about these things to go up there and talk to her.'

'It'll be difficult to get a professional, sir, on Christmas Day.'

'Well, what do you...? No. I can read your expression, Winsome. Don't look at me like that. The answer's no.'

'But you know you're the best person for the job, sir. You're good with people. You listen to them. They trust you.'

'But I wouldn't know where to begin.'

'I don't think there are any set rules.'

'I'm hardly the sort to convince someone that life is full of the joys of spring.'

'I don't really think that's what's called for.'

'But what if she jumps?'

Winsome shrugged. 'She'll either jump or fall if someone doesn't go up there soon and find out what's going on.'

Banks glanced up again and swallowed. He thought he felt

the soft, chill touch of a snowflake melt on his eyeball. Winsome was right. He couldn't send up one of the uniformed lads – they were far too inexperienced for this sort of thing – and time was of the essence.

'Look,' he said, turning to Winsome, 'see if you can raise some sort of counsellor or negotiator, will you? In the meantime, I'll go up and see what I can do.'

'Right you are, sir.' Winsome smiled. Banks got back in his car. The quickest way to reach the woman was to drive up to Swainshead station, just before the viaduct, and walk along the tracks. At least that way he wouldn't have to climb any hills. The thought didn't comfort him much, though, when he looked up again and saw the woman's legs dangling over the side of the wall.

'Stop right there,' she said. 'Who are you?'

Banks stopped. He was about four or five yards away from her. The wind was howling more than he had expected, whistling around his ears, making it difficult to hear properly, and it seemed colder up there, too. He wished he was wearing something warmer than his leather jacket. The hills stretched away to the west, some still streaked with November's snow. In the distance, Banks thought he could make out the huge rounded mountains of the Lake District.

'My name's Banks,' he said. 'I'm a policeman.'

'I thought you'd find me eventually,' she said. 'It's too late, though.'

From where Banks was standing, he could only see her in profile. The ground was a long way below. Banks had no particular fear of heights, but even so, her precarious position on the wall unnerved him. 'Are you sure you don't want to come back from the edge and talk?' he said.

'I'm sure. Do you think it was easy getting here in the first place?'

'It's a long walk from Eastvale.'

She cast him a sidelong glance. 'I didn't mean that.'

'Sorry. It just looks a bit dangerous there. You could slip and fall off.'

'What makes you think that wouldn't be a blessing?'

'Whatever it is,' said Banks, 'it can't be worth this. Come on, Brenda, you've got a husband who loves you, a daughter who needs—'

'My husband doesn't love me, and my daughter doesn't need me. Do you think I don't know? David's been shagging his secretary for two years. Can you imagine such a cliché? He thinks I don't know. And as for my daughter, I'm just an embarrassment to her and that awful husband of hers. I'm the shop-girl who married up, and now I'm just a skivvy for the lot of them. That's all I've been for years.'

'But things can change.'

She stared at him with pity and shook her head. 'No they can't,' she said, and gazed off into the distance. 'Do you know why I'm here? I mean, do you know what set me off? I've put up with it all for years, the coldness, the infidelity, just for the sake of order, not rocking the boat, not causing a scene. But do you know what it was?'

'No,' said Banks, anxious to keep her talking. 'Tell me.' He edged a little closer so he could hear her voice above the wind. She didn't tell him to stop. Snowflakes started to swirl around them.

'People say it's smell that sparks memory the most, but it wasn't, not this time. It was a Christmas ornament. I was putting a few last minute decorations on the tree before Janet and Claude arrived and I found myself holding these tiny, perfect ice skates I hadn't seen for years. They sent me right back to a particular day, when I was a child. It's funny because it didn't seem like just a memory. I felt as if I was *really* there. My father took me skating on a pond somewhere in the country. I don't remember where. But it was just getting dark and there were red and green and white Christmas lights and music playing – carols like "Silent Night" and "Away in a Manger" – and someone was roasting chestnuts on a brazier. The air was full of the smell. I was… My father died last year.' She paused and brushed tears or melted snowflakes from her eyes with the back of her hand. 'I kept falling down. It must have been my first time on ice. But my father would just pick me up, tell me I was doing fine, and set me going again. I don't know what it was about that day, but I was so happy, the happiest I can ever remember. Everything seemed perfect and I felt I could do anything. I wished it would never end. I didn't even feel the cold. I was just all warm inside and full of love. Did you ever feel like that?'

Banks couldn't remember, but he was sure he must have. Best to agree, anyway. Stay on her wavelength. 'Yes,' he said. 'I know what you mean.' It wasn't exactly a lie.

'And it made me feel worthless,' she said. 'The memory made me feel that my whole life was a sham, a complete waste of time, of any potential I once might have had. And it just seemed that there was no point in carrying on.' She shifted on the wall.

'Don't!' Banks cried, moving forward.

She looked at him. He thought he could make out a faint smile. She appeared tired and drawn, but her face was a pretty one, he noticed. A slightly pointed chin and small mouth, but beautiful hazel eyes. 'It's all right,' she said. 'I was just changing position. The wall's hard. I just wanted to get more comfortable.'

She was concerned about comfort. Banks took that as a good sign. He was within two yards of her now, but he still wasn't close enough to make a grab. At least she didn't tell him to move back. 'Just be careful,' he said. 'It's dangerous. You might slip.'

'You seem to be forgetting that's what I'm here for.'

'The memory,' said Banks. 'That day at the pond. It's something to cherish, surely, to live for?'

'No. It just suddenly made me feel that my life's all wrong. Has been for years. I don't feel like *me* any more. I don't feel anything. Do you know what I mean?'

'I know,' said Banks. 'But this isn't the answer.'

'I don't know,' Brenda said, shaking her head. 'I just feel so sad and so lost.'

'So do I,' said Banks, edging a little closer. 'Every Christmas since my wife left me for someone else and the kids grew up and moved away from home. But it does mean that you feel something. You said before that you felt nothing, but you do, even if it is only sadness.'

'So how do you cope?'

'Me? With what?'

'Being alone. Being abandoned and betrayed.'

'I don't know,' said Banks. He was desperate for a cigarette, but remembered that he had stopped smoking ages ago. He put his hands in his pockets. The snow was really falling now, obscuring the view. He couldn't even see the ground below.

'Did you love her?' Brenda asked.

The question surprised Banks. He had been quizzing her, but all of a sudden she was asking about him. He took that as another good sign. 'Yes.'

'What happened?'

'I suppose I neglected her,' said Banks. 'My job...the hours...I don't know. She's a pretty independent person. I thought things were OK, but they weren't.'

'I'm sure David thinks everything is fine as long as no one ruffles the surface of his comfortable little world. Were you unfaithful?'

'No. But she was. I don't suppose I blame her now. I did at the time. When she had a baby with him, that really hurt. It seemed...I don't know...the ultimate betrayal, the final gesture.'

'She had a baby with another man?'

'Yes. I mean, we were divorced and they got married and everything. My daughter's spending Christmas with them.'

'And you?'

Was she starting to feel sorry for him? If she did, then perhaps it would help to make her see that she wasn't the only one suffering, that suffering was a part of life and you just had to put up with it and get on with things. 'By myself,' he said. 'My son's abroad. He's in a rock group. The Blue Lamps. They're doing really well. You might even have heard of them.'

'David doesn't like pop music.'

'Well...they're really good.'

'The proud father. My daughter's a stuck-up, social-climbing bitch who's ashamed of her mother.'

Banks remembered Janet Mainwaring's reaction to the description of her mother as missing: an embarrassment. 'People can be cruel,' he said.

'But how do you cope?'

Banks found that he had edged closer to her now, within a yard or so. It was almost grabbing range. That was a last resort, though. If he wasn't quick enough, she might flinch and fall off as he reached for her. 'I don't know,' he said. 'Christmas is a difficult time for all sorts of people. On the surface, it's all peace and happiness and giving and family and love, but underneath... You see it a lot in my job. People reach breaking point. There's so much stress.'

'But how do *you* cope with it alone? Surely it must all come back and make you feel terrible?'

'Me? I suppose I seek distractions. *A Christmas Carol. Love, Actually* – for Bill Nighy and Keira Knightley – and *David Copperfield*, the one with the Harry Potter actor. I probably drink too much as well.'

'Daniel Radcliffe. That's his name. The Harry Potter actor.'

'Yes.'

'And I'd watch *Love, Actually* for Colin Firth.' She shook her head. 'But I don't know if it would work for me.'

'I recommend it,' said Banks. 'The perfect antidote to spending Christmas alone and miserable.'

'But I wouldn't be alone and miserable, would I? That's the problem. I'd be with my family and miserable.'

'You don't have to be.'

'What are you suggesting?'

'I told you. Things can change. You can change things.' Banks leaned his hip against the wall. He was so close to her now that he could have put his arms around her and pulled her back, but he didn't think he was going to need to. 'Do it for yourself,' he said. 'Not for them. If you think your husband doesn't love you, leave him and live for yourself.'

'Leave David? But where would I go? How would I manage? David has been my life. David and Janet.'

'There's always a choice,' Banks went on. 'There are people who can help you. People who know about these things. Counsellors, social services. Other people have been where you are now. You can get a job, a flat. A new life. I did.'

'But where would I go?'

'You'd find somewhere. There are plenty of flats available in Eastvale, for a start.'

'I don't know if I can do that. I'm not as strong as you.' Banks noticed that she managed a small smile. 'And I think if I did, I would have to go far away.'

'That's possible, too.' Banks reached out his hand. 'Let me help you.' The snow was coming down heavily now, and the area had become very slippery. She looked at his hand, shaking her head and biting her lip.

'*A Christmas Carol*?' she said.

'Yes.'

'I always preferred *It's a Wonderful Life*.'

Banks laughed. 'That'll do nicely, too.' She took hold of his hand, and he felt her grip tightening as she climbed off the wall and stood up. 'Be careful now,' he said. 'The ground's quite treacherous.'

'Isn't it just,' she said, and moved towards him.

They wouldn't let him do it twice. Not even in Amsterdam. Ben hung up, slipped his phone into his pocket. Ah, well. He'd tried. Now he could focus on the job in hand. He'd done the hard bit.

It had taken the best part of two hours and he was sweating like tomorrow was execution day and he'd forgotten to place the order for his last meal. Who'd have thought digging a couple of holes would have been so exhausting?

Found some babywipes in the car. Gave his face a lick with one of them. Then he'd called Amsterdam while he was getting his breath back. So, back to work.

He put his gloves on, grabbed hold of the tongue and tugged. You wouldn't have any idea how hard it was to get the slippery fucker through the gap. Tight fit, and the damn thing wriggled in his hand like it was alive.

This was the sort of job Ben really didn't like. He was supposed to be selling guns, not doing this kind of shite. Could have farmed the job out, maybe. But he hadn't. Too risky. This was something he had to do himself.

He let go of the tongue and dug his fingers through the hole in the corpse's throat. Prised the skin apart. Fumbled for the tongue again and this time forced it through. There. Ya wee beauty.

He yanked on it, made sure there was a good few inches poking through. Ought to be enough.

Sat back for a minute and took a breather.

Dirty work. Still, nothing new there.

* * *

Much as Ben would have loved to have gone home, showered, sunk a couple of beers, watched TV with his cat on his lap and Janice by his side, he wasn't quite finished yet.

The body weighed a ton. He tried lifting it, but the muscles in his arms burned and his spine felt like it was about to snap. He stooped behind the body, stuck his hands under the armpits and dragged it a couple of inches before slumping. Took a deep breath and tried again. Landed on his arse hard enough to make him cry out.

'Jesus,' he said, 'why did you have to be such a fat fuck?'

It was true. The fat fuck didn't contradict him.

'Cat got your tongue?' Well, Ben could see clearly that that wasn't the case. He patted the corpse's plump knee. 'Sorry.'

Truth was, he felt pretty bad. Wouldn't have been so bad if it had been a bloke, but doing this to a woman was tough. Really fucking tough. All joking aside.

He had cut her throat post-mortem so there wasn't an awful lot of blood. Same reason he'd used a .22. Double-tap. Back of the head. Very little spatter. Still, enough blood to attract a couple of flies. He brushed them away.

He needed the money, you see. He wasn't doing this for fun. This was to make an impression. If the big lass was a cake, the Colombian necktie was the icing. But would her husband bite? Ben hoped to Christ he had a sweet tooth.

For Ben, this was the last resort. He'd already let some quack cut his big toe off for twenty grand. That's what he'd been phoning Amsterdam about. See if they'd let him do it again. Well, why not? Lots of medical students out there in Holland needed the practice.

What they did, see, was cut it off at the knuckle, then sewed it back on again straight away. And since it was now a couple of months later, and the toe was working OK – balance was a little off, right enough; and there was a bit of pain occasionally; and he'd never play football; and the scar was fairly unsightly – but all that aside, it had healed well enough for a second operation. Which meant another payment. But a repeat performance was out of the question, apparently.

It only occurred to him now that he needn't have mentioned he'd already had the operation. That way, they could have done the other foot and no one need have been any the wiser.

Bollocks.

Records, though. They'd have had records. They'd have found out. Cancelled the op at the last minute. And then where would he be?

And if they'd found out about the first op, they'd have called off the second one. Having both big toes cut off and sewn back on screws up your balance too much, they'd told him. It's illegal. Even in Amsterdam.

Maybe he could try Brussels.

God, it was the hope that killed you.

Shit, it was better this way. Do this little number. Earn enough to keep the bastard off his back. For a while, at least.

The next payment was due next Thursday. Today was Friday. He had to get a move on.

Four months and counting. That's how long it had been.

The first call had come at three fifteen. He knew that because he'd looked at his watch. Once he'd put the light on. Three fifteen *A fucking M*.

'I know,' the caller had said.

At first Ben hadn't had an inkling what the caller meant.

Ben's mouth tasted like a hamster had died in it, yet he'd been having a very pleasant dream about an old girlfriend. A strange combination of sensations guaranteed to disorientate the most focused of individuals, which Ben, even when alert, wasn't. He said, 'Huh?'

'I know about Freddie.' The tosser had sniggered. Ben snapped awake, shook like hell, felt acid in his stomach and thought he was going to spew. He hung up. He was still shaking when the phone rang again a couple of minutes later.

He heard the same voice say, 'I know all about it.' The man chuckled. Scumbag jizzwad was laughing at him now.

Ben's initial thought was, how could this anonymous caller know about it? Wasn't possible. Nobody knew. It had to be a bluff. OK, so this guy knew about Freddie. But what else did he know?

Ben asked him.

The caller told him and Ben went cold from his stomach to his scrotum.

Fuck. Not only did he know, but the bastard claimed he also had photos.

Ben managed to drag the body over to a tree. Took an age, but he made it. All this exercise, he ought to sleep well tonight. Fetched some rope out of the car boot. Sat the body upright, back against the tree, wrapped the rope around her stomach and used a second piece to hold her head erect. Showed off her new tie to best effect.

Back to the car. Took the camera out of the glove compartment. 'Smile,' he said. She didn't. Just stuck her tongue out at him.

* * *

Thing about blackmail, you knew the payments were going to escalate. Started with a manageable amount, which of course Ben objected to paying, but considering the alternative, he didn't make too much of a song and dance about it. Pay the man, be done with it. And hope that was the end of it.

If those photos got out, Ben was fucked. The blackmailer was back within a couple of weeks and he was asking for a hell of a lot more.

So Ben decided to shoot him.

OK, it wasn't decided quite so matter-of-factly. Ben rarely killed anybody. In his whole life, he'd only killed four people. But the blackmailer had evidence that could destroy everything Ben held dear. Even if the fucker never demanded another penny, Ben couldn't live with the possibility that his life could be ruined at any second.

So, yeah, he was a little hesitant, sure. But once he'd made the decision it was pretty straightforward. All he needed was a name. And a gun. Given that he sold guns for a living, the latter was no trouble. But fingering the blackmailer had been a little harder.

By the third payment, he was ready. Only five grand. Didn't seem like so much now. But at the time it had seemed outrageous. And Ben was getting angry. He hated being controlled.

The whole thing was getting out of hand and Ben decided to put an end to it. Regain control.

He called Joe-Bob. Yeah, a guy from Haddington with a daft American name. Not that Joe-Bob liked it. In fact, he hated it. All stemmed from the fact that he abhorred Country and Western music, so some wit at university had...but that wasn't the point.

Rip the piss out of his name at your peril.

Joe-Bob was a fat bastard with a flat Mohican hair-cut, usually dyed red, but he was nobody's fool. Ben asked him to watch the drop, see who picked up the money bag and follow the fucker.

Well, Joe-Bob had done just that. Tailed the blackmailer all the way to a bar in the Grassmarket. Went inside, saw him disappear into a private back room. Provided Ben with a detailed description. Not somebody Ben recognised.

Ben persuaded Joe-Bob to hang around outside the pub every evening for a week or so in case the blackmailer returned. It drizzled permanently, only letting up during the daytime when he wasn't there. Come to think of it, one night it didn't rain. But it was so cold, Joe-Bob told him, it felt like somebody had wrapped cold cloths around his knees and tied them so tight they'd cut off his circulation.

Had a talent for melodrama, that boy.

Ben had been a little concerned Joe-Bob might get noticed. After all, he was distinctive looking. He'd bought Joe-Bob a hat as a disguise. A fedora. It suited him.

Got a call one night. 'He's here,' Joe-Bob said. It was around midnight by the time Ben joined Joe-Bob on the pavement opposite the pub, and the blackmailer was still inside. One o'clock, he still hadn't left and Joe-Bob had been threatening to go home for the last fifteen minutes. He was soaked. Ben persuaded him to stay with the promise of a bottle of whisky of his choice. On top of what he was paying him already.

The blackmailer finally appeared around one thirty. Joe-Bob pointed him out, and said, 'Laphroaig, please.'

Ben borrowed Joe-Bob's hat and followed the blackmailer.

The rain was great cover. Nobody pays anybody else any attention during a downpour and in any case the streets were almost deserted. Anybody who hadn't already left for home yet was probably going to wait a while longer, see if the weather let up.

There was no one at the bus stop. So Ben double-tapped him. Back of the head, just behind the ear. Quick tip of the fedora and Ben carried on walking with a spring in his step. Five minutes later, he jumped in a taxi.

He gave Joe-Bob the bottle of Laphroaig next day. Kept the hat, though.

The spring in Ben's step was short-lived. Couple of days on, his mobile rang.

'Very naughty,' the caller said. 'Going to have to get myself another messenger boy now. You'll pay for that. Twenty-five grand and a little lesson.' Jesus fuck. The blackmailer was still alive.

When Ben told Joe-Bob, Joe-Bob suggested going to the police. Ben told him not to be a dickhead.

Which is just about the last thing Ben said to his friend before Joe-Bob was discovered eviscerated in Warriston Park cemetery.

Major hassle. The police detained Ben for six hours, which was the maximum they were allowed to hold anybody these days. Any longer, they had to make an arrest. Fortunately, on the evening of Joe-Bob's murder, Ben had been at the cinema with some associates from Manchester. And they'd all gone to a club afterwards. The police checked out his alibi and it held; they released him, but told him to watch his step.

Anyway, that's when he decided to get his toe cut off. One

of the Manc lads had had the operation a couple of months back; said it was money for nowt.

If nothing else, the toe op would force Ben to tread carefully.

Ben placed the last shovelful of dirt on the grave and patted it down. He stamped across it, jumped up and down. Yeah, you could tell the earth had been recently dug up. But who was going to be looking?

He strolled back to his car. He had a long drive back home, which gave him plenty of time to think. He wished he could speak to Janice, but she was the last person he could talk to.

Janice's hair was still damp from her shower. Towel wrapped round her waist and tucked between her breasts. 'Good day?' she asked him.

He planted a kiss on her cheek. 'Tiring,' he said. ''Bout you?'

'So-so.' She untied the towel, dabbed at her chest and neck. Ran it over her shoulders. 'How tiring?'

Ben said, 'Not really that tiring at all,' and started unbuttoning his trousers.

First thing Saturday, he sent off the photo of the dead woman and a note that read: *fifty grand and no police or the boy gets the same*. Yeah, he only needed twenty-five but it wasn't going to stop, was it? Might as well take what he could.

On Tuesday, he called. Told Mr Paul Gardner when and where to deliver the money if he wanted to see his son alive again. Got the expected crap: 'I don't have that kind of money.'

'Don't fuck with me.'

'But, honestly—'

'You live in a million-pound home.'

'Mortgaged to the hilt. My money's all—'

'Be there. With the money. On your own. Or it's bye, bye, little Paul. Your call.'

Thought he handled that rather well. Couldn't raise fifty grand? Who was the rich fuck trying to kid?

Wednesday night and he was trying to relax. Course he was thinking about tomorrow, hoping everything was going to go to plan. He'd get the money. Use it to pay off the blackmailer. That would be it. Not a penny more. He'd stand firm, make sure the fucker understood.

But how could he do that? He'd get laughed at again.

Janice had fallen asleep. She was lying on her back, a tiny snore catching in her throat.

Sex was perfunctory these days. Ben wondered if that was a sign they should get married. She'd like that. She was always hassling him about it. Three years since he'd bought her that engagement ring. Worth a couple of grand, that. If he got desperate... No, he couldn't. There were limits.

He'd have liked to cuddle up to her and doze off. But there was too much on his mind.

How could he tell her?

Janice, something I've got to say.

The information the blackmailer was threatening to disclose was nothing like you'd imagine. No, Ben didn't paedo up some boy or shag his own brother or anything like that. He wasn't a fucking pervert.

It's about Freddie.

Damn it, he couldn't tell her. She'd leave him, go to the police. Even without the photos, the police would nail him. Somehow. Janice's word against his. They'd find something. The blackmailer would tell them. No reason not to.

It wasn't an accident.

The bedroom door burst open and Ben was hauled back to the present. The lights went on, Janice screamed and a masked gunman walked over to her and told her to shut up. Ben thought he recognised the voice.

The gunman swung his sawn-off shotgun at her.

I killed Freddie, Janice.

She kept screaming.

The gunman fired and Janice's head exploded. Bits of her splashed all over Ben. He wiped his face. Dabbed at his bare shoulder. He looked at the gunman.

The gunman shrugged. 'She was making a racket.'

'It *is* you.' The fucking blackmailer. 'You know about the boy?' The blackmailer jabbed him in the chin with the point of the barrel.

Jesus. Felt like the fucker had broken his jaw. He knew about the boy, all right. Must have been following Ben. Shit, Ben should have expected that.

Ben was drooling, or was it blood that was dribbling onto his chest? Was it his own or Janice's? The pain in his chin was excruciating. He wondered if Janice had felt anything. Happened so quickly, he doubted it. He stole another glance at her. Could feel his stomach bubbling.

Freddie was in the way, Janice. I couldn't get close to you whilst he was alive. You understand that?

He tried to speak. Wasn't so much the pain in his jaw stopping him as the fucking ridiculous sobbing that was making his shoulders wildly jerk up and down. Got the words out somehow. Punctuated each word with a sharp breath. 'I'll get you your money.'

'Gardner made me a much better offer.' The gunman levelled the shotgun at Ben's face.

Ben tried to picture the face behind the mask. This, after all, was the man who'd been blackmailing him. But it was hard to concentrate with a shotgun barrel in your face.

The blackmailer continued, 'After I told him I'd seen you in the woods burying a couple of members of his family.'

Ben was fucked. If Gardner knew the boy was dead, that was game over. Ben didn't know what to do, but he knew he had to do something. And quickly. He grabbed a pillow, flung it towards the gun and dived for the floor. Landed in a bruised heap, having achieved nothing.

The blackmailer stared at him, shook his head. After a minute, he turned, started to walk away.

'Where are you going?' Ben asked.

The blackmailer stopped. 'Got to go home. Catch up on my beauty sleep.'

'You're not... you're leaving?'

'You still owe me twenty-five grand.'

'And what's Gardner going to say?'

'Gardner's an arsehole. Gave me half the money up front. Asking to be ripped off. Anyway, if he wants you dead, he's going to have to cough up a lot more.'

'You didn't tell him my name?'

'Information is valuable, Ben. You think I'm the type who'd give it away? Now listen, at the moment, you're worth more to me alive than dead. But that could easily change. All it takes is for you to decide not to pay me. Or for Gardner to offer me more money than I can realistically get out of you. So don't let me down. OK?'

He turned, headed towards the door.

No, it wasn't OK. It was very fucking far from OK. The fucker had shot Janice. And for no reason. And because of that, Ben's main reason for handing over any more money to the scumfuck had disappeared. Thought he was a right clever cunt, but he'd miscalculated. There were worse things than the threat of death. And now that Janice could never find out Ben had killed her husband, Ben felt liberated.

He scrambled to his feet and charged. The blackmailer turned, smacked him on the side of the head with his gun. A box of fireworks exploded in Ben's skull. He swayed, stumbled, and collapsed.

When he woke up in the morning, his head throbbed with a horrific intensity. He looked across at Janice and instantly threw up.

He stopped, eventually. Sat there for a while, not having a clue what he should do. Didn't seem any way out of this hell. Well, there was *one* way.

He fetched his gun. Flopped back onto the floor. Cocked the hammer. Pointed the muzzle at his head.

Didn't seem right.

Put the barrel in his mouth.

Better.

Come on, then. Squeeze.

No joy. Nah, he couldn't kill himself.

He dropped the gun onto the floor.

A shot rang out and something punched through his ribcage.

The gun rattled to a standstill.

He looked down. A red stain blossomed under his right nipple.

And it was hard to breathe.

If only he could make it to his feet. Stagger to the phone. Call an ambulance. Then he'd give himself a chance. But did he want a chance? Was there any point?

The way it had all worked out was pretty funny when you thought about it. But, fuck it, there was nothing worth surviving for.

He took a last look at Janice and closed his eyes.

'So who's coming for Christmas dinner, then, Mum?' asked Joshua. 'Friends, foes or family?'

'Neighbours,' said his mother.

Both her children groaned. Her parents-in-law politely said nothing.

Libby Hawkins smiled round the dining-table at them all.

'Besides, the family are here already – except Daddy, of course.' Her husband's business activities presently lay in a distant land whose national holidays – and Holy Days – did not fall in the month of December.

'Which neighbours?' demanded her son.

'The Viponds...' began Libby Hawkins.

'Oh, no,' protested Joshua. 'I can't stand him and his old jokes. I've heard them all a hundred times before. If not two hundred.'

'The Bentleys...' continued Libby serenely.

'He's so boring,' said her daughter, Clare, 'and I don't like her.'

'Mr Vipond does,' remarked Joshua.

'Joshua,' remonstrated his mother, 'you shouldn't say things like that.'

'Mrs Bentley's a man-eater,' insisted her son unrepentantly. 'Even the milkman runs away from her and the postman won't knock. Ever. If he's got a parcel he just leaves it on the doorstep and scarpers.'

'What we've all got to remember,' said Libby Hawkins, 'is that she's not a nut-eater.' She turned to her mother-in-law. 'Melissa Bentley's got an allergy to nuts so we shan't be having chestnut stuffing in the turkey.'

'We didn't have any of those in my young days,' said the old lady.

'What? No chestnut stuffing, Grandma?' said Joshua. 'What a shame.'

'No allergies,' said his grandmother briskly. 'Tell me, is Mr Vipond's devotion to Mrs Bentley reciprocated?'

'No,' said Libby Hawkins, aware that the elderly were less reticent than the young and even more difficult to divert.

Joshua snorted. 'She's got her claws into someone else, that's why…'

Libby shot her son a warning glance.

'Who else is coming?' asked Clare into the silence.

'All right,' sighed Libby. 'If you must know, the Hellaby-Lumbs.'

There were concerted moans from both her son and daughter.

'What have we done to deserve it?' asked Joshua histrionically, turning in appeal to his grandmother. 'I couldn't have led a better life if I'd tried, now could I, Granny?'

'That I wouldn't know, Joshua,' she said with gentle irony, 'would I?'

'Rumours would have reached you for sure if I hadn't…' he said gloomily. 'Bound to have done.'

'It's not what we've done to deserve it,' pointed out Libby Hawkins. 'It's what they're going to do for us. The Viponds have asked the whole family round for Boxing Day, and the Bentleys are having open house for the entire neighbourhood on Christmas Eve.'

'And the Hellaby-Lumbs?' asked Clare a little breathlessly.

'Don't tell her, Mummy,' interrupted Joshua. 'I bet it'll be the biggest bash of the lot. They're show-offs with attitude and too much money.'

'New Year's Eve,' said Libby mildly. 'With some musical group or other playing.'

'Which group?' asked Clare urgently. 'Oh, Mummy, which group?'

'I don't know, darling. You'll have to ask them yourself.'

Joshua Hawkins was silent for a while and then he murmured something to his grandmother which the rest of the family could not hear.

'It's rude to whisper,' said Clare.

'You, Joshua,' declared the old lady, suddenly sitting up very straight, 'have been reading too many murder stories. That's your trouble.'

'No, I haven't,' said Joshua Hawkins.

'Murder stories,' carried on his grandmother. 'You've always got your nose buried in one.'

'All I said, Granny, was that it would be quite fun to have a really old-fashioned Christmas this year. That's all.'

'And what I am saying,' insisted Arabella Hawkins firmly, 'is that the way you found out what you are pleased to imagine an old-fashioned Christmas was really like has been by reading all those Golden Age detective stories.'

Joshua, as befitted the youth he was, considered this allegation carefully. 'Well,' he admitted, 'I suppose you could say I wouldn't have known much about butlers otherwise...'

'There you are, then.'

'Although,' admitted Joshua, 'I must say that I still don't understand exactly what it was that butlers did...'

'Damned if I ever knew myself,' remarked his grandfather

from the other side of the dining-table. 'A cushy number, if you ask me.'

'Everything,' said Mrs Arabella Hawkins unexpectedly, her stern expression melting with sudden warmth. 'Butlers did everything.'

'I've always suspected that the Admirable Crichton wasn't all fiction...' murmured Libby Hawkins drily. The presence in the house of her two elderly parents-in-law – to say nothing of the absence of her husband – in what was arguably the busiest week of the whole year was not a great help when it came to making preparations for the festive season. But everyone was trying to make the best of it in their own way.

'If we were to have a really old-fashioned Christmas,' went on Joshua persuasively, 'I could be the butler. That would really be fun and I wouldn't have to sit down with everyone either...'

With wry detachment Libby Hawkins watched her son manoeuvring them all into compliance with his wishes. One fine day Joshua was going to make a great salesman – one fine day, that is, when he had finished his education and could get a job: any job at all. At the moment, though, she realised that he was just a very bored young man who was doing his best to inject a little interest into a family Christmas made duller by his father's absence abroad. And, of course, to avoid sitting in his place at the head of the table on the day itself.

Joshua was saying innocently, 'The butler must have done something to earn his oats, Granddad...'

'He saw to the drink, of course,' said old Bertram Hawkins.

'In more ways than one, I expect,' grinned Joshua, adding with mock solemnity, 'Human nature doesn't change.'

'And the cigars...all that sort of thing,' Bertram Hawkins waved a hand.

'Ugh!' exclaimed Clare at once. 'This house is a "no smoking zone". We're not having cigars here, are we, Mummy?'

Libby nodded absently in agreement. Her daughter was a born proselytiser: where she would end up was anyone's guess at the moment. At least Clare herself wasn't smoking anything, – anything, that is, as far as she knew, added Libby mentally, her fingers crossed. That alone was something to be truly thankful for these days.

'And the silver,' Arabella Hawkins reminded them all. 'The butler always looked after the silver. He cleaned it and kept it in the safe in his pantry – you've heard about butlers' pantries and butlers' sinks, surely, haven't you, Joshua?'

Joshua, who had not thought about cleaning the silver, protested, 'That wasn't man's work, surely...'

'Sexist,' said Clare promptly.

'Libby, dear,' Mrs Hawkins leaned forward. 'What happened to that big old silver salver that we gave you?'

'It's in the att...it's upstairs,' Libby quickly amended her response. 'I'll bring it down and Joshua can give it a good polish.'

A polish of any sort was something the salver hadn't had in years but this was not the moment to say so.

'I'm sure that the maids would have laid the table anyway,' insisted Joshua. 'Clare can do that...and bring the food in here from the kitchen.'

'Oh, she can, can she?' responded that young woman spiritedly. 'Well, let me tell you, brother of mine, that...'

'But you'll have to be the maid,' said Joshua unanswerably, 'because there isn't anyone else.'

'There aren't as many maids about as there used to be,'

remarked old Arabella Hawkins with deliberate ambiguity. She patted a stray wave of her white hair back into position. 'Not these days.'

'You can say that again, Granny,' retorted Joshua, with a wicked grin. 'Speaking for myself, I can only say that I haven't met many.'

'The butler would see to all the napery, too,' went on Arabella Hawkins, leaving everyone – but particularly Joshua – unsure whether he had known what she had meant.

Her mother-in-law's circle, decided Libby silently, had probably used coded speech where Joshua's generation dealt in *double entendre*. She sat back and relaxed while her son had it explained to him that 'napery' meant all the household table linen.

'Education isn't everything,' remarked Clare, who hadn't yet decided whether she wanted to go to College or not. 'Besides, we can't have a murder here at Christmas...'

'Why not?' asked Joshua – as she had known he would.

'Because,' said Clare, 'though you can be the butler and I can be the maid, we haven't got a library for the body to be found in, that's why.'

'We're not having a murder, darling,' murmured Libby. 'Just an old-fashioned Christmas.'

'I don't see not having a library as an insuperable obstacle...' began Joshua.

Libby decided against rising to this and said with the skill born of long maternal practice in diversionary tactics, 'Don't forget that there's that lovely big white tablecloth which Granny gave us. I always keep it specially for Christmas...'

'That belonged to my grandmother,' said Arabella Hawkins complacently. 'You don't see real linen like that these days.'

Libby Hawkins made a mental note to see that the tablecloth was properly ironed in time, although exactly when she would do that, she wasn't sure. Her gaze drifted to the old-fashioned mirror hanging over the dining-room sideboard. That, too, had come from her parent-in-law's old house but it, at least, required nothing more than a gentle wipe before being garlanded with holly and ivy for the festive season.

'I do wish so many of the napkins hadn't disappeared over the years, Libby, dear,' her mother-in-law was saying. 'It was the laundry, you know.'

'Paper napkins will do just as well,' said Libby, thinking that it wouldn't be long before 'laundry' was nearly as archaic a word as 'butler'. 'They're so pretty these days.'

'Tell me,' enquired Arabella Hawkins, 'will the gentleman in whom you say Melissa Bentley has got her claws be with us at Christmas, too?'

'Yes. It's Mr Hellaby-Lumb, poor fish,' said Joshua.

'Ah,' remarked Arabella Hawkins. 'How interesting.'

'Anything else, Granny, that you can remember?' asked Clare. 'About Christmas in the old days, I mean.'

A reminiscent look came over Arabella Hawkins' lined face. 'Lots of lovely things to eat but best of all were the Elvas plums...'

Libby made a mental note to lay in a supply of crystallised fruit.

'...But what I really remember about the Christmases when I was young was how lovely the dinner table looked.'

She gave a sweet smile. 'And, Joshua...'

'Yes, Granny?'

'That was the butler's job.'

Clare made a face at him.

'What made it so beautiful?' asked Libby swiftly.

'The epergne,' said the old lady.

'All right, Granny,' said Joshua. 'I surrender. What's an epergne?'

'A table centre with lots of little dishes hanging from it with pretty things to eat in them – bon-bons and chocolates...'

Libby mentally added sugared almonds to her shopping list. Melissa Bentley needn't eat them.

'And,' continued her mother-in-law, well back in her own childhood now, 'the epergne would have been decorated all over with trailing ivy. That looked really lovely against the white cloth.'

Libby relaxed. There was ivy in the garden and she and Clare could do something pretty with it round the old silver candelabrum, another gift that had also been relegated to the attic. It really wasn't any wonder that silver had gone so out of fashion – cleaning that, too, would keep Joshua busy.

'And when I was a lad,' contributed Bertram Hawkins, 'they used something called smilax on the table centre instead.'

He grinned. 'Got you there, haven't I, Joshua? We didn't have any murders but I bet you don't know what smilax is.'

'Sounds like a patent medicine, Grandpa.'

'A climbing species of asparagus that people used to use for decoration.' He sat back in his chair. 'And no, you didn't eat it.'

In the end the smilax was about the only feature that was missing from the table on Christmas Day. Libby had enhanced the effect of the candelabrum and its red candles by placing it on the large silver salver retrieved from the back of the attic and polished back into brightness. She had draped the substitute epergne with ivy and Clare had contrived to hang a little dish of sweetmeats from each branch. Her mother-in-law, pleased, pronounced it as good an epergne as she had seen in years.

Joshua, bustling about with a corkscrew, had paused to admire it, too. 'I like the mirror effect of the salver...'

'Stop slacking, Narcissus,' commanded Clare, 'and give me a hand with these side-plates instead of admiring your own reflection.'

'I don't have a reflection,' said Joshua. 'I'm a vampire...'

By evening all was ready. Joshua answered the front door with aplomb, announced the guests with considerable *empressement* and dispensed the drinks before withdrawing to collapse, helpless with laughter, behind the kitchen door.

'Don't!' pleaded Clare. 'I'm sure I'm going to giggle when I go in. I can't help it.'

'Mr Hellaby-Lumb liked it when I called him "sir",' said Joshua.

'I'll bet.'

He grinned. 'But I could tell that Mrs Bentley didn't care one little bit for the way I called her "madam".'

'Joshua, you are awful.'

'Mr Vipond can't take his eyes off her but she's trying to get her claws into Mr Hellaby-Lumb, the poor fish...'

'Well,' said Clare with the unconscious realism of the young, 'he is the one with the money.'

'Money isn't everything...'

'Want to bet?' she said, starting off in the direction of the dining-room with the soup. 'Just light the candles, will you, and then you can tell everyone that dinner is served...'

Libby Hawkins picked up her soup spoon and relaxed. Joshua and Clare were clearly enjoying acting in their new roles and the guests had entered into the Christmas spirit with evident relish.

'Are they open to offers of work?' asked Gordon Hellaby-Lumb jovially as they reached the coffee stage. 'They're as good as those professionals we've got lined up for New Year's Eve, aren't they, my dear?'

Mrs Hellaby-Lumb gave a remote smile, her eyes not leaving Melissa Bentley. That lady had devoted her evening to chatting up Mr Hellaby-Lumb. And Mr Vipond had spent all his time making sheep's eyes at Mrs Bentley – to her obvious enjoyment and in spite of the equally apparent misgivings of Mrs Vipond.

The boring Mr Bentley, sitting between Mrs Vipond and Mrs Hellaby-Lumb, had been dull but courteously attentive to both whilst studiously appearing not to notice his wife's outrageous flirting with Gordon Hellaby-Lumb and her occasional titillating encouragement of Paul Vipond. Melissa Bentley was sitting between her two admirers, almost invisible from her husband, and was clearly enjoying herself mightily behind the shelter of the epergne. At the head of the table Bertram Hawkins was taking pleasure from watching his grandchildren milking what fun they could from acting as butler and parlour-maid. What Arabella Hawkins was thinking was anyone's guess. Her shrewd old eyes were darting about, watching everyone, and missing nothing.

This was just as well. Her observations were to prove very helpful when she came to describe the evening again and again to Detective Inspector Sloan, Head of the tiny Criminal Investigation Department of the Berebury Police Force. This was after the sudden death of Melissa Bentley from an acute anaphylactic reaction to nuts.

'She drank some coffee, Inspector,' said Arabella Hawkins, 'just a sip, I should say…then she started to complain that her mouth and throat were burning…'

The detective inspector nodded.

'And almost immediately after that her hands and face started to swell. This was before she collapsed, of course. She was dead before the ambulance arrived.' Arabella Hawkins did not sound too disturbed at this. It was Libby and the children who were too distraught to be comforted.

They still had to be questioned, though.

'If,' said Detective Inspector Sloan patiently to Joshua, 'we might go through everything once more…'

'Like I said,' repeated Joshua for the fourth or fifth time, 'Clare made the coffee in the kitchen and brought it through to the dining-room.'

'And?'

'And she stood the pot over there.' He waved a hand in the direction of the sideboard under the big mirror. 'The coffee cups were there already. And there wasn't anything in them then,' he added defiantly.

'What were you doing at the time?' Detective Inspector Sloan wasn't completely *au fait* himself with the arcane duties of Joshua's temporary office but he did not say so. 'Were you still butlering?'

'Putting the nuts and crystallised fruit on the table…' Joshua said dully. 'With the dates and the figs.'

'Then?'

'Clare poured out the coffee and I passed the cups down the table to everyone.'

'You didn't hand them round yourself?'

'No. I just took them from Clare and passed them along the table.'

He looked at the policeman and said belligerently, 'I know that's not the right thing to do but Clare and I were only doing this for a lark. We hadn't ever done it before.'

'What about the cream?' asked Sloan, pointing to a jug.

'I passed it down after the coffee, with the sugar.' Joshua scowled. 'And, no, I didn't put anything in the cups except coffee.'

'Quite so.' Detective Inspector Sloan didn't for one moment suppose that he had. As the policeman saw it, any motive for handing a fatal dose of nuts to Melissa Bentley lay between Mrs Vipond and Mrs Hellaby-Lumb, with her husband, Paul Bentley, also well in the running. The man might well be as dull as everyone said he was, but even so to Sloan's more experienced eye he didn't have the look of a *mari complaisant*: more one of a vengeful man suppressing great anger. 'Then what?'

'Mr Vipond accidentally put some cream in a coffee that Mrs Bentley wanted black.'

'And?' Detective Inspector Sloan didn't think that old aphorism about always killing the thing you loved applied to Mr Vipond but he couldn't be overlooked.

'So Mrs Bentley passed the cup back across the table – round that candlestick thing to her husband who does take cream in his coffee and someone else passed a black coffee back for her instead through – or, rather, round – the centrepiece.' He gulped. 'I think that must have been the one that Mrs Bentley had – the one that had the nut in it.'

So did Detective Inspector Sloan. The fingerprint people

weren't prepared to commit themselves. The elegant little eggshell handles of the hastily cleared coffee cups had been singularly unrevealing in this respect. 'Who handed it to her?'

Joshua suddenly looked defenceless. 'I don't know for sure. It was difficult to see across the table from where I was standing what with all that ivy trailing round and anyway I was still pouring the coffee. All I saw for sure when I looked down from my side of the table was a hand with a cup in it reflected in the silver salver coming out from under all the ivy.'

'Man's or woman's?'

'Woman's.' That, at least, he was sure about.

'Right or left?'

He paused for thought. 'Left from where I saw it reflected on the salver – that means it would have been her right, doesn't it?'

The Inspector didn't answer this. 'Wedding ring?' he asked instead.

'I couldn't see that because there was a cup in her hand.'

Clare had only seen things through the mirror above the sideboard. She stood in front of it now and tried to explain. 'I heard them talking about Mrs Bentley having cream in her coffee when she didn't like it.' She gave a little shiver. 'It reminded me of Cecily Cardew putting sugar in Gwendolen Fairfax's tea just because she didn't want it in *The Importance of Being Earnest*, Inspector.'

'Really, miss?' In his book there were even more important things than being earnest. There was being right in the important matter of murder. 'Now, suppose you tell me exactly what you saw in your mirror...' Sloan went and stood beside Clare, both of them facing the sideboard and the great mirror above it.

Mrs Vipond, Mr Bentley and Mrs Hellaby-Lumb, all sitting on the side of the table opposite Melissa Bentley, had been uniformly vague about what they had and hadn't seen. In fact, they had reminded Detective Inspector Sloan of nothing so much as the three monkeys who saw no evil, heard no evil and spoke no evil. And weren't going to, either. In one way or another Melissa Bentley's behaviour had been a threat to all three.

'I just saw a hand passing over a cup of coffee which was going across the table, Inspector,' said Clare, still very shaken and tearful. 'I had my back to the table, getting the cups ready for Joshua, like we are now, and I was rather in the way of the reflection of the person themselves so I didn't see who it was.' Mr Vipond and Mr Hellaby-Lumb on the other side of the table had declared that they had not noticed anything at all, being busy with passing more cups round. The adult Hawkinses had similarly noticed nothing.

'Left or right hand?' he asked Clare patiently.

Clare raised her own hand in front of the mirror. 'My right, so her left,' she said promptly, 'because it would a mirror-image, wouldn't it?'

Detective Inspector Sloan left her standing in front of the mirror while he went back to the table and sat where Mrs Hellaby-Lumb had been sitting. He advanced his own right hand across the table.

'No, Inspector,' said Clare. 'Your other hand.'

Obligingly, he put out his left hand.

'That's right. That's the one I saw.'

He turned to Joshua and asked him to stand where he had been earlier, looking down at the reflection in the salver. Sloan put out his own hand again.

'Tell me again which hand you saw come round from the other side of the table in the salver...'

'A left hand,' he said promptly. 'Her right, I suppose.'

Detective Inspector Sloan shook his head.

'We can't both be right,' wailed Clare, dismayed.

He smiled benignly. 'Oh, yes, you can.'

'Someone's going to get away with murder,' muttered Joshua, who suddenly discovered that he minded about this.

'No, they aren't,' said the Inspector. 'Two witnesses should be enough for any prosecution...'

'But what about us?' stammered Joshua. 'We don't agree.'

'We saw different hands,' said Clare starting to cry again.

'The lawyers will make mincemeat of either Clare or me,' said Joshua, feeling suddenly less grown-up than he liked.

His sister shivered. 'Of both of us, I expect.'

Detective Inspector Sloan explained himself. 'If a mirror is parallel to an image it reverses it from left to right...'

'That's right,' agreed Clare eagerly. 'Like the mirror on the wall...'

The policeman nodded. 'But when the mirror is at ninety degrees to the image...'

'As the salver was,' agreed Joshua, greatly puzzled. 'It was flat on the table...'

'And you saw the image while you were standing up...'

'True, but...'

'When it reverses the image top to bottom instead of right to left,' finished Detective Inspector Sloan. 'You both saw the same hand over the coffee cup – Mrs Hellaby-Lumb's left one. Mrs Vipond would only have been able to get her right one into that position by leaning across Mr Bentley.'

Clare swallowed as her natural realism reasserted itself. 'I suppose you could say Mrs Hellaby-Lumb had the most to lose...'

'She had means, motive and opportunity,' said Joshua, recovering some of his aplomb. 'And you have two witnesses.'

Turning politely to the police inspector, he resumed his butler mode and asked 'Will that be all, sir?'

'Yes, thank you, Hawkins,' said Detective Inspector Sloan, entering into the spirit of things. 'For the time being, anyway.'

The door slammed shut behind him.

It wasn't exactly that the slamming created a particularly loud bang. It was more that it was a bang of great finality. A very definite closure as it were.

'Rory,' the slammer of the door hissed, sneering through the corner of his mouth, 'so what have you been up to this time? For goodness sake man, don't you realise the Sabbath is only a matter of a few minutes old.'

'Ah, now Inspector Starrett,' Rory Sullivan began, his confidence draining the more Starrett's bloodshot eyes bore down on him, 'I ah, I…well, I suppose I'm what you'd call a victim of circumstance.'

'A victim of circumstance, is it?' Starrett laughed, displaying two rows of snow-white molars, which created a very non-patriotic combination of colours with his eyes and jumper, 'I'd say it was more a case of light fingers not being capable of heavy work.'

'Ah,' Sullivan began, openly dejected.

'You know what, Rory, do you know what's really troubling me?'

'What's that Inspector?'

'I'll tell you, Rory. Even after all these years in the Gardai I'm still bewildered why some people choose the crooked path, the path of deceit, rather than the God-fearing, work for a living type. I mean, take you for instance. It isn't as though we can blame your family. Rory tell me this, I need to understand this, why you do it?'

Rory Sullivan clicked his teeth. He was twenty-eight years

old, the middle of three brothers. His major problem, as far as he was concerned, was that he was born and raised in Ramelton – a village in Donegal, Ireland's most picturesque county – and not in Santa Fe, New Mexico, in the United States of America.

To Rory Sullivan even the line that summed up the States, 'The land of the free and the home of the brave,' was seductive, and compelling. He had been hooked on Americana from the age of eleven.

Like a lot of youths growing up in Ireland in the late Sixties, Rory was fascinated by the whole American culture. He immersed himself completely and utterly in all things American: movies; television shows; Voice of America radio; comics; magazines; vinyl records; Superman; the Lone Ranger and Tonto; *Wagon Train*; Cadillac cars; Harley-Davidson motorbikes; the Beach Boys; the Drifters; cigarette lighters and bowie knives.

He even had a pristine one-dollar bill, carefully folded away in an envelope, which he kept under his mattress. From when he was old enough to count, he automatically converted the local currency directly into dollars – it varied from three to four American dollars to the Irish pound, but the fluctuation always ensured that Rory was ahead in his maths class, particularly when it came to long division.

As a teenager he modelled himself on the new wave of American actors, changing his short back and sides hairstyle, with curls on top, for a Tony Curtis ducktail. Unfortunately the end result, for Rory, was more Karl Malden than James Dean.

Rory completed his American look with an extra-white T-shirt (his mother didn't mind spending the extra few pence on

Persil, 'the results are obvious,' she'd say to anyone who'd listen), grey-black Levi jeans, a cheap leather jacket – black with white piping – and permanently off-white (more Daz than Persil) tennis shoes although few if any who wore them ever got to see a tennis court, let alone play on one.

He was always careful not to smile when he was cutting his James Dean pose. Only his green eyes and apple-red flushed cheeks betrayed the fact that he was Irish and a wannabe American.

'Well?' Starrett asked after thirty-three uninterrupted clicks of the wall-clock.

'Listen, what can I tell you,' Rory said expansively, 'really, what can I tell you? I see myself more as a William H. Bonney character than a real criminal. Like Billy, I've never knowingly taken from someone who couldn't afford it. I've never touched the poor.'

'And you've always proved to be very ingenious in your raids,' Starrett sighed, 'but my point would be that if you used even a small fraction of that guile and cunning on something more worthwhile and honest we'd all be a lot better off.'

'Yeah,' Rory conceded, then following a few more ticks of the second hand of the clock, 'but if I went straight I'd never be able to save enough money to fly Cherry and myself to New Mexico.'

'What? So that you can follow every other Irish immigrant and spend the rest of your life being homesick for dear old mother Ireland? You know, you really should wake up and smell the montbretia and all the other flowers which grace this spectacular countryside of ours.'

'Ah, not Cherry and me Inspector, in our case the other man's grass is definitely greener.'

'Not in New Mexico it's not, sure it's too darned hot there for anything but the flies.'

Rory just smiled.

'And tell me,' Starrett continued, sure to wipe away Rory's smile, 'while we're talking about Cherry, would that be the same Cheryl Mary Teresa Kavanagh who has just sworn a statement charging you with stealing property belonging to her?'

Starrett sighed and picked up the file he'd brought into the badly lit questioning room, which was situated in the basement of Ramelton's Garda Station. He opened the file wide in front of him as if he knew he was going to need to view all of the information contained therein.

'That wasn't theft, Inspector. Sure didn't I get the very same radio for her as a present? I just needed to borrow it to raise twenty dollars to bankroll my next job.'

Starrett needed the file sooner than he thought:

'By any chance would that be the same radio, a Roberts US Valve Special, serial number 23091949 which we found in the back of Edmund Davies' car half an hour ago?'

'Yes…' Rory replied with an implied, 'So?'

'And would that be the same Roberts radio that was originally stolen from Bryson's Electricians in Letterkenny three months ago and mentioned here in their insurance manifest?' Starrett tapped a piece of paper in the file several times with his index finger. The finger was permanently semi-bent as a result of an accident and was always very disconcerting when used to emphasise something. The detective was fifty-four but his finger looked like the finger of a ninety-year-old man. It always looked like it might just break off from the rest of his hand.

'Ah,' Rory replied, this time with nothing implied.

'You see Rory, as I was saying, if you'd just put as much of your energy into going straight as you do into being a highwayman, there would have been a good chance you might have reached your beloved America in the next five or six years, whereas now it's looking like you might be going down for at least that amount of time.'

'Ah but...' Rory cut in, 'I can't be put down for...'

'Armed robbery is a serious offence, Rory.'

'Armed robbery!' Rory screamed in a pitch perfect Little Richard refrain. 'I've never done an armed robbery in my life.'

'Yes,' Starrett said, and again consulted his file, it was an unnecessary but highly effective gesture, 'and a Mrs Mina Bates has also filed a complaint against you. Apparently you threatened her with a knife in the early hours of this morning.'

'Oh, it wasn't anything like that at all,' Rory replied noticeably relieved.

'OK Rory, could you tell me exactly what it was like then?' Starrett inquired, for the record, leaning back in his metallic chair and putting his fine black-shoed feet up on the desk, stretching his arms and clasping his hands behind, and in support of, his head.

'OK, you see Cherry, well she said...'

'Rory,' Starrett began, closing his eyes, 'we'll all be finished here a whole lot sooner if you start at the beginning.'

'OK,' Rory replied and leaned in over the desk earnestly. He was so close to Starrett he could smell the mixture of leather and polish from his shoes. If he'd leaned in a little closer he'd have noticed that they were so well polished he would have been able to see his own refection in the toe-caps.

'Cherry said that was it, we were finished if I didn't come up with the money to buy our tickets to America, like I promised her I would. She gave me one last chance. Now, as luck would have it, it just so happened that I did have a job in mind, over the previous couple of months in fact and I just needed a small job to bankroll it.'

'Bankroll it Rory? What's that all about?'

'Well I needed a getaway car...'

'Edmund Davies?' Starrett said without opening his eyes.

'Well, you caught Eddie and me together so you know he was involved. Anyway, Eddie wouldn't agree to doing the job with me unless I paid him for the use of his car up front.'

'Ah Jez Rory, you don't mean to tell me that your accomplice wanted his money in advance?'

'Well, only the car payment part, he needed that in advance, to get it ready he said, and then I was going to give him a cut as well.'

'Ah Rory son, you've surely been watching the wrong movies. Come on, will you, I'm missing my sleep, let's get back to your story.'

'OK, so I borrowed Cherry's radio to bankroll the job, but I couldn't get anyone to buy it. Eddie wasn't much help either and he downright refused to accept it as payment for his car for the job. Anyway, as you know, I've done Widow Bates' rectory before and she's always good for a bit of cash.'

'Yeah,' Starrett sighed, opening his eyes and looking in the file again. 'I believe you got fifty quid last time.'

'More like about one hundred dollars, I never take more than a hundred dollars from private citizens. Anyway, I break in Saturday morning, in the early hours, to pick up the cash. She always hides it in the same place: in the biscuit tin, which is in the cupboard above the sink in the kitchen. It's always packed with crisp notes, but, like I told you, I never take more than a ton. So I'm in the kitchen, it's five o'clock in the morning and I'm feeling a bit peckish. Cherry, God bless her soul, never has any food in our house, so I think, what's the harm of helping myself to some of Widow Bates' food? I mean she's a widow, her cupboards are always packed to bursting, how much food does one woman need?'

'Come now Rory, it's her money, she can spend it on what she wants.'

'Right, sorry, of course, so anyway, I stick the old rasher-wagon on the gas ring. I'm assuming Widow Bates won't be up for three more hours and because our Cherry is always trying to catch up on her beauty sleep, I've learnt to cook quietly...'

'It wasn't the noise of your cooking that woke up Mina, it was the smell of the bacon frying in the pan, that's what was your undoing Rory,' Starrett offered, unable to resist a smile.

'Yeah, so she sneaked down into the kitchen and caught me...but to claim it was armed robbery, well that's just a downright lie.'

'She claims you waved a knife at her as she walked into her own kitchen,' Starrett said.

'Not guilty your honour,' Rory said becoming animated and leaning up from resting on his elbow on the table. 'She walks in; I've got the bread knife in my hand preparing bread for toast. I pointed the knife to the bread and asked her if she wanted some. Of course I was referring to the bread and not the knife.'

'I sure hope that the judge also believes you.'

'Phew...' Rory tutted, '...with my luck?'

'What exactly did Mrs Bates say to you as you pointed to the bread?'

'Well, she said, "As you've already got the pan fired up Mr Sullivan the least you can do is stick in a few slices of bacon and a couple of eggs for me."'

'And so you, the thief, and Widow Bates, the victim, sat down to break bread and to enjoy breakfast together?'

'Pretty much.'

'Un-fecking-believable, Rory,' Starrett laughed, 'Hardly Al Capone, mate.'

'Al Capone wasn't the toughest of the American gangsters you know,' Rory said with a bit of a whine, 'that honour goes to a Donegal man, Vincent Coll, have you ever heard about him Inspector? He didn't suffer fools gladly.'

'Oh, I've heard all about Mad Dog, Rory,' Starrett said smiling, 'talking about famous people, what was it the *Donegal Chronicle* chap wrote about you after your last job?'

'Ah, he said, "I've seen organised crime in Ireland's future and it's Rory Sullivan,"' Rory said, recalling the quote. To give him his proper due he'd didn't recite the quote with any degree of pride.

'Well, all I can say Rory, is that I hope he's right, so that the Gardai of Donegal can sleep easier at night. Talking about sleep let's get to the last chapter in your recent escapade, the bank robbery, tell me about that?'

When the Gardai patrol car picked Rory up, caught in the act as it were, they left him in the back of the car while they viewed the scene of the crime, the Bank of Erin. The bank building directly overlooked the River Leannan. The two officers discovered nothing, absolutely zero. There were no broken windows, no rammed doors, no sign of explosives, no signs of tunnelling on the inside.

Starrett had to admit that tunnelling had been his first thought. How else had Rory Sullivan managed to get in and out of the Bank of Erin without leaving any obvious tell-tale signs. The River Leannan bridge literally ran at right angles up to the front oak door of the bank. This of course meant, to Starrett's way of thinking, that the final arch of the bridge closest to the Bank, acted as a natural tunnel which had, as one side, the foundations to the one hundred and thirty-year-old ivy-covered, Georgian, two-storey building. Starrett had always considered this to be a vulnerable point in the bank's structure. The bank's manager, the affable Max McDowd, would always cut him off with, 'I'll tell you what, Inspectar,' the 'tar' being the local lazy slant on the word, spoken especially lazy following a few pints, 'if someone wants to try and get in that way, I'll not only provide them with the dynamite, but I'll let them take what they find in the vaults.'

Starrett could never work out if McDowd meant that the bank was impenetrable or that he'd already emptied the vaults himself. Before the conversation went any further, McDowd would add something like: 'Never fear man. I tell you what, let's stop wasting our time on my bank's security and pay a visit to the Bridge Bar for some liquid refreshment and craic.'

Starrett wasn't convinced about the strength of the bank but on the other hand he was rather partial to a pint or three of the Bridge Bar's finest black and cream. So, for now, nothing more would be mentioned about it.

That was of course until Sullivan's daring and intriguing raid.

Sullivan *had* been caught red-handed but *off* the premises. Starrett even visited the scene of the crime himself and his investigation, including a welly-assisted visit under the bridge, produced absolutely nothing, not even a dickey bird in fact.

Starrett examined the area immediately around the locks of the door for tell-tale scrapings of someone trying to pick the locks. Stranger things had happened, particularly involving Rory Sullivan. But the grand door's two Chubb locks and single triple-roll-bar lock were as good as new. Starrett wasn't too preoccupied about the lack of evidence. He knew full well that once Sullivan felt his back against the wall he would be happy to sing sweetly so everyone could stand back and enjoy his handiwork.

Ever since he had started his illicit career, he'd been gaining a bit of a reputation for finding extraordinary means with which to perpetrate his crimes. He'd spend hours working out elaborate ways for his foolproof, he hoped, escapades. Mostly though he'd stumble and fall at the last fence. Just like the time Sullivan carried out the robbery of Bryson's Electricians. He hid away in the lavatory towards the end of shopping hours and then when the shop closed down, he nipped into the stock room and helped himself before returning to the sanctuary of the toilet. His only problem on that occasion was that Bryson's had one of the most luxurious and comfortable men's rooms in Letterkenny so he fell into a deep contented sleep only to be discovered by one of the staff members the following morning. He had the last laugh though. They repossessed their visible goods and let him off with a flea in his ear, but they didn't bother to search deep enough into his shoulder bag where, if they had been more diligent, they'd have found, safely tucked beneath the flask of coffee, and his stash of life-saving Cadbury's milk chocolate bars and banana sandwiches, several other small items *and* the aforementioned Roberts radio; the same Roberts radio that ended up with Cherry, Ramelton's only Doris Day look-alike.

'Look Rory,' Starrett sighed, betraying his impatience, not to mention the thought of his half-finished pint of Guinness still standing on the bar in his corner of the Bridge Bar, 'thanks to Cherry, we've got you on the radio and thanks to Widow Bates we've got you on breaking and entering at the rectory. Listen, I might even be persuaded to see if Mina could suffer a slight attack of amnesia over the knife incident. But there's more, we've got Edmund Davies two doors down and he's singing like a bird about the Bank of Erin job, so why don't you just come clean about it?'

Rory Sullivan rose from his chair and put his hands in his back pockets, Bette Davies style, and walked around the room. Starrett ignored him, for fear of disturbing Rory's thought process.

'Can I plead the fifth, Inspector?' Rory enquired.

'Rory, old son, wrong fecking movie, we're talking more *Lavender Hill Mob* here.'

Forty-five ticks of the second hand later (Starrett counted each and every one of them), Rory said, 'It's all about doing your recce, isn't it Inspector?'

'I'll take your word for it Rory, but what I want to know is, how you got in and out of the bank without causing any disturbance?' Starrett asked, now genuinely in awe.

'Easy, com' 'ere I'll tell you. Your regular drinking buddy, McDowd, never drinks with you on a Saturday night does he?'

'Actually, that's right, how did you know that?'

'Recce, Inspector, reconnaissance, that's what successful crime is all about,' Rory boasted, clearly confident as he sat down at the table again. 'And I'll tell you why he never drinks with you on a Saturday night...'

'Go on, I'm listening?'

'Well isn't Saturday night the night all married men go out for a drink.'

'Yeah, and?'

'And what happens when married men go out drinking on a Saturday night?'

'I don't know Rory, you tell me,' Starrett said and then posted a late, 'they get drunk?'

'Sometimes, but not all of the times,' Rory said, singsong style, 'but what they do all-of-the-time is that they leave their married wives at home by themselves, don't they?'

This woke up Starrett with a jolt. 'You mean McDowd has been...'

'Well, I believe the way he'd put it would be, "distributing a bit of joy around the village."'

'Be jeepers,' Starrett said, grinning from ear to ear, 'and with whom?'

'Well, when you don't drink with your regular drinking buddy on a Saturday night, who do you usually end up drinking with on an average of fifty Saturday nights of the year?'

'Shit, Gary Brittan, you don't mean McDowd and Patsy Brittan. Fecking hell, Gary'll kill him. Kill him dead. The silly...'

Starrett's mind raced forward through several scenarios all of them ending with him undertaking massive paperwork. Most of the little scenes he visualised involved the spilling of blood, and one unsettling little scenario even had some of his own blood splattered around several walls.

Somehow he found his way back to the original track. 'But I still don't understand how you…'

'OK, I'll spell it out for you. The Brittans never, ever, lock their back door do they? Gary's always boasting that no one is ever going to break into his house and heaven help the first one who does. Well McDowd didn't exactly have to break into the house. Patsy welcomed him with open arms. He always leaves his jacket hanging on the inside of the back door. He dallies for a few minutes in the scullery with Patsy, they enjoy a drink or two and then they go off to find somewhere to recline I imagine. I simply slipped into the scullery, borrowed his keys, scooted down the road and opened the bank door. It's a noisy old door so I used the midnight chimes of the church clock to drown out the loud creaking and then I nipped inside and helped myself.'

'Ah Rory, how'd you ever think you'd get away with it?'

'Well I would have gotten away with it; the only thing I didn't calculate was how heavy the jar of money was. I nearly had a hernia trying to carry it to Eddie's car.'

'Why did you go for the auld jar anyway?'

'Well, I'd worked out how to get into the bank sure enough, but I didn't have time to figure out how to get into the vaults. Anyway I didn't really need to. There's the big jar of money by the door, it's called the Staff's Pension Plan pot or something, and sure don't some ejits still go and put some of their hard-earned cash in the big bruiser. Some people just need to give a public display of their generous nature and so they'll throw money at anyone who's collecting. Including the not so charitable bank staff. Then one day I happened to overhear one of the bank tellers say to a colleague that there must be over two grand in the jar. And that was more than I needed to set me and Cherry up in America.'

'Ah Rory, you've gone and gotten yourself into a fine mess.'

'Aye, well, you caught me fair and square and you'll tell the judge I came clean with you, won't you?' Rory said and then stopped.

Starrett figured that he'd something else to say so he just continued to look at the criminal, nodding his head back and forth trying to encourage the final words out of him.

Eventually Rory Sullivan spoke. 'Hey,' he said fighting back emotion, 'I suppose you better tell Cherry not to bother waiting around for me.'

But that wasn't that.

Inspector Starrett proved that the midnight hour is not as much the end of one day as it is the beginning of the next. Some could call his action good-natured; others would call it taking evasive action to avoid a civil riot about the streets of Ramelton.

Starrett proceeded to take a statement from Rory Sullivan. Yes, you could say that he even coaxed Sullivan to using particular words for the statement.

There were none more surprised than Rory when twenty minutes later he signed a statement saying in effect that he, Rory Sullivan, was on his way home from the Bridge Bar when he saw something suspicious occurring around the door of the Bank of Erin. He spotted someone coming out carrying something that appeared very heavy and he shouted across to the stranger. The stranger bolted, dropping the jar and a set of keys to the ground. Surprisingly the glass didn't shatter into a million smithereens. Rory went over, took the keys and, with great difficulty, lifted the jar. He was in the process of returning the jar to the bank when the squad car came upon him. Clearly the strain of lifting the weight confused his bearings, so that it appeared he was actually moving away from the bank rather than towards it at the time he was apprehended. Obviously the Gardai officers *mistakenly* thought Rory was the culprit. But, the statement claimed, he just hadn't had time to return the jar to the bank and lock the door.

Inspector Starrett not only stated, for the record, that he unconditionally accepted Rory's statement, but he also cajoled the Bank of Erin and McDowd, the bank manager, into giving Rory a reward of two grand for saving the bank further loss. Starrett didn't recognise the dollar currency, so he ensured Sullivan was paid his bounty in Irish pounds. Which was how, four weeks later, Rory Sullivan and Cheryl Mary Teresa Kavanagh where sitting on board a Pan Am flight from Shannon Airport to New York City with four thousand dollars to spare.

On Starrett's recommendation, they immediately continued to New Jersey and met up with a colleague of his who made sure Sullivan enrolled as a New Jersey State Trooper. Two years passed and Rory graduated with honours. Many years and scars later, he joined the exclusive Colonel's Row when he became their Superintendent, proving for once and for all that he could use his brain to ensure his fame and fortune on the *right* side of the law.

To this day he still has his first American dollar. It's now framed and has pride of place amongst the awards, diplomas and celebrity photographs busily littered on the wall behind his desk.

Oh yeah, Starrett was happy as well. With Rory out of the way he found he'd a lot more time on his hands to hang out at his favourite retreat, the Bridge Bar.

People are like cars. Since Patrick told me this, I can't get it out of my mind. That's one of his gifts. He comes out with something that makes no sense at first, but the moment he explains, you start to see the world through new eyes. Patrick's eyes. He said people are like cars that day in the showroom, the first time we'd met for years. A throwaway line, but when my eyebrows lifted, he jerked a thumb towards the forecourt. Towards the executive saloons and SUVs gleaming in the sunlight, a line of vehicles as immaculate as soldiers on parade.

'You think I'm joking? Come on, Terry, you work with cars all day, every day, you must see I'm right.' He flicked a speck from the cuff of his jacket. Armani, of course. 'Take a look at that muscular roadster. A mean machine, if ever I saw one. When that beast growls, you'd better watch out.'

I laughed. Same old Patrick. People always laughed when he was around. He never needed encouragement and now he was in full flow.

'And the model with lissom lines over there? Chic and elegant, but beware. You can't put your trust in her.'

'Like Olivia Lumb,' I said, joining in. Out of the blue, our old friendship was being rekindled. 'Remember warning me off that night at the Bali, telling me I'd do better with Sarah-Jane? I wonder whatever happened to Olivia.'

Something changed in Patrick's expression, as if suddenly his skin had been stretched too tight over his cheekbones. But he kept smiling. Even as a teenager, I'd envied the whiteness of his teeth but now they shone with all the brilliance that cosmetic dentistry can bestow. When he spoke, his voice hadn't lost a degree of warmth.

'Matter of fact, Terry, I married her.'

'Oh, right.'

My face burned for a few moments, but what had I said? Olivia was beautiful, he'd fallen on his feet. As usual. Years ago, his nickname was Lucky Patrick, everyone called him that, even those who hated him. And a few kids did hate him, the sour and bitter ones who were jealous that he only had to snap his fingers and any girl would come running. Olivia Lumb, eh? After Patrick himself told me that she was bad news, the night of the leavers' disco?

Frankly, I'd always thought she was out of my league, but that night a couple of drinks emboldened me. When I confided in Patrick that I meant to ask her for a dance, he warned me she was heartless and selfish. Not that she cared so well even for herself. She went on eating binges and then made herself sick. She'd scratched at her wrists with her brother's pen-knife, she'd swallowed her mum's sleeping pills and been rushed into hospital to have her stomach pumped. She dosed up with Prozac because she couldn't cope, she was the ultimate mixed-up kid.

Afterwards, I spent the evening in a corner, talking non-stop and cracking jokes to cheer up Sarah-Jane, whose crush on Patrick he'd encouraged, then failed to reciprocate. Six weeks later I proposed and she said yes. I owed so much to Patrick; his words of warning, and his playing hard-to-get with Sarah-Jane had changed my life.

I mustered a man-to-man grin. 'Lucky Patrick, eh?'

'Yes,' Patrick said. 'Lucky me.'

'She was the most gorgeous girl in the class,' I said quickly.

'Obviously I never had a chance. You did me a favour, it avoided any embarrassment. So you finished up together? Well, congratulations.'

'Know something, Terry? You really haven't changed.'

'You don't think so?' I took it as a compliment, but with Patrick you could never be quite sure. Even at seventeen, at eighteen, his wit used to sting.

'Course not,' he assured me. 'A snappy mover, always smart and reliable, even if your steering is a bit erratic, lets you down every now and then.'

I wasn't offended. No point in taking umbrage with Patrick. You could never win an argument, he shifted his ground with the speed of a Ferrari. Besides, he was right. Occasionally I do try too hard, I suppose. I go over the top when I'm trying to close a difficult sale. I take corners too fast when I'm trying out a new sports car. I'm one endorsement away from losing my licence, I know I ought to take more care.

'It's great to see you again,' I said.

I meant it, and not only because he fancied buying our top-of-the-range executive saloon. The sale would guarantee enough commission to earn the award for representative of the month and win a weekend break for two in Rome, no expense spared. Just the pick-me-up Sarah-Jane needed. More even than that, I'd missed Patrick. We'd hung around together at sixth form college. Both of us were bored with the academic stuff, neither of us wanted to doss around at uni for another three years, simply to help the government massage the employment figures. We yearned to get out into the real world and start earning serious money. I learned a lot from Patrick, he was like a smart older brother, although there were only six months between us. He talked about going into sales and that's where I got the idea for my own career. But I didn't need telling that he'd climbed the greasy pole much faster. The Swiss watch and the cream, crisply tailored suit spoke louder than any words.

Fixing on his Ray-Ban Aviators, he nodded at the forecourt. 'Let's have a closer look, shall we?'

'You'll love her.'

We strolled into the sun, side by side, just like old times. Showing Patrick the features, and as he put the car through its paces on the test drive, I felt confidence surging through me, revving up my engine. This was what I did, it wasn't just selling cars, it was selling dreams. I knew the brochure by heart, the phrases came spinning out as if I'd just thought of them.

The style is very emotive…good looks based on clear reasoning…touch the sports mode console button for a yet more spirited ride…sensuous curves of the door panels and dashboard…suspension, chassis and engine all operate in perfect harmony…the precise synergy…the 15-speaker premium system wraps your senses in rich, true to life, beautiful surround sound with concert hall acoustics…intelligent thermal control seat heating…ultrasonic sensors for the science of perfect parking…real-time enabled DVD-based satellite navigation…twin tail pipe baffles lend a sporting accent…potent, passionate, state-of-the-art…blending priceless power with complete control… not so much the finest car in its class as a definitive lifestyle statement.

They are the poets of the twenty-first century in my opinion, these men (or maybe women?) who script the luxury car brochures. When I borrow their words, for a few minutes I feel like an actor, declaiming Shakespeare on the stage. And guess what Shakespeare would be writing if he was alive today? Not stodgy plays about tempests or Julius Caesar, that's for sure.

'So what do you think?' I asked as we pulled back onto the forecourt. 'Isn't it simply the smoothest ride you've ever known?'

'Yeah, yeah.' Patrick's long fingers grazed the leather upholstery. For some strange reason, a picture jostled into my head, an image of him stroking Olivia's pale face while he murmured to her. 'Lovely mover. So what sort of deal are we talking for cash upfront?'

I clasped his arm. 'For you, I'm sure we can sort out something very special.'

He smiled at me in a hungry way. Like a fat man contemplating an unwrapped chocolate bar.

'You've made a good salesman, Terry, one of the best. I can picture you with other customers, teasing them like an angler with a fish on the line.'

His words cheered me as we discussed figures. I knew Patrick was a skilled negotiator and I did my best to show him how much I too had learned. Working in tandem with Bernard, my sales director, like a comic and a sad-faced straight man, I utilised every – I nearly said, 'trick in the book' – *stratagem* to avoid taking too much of a bite out of our profit margin. It wasn't exactly a success, because half an hour later we were signing up to the biggest discount I'd ever agreed. The commission was much less than I'd anticipated, but even Bernard was no match for Patrick. I could see why my old friend was no longer in sales. He'd made enough to set up his own business. Financial services. While Bernard was making a nervous call to seek head office authorisation, Patrick whispered that he could give me a fantastic opportunity with tax-efficient shelters for my investments. He'd be happy to design a personal balanced-risk strategy for me, as a sort of thank-you for my candour as well as the flexibility on the price of his car.

As we said goodbye, I joked that he'd cost Sarah-Jane and me a weekend in Rome. He smiled and asked after her.

'Lovely girl, you did well there. That cascading red hair, I remember it well. Lot of firepower under the bonnet, eh?'

His cheeky wink wasn't in the least embarrassing. Far from it: his approval of my wife sent a shiver of pleasure down my spine. For years I'd shrunk from the reflection that he'd spurned her advances in the months leading up to the leavers' disco. I hated thinking of her – or of myself, for that matter – as second best. She hadn't hidden her bitterness; that was why we hadn't kept in touch with Patrick. A reluctant sacrifice, but what choice did I have? Besides, she and I were enough for each other.

I contented myself with a smirk of satisfaction. 'Let's just say I don't have any complaints.'

'I bet you don't, you sly dog. How is she?'

'Fine, absolutely fine. Well...'

Honesty compelled me not to leave it there. I told him about the miscarriage and his face became grave. How sad, he said, and then he told me that Olivia didn't want children yet, she wasn't ready and that was fine by him. The fact he was taking me into his confidence at all was flattering; so was the way he talked about Sarah-Jane. It was as though her well-being meant more to him than I had ever realised.

'Remember me to her, now, don't forget. Tell her Lucky Patrick was asking after her.'

'I'll do that,' I said, glowing. This man was a success, he had money, status, a beautiful wife, but he hadn't lost his generosity of spirit. How much I'd missed his friendship. 'Let me give you a ring when the paperwork's sorted.'

'Thanks.' He gripped my hand. 'It's been good, Terry. I heard you'd done well, but I didn't know quite how well. We ought to keep in touch.'

'Too right.' I must have sounded as eager as a teenager, but it didn't matter. He and I went back a long way. 'Maybe we could get together again sometime.'

'The four of us? Fantastic idea, it'll be just like old times.'

It wasn't precisely what I had in mind. Olivia and Sarah-Jane as well? Not like old times at all, strictly speaking. But it was just a figure of speech, I knew what he meant. Time's a great healer.

'I don't think so,' Sarah-Jane said. 'I really don't think so.'

She was perched on a kitchen stool, wearing a grubby housecoat. I'd always liked the way she took care of herself, it's important to have pride in your appearance. But since the miscarriage, she'd become moody and irritable and didn't seem to care about anything. The dishwasher had broken down and she hadn't bothered to call out the repairman, let alone tackle the mountain of unwashed crockery in the sink.

'You mooned after him at one time,' I reminded her.

'That was then,' she said. 'Anyway, I finished up with you, didn't I?'

'Don't make it sound like a prison sentence,' I joked, wanting to lift her spirits. 'Listen, it's just one evening, all right? We're not talking a dinner party, you don't have to entertain them. We'll meet in a bar, so we're not under any obligation to ask them back here sometime. You don't have to see him again.'

'But you'll keep seeing him.'

'What's wrong with that? He's smart, he's intelligent. Most of all, he's a friend.'

She cast her eyes to the heavens. 'There's just no arguing with you, is there? OK, OK, you win.' A long sigh. 'Salesmen Reunited, huh?'

I reached for her, tried to undo the top button of the housecoat, but she flapped me away, as if swatting a fly.

'I told you last night, I need some personal space.'

Of course, I didn't push my luck. During the past couple of months she'd cried so easily. Once, in a temper, she'd slapped my face over something and nothing. I needed to give her time, just like it said in the problem pages of the magazines she devoured. She read a lot about life-coaching and unlocking her personal potential. The column-writers promised to give her the key to happiness, but she was still looking for the right door to open. Fair enough, I could do 'patient and caring'. Besides, she'd agreed to see Patrick again. I could show my old friend exactly what he'd missed.

Sarah-Jane may have had mixed feelings about meeting up with Patrick and Olivia, but when it came to the crunch, she didn't let me down. For the first time in an age, we were hitting the town and she summoned up the enthusiasm to put on her make-up and wear the slinky new dress I'd bought by way of encouragement. We couldn't mourn forever, that was my philosophy. We had to move on.

The evening went even better than I'd dared to hope. Patrick was on his very best form and funny anecdotes streamed from him like spray from a fountain. In front of the girls, he congratulated me on my shrewd negotiating techniques. I thought I had the gift of the blarney, he said, but Terry knows his cars inside out, you know he can torque for England.

I hadn't seen Sarah-Jane laugh like that in a long time. As for Olivia, she'd always been silent and mysterious and nothing had changed. She spoke in enigmatic monosyllables and paid no more attention to me than when we were both eighteen. I stole a glance at her wrist and saw that it was scarred. The marks were red and recent, not the legacy of a long-ago experiment in self-harm. Hurriedly, I averted my gaze. Her own eyes locked on Patrick all night, though it didn't seem to make him feel uncomfortable. It was as if he expected nothing less.

Sarah-Jane did her best to make conversation. 'I'm longing for the day when the doctor signs me off and I can get back to work.'

'Terry tells me you work for an estate agency,' Patrick said. 'I keep trying to persuade Olivia to do a bit of secretarial work to help me out in the business since my last PA left. But it doesn't suit.'

Olivia finished her pina colada and gave a faraway smile. 'I look after the house.'

'I expect it's a mansion,' I said cheerily.

'Seven bedrooms, five reception, a cellar and a granny annexe,' Patrick said. 'Not that we've got a granny, obviously.' He mentioned the address; I knew the house, although I'd never seen it. A long curving drive wandered away between massive rhododendron bushes on its journey to the front door.

Olivia's flowing dark hair was even silkier than I remembered, though there still wasn't a spot of colour in her delicate cheeks. I couldn't help recalling how I'd worshipped her from the back of the class when I should have been listening to the teacher's words of wisdom on some writer whose name I forget. He used to say that all animals are equal, but some are more equal than others. It's the only snippet from those lessons that has stuck in my mind. Of course, it's true we don't live in a fair and just world, no sense in moping about it, you just have to do the best that you can for yourself. Beauty is like money, it isn't divided out to us all in neat proportions. How many women can match the elegance of Olivia Lumb? But I told myself I was more fortunate than Patrick. Looks matter, but a man wants more from his wife.

As Patrick might have said, Olivia was as svelte as the sportiest coupe in the dealership, but never mind. In the early years of our marriage, Sarah-Jane's handling had been tenacious, her performance superb. Of course, nothing lasts forever. It's as true of people as it is of cars. I'd hung my hopes on our starting a family, and losing the baby had devastated both of us. And then, in the course of a single evening at the bar, I saw Sarah-Jane coming back to life, like Sleeping Beauty awoken from a deep slumber. I had Patrick to thank for giving my wife back to me.

For both of us, making friends with Patrick again turned out to be a sort of elixir. He gave me plenty of inside advice on the markets. Tips that made so much sense I didn't hesitate in shifting the money my parents had left me from the building society account into the shelters he recommended. As he pointed out, even keeping cash under the floorboards was far from risk-free. After all, if you were missing out on high dividends and extra performance, you were taking an investment decision, and not a smart one.

As for Sarah-Jane, her eyes regained their sparkle, her cheeks their fresh glow. When I teased her that she hadn't even wanted to set eyes on Patrick after these years, she had to accept I'd been proved right. She was even happy for us to host a barbecue on our new patio, so that we could reciprocate after a dinner party at Patrick's lovely home. Olivia didn't cook the meal, her household management seemed to consist of hiring posh outside caterers. It didn't matter. I sat next to another of Patrick's clients and spent an enjoyable evening extolling the virtues of the 475 while Patrick entertained Sarah-Jane with tales of double-dealing in the murky world of financial services. People talk about dishonest car salesmen, and fair enough, but the money men are a hundred times worse if Patrick's gleeful anecdotes about his business competitors were to be believed.

We asked Bernard and his wife along to the barbecue and it wasn't until we'd guzzled the last hot dog that I found myself together with Olivia. As usual, she'd said little or nothing. I'd drunk a lot of strong red wine, Tesco's finest, and probably I talked too long about how difficult it had been to lay the patio flags in just the right way. She kept looking over my shoulder towards Patrick, who was sharing a joke with Sarah-Jane and our guests. Her lack of attention was worse than irritating, it was downright rude. I found myself wanting to get under her skin, to provoke her into some sort of response. Any response.

'I ought to make a confession,' I said, wiping a smear of tomato ketchup off my cheek with a paper napkin. 'Ease my conscience, you know? This has been preying on my mind for years.'

'Oh yes?' She raised a languid eyebrow.

'Yes,' I said firmly. 'It's about you and me.'

She contrived the faintest of frowns, but a frond of Virginia creeper, trailing from the pergola, seemed to cause her more concern. She flicked it out of her face and murmured, 'You and me?'

I covered my mouth to conceal a hiccup, but I'm not sure she even noticed. 'Well, I don't know whether you ever realised, when we were in the sixth form together I mean, but I had a thing about you. Quite a serious thing.'

'Oh,' she said. That was all.

I'd hoped to intrigue her. Over-optimistic, obviously. Never mind, I'd started, so I would finish. 'You're a very attractive woman, Olivia. Patrick's a lucky fellow.'

'You think so?'

I leaned towards her, stumbling for a moment, but quickly regaining my balance. 'Yes, I do think so. He thinks people are like cars. In my book, you're a high-performance model.'

She peered into my eyes, as if seeing them for the first time. 'Your wife's prettier than I remembered. I might have known.'

That was all she said. *I might have known?* I stared back at her, puzzled, but before I could ask her what she meant, a strong arm wrapped itself around my shoulder and Patrick's voice was in my ear.

'Now then, Terry. You'll be making me jealous, monopolising my lovely wife all the time.'

I could smell the alcohol on his breath, as well as a pungent after-shave. And I could hear Sarah-Jane's tinkling laughter as he spoke again.

'Always did have an eye for a pretty lady, didn't you?'

The next time we got together, for a meal at an Indian restaurant a stone's throw from the showroom, Patrick offered Sarah-Jane a job as his PA. I'm not sure how it came about. One moment they were talking idly about her plans to return to work the following week, the next Patrick was waxing lyrical about how someone with her administrative skills could play a vital role in his business. He needed a right hand woman to rely on, he said, and who better than an old friend?

I glanced at Olivia. She was sitting very still, saying nothing, just twisting her napkin into tight little knots, as if it was a make-believe garrotte. Her gaze was fixed on her husband, as usual, as if the rest of us did not exist.

I assumed that Sarah-Jane would turn him down flat. In the estate agency, she was deputy to the branch manager and stood in for him when he was on holiday. There was a decent pension scheme, too. But to my amazement, she positively basked in his admiration and said she'd love to accept. It would be a challenge, she said merrily, to keep Patrick on the straight and narrow. Before I could say a word, Patrick was summoning the waiter and demanding champagne. One look at my wife's face convinced me it was a done deal. Even though nothing had been said about salary, let alone sick pay or holiday entitlements.

At least I need not have worried on those counts. Within a couple of days, Patrick hand-delivered her letter of appointment. The terms were generous; in fact, her basic rate was a tad higher than mine. When I pointed this out, Patrick was firm.

'I'm sure she's worth it, Terry. And to be honest, I'm a demanding boss. I work long hours and spend a lot of time travelling. I'll need Sarah-Jane by my side. She'll be my right hand, so I'm prepared to pay a premium.'

I shot my wife a glance. 'I don't think...'

'It'll be fine,' she said, patting me on the hand. 'A new environment, a fresh start. I can't wait.'

'But don't you think...I mean, after having so long at home...?'

'I'm ready,' she said. 'I've gathered my strength. You're sweet to me, darling, but I don't expect to be wrapped in cotton wool for the rest of my life.'

'Don't worry,' Patrick said to me. 'I'll take good care of her.'

I can't put my finger on one single incident that caused me to believe that Patrick and Sarah-Jane were having an affair. My brain didn't suddenly crash into gear. The suspicion grew over time. Like when you begin to hear a faint knocking each time your well-loved car rounds a corner at speed. At first you don't take any notice, after a while you can't ignore the noise altogether, but you persuade yourself that it's nothing, really, that if you don't panic, sooner or later it will go away of its own accord. But it never goes away, of course, not ever.

Little things, insignificant in themselves, began to add up. She started to wear raunchy underwear again, just as she had done in those exciting days when we first got together. To begin with, I was thrilled. It was a sign she was putting the miscarriage behind her. But when I turned to her in bed at night, she continued to push me away. She was tired, she explained, the new job was taking so much out of her. It seemed fair enough, but when I suggested that it was unreasonable for Patrick to propose that she accompanied him for a week-long trip to Edinburgh, to meet people from a life company he did business with, she brushed my protests aside. The long hours came with the territory, she said. Patrick had given her a wonderful opportunity. She could not, would not let him down.

Even when she was at home, she was never off the mobile, talking to him in muffled tones while I busied myself in another room. Client business was highly confidential, she reminded me when I ventured a mild complaint. I suggested several times that the four of us might go out for another meal together, but it was never convenient. Olivia wasn't well, apparently. Although Sarah-Jane was discreet, I gathered that her old rival was seeing a psychiatrist regularly. I said that maybe Patrick would want to spend more time with his own wife, but Sarah-Jane said I didn't understand. There was a reason why my old friend buried himself in his work. He didn't need the money, it was all about having a safety valve. A means of escape from the pressures of being married to a neurotic cow.

One night Sarah-Jane announced that she would have to be up at the crack of dawn the next morning to catch the early flight to Paris. Patrick thought the European market was full of opportunities and they were going to spend forty-eight hours there. Putting out feelers, making contacts.

'Are you taking the camera?'

She wrinkled her nose. 'Won't have time for that. You don't realise, Terry, just what it's like. This is high-powered stuff, but it's hard work. Long meetings in offices, talking business over lunch and dinner. One hotel is much like another, it's scarcely a tourist trip.'

'Your mobile always seems to be busy or switched off when I call.'

'Exactly. It's non-stop, I can tell you. I really don't want to be disturbed. And don't fret about the phone bill, by the way. Patrick pays for everything, of course he does.'

An hour later, her mobile rang again. At one time I'd liked the 'I Will Survive' ringtone, all of a sudden I hated it. While she retreated to the kitchen to take the call, closing the door behind her, I did something rather dishonourable. I crept up the stairs in my stockinged feet and opened up the suitcase she'd been packing. There were new shoes I didn't recognise, clothes with designer labels that I'd never seen before. Along with furry handcuffs, a velvet blindfold and a whip.

When at last she came off the phone, I didn't say a word about what I'd discovered. Only for a few seconds had I contemplated a confrontation. But I couldn't face it. Suppose I challenged her and she admitted everything? Said that she loved Patrick and that, compared to him, I was nothing?

How could I deny it? Lucky Patrick, he won every time.

All through their absence in Paris, I felt numb. At the showroom, I was going through the motions, scarcely caring when a customer reckoned he could beat my price by going to the dealership on the other side of town. One lunchtime, when Bernard passed me the latest copy of *What Car?* I left it unopened on the table while I nibbled at a chicken tikka sandwich and stared moodily through the glass at the drizzle spattering the windscreens of the saloons on the forecourt.

Bernard asked if I was all right and my reply was a non-committal grunt.

Of course I wasn't all right, my wife and best friend were betraying me. Worse, they were treating me like a fool. At once I saw that really, it had always been like this. Patrick used people and discarded them like he used and discarded his cars.

And I meant to do something about it.

I still hadn't decided what to do when Patrick dropped Sarah-Jane off at home that evening. I'd seen his car pulling up outside the gate and I'd wandered down the path, to greet them. Good old Terry, I thought to myself as I forced a good-natured wave. Always reliable.

'Good trip?'

'Fine,' Sarah-Jane said. I don't think I'd ever seen her red hair so lustrous, her skin so delicate. 'Hard work, obviously.'

'No peace for the wicked,' Patrick confirmed with his customary grin. 'I don't know what I'd do without my trusty PA…'

'Taking things down for you?' I interrupted, with as much jocularity as I could muster.

'Absolutely.'

He roared with laughter, but out of the corner of my eye, I saw Sarah-Jane start. When she thought I wasn't looking, she shot Patrick a cautionary glance, but he wasn't fazed. The worm – I *knew* he thought this – was incapable of turning.

In bed that night, for the first time in an age, she reached for me. I sighed and said I was tired and turned away. Even though I still wanted her so much, I would not touch her again until I knew she was mine forever.

* * *

The truth dawned on me a couple of days later. I couldn't sort this on my own. I needed help, and only one person could provide it. But I'd need all my sales skills. Before I lost my nerve, I picked up the phone and rang the number of Patrick's house. I held for a full minute before someone answered.

'Hello?'

'Olivia? It's me. Terry. We need to talk.'

'What about?' Her voice was faint. I could tell she was at a low ebb.

'I think you know.'

There was a long pause before she said, 'So you finally worked it out.'

'I suppose you think I'm an idiot, a poor naïve idiot?'

I could picture her shrugging. 'Well…'

'Like I said, we ought to talk.'

'What for? You seriously imagine I'm going to cry on your shoulder? Or let you cry on mine?'

'I want you to come here, to the showroom.' I wasn't going to be swayed by her scorn. Suddenly, I had never felt so masterful. 'We have to do something.'

Another pause. 'Do something?'

'I'll see you at reception at three o'clock. Pretend you're a customer. I'll take you on a test drive and we can decide.'

Looking out through the windows as Olivia arrived in her Fiat runabout, Bernard recognised her and shot me a sharp glance. I smiled and said, 'I finally persuaded Patrick to cough up for his wife's new car. She was ready for a change.'

He raised his eyebrows. 'Oh yes? Well, take care, young man. She's a loose cannon, that one.'

'The two of us go back years,' I said. 'I can handle her. No worries.'

Five minutes later, Olivia was at the wheel of a new fiery orange Supermini. Lovely little motor, alloy wheels, sill extensions and a tiny spoiler above the tailgate, plus bags of equipment for the money. From the styling, you would never guess it was designed in Korea. But this afternoon, I wasn't interested in selling a car.

'Sarah-Jane isn't the first, is she?' I asked, as we paused at a red light.

'So you finally realised?'

'This is different from the others, isn't it?'

'What makes you think that?' Her voice was empty of emotion. I didn't have a clue what was going on in her head.

'Because I know Sarah-Jane. She lost him once, she won't let him slip away again. It's only now that I see the truth. She's been grieving for him for years. He was what she wanted, not me.'

She kept her eyes on the road. 'Perhaps you're right. Perhaps this is different.'

'You've picked up hints?'

'The others never lasted this long. I always knew he would come back to me in the end. This time...'

We moved onto the dual carriageway, picking up speed as we headed out of town.

'What can we do about it?' I asked. 'How can we stop them?'

'Is that what you want, to stop them?'

'Of course. Does that surprise you?'

'He could always twist you around his little finger, Terry. I thought – you were willing to put up with it. As long as you thought he was making money on your investments, as long as he kept flattering you, made you feel like a big man.'

It wasn't the longest speech, but then, I don't think I'd ever heard her put more than three sentences together at one time before.

'I don't care about the money,' I said hotly.

'That's just as well, because there won't be as much for you as you'd like to think. The business is going down the tube.'

'What?'

Her knuckles were white against the steering wheel. 'He's always been lazy and now he doesn't have time for anyone or anything but your wife. The creditors are pressing, Terry. Better watch out, or they'll take your money as well as his.'

I didn't speak again for a couple of minutes, I just gazed out of the window, watching the pylons in the fields, their arms out-stretched as if denying guilt. Until then, I suppose I'd had pangs of conscience. I'm not a naturally violent man. In principle, I think it's right to turn the other cheek. But there are limits, and I had raced past mine.

'You can stop him,' I said eventually. 'That's why I needed to talk to you, Olivia. Not to weep and wail. I just want an end to it.'

Ideas were shifting inside my head, even as I sat beside her. I hadn't been thinking straight. I'd thought: *what if she kills herself?* It wasn't nice, but looking at it another way, you might say it was only a question of time before Olivia stopped crying for help and finally went all the way. Imagining the headlines gave me grim satisfaction. *Faithless financier finds wife dead. Betrayed woman could not take any more.* It would finish everything between Sarah-Jane and Patrick. Their relationship would be tainted for all time. I knew enough of him to be sure he would want to get out of it, make a new beginning with someone else. Someone else's wife, most likely.

But maybe there was a different solution, leaving less to chance. Bernard's words lodged in my brain. He was no fool, he had Olivia's number. She *was* a loose cannon, they didn't come any looser. What if she was fired at Patrick himself?

Signs were scattered along the grass verge warning of police speed enforcement, pictures of so-called safety cameras and a board bragging about how many poor old motorists had been caught exceeding the limit in the past six months. None of it seemed to register with Olivia. The yellow camera wasn't hidden from view, there was no panda car lurking in the bushes, she had every chance to slow down before we reached the white lines on the road, but far from easing off the accelerator, she put her foot down. We leapt past the camera and it flashed twice in anger. I couldn't help wincing, but at the same time I felt blood rushing to my head. This was a sort of liberation. I was manoeuvring Olivia as if she was a car to be squeezed into a tight parking space. And Patrick's luck was about to run dry.

'He deserves to suffer,' she said.

'Yes.'

She tossed me a glance. It was gone in a moment, but for the first time since I'd known her, I thought she was actually *seeing* me. But I still couldn't guess what she thought about what she saw.

'Olivia loves the special edition,' I told Bernard. 'I offered her the chance to take it home, try it out for twenty-four hours before she signs on the dotted line. The insurance is fine, she's not a time-waster, trust me.'

He gave me the sort of look you give delinquents on street corners, but said nothing. No way could he guess the thoughts jockeying inside my head. My voice was as calm as a priest's, yielding no hint of the excitement churning in my guts.

I had made a sale, the biggest of my career.

Olivia had told Patrick she'd be out shopping all day. She was sure he'd have seized the chance, taken Sarah-Jane home so that the two of them could romp in the comfort of the kingsize bed. She was going to drive straight home and catch them out.

What weapon would she choose? From our visit to their lovely house, I remembered the array of knives kept in a wooden block on the breakfast bar. And there was a cast-iron doorstop, a croquet mallet, the possibilities were endless.

Pictures floated through my mind as I shuffled through price lists for gadgets and accessories. Patrick's damaged face peeping from out of the covering sheet in the mortuary. Solemn policemen, shaking their heads. Sarah-Jane, pale and contrite, kissing my cheek. Whispering the question: could I ever forgive her?

Of course I could. I'm not a cruel or bitter man. I'd promise her that we would work at the marriage. Pick up the pieces.

Patrick was right about one thing, I decided. People *are* like cars. They just need the right driver.

My mobile rang. I keyed *Answer* and heard Olivia. Breathless, triumphant.

'So easy, Terry, it was so easy. They were on the drive outside the porch. Kissing, they only had eyes for each other.'

'You – did it?'

She laughed, a high, hysterical peal. 'It's like nothing else. The feeling as your wheels go over someone. Crushing out the life – *squish, squish*. The screams urge you on. I felt so empowered, so much in control. But I reversed over the body, just to make sure.'

'So...'

I heard her gasp and then another voice on the line. A voice I never wanted to hear again. Frantic, horrified.

'Terry, you put her up to this, you bastard. You jealous, murdering bastard.'

It was Patrick, lucky Patrick.

My mind stalled, useless as an old banger. I couldn't take this in, couldn't comprehend what Olivia had done. If Patrick was alive – what had happened to Sarah-Jane?

Dust rose in vortices over the mosque, mingling with the prayers coming from the loudspeaker on the mud brick minaret; but unlike the invocations of surrender, the spirals reached not as far as heaven, nor even as high as the muezzin's tower, instead becoming quickly absorbed into the low orange sky made up of the fine sand of the *khamseen*.

The Americans covered their faces and, following the guide, were soon on the very edge of the desert.

Fused shades of yellow and green blurred into desiccated creams and greys. The landscape empty now but for a few rocks and smaller stones and over the hard ground a thin layer of migrating sand. No sign of man or beast and to the west and south only emptiness that stretched for another thousand miles and more.

The cold *khamseen* wind had been blowing since they got here and some of the Americans grumbled that they were underdressed. Who knew Egypt could be like this, even in February?

Mitchell had a scarf over his mouth and a wool hat on his head. *He* knew.

Taking up the rear he joined a semicircle around the guide who had been talking the whole time. Because of the howling wind, no one had really heard a word. Now that he had stopped in the lee of the step pyramid they could hear properly.

'...the pyramids of Sakkhara are of course very different than those of the more well known examples on the Gizan plateau. Older, with none of the precision architecture we associate with Giza. But even so if you look north it is still very striking. This is the best picture we are going to get today. A real Kodak moment.'

Some of the party took photographs of the step pyramids among the wasteland.

Mitchell did not.

He had seen the pyramids before.

He hobbled over to the guide, a thin, moustachioed man with a white shirt and a hooded anorak.

'I'm not feeling well,' Mitchell said.

'Is it the same as yesterday?' the guide asked without concern.

'Yeah.'

'Do you wish to go back to the bus?' the guide wondered and discreetly looked the elderly American up and down. Mitchell could tell what he was thinking. He had seen the contempt on his face at every glance in the minibus mirror. A contempt hidden sometimes by obsequiousness.

None of the Americans were in what you would call good shape. They were fat, many obese and all – in the Egyptian's eyes – loud and vulgar. They weren't even particularly interested in what he had been telling them. Few of them thought of this as a 'trip of a lifetime' to be savoured at every second. These were retired and quite wealthy people who had the money to enjoy many of these trips. Egypt was just one more country and experience to be knocked off.

But Mitchell seemed an unlikely candidate to have taken ill so early on the tour. He was one of the youngest in the group. He was only about sixty-two or sixty-three and while he couldn't be described as lithe he certainly wasn't as portly as the others. He was six foot tall, perhaps two hundred pounds.

He still had most of his grey hair and if the guide had been more astute he would have seen the alert coldness in Mitchell's blue grey eyes, and maybe he wouldn't have been so blasé about him.

In any case, definitely the fittest and youngest looking of the lot of them.

The guide shook his head.

It was always the ones you least expected.

That ninety-year-old crone from Alabama would probably be perky all the way to Luxor.

'I'm too sick for the bus,' Mitchell said.

'What do you want me to do?' the guide asked on the verge of impertinence.

'Nothing. I'll get a taxi back to the hotel,' Mitchell said.

The guide nodded.

'It should be no more than ten Egyptian pounds. Fix the price before you leave,' the guide said.

Mitchell nodded.

'Thank you,' he said.

Mitchell walked to the car park through the long line of hawkers and hangers on crying out for *baksheesh*. The children were the worst. He distributed a few coins and made it through the rank of underpowered Fiats that were the workhorses of Cairo's taxi fleet.

The ride took him on a slight mystery tour through the southern suburbs and Mitchell didn't even bother to argue when the driver demanded an extortionate twenty Egyptian pounds.

When he walked into the reception of the Marriot, Sandy, the pencil thin, brassy, blonde, Saga Tours rep was waiting for him.

'Mr Mitchell, I was sorry to hear that you had taken ill

again. Do you want me to get you a doctor?' she asked.

'Nah. I know what it is. Doc said I shouldn't have come. Prostate.'

Sandy's botox-tight forty-something face tried and failed to frown.

'Your prostate? Are you sure? Perhaps we should send out for a doctor,' she suggested.

Mitchell shook his head.

'I'm sure. I knew it might be a problem. Doc advised me against coming out.'

Sandy nodded and made a mental note. Lying about a preexisting medical condition would certainly violate any rebate.

'I'm going to call it quits. Seen what I came to see anyway,' Mitchell said.

Sandy's head bobbed up and down like an apple on a stick.

'If you are going to need treatment it might be better to fly back to Europe rather than risk infection in a Cairo hospital,' she said helpfully.

'That's what I was thinking. If you book me on a flight to London tonight I would be most appreciative. Don't worry about the rest of the tour. It can go on without me. Like I say, I've seen the pyramids and that's enough,' Mitchell said.

Sandy nodded. Perhaps that would be best. Certainly one less old codger to worry about.

'I'll try and find you a flight,' she said breezily.

A little too breezily. Mitchell didn't want there to be any delay. He took out his wallet.

'There's an eight p.m. flight to London tonight. First Class please, here's my card,' he said giving her his American Express Platinum Club, which he figured would be the one she'd be most impressed by.

She nodded and went off to make the arrangements. When she was gone he ignored the elevator and took the stairs four flights to his room.

When he got in, he had a shower, towelled off, and was about to call Margaret when there was a knock at the door.

He pulled on a robe and opened the door.

The hotel manager, an older Egyptian man about his own age. Elegant guy, dressed in a three piece.

'Mr Mitchell, I regret to hear of your illness, is there anything I can do for you?'

Mitchell shook his head.

'Everything has been very satisfactory, you guys have been great... Look I don't want to be rude but I really have to call my doctor in Virginia.'

The manager nodded.

'I hope the remainder of your stay will be a pleasant one,' the manager said kindly.

Mitchell nodded and when the man had gone muttered, 'I wouldn't bet on it,' under his breath.

He had a shave, dressed and called Margaret.

'Hi,' he said.

'Frank, how are you?' she replied.

'Good. How are you?'

'I'm fine Frank, we're all fine.'

There was a pause and he wondered if it was wise to spill the beans – but there was no two ways about it, he knew that he had to tell her in case anything went wrong.

'Listen Margaret, I'm going to try for it tonight,' he said simply.

'Oh my God,' Margaret replied and took an intake of breath. There was a pause. He knew she was putting her hand over the receiver and taking a series of deep breaths. He gave her a minute to come back on.

'Frank?'

'Yes?'

'This is the only time I'm going to ask it,' she said slowly.

'What?'

Another pause.

'You do know what you're doing, don't you Frank?'

'I know,' Mitchell said.

'And you'll be careful?'

'Don't worry about me honey. I'll be fine.'

'Oh Frank I—'

'Listen honey,' he interrupted, before the tears came, 'I better go. I love you sweetie, I love you very much and don't worry about a thing.'

An hour later he picked up his airline ticket at the reception desk and had his luggage checked in at the hotel's Sky Cap service.

He was wearing a long black sweater, blue jeans and carrying a small backpack. The backpack was stuffed full of clothes and supplies but the only thing in it that belonged to him was a black ski mask.

He went outside the hotel and hailed a cab.

A blue Fiat that was being held together by rust and prayers.

'Speak English?' he asked.

The driver nodded, as they all did, whether they spoke English or not.

He got inside and gave the driver a piece of paper.

'Can you read it?' he asked in Arabic.

'Of course,' the driver replied.

They set off.

Mitchell had read that hundreds of taxi drivers were seriously injured, many killed, every year in road accidents in Cairo. There were virtually no traffic laws, few traffic police and the rule of the road was: give way to the bigger and more aggressive vehicle, or else. This driver was no different and he nearly got into several collisions before Mitchell had to tell him to slow down.

'American?' the driver asked.

'Yeah.'

'But Americans are always in a hurry.'

'Not me. Safety is my priority,' Mitchell said.

'Our lives are in the will of Allah. *Inshallah* we will be safe.'

'Yeah, doubtless, but keep your eyes on the road anyway pal,' Mitchell said. The man turned and gave him a betel-stained grin.

'I am good driver. For some it is hard to see with dust, the *khamseen*, but not me.'

'That a fact?'

'Yes. Drive good, save, one day I drive cab in Chicago, like my cousin.'

'Great.'

The driver grimaced at Mitchell's unenthusiastic response to his life plan but said nothing.

They drove over the Nile, into the eastern suburbs, well off the tourist trail.

'You are Jewish?' the driver asked after a while.

Mitchell shook his head.

'You Americans help Israel. Let me tell you my friend, the day of reckoning comes for the Zionist Entity. We will destroy it soon.'

Mitchell nodded.

'Yeah, you should invade Israel, it's worked so well the last three times you've tried it.'

The driver had competent English but it wasn't good enough to get sarcasm. He launched into an explanation of the failures of the past and why the next time would all be different.

Mitchell ceased to listen.

One of his qualities.

'Stop right here,' he said suddenly at a busy intersection.

The driver slammed on the brakes.

Mitchell opened the cab door.

'Wait here,' he said and went into what (from all the pots and pans hanging outside) appeared to be a hardware store.

He bought a heavy, steel-headed, claw hammer with a rubber grip. German made. Perfect.

He tried to give the shopkeeper ten Egyptian pounds but the man insisted that he had overpaid him and handed him six pounds in change.

'*Shukran*,' Mitchell said and ran back to the cab.

It took them thirty minutes to get to the address. A rundown neighbourhood filled with shoddily built five storey apartment buildings. Garbage all over the road, slabs of concrete peeling from the tenement walls. There were no cars here, just posters of Mubarak, stray dogs and the occasional motorcycle loaded with three or even four people.

He took out a twenty dollar bill and gave it to the taxi driver.

'Listen to me buddy, we seem to have a pretty good relationship going here, I want you to do me a favour, I want you to wait here for me for about ten minutes, do you understand?'

The driver nodded.

'And when I come back you're going to take me to the airport and I'm going to give you these,' he said showing the man five more twenties.

'Yes sir,' the driver said eagerly.

He would wait, probably a month's wages for him, Mitchell thought.

Mitchell got out of the cab and looked about.

They were really right on the edge of the city here. To the south lost in the gloom there was an old mosque and rows of shanty houses made of cinder blocks and salvaged wood. Then the desert, except that once again there were no undulating dunes of golden sand, just a stony bleak, lifeless and inhospitable plain.

And that biting wind that was beginning to churn up the sand so that it was hard to see fifty yards. Let it blow, Mitchell thought, just so long as the flights aren't delayed.

He walked across the empty street, found the building, put on the ski mask and knocked on the door. He kept the hammer down by his side. He was afraid now. But fear was good, fear kept you on your toes. You needed it. Especially if you were an old geezer retired from this kind of thing for several years.

He knocked again. Footsteps, then a man of about twenty-five answered the door.

He had a moustache and a gold chain drooping over a dirty red 'Ferrari' T-shirt. Mitchell recognised him from the photograph. Aziz's younger brother, Mohammed.

'*Marha-ba*,' Mohammed said before he saw the ski mask.

Mitchell hit him once in the forehead with the hammer. The blow smashed Mohammed's skull and penetrated through the cranium into the frontal lobe. Mitchell removed the hammer with a jerk and Mohammed tottered backwards slowly enough for Mitchell to grab him and ease him to the floor. Blood was pouring from his skull and frothing at his lips. Mitchell watched his legs twitch for a moment and then stop.

He was still breathing but it would be touch and go whether he lived or not.

Jesus. Well now I'm pot committed, Mitchell thought.

He stood and walked down a long corridor. Cracked tiles, flaking plaster and a naked twenty-watt light bulb above his head. Some kind of animal droppings on the floor.

A door to the left that was slightly ajar.

He looked in.

Two men watching a soccer game on TV.

Mitchell ignored them, eased the door closed and walked into the first courtyard.

An odd sight.

Dozens of rabbits running about – nibbling at a pile of lettuce leaves and rotting fruit. In any other circumstance it might have been comic.

He avoided the bunnies and looked for the yellow wooden door to the women's quarters.

He saw it behind a pail of filthy water.

He walked over to the door and pushed it open.

Another smaller courtyard beyond.

The sun peeking out of the orange sky. More rabbits, an emaciated dog tied to a stick, washing hanging on a line.

A woman in a *burka* frozen over a basket, staring at him, open mouthed.

Mitchell put his fingers to his lips, walked across the courtyard and pushed on a second yellow door.

Two more women in full *burkas*.

One of them screamed. Mitchell pushed them out of the way and turned left into a small bedroom. A mattress on the floor, rabbit droppings and, there, in the corner, a crib much too small for a near one-year-old.

The baby was crying and lying on a filthy sheet. She was skinny, pale and they had pierced her ears. She had a diaper on but the diaper was soaked through. Mitchell picked her up in his left arm and held her like a football.

He walked out of the room. One of the two women began yelling and the other tried to prevent him from leaving. Mitchell kicked her in the stomach and she stumbled backwards into a table breaking it. Her companion screamed. Mitchell ran into the inner courtyard, slipped, almost fell, righted himself.

The woman bent over the washing watched him impassively.

He pushed on the first heavy yellow door and ran into the outer courtyard.

A boy of about eleven was standing in front of him shouting something. Mitchell kicked him in the chest and the boy crumpled to the floor.

The kid was out and wouldn't be a problem but by now the TV watching men had appeared from the corridor in front of him blocking the exit to the street. Both were carrying knives.

The men were saying something to him in a hate-filled language of curses and venom. Good, their rage would make them make mistakes. The baby beside him started to cry again.

'*Allahu Akhbar,*' one of the men yelled and ran at him with a large curved meat knife. Mitchell stepped to one side to lower his profile and protect the baby. In the same move he avoided a clumsy knife thrust and hit the man in the arm with the hammer. Before the man could even cry out Mitchell had turned the hammer backwards and smashed him in the head with the two stainless steel claws. They hooked into the man's face with a sickening thud. Mitchell pulled hard and the man's nose and half his cheek came off in a spout of blood and cartilage. Mitchell elbowed him to the ground.

The other man screamed and ran at him, moving so fast that his knife – a small dagger – managed to avoid Mitchell's block and embed itself in his right shoulder. It was a good attack but you don't stab with that kind of knife, Mitchell thought, as he kicked the man in the left kneecap and brought the hammer down twice on the poor bastard's head.

Avoiding treading on the rabbits, he walked across the courtyard, stepped around Mohammed in the corridor, ignored the sounds of screaming behind him and ran into the busy street. There was a bus outside with a noisy diesel engine that would help for a bit, but not too long. Soon neighbours, cops, tourist police, the whole gamut would be showing up, yelling for blood.

He looked for the taxi driver and half expected him to have bolted. His contingency plan was to hijack a private car, but no, that wouldn't be necessary for there he was. With a wince of pain he took the knife out of his shoulder and put it in his pocket.

The driver looked aghast at the hammer and the baby and opened his mouth to protest. Mitchell hooked the hammer under his arm, opened the taxi door, got in the back, set the baby down on the seat and passed the man five twenty dollar bills.

'Airport,' Mitchell said.

'What is going on here?'

Mitchell grabbed the driver around the neck with his left hand and brought the knife to the driver's throat. He tickled the man's carotid artery with the blade.

'Airport now pal. A hundred dollars or this knife in your goddamn neck, your call.'

'I go,' the driver said.

Mitchell released him and the driver set off.

'Any funny business and I'll kill ya, understand?' Mitchell said.

The driver nodded. Mitchell watched him for a minute and then reached in his backpack and pulled out a pacifier, a packet of Huggies and baby wipes. He took off the soiled diaper, wiped the baby girl, applied some rash cream, a Huggy and put her in a sleep suit. He gave her a bottle of formula and a pacifier. Halfway to the airport she stopped crying and in another few minutes she had fallen asleep. She had dark eyes and dark hair and was woefully thin. Maybe twenty pounds at the most. Of course she was still very beautiful.

Mitchell took off the black sweater and looked at the knife wound in his arm. Not bad. He removed his T-shirt and examined it closely. A puncture about an inch deep in the fleshy part of his shoulder, right above the tattooed letters USMC.

He wrapped the wound in gauze which he tightened off with duct tape. He poured water on the black sweater and rinsed the blood out. He put the sweater back on. It didn't look good but there was a leather jacket in his bag at the airport that he'd put on in the lounge bathroom.

'We are at the airport,' the driver said nervously.

'Departures, and take it easy, if you do anything I don't like we can let Allah decide if you live with a knife in your neck.'

They pulled into a parking space at Departures.

Mitchell gave the driver the five twenties and then held out one of two hundred dollar bills.

'You did good. Just remember this, if I'm stopped by the police before I can get on my flight, I'm going to tell them who my accomplice was, the person who helped me get away.'

'I did nothing,' the driver protested.

'Who they gonna believe?'

The driver thought about it and nodded.

'So let me ask you a question, chief, who was your passenger today?' Mitchell said brandishing the Benjamin.

The driver looked at the bill hungrily, took it between his thumb and forefinger and placed it in his shirt pocket.

'An English woman that I drove to the pyramids,' the driver said.

Mitchell gave him the other hundred dollar bill and got out of the cab.

He walked to the First Class lounge, had a cup of coffee, ignored the snooty looks, changed the baby again, gave her a kiss, put on his leather jacket, checked his luggage and then went through security. He showed his own passport and the baby's passport. There was a minor fuss when the inspector couldn't find the baby's entry stamp.

'What was your business in Egypt, Mr Mitchell?'

'I was on a Saga Tour with my wife but the baby got a little unwell, it was a bad idea to bring her, so I'm taking her back to the States and my wife's going on to Luxor.'

'No stamp for the child. Perhaps they stamped your wife's

passport twice?' the inspector suggested helpfully.

'Yeah that's it, I think they did that, is there a fine we should pay or something?' Mitchell asked and finessed the situation with another hundred dollar bill.

He got through security and bought a newspaper.

There was another minor problem at the gate.

The British Airways flight attendant said that his ticket didn't include a passenger. Mitchell said that he didn't think he needed a ticket for the baby since she was sitting in his lap. The flight attendant shook her head and it really might have been a problem if he hadn't been flying First Class. Instead, after some grumbling she cut him another ticket for the baby and let him through.

Mitchell waited until they had left Egyptian airspace before making the call.

'Hello,' he said.

'Frank,' Margaret said and burst into tears.

'Take it easy,' he said.

'Are you hurt?' she asked.

'Scratch. Nothing serious,' he said.

'Thank God.'

She didn't ask if he got the baby – she could tell that from that first syllable.

'Don't do anything stupid like calling the media, or worse, the State Department,' Mitchell said.

'We won't Frank. We know better.'

'Good. OK, she needs to feed, better go. See you in London.'

'Love you Frank.'

'Love you too,' he said and hung up.

The wound in his shoulder started acting up. The bleeding

began again and he had to take a trip to the bathroom to wash the puncture and change the gauze. He took the girl with him in a Baby Bjorn and set her down on the changing platform. He threw away the bloody bandage and put on a new dressing. He took another good look at the dagger's best efforts. Might affect the golf swing, but he'd live.

He put the baby back in the Bjorn and found his seat again.

He stared out the window.

The rough stuff was over but maybe the hard part was still to come. There would be lawyers, there would be questions, there might even be an attempt to extradite him, or kidnap the baby away from his daughter again. He remembered something the instructors had told him at Seal Beach, San Diego, thirty-three years ago: 'the only easy day was yesterday', and for the hundredth time since hearing that it made him feel a little better.

Over Sicily the baby woke and was inconsolable until he fed her a piece of mashed banana and sang the Streets of Laredo three times.

The plane flew over the darkening Mediterranean.

Stars appeared in the eastern sky.

The stewardess went past smelling of jasmine and oranges.

He closed his eyes.

And yes, of course, there would be hardships, there would be hassles, but whatever was coming, they would deal with it as a family this time, united and together.

'We can take it,' he said to himself and then, after what had been a long, long day, with his only granddaughter safe and resting peacefully on his chest, he allowed himself the slightest of smiles and fell into a brief, but untroubled sleep.

Lamb rogan josh. My favourite curry and, once you've got the basic spices, one of the easiest to make. Brown off your lamb cubes and put to one side. Add a generous glug of oil to a wide pan, put the heat on medium high and throw in some cardamom pods, bay leaves, cloves, peppercorns, cinnamon, onions, ginger and garlic. Stir for thirty seconds. Add cumin, coriander, paprika and salt. Stir for another thirty seconds. Add the lamb, some yoghurt and a cup of water. Simmer for as long as you can resist.

I thought I had the curry sussed, until that night in Baba's Bites. Meat cooked until the strands barely hung together, yoghurt and spices perfectly balanced and some other ingredient that brought the dish springing to life. I thought of all the previous times I'd eaten it and knew I'd been stumbling around in the dark.

'Kaz,' I said, hunched over the shallow polystyrene tray, prodding towards the riot of flavours with a plastic fork, 'this is delicious. New cook or something?'

Kaz's brother usually prepared the curries, but I'd only had to smell this one to know it was in a different league. Kaz smiled as he sprinkled his homemade chilli sauce over a doner kebab and held it out to the customer who stood swaying on my side of the little takeaway's counter.

'No, no mate. I mean loads of chilli sauce,' the young bloke drunkenly said, trying to speak slowly and clearly for the benefit of what he thought were foreign ears. In a larger version of the action I'd just made with my fork, the customer jerked his hand up and down to demonstrate that he wanted the kebab to be drowned. The smile didn't leave Kaz's face as he soaked the open pitta bread with gouts of fiery liquid.

'Cheers mate,' said the customer, grabbing the paper wrapped package and staggering out the door, leaving a trail of crimson drops behind him.

Kaz looked over at me and, with an accent that combined the nasal twang of Manchester with the thicker tones of the Middle East, said, 'Yeah mate. It's good then?'

My mouth was too full for any spoken reply. Holding up a thumb, I nodded vigorously. Kaz looked pleased as he turned back to the huge hunk of processed meat slowly revolving on the oil soaked spike. Flourishing a long knife, he began carving away at its outer layer.

Once I'd swallowed my mouthful I said, 'So what's your brother doing then?'

'Oh, he's pursuing a new business interest. He won't be around so much from now on.'

The curry was too good for me to continue talking so, before tucking into it once more, I quickly said, 'Well, compliments to the chef.'

I'd dropped out of my chemical engineering degree halfway through my second year. There was no way I could imagine a career in it. Life, I decided, was too short to spend doing something you didn't enjoy. I sat down and tried to imagine a job that I would enjoy. Twenty-one years old, with a series of mind-numbing McJobs behind me and I was struggling. But during my gap year I went to Thailand (original choice, I know). Though I was far too much of a traveller to ever step inside Koh Samui's flashy tourist hotels full of mere holidaymakers, I watched the tour reps at work. I reckoned I could handle a life working in some of the most beautiful places on earth. Work it out for yourself: Manchester versus the Maldives. Britain versus Barbados. So a degree in Travel and Tourism it was.

Which left me with a new set of course fees rolled into almost two years of student debt. I got a night job in the bakers just down the road from my digs. 'Mr Wing's Chinese Bakers'. There can't be many of those in Britain. But you wouldn't believe the amount of stuff he churns out. During the day it's things like doughy rolls filled with sweet and sour pork, kung po chicken or special seafood mix or batches of little buns sprinkled with sesame seeds and filled with chestnut puree or honey paste. At five o'clock the day shift goes home, the front of shop shuts and the night shift appears round the back. While the rest of the country is slumped in front of the box, or enjoying themselves in pubs and restaurants, the output changes to speciality, or ethnic breads as they're classed on the supermarket shelves. Pittas, naans, raithas, chapattis, lavache, ciabatta – all that stuff. The monstrous silver ovens never get the chance to cool down. Staff scurry around them, transporting away the steady flow of produce like worker ants carrying off the stream of eggs laid by their queen.

My co-workers chat happily away in languages from India, Asia or Africa, but hardly any speak English. It's obvious most haven't got to Britain by legal means either. The cash changes hands just before dawn and, unlike my rate of pay, theirs reflects the twilight world they operate in. The minimum wage doesn't even come into it. It's probably because I'm an official British citizen with a clean driving licence that I got the job of doing drop offs. And, seeing as working next to a furnace half the night wasn't my idea of fun, that was fine by me. I deliver to city centre takeaway joints that need more stock or the Indian restaurants on Manchester's curry mile that prefer to serve freshly baked produce. They all know Mr Wing's never shuts. The phone rings and I'm off in the little van with their order.

Baba's Bites called on my very first night. As soon as I wandered in with the tray of naans and pittas, Kaz spotted me for someone who was prepared to do a deal. And this is how it works: Kaz rings with an order, I pick what he wants from the racks of stuff in the storage room and swipe an extra tray or two. In return he gives me a free curry.

Baba's Bites – it's your typical late night, city centre takeaway place. A few stools and a narrow counter running along the plate glass window at the front. Overflowing bin by the door. Rear of the shop partitioned off by a counter with a glass case on top. Underneath the warm panels of glass are stainless steel dishes full of curry, lumps of sheek kebab on skewers, mounds of onion bhajis, saveloy sausages and pakoras. Above the counter is a huge back-lit menu. A panel of photos showing juicy morsels which generally bear no resemblance to what gets handed over. Along the back wall is the inevitable kebab turning in one corner, a couple of hot trays for the meat he skims off, a chip fryer, a hot plate for flipping burgers, a microwave for pizzas, a glass fronted fridge full of cans and a small sink (never used). In the other corner is the tiny hatchway through to the kitchen. Although you can hear the clatter of pans in the kitchen, you can't actually see into it – a hanging screen of multi-coloured plastic strips ensures that. Kaz shouts through and a short while later whoever is doing the cooking presses a buzzer. Kaz then reaches in and picks up the next batch of burgers, sheek kebabs or boiled rice. When I arrive Kaz always scoops me a portion of lamb rogan josh, then passes it through the hatch for the extra coriander and sliced tomatoes that I like to be added.

Where Kaz was lucky – and why Baba's Bites does so well while countless other similar places just scrape by – is that less than a year ago a massive late-night bar and club opened opposite. Now he's assured of a steady flow of revellers being drawn across the road to the glow of his shop like moths to a flame. Unlike the melting pot of ethnic foods on sale, the clientele are mostly white, mostly male, usually in their twenties. Eyes bright, they burst raucously through the door, vying with each other at the counter, sometimes loudly critical at what's on offer, sometimes reverently appreciative like kids in a sweet shop. Who knows which way alcohol will tip them. As they wait for their orders they discuss all manner of topics. The standard of women in the club they'd just left, how United or City are doing, the lack of black cabs. Sometimes it's stuff from the news – the state of the country's immigration system, scrounging asylum seekers, the flood of immigrants ruining the country. Even when they start to bitterly discuss pakis or ragheads, Kaz's smile remains unchanged as he plays the dutiful patron, quietly carrying out their commands. Serving them food from the very countries they curse.

To the left of Baba's Bites is a Slow Boat Chinese takeaway, on the other side a 24-hour Spar complete with bouncers to stop shoplifters escaping. After that is a dive of a pub. The rest of the row of shops on his stretch of the street consists of daytime businesses – dry cleaners, a newsagent's and places like that. At the other end is a fish and chip shop which, for some reason, always shuts at around eight o'clock. The shutters are drawn down and padlocked long before I ever show up. Above the chip shop is a massage parlour. You'd miss it from the street, but in the alleyway round the back a discreet sign above the permanently open door leading up the stairs reads, 'Far Eastern Massage. Open 24 hours.' I only know this because, when I arrive with a delivery for Kaz, I have to carry it up the alleyway to his shop's rear door.

As you'd probably guess from the swell of my belly, I'm not too fussed about my food. As long as there's enough of it. But I'm sure plenty of people happily gorging themselves at the front would spit it out in disgust if they could see the state of things round the back. The alleyway is narrow and it stinks. While the food places are open for business, the extractor fans sound like a collection of giant vacuum cleaners left permanently on. The grills pump out warm, grease-laden fumes that mingle with the sickly sweet aroma of rotting food. The alleyway is littered with trays of all shapes and sizes dumped from the back doors of the shops. Most usually contain the remains of food: broken eggshells, mangled halves of oranges or overripe tomatoes with skins that are split and weeping. Discarded twenty-five litre drums of economy cooking oil sit piled next to empty beer barrels and crates of bottles from the pub. Industrial size wheelie bins seem permanently stuffed to the top, the lids unable to ever close properly. Crowding round them are broods of bulging bin bags, haphazardly piled onto one another. Water, pooled in the pitted surface of the alley, is either a foul smelling milky colour or tinged with a surface of glistening oil.

Kaz's door is like all the others – heavily metal plated. He's spray painted a large red 29 on it and I kick it twice to let whoever's in the kitchen know I've dropped off. I'm always back in the light cast by the lamps on the main road before the bolts go back and the cardboard trays vanish, dragged inside by, I presume, one of the kitchen assistants.

I found the note in about my eighth curry prepared by the new cook. Because I always have lamb rogan josh with extra coriander and freshly sliced tomatoes, she must have worked out it was the same customer asking for it each time. In fact, I was fairly certain that I was Kaz's only regular customer – the rest just stumble in because it's the first place they find serving food after coming out of the club. Most of them probably couldn't even remember what they'd eaten by the next day. I was halfway through my usual, watching with amusement as three lads attempted to cross the road. After about ten o'clock on a weekend it seems pedestrians, vehicles and the watching police silently agree that daytime rules don't apply. Made impatient by booze, people lurch out into the paths of cars that instantly slow down or stop to allow them to cross. Similarly cab drivers pull up whenever they like or make U turns anywhere they fancy. The whole thing is a mêlée yet, apart from the occasional slanging match, it seems to work.

The three lads had made it through the door and were debating about whether to go for doner kebabs or quarter pounders when I bit on the strange object. At first I thought it was gristle – but it was too hard for that. An exploratory poke with my tongue revealed that it was something folded up. With a forefinger and thumb I extracted it from my mouth, sucking the remains of curry sauce from it as I did so. I held it up and saw that it was greaseproof paper, tightly folded. Carefully I opened it out and there, in the middle of the small square, were the words, 'Help me. I am prisoner here.'

I stared with puzzlement at the paper. Placing it carefully to one side, I decided to show it to Kaz once he'd finished serving the group at the counter. The first two had taken their burgers and wandered out onto the street. The third one waited at the counter, a twenty pound note dangling from his hand. But as he was handed his order, the customer whipped the money from Kaz's reach and spun around to run for the door.

From the corner of my eye, I saw his two mates sprint away up the street. Until then I'd only ever seen Kaz from the chest up. He was of a thickset build and I didn't think particularly agile. But he vaulted across that counter in a flash. The lad had bumped against the door frame and lost a second as a result. Kaz sprang across the shop, grabbed him by the collar and dragged him back to the counter in one movement. With his other hand he reached behind it and produced a baseball bat. He shoved it hard up against the customer's mouth, the wooden tip audibly catching on his teeth. A smear of blood appeared on his lips.

'Pay me,' Kaz demanded, aggression lowering his voice to a growl. All traces of the amiable kebab shop owner with a limited understanding of English had vanished and I looked at the muscles bunched in his shoulders and arms, knowing that he meant it. The prospect of imminent violence hung menacingly in the air and I felt a surge of queasiness in my stomach. Thankfully the customer quickly produced the note from the breast pocket of his Ben Sherman shirt. Kaz snatched it, walked him back to the doorway and said, 'Night then.'

The lad walked shakily off up the street and Kaz returned

to behind the counter. He looked at me and said, 'Why do people have to be like that? I work hard all night, give him what he wanted and he tries to rob me.' He shook his head regretfully. 'It's a bad world Richard, a bad world out there.' His eyes turned to the street and he gazed with sadness at the procession of people flowing past. Then, with a smile and shrug of his shoulders, he picked up a ladle and began stirring the curries.

I couldn't believe how quickly he readopted his previous persona. It was like having a friendly dog snarl at you one moment, then wag its tail the next. Finding it hard to keep the same easy familiarity in my voice, I said, 'You're right there.' I looked at the piece of paper and, having witnessed this new side to him, decided against letting him see it.

Two nights later I was making a delivery at Baba's Bites again, but this time I had slipped my own note into the tray of naan breads. It read, 'Who are you? Why are you a prisoner?'

Not knowing if I would ever get a reply, I banged on the back door and then went round to the front and stepped inside. 'Same as usual?' asked Kaz, already spooning rogan josh onto a pile of rice.

'Yeah, cheers,' I replied and sat down on my favourite stool in the corner. He handed the tray through the hatch and a few minutes later it was returned with a garnish of coriander and tomato. Shielding the food from him with one forearm I sifted through the curry with my fork. A thrill of excitement shot through me when I found the little wedge of paper. Quickly I wrapped it in a serviette and slipped it into my pocket.

And so began a correspondence that would change my outlook on life forever. Over the next two weeks we exchanged a series of notes. Mine written on lined sheets, hers scrawled in a microscopic hand on lengths of greaseproof paper. She'd write them at night, sacrificing valuable sleep to describe to me her plight. Her name was Meera and she was a seventeen-year-old Hindu girl from the war-torn region of Kashmir sandwiched uncomfortably between India and Pakistan. Her father and both brothers had died in the crossfire between militants and government troops. That left her as the eldest of four remaining daughters. After a long and tearful talk, she had persuaded her mother that the only way to prevent the family from becoming destitute was for her to leave the war-ravaged region and look for work. So they had paid almost all their savings to a man who promised to find Meera a well paid job as a cook in an Indian restaurant in London. Abandoning her dream of a university place in Jammu to read law, she had climbed into the back of a lorry with seventeen other people and begun the slow trek overland to Britain. The group was occasionally allowed to emerge at night for a few minutes. Twice they transferred to other lorries – the one taking them on the final leg of the journey was the newest. They sat at its end, crammed in on all sides by crates of tulips. Eventually they were all dropped off at a house, herded inside and the men and women separated. They were told they were in Britain, but certain arrangements still had to be made. After two days locked in a room with only a bucket for a toilet, some bottles of water and a few loaves of bread, a different man kicked open the door. Meera was dragged out by her hair and told the cost of her passage to England had gone up. Her passport was taken off her and she was told that, to repay her debt, she could work in a brothel or a kitchen. Of course she opted for the kitchen and was bundled into the back of a van and driven to Baba's Bites. When she asked me which city she was in, tears sprang to my eyes.

She arrived late at night and was led up the stinking alley, marched through the back door and chained to the sink pipes. She had enough slack to get around the kitchen and reach the toilet and sink in a tiny room at the back. She slept on a camp bed in the corner and hadn't seen daylight since arriving; the nearest she got to that was when the back door was opened up to take in deliveries. But she was made to hide in the toilet when that happened. After cooking from lunchtime to the early hours, she would clean the kitchen. Once Kaz had bolted the back door, he left by the front of the shop, padlocking the metal shutters behind him. Then he went round to the alleyway and bolted the back door from the outside too. Once he was gone she was able to grab a few hours' sleep before he or his brother returned late-morning. Then she would be preparing food – including my curries – until the shop raised its shutters once again at lunchtime.

In one of my first ever replies to her I offered to go straight to the police. But she wouldn't let me. If any officials were involved, she reasoned, deportation would inevitably follow. She needed to remain in Britain, working in a job that paid her cash to send home to her family. All she wanted to do was escape from Kaz's kitchen. She told me that the pipe she was chained to was old and flimsy; she was confident that she could bend or even break it. What she needed me to do was slide the bolts back on the outside of the back door, she would do the same to the ones on the inside of the door, and then she would be free. She didn't want any more help than that.

The situation she was in made me feel sick – and outraged

at Kaz. I agreed to help her and we arranged that the next time Kaz rang, I was to put a note in the tray of breads confirming that tonight was the night. A previous note she sent me had stressed the importance of successfully getting her out; she was terrified of what Kaz would do if she tried to escape and failed. I wished she had room on the piece of paper to elaborate, but I reasoned we would soon have plenty of opportunity to talk face to face.

Friday night and I was sitting in the office, fan directed straight at my face, trying to learn the main aspects of insurance law relating to groups travelling abroad. (One of the less glamorous modules of my course.) At 10:43 the phone's ring put a welcome end to my study.

Pushing the door shut, I picked up the receiver and said, 'Mr Wing's Bakery.'

'Rick? It's Kaz here.'

By keeping to our established patter, I was able to hide the revulsion in my voice. 'Kaz, how's business mate?'

'Busy, my friend. Very busy. I need six dozen more pittas, two dozen naans and one dozen peshwari naans.'

'No problem. Any extras?'

'Just naans my friend. All you can get.'

'Coming right up. I'll be there in half an hour.'

Twenty-six minutes later I pulled up outside Baba's Bites. The place was heaving. A couple were sitting on the pavement outside, he finishing off a burger while she rested her head on her knees and moaned about how pissed she was. In the doorway four boisterous lads were struggling over a pizza, each one trying to grab the quarter with the most pepperoni on. I rapped on the window and once Kaz caught sight of me, I pointed to the trays of bread balanced on my other arm then set off round to the back door. As I picked my way between the debris in the alley I saw shadows moving in the glow of light shining from the massage parlour doorway. Keeping in the shadows, I watched as two men emerged into the alley. Both smiling, they turned round to shake hands with the man who had escorted them to the bottom of the stairs and I realised with a shock that it was Kaz's brother. He patted each man on the shoulder and, as they disappeared round the corner, he headed back up the stairs. So that was the new business interest.

I banged twice on the door and as I leaned down to place the trays on the step, noticed for the first time the bolt drawn back at its base. Looking up I saw another at the top. They hadn't been there a few weeks ago and, knowing the reason for their sudden appearance, anger surged through me – if a fire broke out at night Meera stood no chance of escape.

In Baba's Bites I stood silently in the far corner and waited for the skinny man sitting on my stool to finish his curry. I knew my presence by his shoulder was unsettling him, but I didn't back off. I even wanted him to say something; a confrontation might dissipate the ugly knot of aggression lodged in my chest. Alternatively it might aggravate it further: either way I didn't care. Hurriedly the man wiped up the remains of his curry sauce with a piece of naan bread and popped it into his mouth. Glancing at me from the corner of his eye, he left the shop. I sat down and scowled out the window at the people blundering past, all of their spirits lifted by the arrival of the weekend. I watched and wondered if any had the slightest concern for the army of anonymous workers slaving to keep them served with a plentiful supply of cheap takeaways and taxis. Sitting there I began to think about other parts of the economy that were kept running by illegal immigrants. The people who deliver our pizzas, clean our offices, pick our fruit and vegetables, iron our shirts and wash our soiled sheets. No one on the street outside looked as if they could care less. A minute later Kaz called me over and handed me my curry. Hardly able to meet his eyes, I took it with a brief smile and reclaimed my seat.

Looking at the bright red curry I guessed that I'd put on a good half a stone over the past fortnight. It was as delicious as usual; Meera had explained in one note that it was Kashmiri rogan josh I was eating: she used fennel, cloves and a pungent resin called asafetida. As I finished it off I saw the tiny scrap of greaseproof paper. Surreptitiously I unfolded it and saw she had just been able to scrawl the words, 'Please do not fail me.'

Raising my voice unnecessarily, I said goodnight to Kaz, hoping Meera was able to hear me in the back kitchen. The bakery night shift finished just after 4 a.m. and immediately I drove back to Baba's Bites.

Most of the clubs had shut around an hour before and now just a smattering of mini cabs roamed the streets searching for their last fare of the night. The shutters at Baba's Bites were drawn down and padlocked, the bin outside overflowing with the remains of that night's sales. Polystyrene trays were thrown into the doorways of the neighbouring shops, chips dotted the pavement like pale fat slugs. I pulled up at the corner and quietly made my way up the alley. The council bin lorry came round every Sunday and Thursday – which meant the refuse had been cleared from the alley only last night. However Fridays were probably the week's busiest night and already the alleyway was piled with bags of rubbish, boxes and packaging hurled from the back doors of the shops. At the other end light shone from the massage parlour's open door. It spilled across the narrow passageway, helping me pick my way forward. Up ahead an enormous rat heard my approach. We looked at each other for a few seconds then, to my relief, it casually crept back into the overflow of a nearby drain. At the back door of Baba's Bites I put my ear up against the cool metal surface and listened. But there was nothing to hear. Tentatively I knocked twice. Instantly a knock was returned. She must have broken free of the pipe and was sitting on the other side of the door listening for my arrival.

Urgently I whispered, 'Meera, is that you?' Instantly I felt stupid: it could hardly have been anyone else.

Her voice was light and sonorous, and would have been beautiful to hear if it wasn't packed with so much fear. 'Yes Richard, it's me. I have broken the pipe, the kitchen is flooded.'

Looking down I saw water seeping out from the bottom of the door. Metal began to clunk and rattle as she started undoing the bolts on her side of the door. I stepped back to slide open the ones on my side – and to my dismay saw they were secured with two heavy-duty padlocks. I shut my eyes and silently swore. I didn't think Kaz would bother padlocking a door that was bolted shut from both the inside and out. But now it seemed an obvious precaution, especially considering the prisoner he kept inside. Meera's trembling voice sounded through the thick barrier separating us. 'I have done it. Can you open the door?'

'Meera,' I whispered. 'He's padlocked the bolts. I can't unlock them.'

'You must,' she cried, now panic-stricken. 'I must leave here!'

I needed a hacksaw; and nowhere would be open until morning. By then our chance would be gone. Even if Kaz turned up late, I couldn't stand there in broad daylight breaking into the back of a shop. 'I'm so sorry Meera, I need a hacksaw. I'll get one later and come back the same time tomorrow.'

'No!' she pleaded. 'I cannot be here when he comes. He will know what I have done.'

I looked at the tamper-proof screws protecting the door hinges: there was no way I could free her. I slapped the palm of my hand against the wall in frustration. 'I'm sorry Meera. I promise to come back.'

She began to sob, 'He beat me for burning the rice. He said he will send me somewhere far worse than here if I do wrong again. Help me Richard.'

Desperately I whispered back, 'I will, tomorrow.'

I heard her slump against the door and start to cry. At the other end of the alley male voices were audible coming down the stairs of the massage parlour. Pressing my hands against the door, I could only whisper, 'I'll come back tomorrow night,' before quickly walking back out onto the street.

As soon as B&Q opened I was searching the place for hacksaws. An elderly assistant saw me scanning the aisles and took me to the correct section. 'It's a big padlock. The hasp is about a centimetre thick,' I told him.

'Well,' he said, rubbing his chin with one hand. 'This will get through it in about five minutes.'

'Great,' I said, taking the saw from his hands and hurrying to the tills.

After that I went to the supermarket and bought a load of food, including a pile of fresh fruit and vegetables. I had already decided to insist that Meera stay at my place until she was sorted out with a job. I was confident I could get a place for her in Mr Wing's bakery, even if it would be for a pittance. Now, given what she had said about Kaz beating her, I wasn't sure what sort of a state she might be in when I finally got that door open. I had formed an image of her face – long dark hair, fragile features and large brown eyes. Picturing her now covered in bruises, I added bottles of ibuprofen and paracetamol to my trolley.

The rest of the day was spent dozing fitfully on my sofa. I kept waking up, my mind dwelling on what he'd do to her. He wouldn't hurt her too badly, I reasoned. After all, he needed her to cook. But I'd seen the flash of his temper and an uneasy feeling sat heavy in my mind. Flicking on the telly, I caught the lunchtime news. The presenter was describing how a major ring in peddling African children into the British sex trade had been broken up by the police. The implications of Kaz's brother's new business interest suddenly hit me like a slap in the face. Kaz himself had said she would end up somewhere far worse if she did anything wrong again. An image of a grimy bed in the Far Eastern Massage Parlour forced its way into my mind. Meera chained to it, a queue of punters at the door, pulses racing at the prospect of a new girl in her teens. I tried to push the thought away.

In Mr Wing's that night I sat staring at the Chinese calendar on the wall of his office. It was the Year of the Monkey, judging by the number of little primates adorning the pages. The relief I felt when the phone finally rang was instantly diminished when I heard Kaz's voice. Sounding unsettled, he asked for double quantities of just about everything. He hadn't time to make it to the cash 'n' carry, he explained. At least I now could make a delivery and then sit at the counter and observe him. Try and gauge by his behaviour just what he might have done to her.

So, after dumping the trays at the back door and kicking it twice, I marched round to the front of the shop. As soon as I stepped inside it was obvious something was wrong. For a start there was no lump of doner kebab turning on its vertical skewer in the corner. The fridge of canned drinks was almost empty – just cream soda and cans of shandy remained. People were waiting restlessly for their orders while Kaz hurried around behind the counter looking totally stressed out.

'Forget the chicken,' said one customer. 'I haven't got all night. How much are those things?' He pointed down at the skewers of sheek kebabs lined up under the counter.

'£2.50 each, including pitta bread and salad. How many?' asked Kaz, acknowledging me with a quick wave and passing a portion of lamb rogan josh through the hatch.

'Two,' the young man snapped, rapping a pound coin impatiently against the counter.

I took my corner seat and after a longer wait than usual, my curry arrived. 'You alright?' I asked as Kaz handed it to me over the counter.

'Yeah, staff problems that's all,' he replied distractedly. As I took the polystyrene tray I noticed a long scratch running across the back of his hand. Pretending I hadn't seen it, I took my curry and sat back down. With the first forkful I knew it hadn't been cooked by Meera. The sauce was watery, my extra garnish of coriander was missing, the lamb was burnt and the rice had been left in the pan until the grains were bloated and soft. As soon as it entered my mouth it turned into something that resembled semolina. I struggled through it, wondering what this meant. Was Meera beaten so badly that she couldn't cook? Or had she already been bundled up the alley and into the massage parlour?

Binning the container, I waited a few moments to try and ask Kaz where his usual cook was, but the shop had grown too busy again. Drunken men milled around at the counter, confused by the lack of doner kebab and settling reluctantly for the poorly prepared alternatives. Not wanting to arouse Kaz's suspicions by lingering for too long, I slipped back out and returned to Mr Wing's.

As soon as the bakery shut, I said my goodnights and hurried along the street to my car. Checking that the hacksaw was still safely stashed on the back seat, I set off straight back to Kaz's. In the alleyway I picked my way through the debris, nose wrinkling at the fruity smell being given off by a tray of rotten bananas.

Now, at the door, I knock on it twice and wait for a reply. Nothing. 'Meera?' I whisper loudly. 'Can you hear me?' On the other side of the door is only silence. Dark thoughts crowd my brain. Have they gagged her? Can she no longer speak because her mouth is so badly swollen? I raise up the hacksaw but, just as I start to saw, I realise that without her to unlock the inner bolts, the door will be impossible to open. Voices at the other end of the alley cause me to crouch behind a pile of bin bags. Four men emerge from the massage parlour. They step out into the alley, laughing and patting each other's backs. One mimes a whipping motion as if he's urging a horse to the finish line and they all roar with laughter again. Holding up hands to slap each other's palms, they head back onto the street and disappear round the corner.

The image of Meera chained to the bed, legs spread,

reappears in my mind and I throw the hacksaw angrily down. Looking at the entrance to the massage parlour, I consider barging my way up the stairs and demanding to see her. Two more men appear at the corner and disappear into the open doorway. Angrily I pull out my mobile phone and dial 999. Once connected to the operator I ask for the police. I'm put through to a tired sounding man and I explain that I have reason to believe there is an illegal female immigrant being held against her will in the Far Eastern Massage Parlour, just off Cross Street in central Manchester. The person asks how I know this for certain and when I reply that I don't, he says they'll try and arrange for a patrol car to call the next day.

'But you need to send someone now. She's probably up there being raped this very moment,' I almost shout.

The person at the other end of the line barely attempts to mask their boredom, assuring me that my report has been logged and will be dealt with at the earliest opportunity. But, he adds, with it being Saturday night, that may well be some time.

Furiously I yell, 'Now! You must send someone now!' and kick out at the nearest bin bag. The thin plastic splits and among the scraps of shredded cabbage, tomato and cucumber that tumble out, is a human hand. Long feminine fingers, bone and gristle visible at the neatly severed wrist. I think of the rows and rows of sheek kebabs Kaz was so eager to sell and the lumps of crudely butchered meat in the curry I'd eaten earlier. As the vomit erupts from my mouth all I can hear is the officer saying, 'Sir, are you all right? Can you hear me sir? Sir?'

The Walthamstow locals were unanimous when Harriet
Blackstone died. Standing in the doorways of Gladstone Road
(the renamed O'Connor Street), watching the police horse
and cart clip-clopping away to the morgue, they looked at
each other, and either said it or left it unsaid but understood:
'She asked for it.'

It was in truth, only what they had been saying about Mrs
Blackstone for years. When they saw her cleaning her attic-
floor windows on long ladders borrowed from Mr Dean the
builder (what had she got on *him*? they asked themselves),
when they saw her sharpening her kitchen knives at the front
door, saw her buying arsenic (for the rats) and cyanide (for
the wasps) at the chemist's or the general stores, they always
looked on these habits as hubristic, without ever using the
word. 'She's asking for it,' they had said, shaking their heads.
Now there was the satisfaction of seeing their prophecies
come true, as well as a more general satisfaction. That night
they had a street party, with Eccles cakes and muffins, and
bottles left over from the Diamond Jubilee. Everyone came
except Harriet's daughter Sylvia, and she seemed regretful at
missing the fun.

'Don't get many chances of a good knees-up,' said Mr
Rowlands at number twenty. 'Won't be decent when the old
Queen goes.'

'Not decent at all,' said Mrs Whitchurch, his neighbour.
'Mind you, after that there'll be the Coronation...'

And the thought of the first coronation for sixty-odd years
gave an added zest to the evening.

Harriet Blackstone had married beneath her, after some years of trying for someone above or on a level with her. Her father had run a failing ironmonger's in Deptford, and her husband had peddled insurance in the poorer areas of cockney London. 'Poor blighter,' everyone said about him when she made him the happiest of men. Nine years later he had gone to his well-deserved rest, having fathered a sickly but determined little girl. The neighbours suggested 'For this relief much thanks' as an appropriate inscription for his gravestone, but the one Harriet had erected merely said 'Sacred to the memory of' and left room for two more names. Harriet did not intend Sylvia to marry. She was needed for the heavy work.

'All men are good for nothing,' she told her daughter, but Sylvia had heard about one or two things that they were good for, and began marking out potential husbands from an early age. They represented not only satisfactions of an earthly kind, but escape as well. So when the jollifications were going on down in the street below, Sylvia watched them from behind the curtains of her cramped little two-up-two-down, wishing she could go down and have a dance and a glass of something nice. She sighed, but she felt that it would not do, and soon she went back to bed with her plasterer husband, and had a giggle and a good time with him.

Relations with her mother had, in fact, been resumed two months before. The marriage had been marked by Mrs Blackstone only by curtains drawn as for a funeral, but some weeks later she had sprained her ankle while unblocking a drain, and had sent one of the neighbouring boys with a note to her daughter, rewarding him with a ha'penny (half the going rate). The note had simply said, 'Sprained ankle. Come.' When Sylvia came round she had finished unblocking the drain, peeled a few potatoes, cut a few slices of cold meat, and then left. All this had been done to a continual ground bass of complaint and criticism not one whit lessened by the fact that her daughter was doing her a favour.

'I could forgive treachery,' Mrs Blackstone said at one point, 'I could forgive the disobedience and the loose morals – because what had been going on *before* the wedding I shudder to think – but what I *cannot* forgive is my daughter taking her sheets to the Communal Wash House to be boiled. The shame of that will be with me to my dying day.'

Sylvia had said nothing and left. But she went back at least once a day during the next week, and now and then thereafter when the ankle was recovered. 'Blood is thicker than water,' she said when the neighbours commented. Behind her back they nodded sagely.

'Who else is there to leave the house to?' they asked each other. When such remarks were repeated to Charlie Paxman, Sylvia's husband, he licked the foam off his lips and said:

'Silly old buzzard will probably leave it to the Primitive Methodists.' So far, at any rate, she had not. All the neighbourhood would have known if she had taken the momentous step of going to a solicitor's.

Harriet was indeed a regular worshipper at the Ebenezer Chapel in Trafalgar Street, where the rigorous and belligerent tone of the services matched her own martial spirit. She was no Sunday Christian, but had brought her values into every corner of everyday life. She had a withering glance that could have felled a bay tree, and she used it against young people holding hands, sometimes followed by 'Shame on you' or some variant of it. Children playing ball in the street were sent scurrying for cover by her shrill objections, and any woman whose clothes were visibly dirty would be assailed by words such as 'slattern' or 'slut'. Cleanliness and teetotalism were up there beside godliness in her scale of values: boys emerging from the Gentlemen's convenience in Trafalgar Street would be asked to show her that they'd washed their hands, and the smell of beer on the breath of a passing labourer would elicit the outraged cry of 'Drunken beast!'

'Give it a rest, old woman,' said one of her victims. 'Just because your tipple is vinegar doesn't mean the rest of us can't enjoy a pint or two of summat nicer.'

But the object of her particular wrath in the months before her death was the house on the corner of Trafalgar Street and Gladstone Road, one whose entrance she could see from all the front windows of her own house. After the death of Mr Wisbeach, the house had been sold (his son lived in Wimbledon, and had no conscience about what happened to the neighbourhood he grew up in). It soon became clear to Harriet Blackstone that the new owners were unusual. There were several women apparently living there, but no man. To be precise, the house contained no man, but from time to time it did contain men. Several members of the frail sex came and went, often regularly, but none of them lived there. Harriet soon began to suspect that some of the women were also only there on an occasional basis. The explanation for this irregularity eventually occurred to her.

'The place is no less than a brothel!' she said to the Ebenezer's minister.

'I should prefer the phrase "House of Pleasure",' he said. There was no inconsistency in his rebuke. 'Pleasure' was always, for him, a dirty word.

Steady and prolonged observation of the house only

strengthened Harriet's conviction. One fine afternoon she marched around to the Walthamstow police station and demanded to see the inspector in charge, refusing to say what she wanted to talk to him about. Such was her force of personality that she got her way, though normally the constable on the duty desk would have shielded his boss from the force of any public indignation.

Inspector Cochrane took his feet off the desk (he wore size thirteen boots, which had for a long time hindered his promotion, as being more suitable for a walker of the beat rather than one undertaking a more thoughtful role, but eventually merit had won out). He welcomed Mrs Blackstone and heard her detailed account of the occupants of number three, Gladstone Road, and the male visitors that had been seen going there. He took no action to cut her short, merely lighting a cigarette and enduring the vicious glances she cast at it. When at last she drew to a close, he tipped the ash off the end of it and got a word in himself.

'Right,' he began. 'Now, it may surprise you to know that you're not the first to come to us over this little matter. I feel people might have done better to talk to the inhabitants of number three, so they got their facts right first, but new residents always take time to be accepted, don't they? Anyway, we've made enquiries, and the family who bought the house from Mr Wisbeach are called O'Hare. Their grandfather came over from Ireland to work on the Manchester to Leeds railway, and their father came south to work on building the station at Liverpool Street and on the lines going out from it. He died last year. It's a big family, and the men in it are either married or working here and there around the country.'

'One of the regular visitors bears a distinct resemblance to the constable who directs the traffic at one end of Walthamstow High Street,' said Harriet waspishly.

'PC O'Hare. Quite,' said Inspector Cochrane. 'Some of the men of the family visit regularly, some less often if they live further away – just as you'd expect. The mother, widow of the man who worked on Liverpool Street station, is not too badly off, and one of the daughters works for a dressmaker in Clerkenwell. I'm not sure I should be telling you their business, but I feel I should save time. So there you are. Problem solved.'

Harriet Blackstone, after a few moments' meditation, cast him one of her bay-tree-withering looks.

'You're telling me I've been wasting my time,' she said.

'I've said nothing of the sort.'

'Well, let's wait and see: it's Time as will tell,' she said, and she marched out of his office and the police station without so much as a goodbye.

As ill luck would have it, it was later that afternoon, when Harriet was still in a foul mood, that Charlie Paxman made his first visit to his new mother-in-law's home. He had seen Sylvia going in when he was arriving back early from a job, and he had knocked at the front door to tell her he was off to the Wolf and Whistle for a pint.

'Bring him in. Let's have a look at him!' shouted Harriet in the kitchen to her daughter at the front door. Charlie went through sheepishly and she surveyed his white-spattered and overalled form from top to toe.

'Well, you're never going to set the Thames on fire,' she said.

'Such was never my ambition,' said Charlie genially. 'And I

doubt if Mr Gladstone 'imself could 'ave achieved it.'

Mrs Blackstone continued sharpening her carving knife on her whetstone, her way of relieving her frustration, and continued the attack. 'Don't you take the name of that godly man in vain,' she said (never having heard of the great man's determined work among the fallen women of the Westminster area). 'He was worth a hundred of you. I suppose you're off to the pub?'

'Just called in to tell Sylv I'm off to do a little job in Trafalgar Street,' said Charlie, winking at his wife. 'You're doing a fine job on that knife, Ma. I could use that in my job, a fine sharp one like that. Just take care you don't whetstone the 'ole thing away, though.'

'When I want advice from a sot like you, I'll ask for it,' said Harriet. 'Get off to your beer palace and your drunken mates.'

'Yes, I could do with a good sharp knife like that,' said Charlie meditatively as he left the house.

'Don't know what you've got against drink,' said Sylvia, greatly daring. 'I like the odd Guinness myself these days. Or a port and lemon.' And she put down what she was doing and followed her husband.

Three days later, when she was putting out cyanide against the insects and hoping it would also tempt any stray dog in the neighbourhood that penetrated her backyard to have a lick, Harriet had a set-to with Jim Parsons in the next house. Jim had worked on the roads, and was now invalided out with a pittance of a pension.

'That stuff smells like a charnel house,' he shouted. 'I wonder you don't drop dead on the spot, just putting it out.'

'You wouldn't understand the first thing about hygiene,' she shouted.

'No, I wouldn't. But I tell you, if one of my pigeons dies, there'll be another death follows on.'

Jim Parsons loved his birds more than he had ever loved mortal, and his love of them made Mrs Blackstone wish she could wipe out the entire loft of them, and make a feathered carpet of Parsons' backyard.

The end, when it came, was sudden. It was an early morning death, so most of the activity in Gladstone Road was centred on the back kitchens. Paul Dean, the builder, had left his long ladder outside the Blackstone residence at half past six (he was not being blackmailed by Harriet, and merely did it for a quiet life). Since it was the second Thursday in the month, everyone in the street knew it was Mrs Blackstone's day for cleaning her windows. Being convinced that everyone had a duty to do the difficult things first – as they should eat their vegetables before their meat, if any – Harriet always began with the attic windows. She climbed the stepladder, as always soon after seven o'clock. Her long skirts did not make things easy, but she was used to that problem, and she coped with that and with the bucket she was carrying. The police ascertained later that the glass in the right-hand side of the double window had been cleaned, and she had just begun on the left-hand side, abutting Jim Parsons' house, when she fell. She dropped her bucket immediately, and managed to grasp the guttering along the top of Jim Parsons' house. The iron was much eroded by the pigeon droppings, of which the gutter itself was nearly full, and the whole section broke off with her weight. She fell to her death on the pavement below, hitting her head on Parsons' front step. She lay face up, the face half-covered with pigeon dirt. The doctor at the other end of Trafalgar Street was called out from his breakfast, and he pronounced her dead.

'Any fool could have seen *that*,' said Charlie Paxman, who nevertheless stood guard in the street and moved people on when they were inclined to gossip or crow.

The police investigation was brief, not to say cursory. The foolishness of a woman in long and bulky skirts cleaning regularly the windows of a room that was never used, at a level too high for the dirt to be seen from the road, was evident to all the (male) members of the force who looked into the matter. The details of the accident hardly seemed of any moment, and in any case were irretrievable. A man on his way to an early start at a factory in Ilford had walked along Gladstone Road on his way to the omnibus in Trafalgar Street. He had seen Harriet Blackstone up her ladder but had seen nothing untoward about her activity, which he'd seen her at regularly over the years. He had seen a boy running down a side lane in the direction of Gladstone Road at a great tilt, and said he had the look of Dick Gregory, who had lived in the area up until six months before. After he turned the corner into Trafalgar Street he had heard a crash, but his omnibus was approaching his stop, so he had no time to investigate even if he'd thought it important. In fact he hadn't thought twice about it. No one had heard anything of Dick Gregory since his family had moved away, and they were not to hear anything of him again for six or seven years, at which time he joined the police force and was frequently to be seen trying doors and reprimanding children and vagrants along a regular beat, splendid in his hard helmet, with his truncheon swinging from his belt. At the time the police paid very little attention to the workman who brought up his name. All boys look pretty alike, they said.

On the night of her death, when the jollifications had died

down in the street and her daughter was sleeping in the arms of her lawful husband, there was quite a lot of activity in number three, the house that had engaged so much of Harriet's attention in the last week of her life. In one of the front bedrooms a man and a woman were preparing for bed, he undressing with enthusiasm, she with a practised routine. They were laughing over the events of the day. The woman, in bed first, lay back against the pillow, looked at his boots beside the bed, and giggled. 'Funny, all the times you've been, and I don't even know your name. I always think of you as size thirteens.'

'Come to that, I don't know yours,' said the man.

'Call me Collette. Collette O'Hare.'

'O'Hare, of course. And you can call me Prince Albert.'

And then, with the sort of thoroughness and dedication for which that prince was famous, he got down to the job.

'Where on earth have you been?' asked Henry Redmayne, petulantly. 'You must have received my letter hours ago.'

'I came as soon as I could,' said Christopher.

'Well, it was not soon enough. Heavens, I'm your brother!'

'I was busy, Henry. My client wanted to be shown over the house.'

'And does the demand of a client take precedence over a heartfelt plea from your only sibling? I declare, Christopher, that your memory is wondrously short. But for me,' said Henry, striking a pose, 'you would have no clients.'

'You did help me to launch my career, it's true, and I'm eternally grateful.'

'Then why not show your gratitude by responding to my summons?'

'I've done so.'

'Hours too late.'

Arms folded, Henry turned his back to show his displeasure. Christopher was far too accustomed to his brother's irritable behaviour to let it upset him. Over the years, he had endured Henry's bad temper, his capriciousness and his blatant selfishness, with a weary affection. They were in the drawing room of Henry's house in Bedford Street and Christopher was waiting patiently for his brother's ire to cool. A gifted young man, he was one of the many architects helping to rebuild London after the ravages of the Great Fire, and he had achieved marked success in his short career. He never forgot that it was Henry who, by introducing him to a friend, provided him with his first client.

Christopher always dressed smartly but his brother wore nothing that was not flamboyant. As he swung round to confront his visitor, Henry was wearing a pair of red velvet petticoat breeches, edged with ribbon and hanging from his hips, a blue and gold doublet over a billowing linen shirt and a pair of shoes whose silver buckles positively gleamed. To hide his thinning hair, he had on a full periwig but it did not disguise the clear signs of dissipation in his face. With his handsome features, his healthy complexion and his long hair with its reddish tinge, Christopher looked as if twenty long years separated them and not merely a short few.

Henry put a hand to his chest. 'I face a terrible dilemma,' he announced.

'There is no novelty in that,' said Christopher with a tolerant smile.

'Do not mock me. I speak in earnest.'

'What is it this time – gambling debts?'

'No.'

'A stern warning from Father?'

'The old gentleman has not written for a month, thank God.'

'Then there must be some vexing problem at your place of work.'

'The Navy Office is an agreeable sinecure.'

'That leaves one possibility,' decided Christopher. 'There's a woman in the case. You've put yourself in a compromising position yet again.' He heaved a sigh. 'Will you never learn, Henry?'

'Stop sounding like Father,' retorted the other. 'It's bad enough to have one clergyman in the family. Read me no sermons, Christopher. Every supposition you make is entirely wrong. Do me the courtesy of listening to me and you'll hear why I'm in such a dire predicament.'

'Very well,' said Christopher, sitting down. 'I am all ears.'

'Last night, I went to the theatre with a friend to watch the Duke's Company. The play was called *The Comical Revenge*.'

'I remember it well. I saw it some years ago when it was first performed. George Etherege has a wicked eye and sparkling wit. *The Comical Revenge* is almost as good as his new play, *She Would If She Could*.'

Henry stamped a foot. 'Damnation! Who is telling this story – you or me?'

'I'll say no more.'

'Thank you. Now, where was I?'

'Going to the theatre with a friend.'

'Will you please be quiet, Christopher!' His younger brother put a hand to his lips to signal that he would remain silent. 'Let me try again,' said Henry, measuring his words before he spoke them. 'What I tell you is in the strictest confidence and must be divulged to nobody. Do you understand?' Christopher nodded obediently. 'The friend whom I accompanied last night was Sir Beresford Tyte, an odd fellow in some ways but generous to a fault. He has saved me time and again with a providential loan. Now, however,' he went on, grimacing, 'Sir Beresford wants repayment.'

'I knew that it was a gambling debt!'

'But it's not – at least, not entirely. Sir Beresford had an unfortunate encounter at the playhouse. We chanced to meet the egregious Lord Plumer there. Sir Beresford – and here I must remind you how crucial discretion is – has become closely acquainted with that divine creature, Ariana, my Lady Plumer. It seems that her husband finally learned of the attachment,' said Henry, rolling his eyes. 'There was a frightful scene. My friend denied ever having seen the wife, as any decent man would have done, but my Lord Plumer insisted on revenge. He challenged Sir Beresford to a duel.'

'That was very rash,' observed Christopher. 'Sir Beresford must be thirty years younger than him. He's bound to triumph.'

'Sadly, he is not.'

'Why?'

'Because he will not be crossing swords with that old cuckold, that's why. He has a substitute,' said Henry, ruefully. 'I've been engaged to fight in his stead.'

Christopher was astonished. 'You?'

'Yes,' confessed the other, taking a seat opposite him. 'My friend and I are of the same height and build. If I wear that black periwig of his and don his apparel – years out of fashion, though it be – I can pass for Sir Beresford Tyte easily enough.'

'But why should you have to?'

'To settle my debt to him.'

'On such demanding terms.'

'I owe the fellow hundreds of pounds.'

'Let me help you to pay it off.'

'If only it were that easy, Christopher,' said his brother, woefully, 'but it is not, I fear. After the play, we adjourned to a certain house to take our pleasure with the ladies of the establishment. A modicum of drink was consumed.'

'In short, you became hopelessly drunk and gave him your word.'

'As a matter of honour, I have to keep it. Yes,' he added, seeing his brother's look of disapproval, 'honour is at stake here. When the idea was first put to me, I found it rather appealing. Just think of it, Christopher. Five minutes of swordplay and I wipe out debts that took me years to build up. I'd be free of obligation.'

'Sir Beresford is the man with the obligation. It is he who was challenged last night. If honour has any meaning,' insisted Christopher, 'he should face his mistress's husband with a sword in his hand. Is he too cowardly to do so?'

'No, he's too fearful of losing Ariana's love. It's one thing to put horns on the head of my Lord Plumer. To thrust a rapier through his heart is a different matter.'

'So he expects you to kill the old man in his place?'

'He'd prefer me to wound and disable him.'

'That's a monstrous imposition to place upon a friend.'

'It did not seem so at the time,' said Henry. 'I am no mean swordsman and have no fear that the old goat will get the better of me. If I drew blood from him, I foolishly assumed, he'd turn tail and quit the field. Duty done, debt discharged.' He ran a worried hand across his chin. 'Then I learned a little more about my Lord Plumer.'

'I think I can guess what you are going to tell me,' said Christopher. 'If this lady is the young and beautiful wife of a much older man, she will have more than one suitor after her. Sir Beresford Tyte may just be the latest.'

'You've hit the mark, brother.'

'My Lord Plumer will have challenged others to a duel before now. Why does he do so when he has little chance of prevailing with a sword in his hand?'

'Because his bullies have cudgels in theirs, Christopher.'

'Ah, I see. He is determined to win at all costs.'

'The last man whom he accused of a liaison with his wife

was found battered almost to death. The one before that had his nose slit.' Henry shivered. 'I prefer my nose as it is, thank you. It's one of my best features. And I've no wish to be cudgelled until every bone in my body is broken.' He spread his arms in despair. 'What am I to do?'

'Let your friend suffer the consequences of his dalliance,' said Christopher. 'Sir Beresford must have known the risk that he was running. Husbands do not like it when their wives are led astray. This is a mess of his own making.'

'But I'm the one who has to get out of it somehow. Whatever I do, I'll not go back to Sir Beresford. He's counting on me.'

'To take punishment on his behalf. That's an unjust contract to enforce.'

'Teach me a way to escape from it, Christopher. I need your counsel.'

'Why? You always ignore it. I've been telling you for years to shed the company of rakes like Sir Beresford Tyte, but you'll not hear of it. You see the result of it now.'

Henry put up his hands defensively. 'Not another homily – please.'

Christopher bit back what he was going to say. His brother was in great distress but censure would not help him. Only positive action could rescue Henry Redmayne. The difficulty lay in extracting him from a desperate situation while keeping his honour intact. Christopher pondered. Henry reached out to touch him.

'Will you protect me, Christopher?' he asked. 'Will you act as my second?'

'That will not suffice.'

'Do not betray me in my hour of need.'

'I'd never do that,' said Christopher, smiling as an idea suddenly popped into his head. 'Where is this duel to take place?'

'At a time and spot of our own choosing.'

'Then the problem is solved.'

'How?'

'All will become clear in time, Henry. Talk to Sir Beresford,' he instructed. 'Let him send word that the duel will take place at seven o'clock on Sunday morning.'

'Sunday?' Henry was surprised. 'A sword fight on the Lord's Day?'

'There's a reason behind it.'

'And where will Sir Beresford – or his deputy – meet his challenger?'

'At the new house that I've designed,' said Christopher. 'It's only half-built but the garden has been walled. It's very private. Sunday is the one time when none of the builders or gardeners will be there.'

'But I hoped you'd find a way to get me out of this duel.'

'Trust me, Henry. I'm doing just that.'

The house was in Baynard's Castle ward, a district that had suffered badly during the Great Fire and lost its parish churches as well as a large number of other properties. Christopher Redmayne had designed one of the many new houses to fill the vacant gaps. Tall, stately and with an impressive façade, the building had a garden that ran down to the river where, in due course, it would have its own landing stage. Trees, bushes and flowers had already been planted but most of the garden was given over to a series of rectangular lawns. It was on the biggest of these swards that the duel was to take place.

Christopher did not recognise his brother when they met. Henry had not only put on apparel belonging to Sir Beresford Tyte, he was wearing the man's periwig and had adopted his friend's posture and gait. It was a convincing disguise. Christopher used a key to let them into the house. They went through it into the garden. Henry was tense and uncharacteristically reticent. His brother led him into the shadow of some bushes. They did not have long to wait. Within minutes, the garden gate opened and Roger, Lord Plumer, entered with two brawny companions.

'I thought you said I would not have to fight,' complained Henry.

'Take up your position,' said Christopher. 'That is all.'

'And then?'

Henry's question went unanswered because his adversary was bearing down on them. Lord Plumer was a short, fat, waddling man in his late fifties with a neat grey beard. Identifying Henry as his opponent, he got close enough to sneer at him.

'So you had the courage to turn up, did you?' he said with disdain. 'I'll make you rue that decision, Sir Beresford. You tried to steal my wife's affections away from me, you libertine. By the time I've finished with you, my friend, you'll not be able to consort with any lady. Make yourself ready, sir!'

'Not so fast, my lord,' said Christopher, stepping forward. 'If a duel is to take place, it must abide strictly by the rules.'

'A plague on any rules!' snorted the other, drawing his sword. 'Defend yourself, Sir Beresford. I'm coming to relieve you of your manhood.'

And without further warning, he charged forward,

brandishing his rapier. Henry barely had time to unsheathe his weapon in order to defend himself. Parrying the first thrust, he backed away. Christopher kept one eye on the two seconds as they tried to move in behind his brother to distract him. It was clear that, if their master faltered, they were to rescue him and overpower Henry. As a precaution, Christopher kept a hand on the hilt of his own sword but he did not have to draw it. Salvation appeared in exactly the way that he had planned.

'Hold, sirs!' yelled Bale. 'You are breaking the law!'

Two constables had just burst in through the gate. Jonathan Bale, the first of them, was a big, powerful man with an authoritative voice. There was disgust in his face as he strode across the lawn.

'Shame on you both!' he cried. 'Is this how you celebrate the Day of Rest? Would you defy God by fighting on the Sabbath?'

Relieved by the interruption, and recognising Bale as his brother's close friend, Henry backed away. He had been rescued. In turning up in place of another man, he felt that honour had been satisfied. Tossing a smile of thanks to Christopher, he sheathed his sword. But his opponent was not so ready to abandon the duel. One of his seconds pulled a pistol from his belt and handed it to his master. Lord Plumer took aim. Before Henry realised what was happening, there was a loud report and something stung him on the temple. With blood streaming down his face, he collapsed to the ground.

Shocked by what he had witnessed, Bale ran towards the injured man. The other constable, meanwhile, tried to arrest Roger, Lord Plumer, but he was brushed aside by the two seconds. They ran to the gate with their master and got away in their carriage.

Christopher paid no attention to their escape. His only concern was the fate of his brother. Bending solicitously beside him, he eased the wig off so that he could examine the wound properly. Bale looked anxiously over his friend's shoulder at the fallen man.

'You did not tell me that it was your brother, Mr Redmayne,' he said.

Christopher did not mince his words. As he stood outside his brother's bedchamber, he let Sir Beresford Tyte know exactly what he thought of the man's behaviour.

'What you did was unforgivable,' he said with controlled passion. 'It was cruel, ungentlemanly and tinged with cowardice. Thanks to you, my brother might easily have been killed.'

'I did not mean this to happen,' said the other.

'Then you should have met your own obligations, and not shuffled them off onto Henry. You exposed him to unnecessary danger.'

'I thought he would simply wound my Lord Plumer and put him to flight.'

'While you were hiding at home. Really, Sir Beresford, I thought better of you.'

Sir Beresford Tyte had the grace to look shamefaced. He was a tall, thin man in his late twenties with an air of prosperity about him. Unlike Henry, his life of debauchery had left no visible signs on him. He was undeniably handsome and Christopher could see why the lady in question had been attracted to him.

'How is Henry?' asked Tyte with obvious concern.

'We shall know when the doctor has finished examining him.'

'I was horrified when I heard the news.'

'Had you fought the duel yourself, my brother would not have been shot.'

'No,' rejoined Tyte, 'but I might have been. How was I to know that that old fool would have a pistol at hand?' He tried to mollify Christopher with a smile. 'Do not be too harsh on me, Christopher. Your brother has profited from this venture. All his debts have been paid off in this action.'

'That is no consolation to him – or to me.'

'I'll be revenged on my Lord Plumer for this!'

'And who will you get to do that on your behalf?' asked Christopher, sharply.

Tyte looked embarrassed. The next moment, the door opened and the doctor, an elderly man with a pronounced stoop, came out of the bedchamber. They turned to him.

'Well?' asked Tyte.

'He's a fortunate man,' said the doctor. 'The bullet only grazed his temple. It drew blood and will leave a scar, but there's no lasting damage. The patient, however, is still badly shocked by the experience. I've given him a sleeping draught.'

'May I not speak to him?'

'You may try, Sir Beresford, but do not expect a conversation with him.'

Tyte nodded and went quickly into the bedchamber to apologise to his friend. Reassured by the diagnosis, Christopher led the doctor downstairs and showed him out of the house. He then went across to Jonathan Bale who had been waiting in the hall. The constable was trying not to look at a painting on the wall of naked women in a Roman orgy.

Christopher repeated what the doctor had told them.

'I'm relieved to hear it,' said Bale, seriously. 'I could never bring myself to approve of your brother's way of life,' he added, glancing at the painting that troubled him so much, 'but I do not wish him any ill. He was the victim of attempted murder and the culprit must answer for it.'

'He will do, Jonathan,' promised Christopher.

'Tell me his name and I'll obtain a warrant for his arrest.'

'That would not achieve anything, alas. The gentleman is far too well connected to fear the process of law. His brother is a judge and he has a dozen politicians in his pocket. Besides,' he went on, 'Henry would not want this matter to go to court or he will be charged with taking part in a duel.'

'Why did he do so in disguise, Mr Redmayne?'

'I will tell you when this whole business has blown over.'

Christopher was very fond of the constable but he knew that his friend's Puritan conscience would be aroused if he heard the full facts of the case. Infidelity and large gambling debts lay behind the affair. Both were anathema to Jonathan Bale. At a later date, Christopher resolved, he would give his friend an edited account of events.

'I'll not let this crime go unpunished,' warned Bale.

'Nor will it be, Jonathan. I am already devising a reprisal.'

'I hope that you do not intend to challenge the fellow to a duel.'

Christopher grinned. 'I'd never do that,' he said. 'Duelling is illegal. You'd have to arrest me and I'd hate to put you in a position to do that.'

'Thank you,' said Bale with a rare smile. 'My wife would never forgive me, if I arrested you. Sarah would not let me hear the end of it.' He became solemn. 'As long as an attempt to kill your brother does not go unanswered.'

'It will have the most appropriate answer of all, Jonathan.'

'And what is that?'

'A comical revenge.'

Convinced that he had killed his wife's lover, Roger, Lord Plumer, returned to his house in high spirits. He found his wife, Ariana, alone in the drawing room. She looked up with disappointment when he entered.

'Yes,' he said, knowingly. 'You may well be surprised to see your husband when you were hoping that Sir Beresford Tyte would call on you.'

'I awaited only your return,' she said, retaining her composure.

'That is how it will be from now on, Ariana. Whether we are in London or on our estate in the country, you'll keep to the house and await my return.'

'Would you make a prisoner of me, sir?'

'I thought I'd done that when I married you. But I see that I'll need to put more formal constraints upon you. Do not stir abroad without my permission.'

'This is intolerable!' she complained.

'It is what befits a Lady Plumer.'

'I'll not be kept behind bars like that.'

'You were allowed far too much licence, Ariana. Those days are gone.'

His wife rose from her chair and crossed to the window. Still in her twenties, she was a shapely woman of medium height with a quiet loveliness that was now vitiated by a deep frown. Having married her husband for his title and his wealth, she had soon regretted her decision. It was not long before she was seeking interest and affection from outside the bonds of matrimony. Without such diversions, her life would be unbearable. The future suddenly looked bleak.

'Forget him, Ariana,' said her husband, moving to stand behind her. 'You'll never see Sir Beresford again – unless you attend his funeral, that is.'

She spun round in alarm. 'His funeral?' she gasped.

'Yes, my wayward darling. I killed him in a duel this very morning.'

The sleeping draught administered by the doctor was quick to take effect. No sooner had Sir Beresford Tyte told his friend how deeply he regretted what had happened than Henry Redmayne drifted off. When he woke up again a few hours later, he found Tyte still at his bedside. Christopher was also there.

'How do you feel now?' asked his brother, softly.

'In agony,' replied Henry, determined to get maximum sympathy from the situation even though he was in no pain. 'My stomach churns, my heart is about to burst and my head stings as though someone inserted a dagger in my ear. The wonder is that I'm still alive after that ordeal.'

'I blame myself for that,' admitted Tyte.

'So you should,' said Christopher.

'Tell me how I can make amends and I'll do it.'

'A loan of fifty pounds would be an admirable gesture,' suggested Henry.

'Take it as a gift,' insisted Tyte. 'You've earned it, my friend.'

'I've an idea how it might usefully be spent,' said Christopher. 'An attempt was made on your life this morning,

Henry. A sly and cowardly attempt. The culprit must pay for that. Jonathan Bale wanted to arrest him but the deception would then be exposed in open court.'

'We must not have that, Christopher!'

'Dear Lord, no!' agreed Tyte. 'If it were known that I let Henry deputise for me, my reputation would be ruined.'

'It's already been seriously compromised, Sir Beresford,' said Christopher, 'but enough of that. Let us turn to my Lord Plumer. Though he is swift to denounce anyone who dallies with his wife, I hear that he is not above straying away from the marital couch.'

'Indeed not!' declared Henry, sitting up in bed. 'For all his wrinkles, he's a rampant satyr at times. His mistress is one Betty Malahide, a comely creature and worthy of far better than him.'

'The lady is aware of that,' said Tyte. 'From what I hear, Betty Malahide tired of him and brought an end to the liaison. That made him choleric. It also forced him to spend more time at home where he found evidence that Ariana and I were more than passing acquaintances. Had he still been involved with his mistress,' he went on with rancour, 'then I would still be enjoying favours from his wife.'

'And I would not have had to face a madman with a pistol,' said Henry.

Christopher was curious. 'Do either of you know this Betty Malahide?'

'We both do, Christopher, and I would sue to know her better.'

'If she discarded my Lord Plumer, she would have only bitter memories of him. Do you think she would help us to wreak our revenge on him?'

'At a price,' said Tyte. 'Betty will do anything for a price.'

'Then the fifty pounds you offered Henry will be a sound investment.'

'But I need the money,' wailed his brother.

'You need satisfaction,' said Christopher, 'and the only way you can get that is by humiliating my Lord Plumer to the point where he has to quit London.'

'Yes,' said Tyte. 'I'll subscribe to any plan that does that. I want him well and truly out of the way. While he's in the city, he remains a danger to me.'

'Return home, Sir Beresford. Give out that you've been injured and are lying at death's door. That will content my Lord Plumer and put him off guard.'

'What of Betty Malahide?' wondered Henry.

'You must introduce me to her,' said Christopher. 'I have a proposition that might appeal to the lady.'

Lord Plumer was at his favourite coffee house when the letter was delivered to him. It was a request from his erstwhile mistress and he responded with alacrity. Excusing himself from his friends, he went out to his carriage and told his coachman where to take him. He was certain that Betty Malahide had repented of her decision to end her relationship with him, and was going to beg him to return to her bed. That put him in a position to exact conditions from her. He whiled away the journey by musing on what those conditions might be.

Admitted to her house, he was immediately conducted upstairs and that confirmed his belief that she wished to be reconciled with him. As he tapped on the door of her bedchamber, he expected a welcoming call to enter the room

EDWARD MARSTON

where he had enjoyed so much pleasure in the past. All that he heard, however, was a frightened voice.

'Is that you, my lord?' asked Betty Malahide. 'Do please come in.'

As he opened the door, a second surprise awaited him. Hoping to find her contrite and anxious to atone for the unkind way she had spurned him, he instead discovered that his mistress was not even alone. Betty Malahide, a buxom woman with a swarthy hue that he found irresistible, was perched on the edge of the bed. A plump man in black attire seemed to be examining her. Pulling her gown around her with embarrassment, she shot the newcomer a glance of apprehension.

'Thank you for coming so promptly, my lord,' she said. 'This is Doctor Cooper and he has grim news for both of us.' She flitted towards her dressing room. 'I'll leave you alone so that he can divulge what he has found.'

'What ails you, Betty?' asked Lord Plumer but she had already vanished into the adjacent chamber. He turned to Doctor Cooper. 'Well?'

'The lady requires treatment, my lord,' explained the doctor. 'Not to put too fine a point on it, she has the French disease.'

'Well, she caught it not from me!' exclaimed the other.

'Perhaps not, my lord, but she would certainly have given it to you.'

'How do you know, man?'

'Because it's a virulent strain that I recognise,' said Doctor Cooper, 'and it is highly infectious. If there have been intimate relations between the two of you in recent weeks, there is no way that you could escape contracting the disease.'

'The devil take her!'

'Mistress Malahide deserves compassion rather than reproach.'

'The wanton will get no compassion from me,' snarled the other, pacing the room in agitation. 'If she did not catch the disease from me, then she caught it from another man. Betty has both infected and cuckolded me!'

'That's a private matter between the two of you, my lord. Fortunately, we have caught it early and I have a cure that will restore the both of you to perfect health.'

'What sort of cure?'

When the doctor explained in detail, Lord Plumer was so shocked that he had to sit in a chair to recover. He agreed to present himself later that day so that the first stage of the treatment could begin. The doctor left him to reflect on the consequences of his doomed romance with Betty Malahide. He was still basking in remorse when she came back into the room. Her manner had changed completely. Hands on hips, she was now angry and vindictive.

'I curse the day I ever met you, my lord!' she yelled.

'I am the victim here, you harlot!'

'I offered you my love and you infected me in return. The French disease is a poor reward for all the efforts I made in this very room to pleasure you.'

'What are you saying, woman?' he demanded. 'You are the villain here. While swearing that you were true to me, you grant favours to another and let him pass on his hideous infection. I caught it from you in turn.'

'How can that be when no other man has touched me?'

'Do not lie to me, Betty.'

'You are the liar, my lord,' she accused. 'This condition

from which we both suffer was picked up by you between the thighs of some common whore. Admit it.'

'I'll admit nothing of the sort,' he said with righteous indignation. 'Unlike you, I kept my vow of fidelity. In all the time that we were together, I never looked at another woman. I swear it, Betty! I'd take my Bible oath.'

Betty Malahide could see that he was telling the truth. It put a malicious glint into her eye as she came forward to confront him. She produced a cold smile.

'What about your dear wife, my lord? Did you not sleep with her?'

He flicked a dismissive hand. 'Ariana does not count.'

'Oh, but she does. In view of what Doctor Cooper told us, I think that she counts for a great deal. There is the root of our trouble,' she urged. 'It's my Lady Plumer who is to blame for all this. Your wife infected you and you passed on the disease to me.'

'Dear God!' he said, clutching at his throat. 'Can this be so?'

'It is so, my lord. And that raises another question. Who gave it to her?'

Lord Plumer gulped. A day that had begun so well had ended in disaster.

Christopher Redmayne had never thought of his brother as a tactful man but he was proved wrong. When the two of them called on Lady Plumer, Henry was both suave and politic, passing on the information with a degree of charm and wording it in a way to upset her least. Henry had recovered from his brush with her husband. Wearing his new suit, he looked as resplendent as ever but his serious manner counteracted the impression that he usually gave of being a decadent fop. Christopher also admired Lady Plumer's poise. She did not falter for a second.

'I am vaguely acquainted with Sir Beresford,' she said, 'and I'm sorry to hear that he was injured in a duel with my husband.' Her voice hardened. 'I'm even more sorry to learn that Roger disgraced himself by shooting a pistol in that way. Yet you tell me that Sir Beresford will recover?'

'Yes,' said Henry. 'My brother has just been to see him.'

Christopher took over. 'Sir Beresford was badly wounded but the surgeon managed to save him. What he needs now,' he said, 'is a period of rest. His wife has been a tower of strength to him. When he feared that he was about to die, he confessed his sins to her but she was a true Christian and forgave him, provided,' he added, 'that her husband did not go astray again.'

It was a polite hint to Lady Plumer that the affair was over. In view of the trouble that it had caused, Sir Beresford Tyte was eager to abandon his relationship with her and, while he had not, in fact, confessed all to his wife, he had resolved to commit himself to a period of fidelity. Though she gave no hint of understanding what Christopher meant, Lady Plumer was, for her part, quite content. Since her husband had learned of her clandestine romance, it could not, in any case, continue.

She was grateful to the brothers for confiding in her. What they told her gave her a lever to use against her husband. Even someone as ruthless as Lord Plumer would not wish his friends to know that he had broken the unwritten laws of duelling so brazenly. Knowing the truth about what he had done would purchase her freedom once more. Of the two brothers, she thought Christopher by far the more handsome and appealing but she sensed that he was too responsible to become involved with a married woman. She dismissed Henry as a possible lover because of his resemblance to Sir Beresford Tyte. In time, she would have to look elsewhere.

'I thank you both for this intelligence,' she said, smiling at Christopher.

'We felt that you had a right to know,' he replied, 'even though Sir Beresford was only a distant acquaintance. But your husband must be warned, my lady. The duel was interrupted by two constables. Had they managed to apprehend my Lord Plumer, he would have been arraigned on a charge of attempted murder.'

'Goodness!' she cried, secretly wishing that he had been.

'It might be better if he were to quit London for a while.'

'I'll insist upon it, Mr Redmayne,' she said. 'When he returns home, I will have a great deal to say to Roger. The time has come for stern words.'

'Do not be too harsh on him, my lady,' said Henry, suppressing a grin.

'No,' said Christopher. 'You may find him in a weakened state.'

Lord Plumer could not believe the severity of the cure. Stripped naked in the doctor's private chamber, he was forced to sit in a hot tub from which mercury vapour rose to invade his eyes and ears. It was agony but it was also the only known way to deal with venereal disease. If this first ordeal did not work, Doctor Cooper had warned him that he would have to endure isolation, semi-starvation, enemas, ointments and pills, each involving the hateful mercury. Lord Plumer felt as if he were being boiled alive. The worst of it was that he did not know whether to blame his wife, his mistress or himself. His dilemma was an impossible one. He could not challenge his wife without revealing that he had caught the disease, yet he could not sleep with her for fear of contracting the infection again. All that he could do was to grit his teeth and suffer.

'No!' he howled as the doctor added more mercury. 'I am burning in Hell!'

Jonathan Bale had been so helpful that Christopher felt he deserved an explanation. They met at the architect's house in Fetter Lane, one of the few buildings that had escaped destruction from the fire. It was so much larger and more comfortable than his own house that it always made Bale slightly uneasy. Christopher told him about his brother's folly in agreeing to represent another man in a duel though he did not disclose Tyte's name or that of Lord Plumer. Bale's sense of duty pricked him.

'I should, by rights, arrest your brother and this false friend of his,' he said.

'Leave them be, Jonathan. Thanks to your prompt arrival, the duel did not, in fact, take place. You prevented the crime. But you inadvertently set off another. Henry's opponent did not behave like a gentleman.'

'Neither will I when I call him to account. Who is the rogue, Mr Redmayne?'

'A man who has been truly chastened.'

'He deserves to be locked up in Newgate.'

'Have no fear,' said Christopher with a chuckle, 'he has

suffered worse than mere imprisonment. He has been deprived of his peace of mind.'

Christopher did not dare to tell him how they had employed an actor to play the part of Doctor Cooper or paid Betty Malahide to collude with them. Lord Plumer had been given a fright and that was the object of the exercise.

'You talked about a comical revenge,' recalled Bale.

'Yes, Jonathan. It's the title of a play by George Etherege.'

'You know my opinion of playhouses. They are dens of sin and iniquity.'

'They are also places of entertainment,' said Christopher. 'And they excite the mind as well. It was only because I once saw Mr Etherege's play that I was able to arrange this comical revenge. I look upon it as a fine piece of architecture.'

Bale was mystified. 'How is this play linked to the punishment that has been inflicted?' he asked, scratching his head.

'*The Comical Revenge* has a significant sub-title.'

'Oh? And what might that be, Mr Redmayne?'

Christopher smiled to himself. '*The Tale of a Tub*,' he said.

17 Bridgnorth Street
Kidderminster

10 August

Dear Ronald,

I was sittin' only a coupla feet away on the night Big Jimmy was shot through his underachieving brain...

That's my opening gambit. No – that *was* my opening gambit.

Remember how our guru gave us those three guidelines? First, grab 'em all with that first sentence of yours. Second, don't get too worried if you find yourself writing a load of crap. Third (this is it!), if you want a short cut to 'ideas', just take any situation you've experienced recently, doesn't matter how pedestrian and trite, write it up as quickly as you can, and then just change one of the incidents in it, just the *one*, and see how your story suddenly leaps into life.

So please read my entry (enclosed) for our competition. How I need that prize money! There's not much 'grab' about the new opening, but plenty of 'crap' in the rest. I'm not bothered. It was the *third* guideline that struck in my underachievin' brain, and you'll soon spot that one fictitious incident in the story. Forgive me! Here goes.

There were twenty-three of us on that trip, with me the youngest but one. Mistakenly, I'd never expected things to live up to the brochure's promise: 'Ten days amid the cultural delight of Prague, Vienna and Budapest, with a unique mix of travel, guided tours and group seminars in creative writing. Travel is by rail, coach and boat. Each of our experienced guides is fluent in English. The leader of the seminar is himself a published author with four acclaimed novels to his name.'

I fell for him a bit from day one, and once or twice I thought he might be vaguely attracted to a single woman about ten years younger than he was. So I was disappointed when it was another man in the group who came to sit beside me as we travelled on the long train journey from Prague to Vienna. It happened like this.

The first-class carriage into which the group was booked was already uncomfortably full when the porter finally lugged my large, over-packed case up from the platform and told me it would have to be stowed away in the next carriage. Not a problem really. Since I was determined not to let my precious case out of my sight, I decided to leave the rest of the group and move along into the next carriage myself; and in truth I almost welcomed the thought of being alone and of concentrating my mind on that glittering short-story prize. I had already taken my seat and was reconsidering my opening sentence...

But I got no further.

'Mind if I join you?' (Did I?) 'I thought you'd probably be a bit lonely and—'

But before Ernest Roland, one of our group, had any chance of continuing, the automatic doors opened and two latish-middle-aged women made their way breathlessly into our comparatively empty carriage, each dragging a vast, wheeled case behind them. For a few seconds they stood beside us, glancing indecisively around, before pushing the two cases into the empty space on the carriage floor across the aisle, and finally settling down into the vacant twin-seats immediately in front of us, their backs towards us. From the window seat she had taken, it was the larger of the two ladies who spoke first: 'Well, we made it, Emily!'

Emily was a much slimmer, smaller-boned woman with a rather nervous-looking face – a face I could see quite clearly slantwise, for a slightly curious reason. Throughout the carriage the backs of the seats were designed in such a way that an opening was left running down the middle, fairly narrow at the top and the bottom, but with a bulbous swelling in the centre, some four to five inches wide, the whole gap shaped like an old-fashioned oil-lamp. From my seat therefore, also by the window, my view of her was pretty well unrestricted, as was the view of the broad adjustable arm-rest in black leather which separated the blue-upholstered seats. The whole design was light and airy: a comfortable arrangement for passengers' comfort, if not for the passengers' privacy. Indeed, we could follow the newcomers' conversation quite clearly since we each spoke English, albeit with an odd transatlantic twang that almost sounded *un*-American. Very soon we learned that the window-seated widow (?) was named Marion; and it was Ernest who turned to me, eyebrows lifted, as he pointed to Marion's chubby right hand on the arm-rest, the middle finger displaying one of the largest solitaire diamonds I have ever seen. And I was wondering what beautiful brilliants bedecked her other hand when the connecting doors opened behind us. 'Listek, prosim.' Then with a change of gear to a moderate semblance of English, 'Teekits, please.'

Ernest managed to explain that we were both members of the...he pointed back over his shoulder.

The ticket collector nodded and moved a pace forward. 'You English also as well?'

'No,' Marion, 'we – are – from – Quebec – in Canada. You understand?'

The man shook his head and both women were now dipping their hands into their hand-luggage.

'Don't worry, dear,' said Emily.

But Marion's fingers continued to scrabble around the bottom of her bag, trawling a collection of brochures, tour-guides, papers, documents and whatever; and was placing them all in a pile on the arm-rest beside her when Emily gave a sotto-voce squeak of delight. '*I've* got them – *both* of them!'

The man checked and clipped each ticket, and moved on a few paces before turning around and eyeing the cases.

'Yours?'

'Yes.'

'I am sorry but...'

'You want them moved?' asked Marion belligerently.

'Next stopping per'aps many people...'

'We understand,' said Emily.

Ernest grinned at me: 'I think per'aps, er, we ought to...'

'So do I.'

We both stood up and joined Marion, who was already out of her seat and staring fecklessly at the luggage when Ernest laid his hand gently on her shoulder.

'Why don't you sit down and relax. *I'll* move the cases to the luggage place at the end of the carriage. They'll be fine there – it's where my friend here has left hers.' He smiled sweetly; and Marion expressed her gratitude equally sweetly as she sat down again – as did I when Ernest insisted that he could manage well enough – better, in fact – without any help from me.

Quickly the cases were stowed; and with my companion back beside me I had no opportunity of developing a second dazzling sentence that would follow my daring murder of big Jimmy. In any case there was soon a further interruption.

Two uniformed Czech soldiers stood beside us, asking in good English to see our passports. Ernest and I were immediately cleared. As was Emily. But Marion was once again scrabbling away in her bag in a state of incipient panic.

'Don't worry, madam. We'll come back.'

They moved along the carriage, and a flushed-faced Marion turned to Emily. 'It's in my wallet. I *know* it is. But where *is* the wallet?'

'Didn't you see it when you were looking for your ticket, dear?'

'I just can't remember and then you found my ticket and... I'm going mad... I just—'

She broke off, very close to tears now as, for the second time, she began piling up the bag's contents on the arm-rest, and as a kneeling Emily was spreading her small hands over every square inch of carpet around them. And we joined her. With no success.

'I had it when...' bemoaned Marion. 'I just wonder if... You know those sort of zip-up things on the side of my case? Yes! I'll just...'

She got up and walked to the luggage area, only to return almost immediately, her face betraying disappointment.

'Do you know exactly what else was in the wallet, Marion?'

'Not exactly.'

'How much money?'

'About a thousand euros – more, I should think.'

'As much as that?'

'You don't have to rub it in, Emily!'

A knight in shining armour now rode upon the scene in the form of a dark-suited middle-aged man who had been seated further along the carriage and who spoke excellent English, albeit with an obvious German accent. 'Excuse me for intruding, ladies. My name is Herr Steiner. I just wonder if I may be of some help to you?' He explained that he worked with the Canadian Consulate in Vienna, and that he couldn't help overhearing about the wallet, containing passport, money and (surely?) plastic cards as well. (Marion nodded.) Above all the good lady should be worried about the cards, because even without a PIN number the thief would for a while have unlimited access to the big stores in the major cities.

For the first time Marion seemed aware of the full implications of her loss: 'I shall have to cancel the cards, yes.'

'That's where I can help you, if you wish it. You have a mobile phone?'

'My good friend here—'

'It's not charged, dear,' confessed a contrite Emily.

'Do you have any details about your passport number, card numbers...?'

Temporarily at ease, Marion produced the sheet of A4 which we had already observed on the arm-rest.

Herr Steiner perused the sheet carefully: 'My goodness! Passport number, copy of your photo, card numbers – even your PIN number. You really shouldn't let anyone see *that*, you know. But it won't be difficult to sort out the passport and cancel the cards. And if you would like me to do it for you...?' The offer was gladly accepted; and very soon we heard Herr Steiner back in his seat, reeling off strings of numbers in German into his mobile phone.

Ten minutes later all arrangements had been made: cards cancelled, and the address given of the consulate offices in Vienna. Herr Steiner was back in his seat resuming his reading of Heinrich Heine's biography. Marion and Emily were now conversing almost normally. Ernest and I were swapping our assessment of the tour so far, and promising to send each other a copy of our short-story entry.

After crossing the Czech-Austrian border, it came as no surprise that we were subjected to a further passport inspection with (we had been warned) the Austrian police somewhat more officious and perhaps a little too efficient than their Czech counterparts (who, incidentally, had not reappeared). The two men considered our passports carefully, like scrutineers at some electoral recount; then moved on to the Canadian travellers, and it was Herr Steiner who came forward and encored his guardian angel act. He took the A4 sheet Marion handed to him and showed it to the policeman, itemising the information given in rapid yet quietly spoken German. After some note-taking, and some discussion, their faces impassive, the policemen passed on up the carriage and Herr Steiner translated their instructions to Emily and Marion: when the train reached its destination in Vienna, both of them must remain in the carriage where the station official would meet them.

And that was about it really. Well, no – it wasn't.

Just before we reached Vienna, our group leader came through to ask us to join the main party for a short briefing. Ernest fetched my case and the pair of us left the carriage, bidding farewell to the Canadian ladies, but not to Herr Steiner, who must have been temporarily elsewhere since Heinrich Heine was still lying on his seat.

And what of Marion's wallet? Well, it will perhaps surprise

my readers to learn exactly what had happened to it because I know the full truth of the matter.

It is easy enough to make a couple of intelligent guesses: first, that the wallet was not lost, but stolen; second, that the theft occurred on the train, and most probably in the very carriage in which Ernest and I found ourselves. Again, motives for the theft are variously obvious: in themselves passports are valuable items for much criminal chicanery, particularly for falsifying identities or legitimising bogus immigrations; the possession of other people's credit cards, especially with PIN numbers presented on a plate, can be extremely profitable – at least in the short term; and the attraction of a thick wodge of banknotes... Need I say more?

But *who* was the guilty party in all this?

Plenty of suspects. The Czech police would be the obvious ones, since anyone finding the wallet would probably give it to them, and they were on the scene from the start. The Austrian police? If they'd had a little more opportunity of finding the wallet itself, they'd had ample time to note down its key contents, so obligingly set forth on the sheet Marion handed them. But why, if they were the guilty party, did they bother to arrange a meeting with the 'station official' in Vienna? If, in fact, they had done so...

But no! Cross all four off the list, as well as the ticket collector – no, I'd not forgotten him! I know that in detective stories it is frequently the unlikeliest who turn out to be the crooks; but in real life it is usually the *likeliest*; and for me it was that smoothie of a 'diplomat' (ha!) who had moved into the top spot. Was it really necessary for him to spend so long studying Marion's sheet when he'd phoned – if in truth he was talking to *anyone*? And where was he when he left the carriage? Not in the toilet or the buffet-car because he would have had to pass us if he'd visited either. And he didn't. And incidentally, *he* wasn't the thief either.

So what we needed was a sharply observant detective like Poirot, say – or someone like me. For *I* was the one who observed the thief bend down to pick up a deliberately dropped Vienna guide from the dark blue carpet at the side of the aisle and to pick up something else at the same time – the camouflaged wallet, also dark blue – and casually slip both into what he called his Fisherman's Bag. That person was Ernest my companion.

How he profited from his theft I do not know, and have no desire to know. But it was a sad day when he came to sit beside me on that journey. The saddest recollection of all, though, is a small thing, yet one I always shall remember. As the train was slowing down at the outskirts of Vienna, Emily got down on her knees and felt along the whole carpet once more. I could have – should have – told the poor dear that she was wasting her time. But I didn't.

Finis

Well, there it is Ronald. Sorry I couldn't think of a decent anagram of your Christian name: 'Roland' is far too weak. But your surname came to the rescue, tho' I've never been too fond of 'Ernest'. Do read the story and let me know what you think.

Fond regards,

Diana (Duncan-Jones)

P.S. No Brownie points for guessing the 'one incident' that's changed!

* * *

29 Emmanuel Road
Cambridge

14th August

Dear Diana,

Thank you for your story – much enjoyed – although the last two paragraphs were a bit painful, to tell you the truth. I understand why you had no joy in trying to anagram Ronald, but I trust I've done better with you! I haven't got your skill as a writer since (until your dénouement) you describe the sequence of events with accuracy and economy and you quite certainly took our leader's injunction to heart about just changing one of the incidents. I've decided not to enter the competition myself but I've girded my loins and written an ending which relates far more closely to the truth. Ready? I begin with 'So what we needed...'

So what we needed was a sharply observant detective, like Poirot, say – or someone like me! For I was the one who had noticed Nadia bend down on the pretext of retrieving a deliberately dropped guide-book and picking up the wallet with it and nonchalantly slipping both into her capacious handbag. I cannot believe she was sufficiently street-wise to understand the full potential of the wallet's contents. But I do know (she had told me on the tour) that she was getting uncomfortably short of ready monies. How she profited from her theft I have no desire to know but it was a bad day for me when I went through to join her on our railway journey. I said nothing to Nadia who looked as if she'd been stuffing her stomach with the most expensive meals in the most expensive restaurants in Prague – probably at the expense of the emaciated Emily.

Finis

Now listen Diana! For *me* the saddest thing of all is that we should both have come out of this with our reputations tarnished at least on the printed page since clearly neither of us has a particularly high opinion of the other. I must admit though that I took a bit of a shine to you and I think I still would have but for our time on the train together. What a pity things have ended like this! I shall put to paper no more about that strange morning since I am not such a big fan as you are of the 'changed incident' guidelines. But as you will have noticed I *have* changed just the *one* little thing: I did not actually see you pick up the wallet. I *did* however see the wallet in your handbag and I *did* see you push it down deeper so that it was no longer visible.

On a final and more constructive note let me congratulate you on your much more economical use of dashes and let me congratulate myself on using not a single comma in this letter to you.

Ronald Sterne

Extract From a Diary

Feb 5th 2005

I've only a few weeks to live, they tell me, and tho' I was brought up as RC I've never been into a confessional to tell of the sins I've committed. In any case I've no real regrets for any of them. My only confidante in life has been you, dear diary, and this will almost certainly be my last entry.

Marion and I were in the same class in secondary school; but after leaving we had exchanged only a few perfunctory letters over the years. So it came as a surprise when she wrote to me early last year informing me that her (second!) husband, a bigwig with a BA, had died, and inviting me, a lifelong spinster, to join her on a fortnight's Hapsburg Holiday, dividing our time between Prague, Vienna and Budapest. An additional carrot was Marion's promise of an upgrade to Club Class (thanks to her late husband), and it was that which swayed me. I felt fairly sure that I could, in spite of my deteriorating health, just about cope with the travel, and almost everything else really – and I accepted the invitation.

Marion had always been a big and bouncy and bullying girl at school, and I had been hurt deeply (we were only seventeen) when she had robbed me of the only boyfriend I've ever had in my life, one of the sixth-formers a year ahead of us: Jonathan. And it took a very short time for me to realise that her boisterous nature had blossomed over the years (thirty-five of them) and developed into a selfish bossiness that I found well-nigh intolerable on occasions. Increasingly I found I had no real say in where we went, what we ate, at what time we did whatever she'd decided to do. I won't go on.

At one point tho' things did become intolerable.

Many times when we were sitting together over a meal or over drinks, we spoke of our school days; and the evening before we were to catch our train from Prague to Vienna she asked me a question quite out of the blue.

'Did you ever keep in touch with Jonathan?'

'No.'

'He was very sweet on you, you know.'

'Not as sweet as he was on you.'

'I don't know about that. After you'd left school and gone off to Shropshire – and after things cooled down between us—'

'Yes?'

'He asked me if I had your new address.'

'Which you did have.'

'Of course. But he would have been no good for you, Emily dear.'

'Did you give him my address?'

'No, I didn't. He was a bit of a wimp, you know, and I thought you'd got over him by then – like I had.'

'Don't you think that what *I* thought was more important than what *you* thought?'

'To be truthful, Emily, I don't, no.'

That was it – virtually verbatim, I swear it. I didn't want to murder Marion, not quite, but I desperately wanted to hurt her. How? I'd no real idea, but someone was smiling down on me the morning we boarded the Vienna-bound train.

Seated immediately behind us were two youngish things on a group holiday; he, Ronald by name (we could hear all they said), seemed a pleasant enough fellow, with a diffident manner, in sharp contrast to his companion, named Diana, who sounded a selfish little bitch, openly flirting with her beau and equally bemoaning her shortage of cash. But both of them got up to help Marion when the ticket-man told us to move our luggage. So I was left alone for a couple of minutes, and all I needed was a couple of seconds. My opportunity! I took Marion's wallet from her bag and through the gap at the back of our seats I pushed it down into Diana's open hand-luggage. A lightning impulse and so risky. If the girl had told us of her great surprise at finding the wallet in her bag, who could have done the deed – except me? And I have never in my life felt so relieved as when we finally reached Vienna without her saying a word about the matter.

Marion soon bounced back of course from this slightly distressing experience. The station official at Vienna was charming and helpful; the consulate had already made arrangements for the passport, all cards had been cancelled; the insurance company later coughed up not only for the euros but even for the wallet. This last information I learned when she rang me a few weeks later, but we have not communicated since. My one remaining hope is that she will not hear of my death and turn up to shed a perfunctory tear at my funeral. I mustn't be too hard on her. At least I enjoyed flying Club Class.

Just one thing I'm vaguely curious about: I wonder whether Diana and Ronald kept in touch after they reached home, and if so what they said to each other. At least *he* would have had knowledge of her address, surely so – which, alas, is more than Jonathan had of mine.

The court was so packed they had had to close the doors on more people trying to wheedle or push their way in. But of course I had known it would be, how could it be anything else, in the circumstances? Alan Davidson was being tried for the murder of his brother. I was sitting in my appointed place, very smart in my black skirt with high-necked white blouse, single pearls on my ears, and my wig itching like a hat that didn't fit.

My name is Judith, and some of my friends call me Jude, very appropriate – St Jude is the patron saint of lost causes, and if ever there was a lost cause, defending Alan Davidson was it!

What on earth had made me accept?

Counsel for the Crown, Sir Peter Hoyle, was questioning the police witnesses who had found the battered body of Neil Davidson on the living room floor of his house. They were making a good job of the horror of it. It was all quietly understated, no melodrama, no playing for effect, and above all, no exaggeration for me to find fault with. Not that it would have made any difference. It would alter none of the facts that mattered, and they were all there in hideous detail.

As I sat increasingly uncomfortably, I remembered the message asking me to go to Lord Justice Davidson's office. At the time I had had no idea what it was about. I did not connect it with the crime in every newspaper headline. My first thought was that I had committed some solecism of legal behaviour of which I was unaware, and I was preparing a suitably profound apology. After all Lord Justice Davidson

VC was one of the most senior judges in England, a man renowned for his wisdom, his heroism and his justice, even toward those who had been his enemies. And he certainly had those! Success such as his breeds envy.

And it had come to him young. During the darkest days of the war in 1942, aged barely twenty, he had taken a German gun position almost single-handed and saved the lives of a score of men. He had won the Victoria Cross for it, one of the highest decorations in the world for gallantry on the field of battle.

From then on it had been up all the way. Even his wife was a legendary beauty! And he had had two fine sons, and a daughter, by all accounts a beauty also.

I had knocked on his door five minutes early, and been told to enter straightaway. I had only ever seen him in the distance before. A couple of yards from me, in his late fifties, he was still one of the handsomest men I have ever seen. Many a woman would have paid a fortune for a head of hair like his, or eyes! Even the dark hollows around them and the ashen pallor of his skin could not mask the vigour of life within him.

'Yes sir?' I had said haltingly, only beginning to realise that whatever it was he had called me for, it was to do with him, not with me.

'As you will know, Miss Ashton,' he said gravely, 'my elder son, Neil, was murdered four days ago. This morning they charged my younger son, Alan, with the crime.

'I would like you to defend him.'

For a minute I had had no breath to reply, no words even in my mind. My awe of him vanished, the distant, excited respect I had felt ever since I had been called to the bar was obliterated by my overwhelming human pity for him as a man, a father who in one terrible blow was losing both his sons.

'I...I...' I had stammered, knowing that I sounded like a fool.

'Please?' he had said simply.

I am a good barrister, sometimes very good, but there are still a score of people better than I, longer established, and with far more respect within the profession. He could have asked any of them and they would have been honoured to accept.

I had drawn in my breath to say 'why me?' but I hadn't said it. I had been flattered. I wanted to do it. He must have heard something about me, some brilliant defence I had made, perhaps of the Walbrooke boy last spring. I was proud of that. Maybe this was my reward?

I had not argued or made excuses or protests of mock modesty. I had simply accepted, and promised him I would do everything I could to help Alan.

Of course that had been before I met Alan Davidson, or knew the facts of the case.

Now here I was listening to Peter Hoyle asking the police surgeon to describe Neil Davidson's injuries, and watching the jury's faces as the pity and revulsion spread through them, and then the anger. I saw how they looked across at Alan, sitting motionless, his face frozen in misery. He refused to defend himself even by a second's shame or remorse in his expression, or the softening in the angles of his body. He sat as if already condemned, and I have never felt so helpless in my life.

I hated looking at Lord Davidson where he sat on the front row of the public seats, his face stiff and pale, his shoulders hunched. Beside him his wife had her face turned away from me.

The surgeon was waiting for me to say something, but what could I ask? The facts were incontrovertible. Someone had beaten Neil Davidson to death. There were bruises and abrasions all over his body, and one final blow had broken his neck. He was a strong man, not yet in the prime of his life. His knuckles were bruised and raw. Whoever had done that to him had to be badly marked themselves. And there was Alan with the scars on his cheek and the purple not yet faded from his brow and jaw.

'Miss Ashton?' the judge prompted and I could hear both the impatience and the pity in his voice.

'No, thank you, my lord,' I declined. The last thing I wanted was for the surgeon to say anything further!

Peter Hoyle glanced at me, and called his next witness. I have never liked him much, and at that moment I suddenly found him almost intolerable. He looked as if he were secretly enjoying all this misery.

Of course I understood now why Lord Davidson had chosen me. He would not embarrass any of his friends by asking them. No matter what passions of rage or love tore through his heart, the lawyer in his brain would know that there could be no defence. Perhaps only God understood the reasons why Alan had killed his brother, but the facts were being unrolled relentlessly in front of us as I sat there, and I was helpless to argue against any of them, or even to reinterpret them in any kinder light.

'And was there any evidence whatever of forced entry?' Hoyle was asking.

'No sir, none at all,' the police sergeant answered.

'And was there anything missing, as far as you could determine?' Hoyle pressed.

'No sir. According to the insurance records, and they were pretty detailed, there was nothing of value taken. All his ornaments and pictures were accounted for. His coin collection, which is very valuable, was all around in glass cases, and untouched, and there were nearly two hundred pounds in notes in the desk drawer.'

'Then it would be reasonable to conclude that robbery was not the intention of his murderer,' Hoyle said with a glance at me, and then at the jury. 'Thank you, Sergeant, that is all I have to ask you. But perhaps Miss Ashton can at last think of something?' He left the rest unsaid.

I only wished I could, but every time my brain scrambled furiously in the jumble of facts, I remembered Alan Davidson's white face and blank eyes filled with fury and despair, but no will to fight. No matter what I said or did, or how I pleaded, he would barely talk to me. Even the little he did say was of trivia, small duties he wanted done for him, as if he expected to die and needed an executor rather than a defence. They were waiting for me...again. Not only could I not help Alan Davidson, this was likely to be the end of my own career. Memory of this would wipe out all my past successes.

'No thank you, my lord.'

There was a faint titter somewhere in the body of the court, stifled almost immediately, but I heard it and I knew what it meant. It was a mixture of nervousness for the reality of the pain, and pity not for Alan, but for me, because I was a failure.

Hoyle next called the elder of the two friends who had gone

to the airport to meet Alan on his return from abroad. 'And what date was that, Mr Rivers?' he asked politely.

'The twelfth, sir,' Rivers replied. He was a tall man, a little thin, although that might have been exaggerated by the pallor of his face and the pinched look around his mouth. I would have guessed him to be in his middle thirties, but today he looked more like fifty, and yet also oddly vulnerable.

'At what time?' Hoyle enquired.

'Half past eight in the morning. It was an overnight flight from New York.'

'Alan Davidson had been in New York?'

'No. He'd been doing botanical and ecological research in the Amazon Basin,' Rivers corrected with sudden asperity. 'He simply returned via New York.'

'I see,' Hoyle said, as if he saw nothing at all. 'And you met him at one of the London airports?'

'Yes, John Eaves and I met him at Heathrow.'

I looked across at Alan, but as almost always, he avoided my eye.

'Will you please tell us where you took Mr Davidson,' Hoyle asked.

Rivers clenched his jaw. Even from where I sat I could see the tightening of his muscles. He was obviously loathing every word he was forced to say, but there was no escape for him. Oddly enough, the transparency of his emotion made his evidence the more powerful.

'To the hospital at St Albans,' he replied.

Hoyle opened his mouth, a slightly sarcastic expression flashing across his face, then he changed his mind. 'Why was that, Mr Rivers? Did he ask you to?'

'Yes.' His voice was so quiet the judge directed him to raise it so the court could hear him. 'Yes!' he repeated, staring directly at Hoyle with such misery in his eyes that for the first time since the trial had begun I had a sense of some real and intense personal tragedy far deeper than sibling rivalry turned so sour it ended in murder.

'And the reason?' Hoyle pressed.

Rivers looked once at Alan in the dock, then spoke quietly but every word was distinct. 'He was very close to his sister, Kate. He'd been abroad for a long time with no way to send letters from where he was, or to receive them, I suppose. Almost the first thing he did was to ask after her.' His voice shook a little. 'He didn't know...' he stopped, blinking his eyes several times, and looking at Hoyle with such loathing I had a sudden vision of how he would look at me when I failed to do anything to help his friend. I dreaded that day, just as I knew that it was inevitable.

'And you answered him?' Hoyle said after a moment.

'I had to,' Rivers mastered himself again. 'He had to know. I just wish to...to God...' he took a deep breath, 'that I'd done it later! Or stayed with him...or something.'

In spite of himself Hoyle was suddenly gentle. 'What did you tell him, Mr Rivers?'

Rivers's whole body was tight. 'That Kate had...had some kind of mental breakdown. Nobody knows what caused it...and...and she was in the hospital, and there was no real hope of her ever coming home.'

The court was silent. Hardly anyone moved, even in the public gallery. I knew the story, of course, but told again like this it was still horribly jarring. It was so easy to imagine the joy of homecoming, the reunion of friends, and then suddenly everything had changed, broken. The heart of it was gone. I could see their faces as they turned to look at Alan sitting blank-eyed in the dock.

Lord Davidson put his arm around his wife and she moved a little closer to him.

Rivers went on with the story, how he and Eaves had taken a shocked Alan to the hospital in St Albans and waited for him, pacing the floor, talking in snatched sentences, drifting from desperate hope into silence, then fractured words again, and more silence.

It had been nearly two hours before Alan had emerged, ashen-faced, walking so blindly he stumbled into the doors. They had taken him home where he had asked them to leave him, and reluctantly they had done so, not knowing what to do to help. Of course Hoyle made the most of Alan's state of mind, making him appear to have been planning murder even then.

'I thought he needed time alone,' Rivers said in an agony of apology. It was Alan he looked at, not Judge Davidson or Barbara beside him, her face at last turned towards me so that I could see her features, still exquisitely chiselled, her hair barely dimmed from the russet beauty of her youth, only a little softer, like autumn leaves as the year fades. I could not bear to see the pain in her, it was palpable, like a storm in the air. In a sense she had lost all her children, but in a slow and hideous fashion, worse than disease.

The following day Hoyle called more police witnesses to show that Alan had tried to cover his crime. When questioned he had denied any guilt, then when the net inevitably closed around him, he had fled, making him both a liar and a coward.

As I sat watching Hoyle close his case, without offering

more than a token resistance, I felt utterly beaten. I have never prayed to saints for miracles. It is not part of my faith, and to be honest I did not think any form of intervention, divine or otherwise, would help Alan Davidson now. There was no shred of doubt, reasonable or otherwise, that he had gone straight from the hospital in St Albans to his home, and a few hours after Rivers and Eaves had left, he had gone to his brother's house and fought with him so savagely and relentlessly as to leave him dead. To escape so lightly himself he had to have taken Neil by surprise. He had not been larger or heavier, simply possessed by a rage which lent him superhuman strength.

Hoyle rested his case. Thank heaven it was too close to the end of the day for me to begin. I had nothing but character witnesses, for any real good they would do.

I left the courtroom. I had to see Alan and try one more time to persuade him to speak to me. I could not argue with the facts, I must try the reasons behind them, if only he would trust me. There had to be more than the few bitter details Hoyle had brought out.

He was alone, staring at the small square of sky through the high, barred window. He turned as he heard the door unlock and the very slight squeak of the iron hinges.

He stared at me as the warder locked us in.

I was there for nearly an hour and a half. I tried every argument, every plea I could rake out of my imagination. I begged him, but he would tell me nothing. He just sat patiently on the stool waiting for me to exhaust myself, then spoke in his quiet voice, denying me anything at all. I left again with not a single weapon in my hand to defend him, and I had to begin the next morning.

I thought of Judge Davidson and how I would face him when it was all over. I felt that the largest, most vital part of my life was also going to be consumed in this apparently meaningless tragedy.

And yet I had spent some hours with Alan and had had no sense of a psychotic personality, and perhaps that was the most frightening part of it. Where *was* my own judgement? I used to think I was good at understanding people, that I had a sensitivity, even some kind of wisdom!

It was that moment that I decided to go to the hospital in St Albans for myself, and see if I could learn anything more as to what happened the night Alan had gone to see his sister. Of course I had questioned each of the witnesses Hoyle could call, but all they did was prove that Alan had been there, and had left white-faced and almost as if walking in his sleep. It hardly seemed possible he could hate Neil so passionately simply because he had not told Alan of Kate's illness. He had been in the Amazon jungle and unreachable to anyone except by the most primitive means. And that was not the sort of message you give except face to face, and when you could be there to explain all you knew, and assure them that everything was being done for her. He could not have helped, and a fractured wireless communication would hardly make him feel better.

Perhaps they had not handled it in the best possible way, but it was a genuine mistake, not worth a quarrel, let alone a murder!

I took the train, and sat thinking about it all the way. It was not a very long journey, just under an hour on the express. By seven o'clock I was in a small side room where one of the doctors patiently explained to me that Kate Davidson would not be of any assistance to me as a witness, even were she able to leave the institution and appear in court, and that was out of the question.

'I am afraid nothing she said would carry any weight.' He shook his head ruefully, pushing his hand through his hair and leaving it sticking up in long, wavy strands. 'She's completely delusional. Sometimes she is very depressed and we have to restrain her, in case she were to damage herself. At other times she simply sits and stares into space. I'm sorry.'

'But when she does talk?' I insisted.

'I'm sorry, Miss Ashton, but as I said, she is delusional. She wanders from past to present. She's very confused even about her own identity some of the time.'

I had nothing else to cling to. 'May I speak to her?' I asked.

He looked doubtful, his tired face puckered with lines of strain. 'She doesn't know about her brother's death, or that Alan has been charged with killing him,' he answered me. 'I'm afraid that news might be more than she can deal with. I'm sorry.'

I refused to give up, I don't really know why. I had no clear ideas. 'If I promise not to tell her?' I insisted.

He still looked dubious.

'You can be there with me,' I went on. 'Stop me, throw me out, if you need to for her sake. I'm at my wits' end, Dr Elliot. I have no idea how to defend Alan Davidson, and I have to start tomorrow. She and Alan used to be very close, she would want me to try everything I could, wouldn't she?'

He stood up slowly. I thought it was a refusal, but he opened the door and said 'Come on, then,' almost over his shoulder, and I followed his white-coated figure, a little stooped, sleeves too short, all the way up three flights of stairs and along what seemed like miles of corridor to a sunny attic. Inside a young woman sat stitching a piece of white linen. There were two other women there, also working at something or other, but no one needed to tell me which was Kate Davidson. She had the same beautiful hair, except that her face was marked with grief of such an intensity it caught my breath in my throat, and even in the doorway I almost wished I had not come.

'Kate, I have someone who would like to see you,' Dr Elliot said gently. 'You don't have to speak to her if you'd rather not, and I'll stay here all the time, if you wish.' That was a statement rather than a question, as if he already knew the answer.

She raised her eyes from her linen to look at me, and I felt a sense of her mind as sharply as if she had reached out physically and touched me. I did not see insanity, and certainly not any kind of foolishness, only a pain and a fear so profound that she had to shelter from it by removing herself from reality.

'Kate?' Dr Elliot asked gently.

'If you wish,' she said, her voice low, a little husky. Looking at her I had an overwhelming sense of what Barbara Davidson must have been like thirty years ago, and why the judge had fallen so passionately in love with her.

'Thank you.' I walked in and sat on the chair opposite her. I had already changed my mind about how to approach her. All idea of treating her like a child had been swept away the moment I met her eyes. It was not a retarded woman who faced me, but one hiding from an unbearable wound. Only one question beat in my brain – did I need to know what that wound was?

By the time I left three hours later I knew at least what she had told Alan the night he visited her. I was not certain whether I believed it myself. Surely it was too bizarre, too dreadful? But the only question that mattered was had Alan believed it? If he had, it would explain both his actions and his silence now.

I left her weeping quietly, but I thought with some kind of inner peace beyond the pain, because I had listened, and I had seemed to believe her. Or perhaps the truth was that in spite of its horror, its apparent impossibility, in my heart I had believed her, and she knew that.

Dr Elliot walked with me as I stumbled into the street and the glare of the lights and the noise of the traffic.

'What are you going to do, Miss Ashton?' he asked me.

'The only thing I can,' I replied. 'Try to prove that Alan believed her.'

'You won't succeed,' he said, biting his lip. 'And she can't testify. She was more lucid with you than I've seen her with anyone else. You might not find her like that again for weeks, maybe months. I wish I could tell you she was getting better, but she isn't.'

'I haven't got weeks or months,' I answered. 'Anyway, they don't call me Jude for nothing. It's what I do – increasingly often lately.'

He looked totally confused.

'St Jude – the patron saint of lost causes?' I explained. 'My name is Judith.'

He smiled, making him look younger. 'I got there rather before you,' he said. 'With the lost causes, I mean.'

I smiled at him, and thanked him. I had a lot of work to do and it would take me all night, and I'd be fortunate to be ready for the court to open in the morning.

* * *

My first witness for the defence was the Davidsons' cook. I had dug her out of her bed in the middle of the night, but I had asked her only the briefest of questions. She had very little idea why she was now on the stand testifying, and she kept glancing from me to Lord Davidson where he sat on the public benches. I could hardly blame the poor woman for being unhappy. She was confused and her loyalties were torn.

'Mrs Barton,' I began. The room was totally hushed. I don't really think anyone imagined I was going to get Alan Davidson acquitted, but they were all curious to know what I was going to try. The mixture of embarrassment and pity was about equal. 'Were you employed as cook in the house of Lord Justice Davidson on September ninth last year?'

'Yes, ma'am,' she said steadily, staring at me as if I were trying to hypnotise her.

'Was Mr Neil Davidson living at the house then also?'

'Yes, ma'am.'

'What was the state of his health, do you recall?'

There was a slight stir in the court. Lord Davidson shifted in his seat.

Mrs Barton swallowed. 'That weekend he was taken very poorly with the flu,' she replied.

'Was the doctor sent for?' I questioned.

'Oh yes, and he came. But there really isn't much you can do for it. Just stay in bed, and drink all you can.'

'Did anybody look after him?' I pressed. Please heaven she was not going to go back on her testimony now!

'Yes, ma'am.' Her voice dropped to barely more than a whisper. 'His valet did, and then Miss Kate, his sister.'

I let my breath out slowly. 'How do you know that Miss Kate did?'

'Because she came into the kitchen and cooked something for him herself. Seemed Mr Neil asked her to. Said she was the only one who could cook egg custard just the way he liked it, and would take some up to him on a tray.'

Hoyle rose to his feet. I knew he was going to object that this was all irrelevant, but in the event he did not bother. With a patronising smile he shrugged and sat down again, as if nothing I could do would harm his case anyway and he might as well be generous to me.

'And did she cook the egg custard, and as far as you know, take it to him?' I asked.

Judge Davidson stiffened.

'Yes, ma'am,' Mrs Barton replied. 'She certainly left my kitchen with it.'

'Thank you.' I turned to Hoyle and invited him to question the cook.

He stood up and spoke with elaborate weariness, adjusting the front of his gown very slightly. 'Mrs Barton, has this touching story of sisterly affection nearly a year ago got anything whatsoever to do with Neil Davidson's death...by any stretch of your imagination, or ours?'

'I don't know, sir,' Mrs Barton answered. 'That was the night Miss Kate was took ill herself, an' I never saw her again.'

Suddenly the courtroom was alive. The ripple passed through the public benches like a shock of electricity before a storm. Davidson looked startled. Beside him Barbara was close to tears. In the dock Alan was rigid, glaring at me with panic in his face.

Hoyle for once looked as if he had bitten into an apple and found a worm in it.

The judge leaned forward. 'Miss Ashton?' He did not put words to a question but it was there in his face.

'I have no redirect, my lord,' I replied.

He sighed and sat back. I had not answered him, but he had understood that there was a story I was going to draw out, and he was prepared to wait.

I called Neil's valet. This was going to be the most difficult. He was a lean, dark young man with a troubled face, as if anxiety sat heavy on his shoulders, and he never once looked toward Lord or Lady Davidson.

'Mr Clark, were you valet to Mr Neil Davidson while he was living in his parents' home last September?' I began.

'Yes.' I already knew what he had done, and why, from the few words we had exchanged in the small hours of this morning, but this was still going to hurt, and I was sorry for that.

'Do you remember his illness on the ninth?' I asked.

'Yes,' he answered very quietly. For a moment I was afraid he was going to lose his courage.

'Of course,' I agreed. 'It is not something a competent manservant would forget, far less a good one, and as close as a valet. Did you look after him during this time, fetch and carry for him, help him in every way he needed?'

There was only one reasonable answer he could give.

'Yes,' he agreed.

I smiled and nodded. 'And were you there when his sister Kate brought him the dish of egg custard she had prepared for him?'

Now he looked confused, but if anything, less frightened than before. 'No.'

I knew he had been on duty that night. I did not want the

trouble of having to call other witnesses to prove that. But if at this last moment his nerve failed him, I would have to. I could not succeed without him. I raised my eyebrows as if mildly surprised. 'You were off duty that evening? I must have misunderstood my other witnesses.'

His eyes narrowed and he turned even further away from Barbara Davidson. 'I was on duty,' he said miserably. 'I just wasn't in the room when he asked for her or when she came.'

'Do you know who was?' I said quickly.

This time his hesitation was so long that the judge intervened. 'Mr Clark, you must answer the question.'

'Yes,' he said at last. 'Lord Davidson.'

'Both times?' I pushed him. 'Or just when Neil asked for her?'

'When he asked for her,' he said grimly. 'It was he who told her to go.'

I felt a fraction of the ache ease inside myself, and a different kind of pain take over. 'Did you see her go in with the custard?'

'Yes.' Now it was a whisper, but in the utter silence of the room everyone must have heard him, even though they had no idea what they were waiting for. I prayed that none of them knew how much I also was feeling my way.

'Was anyone else in the room then, apart from Neil himself?'

'No.'

'And when she came out?' That was the question on which it all turned.

The man was ashen, and there was a sheen of sweat on his skin. Now at last he looked at Lord Davidson, but Davidson was sitting with his body forward, staring at Alan as if he recognised him for the first time.

Barbara looked at her husband, then at her son, then at me, and I was twisted inside with guilt for what I was going to do to her, but I could not pull back now.

'Mr Clark?' the judge prompted.

The valet stared at a space on the wall somewhere ahead of him. 'Yes, I was there.'

'Would you describe it, please?' I requested.

'My lord…' Hoyle began. 'Miss Ashton is an actress of considerable skill, not to say ambition, but the tragedy of Lord Justice Davidson's daughter is not part of this trial, and ordinary decency requires…'

The judge was miserable.

Davidson himself had not said a word, but his distress, and that of his wife, was a presence in the court so powerful there can have been no man or woman unaware of it.

His voice cutting like acid, the judge adjourned the court and requested me to see him in his chambers immediately.

'Miss Ashton,' he said the moment the door was closed behind me and I stood in front of him, 'I will not permit you to exploit the tragedy of Katherine Davidson's illness to divert the jury's attention from her brother's guilt. For God's sake, have you no sensitivity at all to her family's agony?'

I had been expecting him to say something of that sort.

'My sorrow for their grief does not allow me to conceal facts that are relevant to a murder case, my lord,' I answered. 'No matter how much I may regret the additional pain it causes, it isn't right to judge between one person and another, whose feelings may be spared and their sins hidden, and who has to have their wounds exposed.'

'You say that so easily,' he replied, and for a moment there was a flash of anger at what he saw as my blundering ignorance. 'You're what – thirty? Have you any idea what Davidson, and men like him, did for this country?' He leaned forward over the desk. 'You have no concept of what we endured during the war, what fear there was under the masks of courage we put on everyday, or what that cost. Davidson's heroism gave us hope, and belief in ourselves and the possibility of victory, if we could just hold on.'

I did not interrupt. I knew he needed to say it, and it was probably true.

'You look at him now with honour and prosperity, and you assume it was all easy for him,' he went on, now thoroughly consumed in his own emotional memories. 'But Barbara was married to Ernest Upshaw when she and Davidson met. It was passionate and total love at first sight, at least for him. He saw her across the street, and from that moment on he could think of no other woman.' There was a softness in his eyes, as if vicariously he tasted the fire and the tenderness of that long ago love story.

His voice dropped. 'They had to wait. In those days you did not divorce. It ruined a woman.' He was staring, soft-eyed, far beyond me or anything within the room.

'Ernest Upshaw was a hero too, in the same regiment as Davidson. He was seconded to a raid across enemy lines. He didn't come back. As soon as a decent period of mourning was over, Davidson and Barbara married.' Suddenly his eyes focused sharply on me again. 'They've lost their eldest son, but I will not have you drag their daughter's tragic breakdown into the public. Do you understand me, Miss Ashton?'

'Yes, my lord, I understand you,' I answered without wavering my gaze from his. 'I am sure you will not allow me

to overstep the boundaries of the law, but within them, I am
going to do everything I can to help my client—'

'Your client is beyond help, Miss Ashton!' he said bitterly.
'You know that, and so do I. We'll go through the motions of
the law, as we must, but he is guilty, and we can't redeem that.
I will not permit you to crucify his father as well by exposing
that poor young woman's mental or emotional collapse for
the public to pore over and speculate about, and the
newspapers to make money out of.' His face was hard, his lips
tight, exaggerating the deep lines from nose to mouth. 'No
ambitious young lawyer is going to save her own career, or
rectify the mistake of having accepted an impossible case, at
the expense of one of our greatest families, which has already
suffered more than its share of tragedy.' It was not even a
threat, just a statement of fact.

I felt a flicker of real fear in the pit of my stomach, like an
awakening sickness, but I had believed Kate Davidson, and I
still did. It was belief, it was certainly not knowledge, and that
doubt was like a needle in my side. I knew what I was risking.
But to back away now, to run from the battle because victory
was not sure, would be cowardice that would cripple me
forever.

'Of course, my lord,' I said steadily. 'If the case could be
heard in private it would be the easiest, but since there is no
question of national security involved, I don't think that will
be possible.'

A dull flush spread up his cheeks. 'Are you attempting to
mock me, Miss Ashton?'

My knees were suddenly barely strong enough to hold me
up. 'No, my lord. I deeply regret the fact that evidence I may
elicit from witnesses will be distressing to the Davidson family

– and that is not just words – I do mean it!' I did, more than he could know. 'But my feelings are not the point. The truth is, and the nearest to justice that we can come.'

'Then you had better get on with it,' he said grimly. He seemed to be about to add something else, then changed his mind.

We returned and I resumed questioning the valet. The judge reminded him that he was under oath, and faced me with a spark of hope in his eyes. I killed it immediately. I hated doing it.

'Did you see Kate Davidson when she came out of her brother Neil's room?' I asked bluntly. He must have seen in my face that I knew the answer and that all the power of emotion in me was bent on dragging it out of him, whatever the cost to either of us, or to anyone else. He did not even look at Lord Davidson for help, or to the judge, and I refused to look at them either, in case it robbed me of my courage.

'Yes,' Clark said very quietly. But there was not a sigh or rustle in the room and every word was as dense as a scream.

'Describe her,' I ordered. 'Tell us exactly what you saw, what you heard and what you did, Mr Clark.'

He was a man defeated by a weight too vast for him and finally he surrendered to it. He spoke in a tight, almost colourless voice, as if to add emotion to it would be unbearable. 'I heard Mr Neil shouting for me and the dressing room door swung open so hard it crashed against the wall, and he stood there in a rage like I've never seen him in before. His face was red and he had scratches on his cheeks and one eye was already swelling up. "Throw that garbage out!" he shouted at me, gesturing behind him.'

Lord Davidson started up in his seat, and then stood

frozen, staring first at me, then slowly and with horror darkening his eyes, at Alan.

Barbara looked as if she were confused, like a lost child, growing more and more frightened with each moment.

Clark rubbed his hands slowly up over his face, digging the heels of them into the sockets of his eyes. I did not prompt him to go on, I knew he would.

Even Hoyle was silent.

'I didn't know what he meant,' Clark said hoarsely.

I was afraid for an instant that he was going to break down, his voice was so thick, so choked. But he mastered it, lifting his head a little and staring at me, as if I were the one person in that whole room who already knew what he was going to say, and somehow that reality helped him.

'Then I saw Miss Kate lying on the floor. Her hair was over her face and there was blood on her clothes. Her skirt was torn and up around her waist...' He took a deep, shuddering breath. 'And I knew what had happened. God...I wish now I'd done something different!' The pain in his voice was so sharp it cut the mind. 'But I was a coward. I was afraid of him, and...what he would do to me. I did as he told me. God forgive me, I put her out.'

I was sorry for him. He must have been in hell, the real hell of guilt. But I could not afford pity there or then.

'You knew she had been raped by her brother, and you picked her up and put her out? Is that what you're saying?' I asked.

He looked at me as if I had struck him, and that he deserved it. I admit even now that I can still feel the twist of guilt in my stomach I did at that moment.

'Yes,' he whispered. 'I did.'

I gave him his chance. 'Why? I asked. 'Why did you not help her? At least tell her father and mother what had happened?'

His voice was not much more than a whisper. 'Because a couple of months before that I had taken some money from Neil's dresser, just a few pounds. My mother was ill. I got something special for her, to help. Neil knew, and he told me he would fire me if I said anything about Kate. My mother's worse now. I can't afford to be without a job. There's no one else.'

'So you were blackmailed?' I wanted the jury to be sure of that.

'Yes. She locked herself in her room for several days, until they broke the door and the doctors took her away,' he said hoarsely.

It was even worse than I had expected. I don't know why. I had believed Kate when she told me. At least I think I had. I looked across at Alan. He sat in the dock with his head bowed and his hands over his ears, as if he could not live through hearing it again.

I meant to look at Lord Davidson, but it was Barbara's face I saw as she stared up at him, and in a dawn of horror more intense than anything I could have imagined before, I realised that he had known! I saw it just as she did. It opened up an abyss in front of me. It must have hurled her into one so deep she felt as if she would never escape the darkness again. He had known and he had done nothing!

She was so white she looked as if she must be dead! Perhaps in that moment something inside her did die.

I thought of the great love story of their meeting, her first husband, Ernest Upshaw, in Davidson's regiment – sent on an impossible raid – to die a hero! So his exquisite widow could marry Davidson?

Was that also the understanding I saw in her face as she stared at him now, as if she had never truly seen him before?

Lord Justice Davidson VC looked at the judge, then to the dock and the son who had avenged his sister because no one else would. Then at last, slowly like a man mortally wounded, he turned to his wife. I can't ever know, but I believe that in that moment at last he began to understand himself, and what he had done, what manner of man he was, and what it had cost him.

His elder son also felt that if he wanted a beautiful woman badly enough, then he could take her. He was cut from the same cloth – handsome, passionate, selfish at heart. The world had loved his father! Why not him too?

The court was still silent, like people who have witnessed something too terrible for speech. I don't know how much they understood, but they felt it.

Davidson turned to me. I expected to see hatred in his face. No man could ever forgive what I had done to him! And I had done it in public, in a courtroom, the realm where he was all but king.

But it was not hate that brimmed his eyes, it was the first white dawn of understanding of what sin truly is, and the hunger above all else in existence, to tear it from his soul.

Defending Alan from conviction was a lost cause, it always had been, he would have to serve something, even if the court accepted my plea for him of diminished responsibility – but perhaps I had saved another cause no one had even known was lost, until that moment? The path back from such a place as Lord Davidson had gone to is very long indeed, but it is not impossible. It takes more courage than facing an army's guns because the enemy is within you, and there's no armistice.

Thank you St Jude, for the miracle after all.

I turned back to the judge, my voice hoarse, but all uncertainty fled away.

Acknowledgements

'Home' by John Harvey © 2005 by John Harvey. First appeared in *Ellery Queen Mystery Magazine*. Reprinted by permission of the author.

'The Greatest Trick of All' by Lee Child © 2005 by Lee Child. First appeared in *Greatest Hits*, edited by Robert Randisi. Reprinted by permission of the Avalon Publishing Group.

'He Loved to Go for Drives with His Father' by Alexander McCall Smith © 2005 by Alexander McCall Smith. First appeared in *A New Omnibus of Crime*, edited by Rosemary Herbert & Tony Hillerman. Reprinted by permission of the author's agent, David Higham Associates.

'Toupee for a Bald Tyre' by Robert Goddard © 2005 by Robert Goddard. First appeared in *The Detection Club Collection*, edited by Simon Brett. Reprinted by permission of the author and the Orion Publishing Group.

'No Flies on Frank' by Danuta Reah © 2005 by Danuta Reah. First appeared in *Sherlock Magazine*. Reprinted by permission of the author.

'Cain Was Innocent' by Simon Brett © 2005 by Simon Brett. First appeared in *Thou Shalt Not Kill*, edited by Anne Perry. Reprinted by permission of the author and his agent, Michael Motley.